# TULISIA

# TULISIA

## Richard Brunke

Copyright © 2002 by Richard Brunke.

Library of Congress Number: 2002093163
ISBN :    Hardcover    1-4010-6654-2
          Softcover    1-4010-6653-4

All rights reserved. No part of this book may be reproduced or transmitted in any form or by any means, electronic or mechanical, including photocopying, recording, or by any information storage and retrieval system, without permission in writing from the copyright owner.

This is a work of fiction. Names, characters, places and incidents either are the product of the author's imagination or are used fictitiously, and any resemblance to any actual persons, living or dead, events, or locales is entirely coincidental.

This book was printed in the United States of America.

**To order additional copies of this book, contact:**
Xlibris Corporation
1-888-795-4274
www.Xlibris.com
Orders@Xlibris.com

# CONTENTS

**PRELUDE**
    UNDER A CANOPY OF INDIFFERENT STARS ........... 9
**ONE**
    THE CLANS OF THULISTAN ......................... 13
**TWO**
    S'HAPUR ................................................ 18
**THREE**
    THE CITY OF TWILIGHT .............................. 27
**FOUR**
    THE RULER ............................................. 41
**FIVE**
    THE TORSCH ........................................... 49
**SIX**
    LESSONS IN HUMILITY ............................... 63
**SEVEN**
    SMALL WORLD ........................................ 78
**EIGHT**
    BITTER PARTINGS .................................... 91
**NINE**
    DANGEROUS PLANS ................................. 100
**TEN**
    OUT OF THE FRYING PAN . . . ..................... 113
**ELEVEN**
    MEETINGS ............................................ 130
**TWELVE**
    THE ADVANTAGE OF FRIENDS .................... 146
**THIRTEEN**
    AWKWARD SITUATIONS ............................ 160

**FOURTEEN**
    FOR THE GLORY OF GOD ......................................... 174
**FIFTEEN**
    THE MEEK SHALL INHERIT .................................. 177
**SIXTEEN**
    RISE TO GLORY .................................................. 182
**SEVENTEEN**
    THE BREATH OF DRAGONS ..................................... 190
**EIGHTEEN**
    BROKEN MINDS, BROKEN PLANS ........................ 197
**NINETEEN**
    WINDS OF WAR ................................................... 205
**TWENTY**
    THE HAPPY WIDOWER ............................................. 220
**TWENTY-ONE**
    A MOMENT'S CLARITY ........................................... 237
**TWENTY-TWO**
    SOLDIER'S OATH ............................................. 250
**TWENTY-THREE**
    DIVINITIES FALL ................................................ 269
**TWENTY-FOUR**
    DUTY AND HONOR ................................................. 279
**TWENTY-FIVE**
    ONE DESTINY UNVEILED ....................................... 292
**TWENTY-SIX**
    UNIFICATION ................................................... 305
**AFTERWARDS**
    FORGED IN THE DEEPS ........................................... 321

For everyone who put up with me when I needed time to write this; especially my wife Margaret, and my children Connor and Mackenzie who would rather be playing with me. And to my mom, who always loves whatever I write.

# PRELUDE

## UNDER A CANOPY OF INDIFFERENT STARS

The embers of the campfire cast a dim pool of light, insufficient to hold back the stifling nighttime darkness in the wilds of the Long Wood. Surrounding the campfire, huddled within dirty blankets and rags, slept a group of outcasts and thieves.

A short distance outside of this pool of light a silent procession of shadows moved through the wood.

Nothing stirred in the camp. The majority of those around the fire were sleeping off the effects of a keg of brandy that they finished off several hours before. The brandy cost a group of miners their lives. However, life was cheap in these parts, and brandy was valuable. Those in the camp had little need for morality or guilt.

Within the camp one man awoke, an unnamed terror causing the hair on his neck to stand. He peered out from under his filthy blanket, scanning the trees about the camp. He looked for a moment into the forest, peering closely in the direction from which he thought he heard the noise; perhaps made by a small animal. He could not see anything, but the unknown fear that woke him led him to investigate further.

He spat to clear the foul taste from his mouth, crawled from under his blanket, and rose quietly to his feet. His many years as a thief taught him how to move silently at need, and he exercised that skill now despite his sleep and drink befuddled mind. He stepped over the other sleeping forms clustered by the nearly burnt out fire. The air smelt of evergreen and pitch, only lightly tinged with wood smoke. With curiosity that was beginning to overcome fear, he approached the edge of the camp, looking away from the fire to give his eyes time to adjust fully to the near complete darkness.

At first, he could not make out the source of the gentle noise he heard as he crept slowly away from the clearing. Then, the fire popped behind him, startling him into a small forward jump and a barely audible yelp. A fraction of a second later, he recognized the sound and began to calm himself. It was only then, as the fire fed briefly upon the sap inside the small piece of wood, which popped open, that he saw the source of the fear that had awakened him.

No more than twenty feet in front of him, the firelight reflected from a shiny, dark, almost manlike shape. While the short-lived light lasted, the man saw an unknown number of like creatures further away from the camp. With instinct borne of years of survival, he jumped away from the nearby alien figure with a screech of terror. This screech turned into a shout of warning to the rest of the camp as he backed further away, scrambling to find a stick or stone to defend himself with. "Wake up—help, they're in the forest! Wake up, we're under attack, wake up!" He continued his shout, awaking the camp.

Many men rolled groggily to their feet, unable to think past the pain in their heads. Others, more alert, rolled quickly to their feet, searching for weapons. A few of the women with their wits about them threw fuel onto the fire.

As the growing fire pushed the darkness further from the camp, other men in the camp began to see the dark shapes moving amongst the fir trees. Their cries of alarm and fright joined those of the thief. After a minute of panic and confusion in the camp, the camp leader came out of his tent, armored and armed. Following the shouts and directions of his men, he quickly identified the source of the threat to his camp.

"We're beset men—ware the camp! To arms!" His loud voice cut through the generalized panic. "Form up, swords to me, archers fire at will! Protect the women and children!"

A dozen men began to fire arrows into the forest at the moving shadows. For the most part, their shots were wasted, flying off into the forest to either strike a tree, or land harmlessly in the soft loam. A few struck their targets, but not with the results intended.

The ill aimed arrows bounced harmlessly from the hardened shells of the creatures in the forest. Although they did not injure them, they did serve to turn them from their course, a course that led away from the camp. The creatures sensed a threat. One of them, indistinguishable from the rest, paused in its progress, silently communing with an unknown source. After a moment, it turned its attention once again outwards to those surrounding it, and those attacking them.

With gentle clicking sounds and motions of its clawed hands, it instructed its companions to defend themselves. At once, a number of the creatures turned their attention away from their journey, towards the humans in the encampment. Instinctively, without compassion or any sign of emotion, they returned the attack.

As they entered the camp, they were fully revealed to their attackers. The sight of the larger than man sized insect like creatures sent the entire camp into panic, all plans of defense lost in the turmoil.

The next morning found the forest silent but for the chirping of the birds and the whistle of the wind through the trees. Somewhere, just inside the southern edge of the forest, a group of insect like, bipedal creatures moved southward. They showed no signs of the conflict—no noticeable injuries, no sign of fatigue, no remorse.

Within the forest encampment of the brigands, things were quite different. A few men that had chosen to flee instead of fight, along with the women that were overlooked in the slaughter, searched for survivors. Amidst the crisscrossed patterns of sun and shadow that filled the glade, they instead found the torn up parts of people they knew. The bodies, thoroughly hacked and torn by the claws of the creatures, were unrecognizable, and the stench unbearable. Over forty men and women lay dead and mutilated on the ground.

In the midst of the carnage lay one dead figure that none dared approach. The black shell of the creature was covered in human blood. A long spear stuck from its throat, wedged into a small gap between two neck plates. A small puddle of viscous, yellowish fluid had seeped from the mortal wound to the ground below, where it puddled around the fearsome form of the deceased creature.

The ten survivors, two of whom were wounded, possibly mortally, left the bodies as they lie. They left the camp, fearful that the horrible creatures may return. Afraid even to remain in the forest, the four men and six women made for the mountains to the south, back towards the more established camps of the mountain miners. With them they carried the first stories of the dark, deadly creatures later identified as the d'rakken mahre; stories filled with terror, both real and imagined.

These tales spread widely, and as is the way of such things, were greatly embellished around many a taproom fireplace. This story, coupled with other rumors and legends, began a series of events that would change the civilized world; and shift forever the balance of power of Tulisia, the greatest of the ancient Empires.

# ONE

## THE CLANS OF THULISTAN

In the University of Ancient Learning in Desil, the learned teach their students the histories of the lands and the peoples. Among the most popular of the courses, well attended as a prerequisite to military service for officers in the Tulisian Army, was one focused on the people and history of the Empire of Thulistan. The professors of the universities, caring little for the pride of their Tulisian students, teach history as it is written, not as the Tulisians wish to hear it. Some students were able to push past their fundamental disdain and hatred of the Thulistans, and were thereby better able to grasp the nature and strengths of their enemy. Others; less enlightened and more in love with their innate superiority, typically dropped the class and opted for a carreer in the lesser, but still respected, elite mounted cavalry of the Tulisain army.

During the first day of the new semester, a stern faced professor, wearing a gold belted white robe, prepared to give his well-rehearsed introduction to his History of Thulistan class. After sweeping the assembled students with his 'settle down' look, he began abruptly.

"It is taught that the harsh climate of the great northern Empire of Thulistan breeds fierce men, trained from birth to battle and survival. The hardy Thulistans are known to have migrated from even more northerly lands during a period of history, several thousand years ago, when the ice flows permanently landlocked their ancient homeland, forcing them south across the ice in search of new hunting grounds.

"Thulistans," the professor continues, "are bred to protect the honor of complex family and clan organizations. Inter-clan warfare filled much of their early history, and the skills of battle were refined to an art form among their men. This tradition of honor, pride, and conflict defines the earliest roots of the oral histories cherished and shared by the family leaders, called the S'hapur.

"The early Thulistans were prolific, and they quickly expanded southward from their original far northern homes at the tip of the continent of Tulisia, seeking new lands to claim for their families and clans. In the lands later known as Barstol, they first met with other humans, humans not of their 'true blood'. These strangers were the colonists from Tursys, at the time an advanced civilization spreading from its overpopulated island home to the southeast. These early meetings resulted in mistrust, then hostility, and finally bloodshed as the Tursysians, and later the Tulisians sought to protect land they had laid claim to.

"At first, the Thulistans simply withdrew from the lands of Barstol and tried to ignore the races to the south. Soon, however, they were forced to unite to face the threat of the other races migrating northward, seeking additional lands to colonize. Individual families sought protection under their clan names and selected from within their family S'hapur a leader for the entire clan, known as the S'hapur-la. These leaders met to form a loose government lead by another leader selected from among the S'hapur-la to symbolize the unity of the Empire. This leader was known as the Mal S'hapur-la."

The professor began to pace as he spoke. "A nation was forged from this structure, with an understanding of its power, its past, and its future challenges. Clan warfare was abolished, and matters of clan honor were satisfied through elaborate games of strength and skill, and matters of personal honor were met with personal challenge, not clan warfare. The result was a loosely governed, strong, independent nation. As the Tursysian, and later the Tulisian, armies swept through the vast southern lands of the continent, drawing all under their control, the Thulistans remained unvanquished in their holds in the frigid and harsh Rhunne Mountains.

"Throughout the ensuing centuries, the Tulisian's ascended in power and took hold to the south and steadily expanded their empire. During this period of constant strife, many nations formed in the ebb and flow of warfare across the continent. Many of these nations were great in their time, such as Barstol, Carstan and Tursys. However, even these nations were nearly destroyed by the growth of the Tulisian Empire. Tulisians, agree most scholars, were and are an imperial race that destroyed or absorbed all that stood in the way of their expansion. Barstol was utterly destroyed by the armies of Tulisia, and the greatness of Tursys was reduced to subtle schemes and dreams of a return to power.

"Other countries . . ." the professor paused to take a small sip of water from a glass on his podium, "developed and survived by never achieving enough greatness to attract the greedy eye of Tulisia; such as Maldin with its endless farmland, and Carstan who courted the Tulisians as an ally against their avowed foe: Elindar. Only Desil remained relatively unchanged within the pall of the Tulisian Empire. Desil existed on the power of wealth. The leading families of Desil purchased guarantees of freedom for their people with bribes, lones, and other displays of financial power. Desil provided the wealth that the Tulisians required to maintain its war efforts; at a reasonable interest rate of course. Tulisia and Desil became interdependent, and Desil became a willing member of the Tulisian Empire.

"With the vast majority of the continent currently under their rule, the Tulisians, one would think, should have nothing to fear." The professor paused for effect. "They—you—", he looked directly at a young Tulisian student, "do fear, however. History shows that Tulisians fear the one nation that has withstood their military might; and fear the ancient wisdom and power of the Thulistans. Tulisians fear the one people that they can not control. During the next semester," concluded the professor, "you just may come to understand why."

Pleased that his speech had gone well, as it always did, the professor sat down at his desk and allowed an assistant to take over the lecture for the day.

In the fastness of Thulistan's Rhunne Mountains, however, the fears and plots of the Tulisian Empire meant little. Survival in the bitter climate bred an awareness of life, and an expectation of challenge and struggle. There was no time for concern over tomorrow and what it may bring. Today was enough. Survival, family, and clan were enough for the men, women, and children of Thulistan.

What was not taught to the Tulisian students, because it was unknown outside of Thulistan, was that the Thulistans struggled against more immediate problems than the might of the Tulisian army.

The Thulistans knew they were relative newcomers to the land they lived in. They had a deep understanding of time and history, and understood that others creatures had come before them. Currently it was one of their predecessors to the land that demanded their attention.

The oldest histories made mention of the k'aram mahre, the winged peoples that flourished upon the world when it was young.

When the Thulistans first came to their new homes in the Rhunne Mountains, the k'aram mahre lived near them and shared the lands with them. Shortly after their coming, however, the winged ones began to diminish. Before the end of the tenth generation of Thulistans upon the Tulisian continent, all of the k'aram mahre had disappeared from the skies. It was rumored that the beautiful winged creatures had gone into the earth, though it was not understood why, or what happened to them after.

Some generations later the first encounters with the d'rakken mahre, or 'hard people', began. The name seemed a parody on that of the k'aram mahre, or 'beloved people'.

Much was said about the d'rakken mahre. Early explorers of the deeps made claims that they encountered human shaped insect like creatures, living in great cities in the dark. Despite the similarity of names, and the rumor that the creatures were connected with the k'aram mahre, these aggressive and dangerous creatures had little resemblance to the beauty of the passive k'aram mahre.

During recent months in Thulistan, bands of d'rakken mahre had been reported on the surface, in various areas throughout the Rhunne Mountains. These bands were reported to be uninterested in the people they encountered, unless they somehow interfered with their progress. Attempts at communications, or capture, resulted in the slaughter of many unfortunate Thulistans.

So, with armies poised to attack along both borders; the Carstans to the southeast and Tulisians to the southwest, each searching for signs of weakness, the Thulistans were paralyzed from within. No foe had ever daunted their people before, and yet there was a prophecy regarding the d'rakken mahre. The d'rakken mahre were believed to be part of an unknown cycle begun by the Gods, possibly linked with the k'aram mahre. They were spoken of as beings of power and unknown potential by the oral histories, and were to be respected as creatures of the earth, and possibly descendants or relatives of the long missing k'aram mahre.

And yet, despite this, the d'rakken mahre were alien and frightening to the Thulistans. They did not communicate their need. They searched the valleys of the mountains for some portent or talisman. They slaughtered without any trace of guilt or understanding any that got in their way.

The truth was that the Thulistans were unsure of what the emergence of the d'rakken mahre signaled. They watched the progress of the d'rakken mahre and kept their people clear of them. They noticed with dismay that the groups of the creatures were growing larger, and were emerging more frequently from the depths of the earth.

The leaders of the clans of Thulistan waited for answers, seeking some sign of the intent of the creatures.

# TWO

## S'HAPUR

In his early thirties, Morgan was the youngest S'hapur, or family leader, ever selected by the Partikson Family of Clan Piksanie. It was universally believed that he was destined to be the S'hapur-la of Clan Piksanie in time.

He was tall for a Thulistan, being close to six feet in height, was broad in the shoulders, and had the dark complexion typical of the race. His long jet-black hair was tied into a warriors braid and hung down the center of his back. He possessed rare ice blue eyes that could pierce one to the soul. A solid, square jaw, generally set in stubborn resolve, dominated his clean-shaven face. A deep scar ran down his cheek to the mid-point of his chin, deepening his typical frown. The scar was the result of a mistake in battle. It was his last mistake in battle, and the scar served to remind him of his commitment to perfection in the arts of the warrior. The overall impression he generated was of confidence, competence, and a subtle sense of danger.

Although his prowess in battle made him one of the most respected and feared men in Clan Piksanie, it was his conventional wisdom, natural leadership, and keen intellect, that made him the youngest S'hapur ever selected by the Family. Under his leadership, Family Partikson flourished, and had come to prominence among all families in the clan. A new S'hapur-la would be selected at the Piksanie Games during the upcoming year, and Morgan's name was spoken of among the elders as the leading contender for the honor.

The families of Clan Piksanie inhabited the mountain vales to the northwest of North Post, one of Thulistan's few large trading cities. Family Partikson lived in a high valley far into the Rhunne Mountains. Their summer encampment boasted over two thousand tents: The Family Partikson included almost six thousand men, women, and children. This made the family the largest in Clan Piksanie, and among the largest in the Empire.

Morgan rode down towards the encampment with the small band of trackers he led into the mountains to search for signs of d'rakken mahre scouting parties. Rumors from the north led Morgan and his men to undertake the mission, in hopes of discovering the danger represented by the creatures. He was chewing his lip in vexation at the overall failure of the mission. They hadn't found any sign of d'rakken mahre parties during their two-week trek deep into the mountains, but had warned a number of small communities of trappers and miners to band together for protection.

They also heard many stories of d'rakken mahre parties searching through valleys to the far north. It seemed that the parties of d'rakken mahre were still far from the lands of the clans. Satisfied that the family was not at imminent risk, had Morgan decided to return to the encampment. It had been a long ride, and the sun was just beginning to dip below the peaks of the mountains, throwing the valley into shadow as they rode down the steep trail. Morgan shivered slightly in the early evening chill.

As Morgan galloped down from the high trail at the far end of the valley in which his people lived, his chest tightened involuntarily with pride. The encampment below was a bustling, successful community. Shepherds guided large flocks of prize sheep away from the incoming horseman. Down the valley, closer to the great cluster of multi-colored tents, a herd of horses ran restlessly in a large wooden pen. These horses were the key to the family's success. Family Partikson boasted a herd of some of the finest war-horse stock in the empire.

The two trackers that accompanied him in his search followed doggedly behind him, eager to return to hearth and home.

As they came nearer the camp, people began to wave at their returning leader and his men. Morgan acknowledged their shouts and waves with only a nod of his head. Despite his satisfaction at having been selected S'hapur, Morgan was uncomfortable with the prominence of the position. He masked his discomfort behind a stern gaze, feigning indifference to the crowd's adoration. The past weeks had been hard, with too many hours spent in the saddle amongst the forested hills of the mountains. Morgan felt worn and was in need of a bath. His leather breeks and jacket were stiff with sweat and dirt. Given a choice, he would ride over to the small lake and bathe himself, but he knew his men wouldn't allow him to compromise his dignity by doing so, so why bother trying? He released the thought with a sigh. Morgan missed his independence.

Morgan's long sword slapped lightly against his thigh as his horse cantered the final distance to the center of the camp. The sword had been handed down through generations of S'hapur. The sword and the oral histories were the traditional badge and responsibility of the S'hapur. Morgan blinked himself back to full awareness as he rode past the many skins curing on long wooden racks; he didn't want to be caught daydreaming.

At the center of the camp was a large semi-permanent structure of wood and canvas that served as Morgan's home, and community meeting place. The men with Morgan had already split off towards their own tents and families, calling their farewells. Morgan rode the final distance alone, enjoying the smells and sights of home. He had missed the familiar sights and sounds. Strangely enough, he found that he missed the familiarity of his home more than the anticipated comforts it would provide. Comfort meant little to Morgan, it took time and energy to provide, and time and energy could always be used to better effect in his opinion.

News of his approach preceded him, and other prominent members of the community were awaiting his arrival at his pavilion, as well as a small crowd of onlookers. Morgan groaned inwardly at the gathering.

The assembled leaders watched his approach quietly, looking at him closely in search of clues to the success of the mission. Others among the crowd weren't so circumspect and shouted their inquiries. Morgan distinctly heard cries of "What news Morgan?" and "Shall we have to move?" as well as many other shouted questions. He would not answer, however, he did not wish to admit his ignorance or the failure of the mission in so public a place.

He dismounted in front of his pavilion and left his horse to the care of a groomsman. He patted the tired beast on the neck before greeting the men awaiting him at the entrance of the pavilion. He looked at the assembly, and visibly sighed, knowing his bath would have to wait until much later. He enjoyed the responsibility of leading and caring for the Family, but sometimes found that he lacked the patience to explain himself to his followers.

The men awaiting him were the family's elders, a group of men selected by the community for their wisdom, and battle leaders, Morgan's sub commanders in matters of war. There were six elders and four battle leaders. Morgan stalked past them into the pavilion silently, refusing to speak until he was seated on a pile of furs with a warm cider in his hands. He knew he would have to answer their needs, but at least his position gave him the small pleasure of doing so on his own terms.

After sipping slowly at the cider for a moment he looked up to meet the expectant eyes of the assembled men. They did not seem in the least bit put off by his reticence. His habits and nuances were well known, and none would break the silence until their leader invited them to do so. Having been given the peace and respect he desired, Morgan smiled gently and set down his flagon of cider.

"I suppose you have some small interest in the results of our search of the surrounding mountainside in regards to the d'rakken mahre?" His voice was a well trained, even baritone, that created a sense of confidence. The absurd obviousness of his statement broke the tension of the men surrounding him.

Halnan, one of his battle leaders, and a childhood friend, was the first to speak. "It is of, as you say, some interest to us—yes.

Were it not important Morgan, why by the Gods, would we be here in an enclosed space with you and your ripe leathers?"

The elders seemed shocked by the casual banter, and sat motionless awaiting Morgan's response to Halnan's well-aimed jibe.

Morgan, however, was amused by the response, his face coloring slightly in embarrassment. His friend always managed to bring him down a notch, providing him with a dose of humility when he most needed it. He leaned back and took another sip of his cider, trying to conceal his unusual display of emotion behind the mug. After regaining his composure, he set the mug back down on the floor beside him and responded. "Well spoken, old friend. I should indeed speak of my mission so that I may bathe before I further offend your olfactory senses. Ah, would that you had any other senses as sharp—a sense of respect for your S'hapur for instance."

Some of the assembled elders looked with consternation at Halnan, showing their distaste at his comment and support of Morgan's rebuke. Halnan simply smiled, understanding that his friend had scored the final point in this particular round, and bowed low in mock abasement.

Morgan nodded acceptance to his friends surrender and began his long awaited story in the even voice of one trained in the story telling arts of the S'hapur. "We rode deep into the upper valleys between Northpeak and the Westridge. As we reached deeper into the mountains we began to find small communities of miners and trappers who had heard increasing rumors of d'rakken mahre traveling the lower valleys on the other side of the mountains, in the Long Wood. It's said that the d'rakken mahre parties are moving increasingly south, up into the mountains. We also heard rumors of small villages destroyed for no other reason than being in the path of the d'rakken mahre scouting parties.

"We warned those who had not heard the rumors of the d'rakken mahre to seek the safety of numbers, and found not a few who asked to be allowed under the protection of the family. Of course I granted the request. We should see some fifty or sixty men and women wandering into camp during the next week. Outside of that, we only had the mild excitement of an encounter with two rogue morkai. I seem to be out of practice in my defensive skills. One of the damned beasts fell on me after I killed it. I nearly suffocated from the smell before Darin and Thorm pulled the rank thing off of me. Nothing is more vile than the smell of a wet morkai."

The casual statement regarding the morkai caught the assembled men by surprise. Morkai were a rare giant being of low intelligence that inhabited the upper reaches of the mountains. In the past, on occasion one of the vast hairy beasts would roam into the camp. It often took a full squadron to kill the beast or chase it off, and rarely would the squad manage to do so without casualties. Morgan, apparently had killed at least one single handedly, and in truth thought nothing of it. His battle leaders eyes shown with awe and pride—and the elders with concern and fear for the safety of their leader.

Morgan read the varied thoughts of the men assembled about him. He was equally uncomfortable with the concern of the elders as he was with the awe of the battle leaders. His battle prowess was a matter of fact, not pride for him. Battle skills came easily, and Morgan felt no particular pride in anything that came easily to him.

"Anyhow," continued Morgan, "Thorm has the hides, they should bring a fine price in the markets of North Post." He broke off his narration, giving the men a chance to question him.

Brandon, one of the elders was the first to speak. He was one of the oldest members of the community; it was believed that he was over one hundred and thirty years old. The Thulistans were long lived, when war did not interfere. His voice was high and broke frequently when he spoke. "It seems that for now we are safe from the d'rakken mahre. But what of the future? The Family has grown and we would be hard pressed to move quickly, should it be needed, to protect ourselves. We must know the purpose of the d'rakken mahre. We must better understand their threat. How, Morgan, will we meet this need?"

Morgan listened quietly to the words. Brandon had wisely

counseled the previous four generations of S'hapur of the Partikson Family. In his wisdom, he asked the one question that struck dead on the head of what Morgan perceived as his failure.

The question had haunted Morgan ever since he first heard of the threat that the d'rakken mahre posed. He had almost hoped to meet with a scouting party of d'rakken mahre just to determine the scope of the threat. Although the danger was still far off, it was an unknown. He could not abide by an unknown threat endangering his Family. He was the leader. He had been entrusted to protect and guide. He was expected to give answer to the question posed by Brandon, and he had no satisfactory answer.

"This question deserves an answer and I shall give the best answer that I may. The fact is, I do not know what risk the d'rakken mahre poses the family. However, as the S'hapur of Family Partikson of the Clan Piksanie, I vow to find out. I will undertake a Quest to meet our need. I swear before those of you assembled that I will not rest or return to the family, that I will not hold myself worthy of the esteemed position you have given me, until this Quest is met."

Morgan was known to take dramatic personal risks, and often assumed the responsibility of the community squarely on his shoulders, but the extravagance of his vow caught all of the assembled men by surprise. S'hapur did not Quest, they were too important to their people to be risked so.

"Morgan, please reconsider, another must be selected to take your place!" The voice of Kallis, the newest of the communities elders rose above the general commotion.

Morgan stood slowly from the rugs, and began to untie his jerkin. "I have spoken, and as the S'hapur, I expect my decision to be respected." He then walked away from the now quiet assemblage, continuing to loosen his clothing. His bath had waited long enough, and he was going to clean up. He was no longer needed in the council meeting. They would argue for hours before realizing they had no choice in the matter, and then would grumble their way to acquiescence—it always worked out. He entered the room to the rear of the building that he lived in with a smile, mostly in anticipation of the bath awaiting him, but also for the prospect of the men he left behind. They would learn someday, he supposed. His room was comfortable but austere. Deep furs were piled upon his pallet and a great copper tub sat steaming near the fir pit.

The elders and battle leaders argued late into the night, and when that failed to produce any answers they sent Halnan as an emissary to plead with Morgan to change his plans. He knocked on the door to Morgan's room and then entered, before any reply was made from within. He found Morgan sitting in a large chair, reading from a worn book by the light of a bright brazier standing next to him.

Halnan entered the room and stopped, seeing the vexed look on Morgan's face at the intrusion. "They have asked me to come and ask you, in the name of our friendship, to change your mind. I told them that I would be lucky if you didn't beat the crap out of me for challenging your authority, but they were willing to risk my beauty."

Morgan's vexation had not lessened. This was getting ridiculous. They were supposed to argue, and then give in. Sending in his friend was not a part of the program. He was not truly angry with Halnan, though. His friend knew he would not change his mind, and was only here, going through the motions, to please those outside.

"Well," Morgan spoke slowly, "I may leave your precious hide intact if you leave very soon, and ensure them that I will not be deterred. The vow has been taken. What kind of man goes against a vow sworn in front of witnesses? By the ancient tradition of the Quest, I am committed, and my pride, and that of the family require that I fulfill my vow."

Halnan nodded in answer. He expected no less, and would not allow the council to waste any further time on discussing if Morgan would Quest. The Quest was a foregone conclusion. Preparations must be made to ensure its success. He turned and left his friend to his book.

Having decided to back the Quest, the council turned itself to planning. Late in the night, after the council completed its deliberations, an exhausted Morgan was pressed to accept one concession. Halnan, his childhood friend, and one of the families best trackers and warriors would accompany him as his Torsch, or second, vowed to fulfill the Quest should he personally fall or fail.

# THREE

## THE CITY OF TWILIGHT

In the far west of the Thulistan Empire, nestled at the apex of Talon Valley in the Moghin Mountains, the city of Torance paid little head the concerns of the Empire. The city itself was a little known outpost peopled by various outcasts and adventurers. The reason for their indifference was not because they did not know of the threat of the Tulisian Empire, or the depredations of the d'rakken mahre. Quite to the contrary, their indifference was precisely because of how well they understood these things.

The city itself was too remote, too well protected to concern itself with conquering armies. The rugged eternally snow capped mountain range surrounding it ensured armies could not approach from east, west, or north. From the south, the approach was wide open, but involved a long trek up the valley with little reward to gain even assuming any army could penetrate the high walls and massive fortifications. Regarding the rumors of the d'rakken mahre, they were unconcerned because they already knew of them. In fact, unbeknownst to the outer world, they had been actively trading with them for over a decade. This closely guarded secret was the unlikely source of the city's riches.

Its inhabitants, some five thousand men and women, knew Torance as the City of Twilight. Although protected by a castle with stout walls above, the secret of Torance remained hidden hundreds of feet underground. Beneath the castle walls, deep under the earth, the city of Torance existed in a series of natural and man made caverns. Within the protective depths of the earth, they built homes, shops, streets, and even parks.

Here they labored in secret from the upper world, garnering wealth and power. Here, over a decade ago they had discovered an entrance to the myriad highways and byways of the underworld. From these passages came creatures from the earth's womb, seeking an exchange of wealth for food and raw materials. Chief among those encountered from the depths were the diplomats of the d'rakken mahre, seeking to negotiate trade. This trade made the residents of Torance very wealthy, secretive, and unconcerned about a threat from the well-understood d'rakken mahre.

Amongst the well-populated caverns and halls of Torance lived peoples of many backgrounds and races. Carstans, Thulistans, and Barstolians worked alongside each other. Dwarves mined the rock, tending to the body and bones of mother earth. One thing shared by all was a sense of independence from all governments other than that of the castle itself, and a toughness borne of having carved out such an improbable home.

Torance was a bustling, successful, content community—at least by most accounts.

At least one inhabitant, however, was not content or happy.

Taire had been brought to the city years ago by his father. His father Arn was an adventurer who had left the green farmlands of Maldin seeking fame and wealth on the Tulisian continent. He had also hoped to escape the drudgery of farm work, the primary occupation on the island kingdom of Maldin. He was a hulking man, but kind and soft-spoken. Leaving his village and family had troubled Arn greatly as he had already possessed a deep sense of his debt to those that had supported and raised him. Despite this, he knew that his was not to be a farmer's life.

In the process of escaping one type of drudgery, Arn landed in another. Shortly after arriving on the main continent, he found himself conscripted in the Tulisian army, and after a brief training received orders to join a detachment along the Thulistan border.

He escaped the daily hell of army life by seeking romance on the lice infested cots of the Barstolian camp followers and tavern whores. One of his indiscriminate couplings had the unfortunate side effect of impregnating one of his acquaintances, a friendly, if simple Barstolian barmaid. Due to increasing discontent with military life, and the vengeful father of the barmaid, he found himself forced to flee across the border into Thulistan, seeking refuge for himself and his new wife.

They fled north into the lush Talon Valley and made a temporary home in its forested hills. He and his wife lived happily for a time, until the baby was born, taking its mother's life in the process. Arn fled the memories of their home with his newborn son, whom he named Taire after his own father, in his arms. Within a few days he had reached the head of the valley, and found the Castle Torance. He gained admittance into the castle, and in time was allowed to enter the city as a watchman of the guard.

Taire lived happily with his father during his early years. He was a playful child, growing quickly beyond the size of other children his age. He and his father frequently visited the park in the large central cavern, playing by the riverside under the artificial sunlight. The river burbled softly in its course, forming a deep and swift moat around an island of grass occupied by the lavish mansion owned by The Ruler, the master of the city and the castle above. The mansion evoked fantasies of grand adventure and wealth within Taire's young mind.

The central cavern was the only place truly lit to daylight standards, with growing grasses, plants, and many small pens for herd animals. It projected a sense of comfort and closeness, and smelled of things green and earth-like. He and his father played amongst the lights and grass and were content under the earth.

Occasionally, his father's position with the guard allowed him to bring Taire up through the upper levels of the cavern complex and into the military complex on the highest level. Once, he even accompanied his father to the castle, to the highest levels to attend a formal ceremony led by The Ruler. The Ruler seemed a great and imposing man standing in the distance of the bright hall, wearing shining silks and satins.

From the castle, he got his first glimpse of the outside world through a high window. The outside seemed a sterile, bright place full of oddly bold colors and unknown hazards. It completely lacked the comforting twilight of the under-city. It smelled similar, but lacked the comforting earth smell. The net effect was disconcerting to Taire, and he was eager to go back home to its known comforts and enclosed spaces.

The years passed with comforting regularity and with little to demarcate one from the next, until, at the age of thirteen, Taire's happiness came abruptly to an end.

Taire came home from school to find his father waiting for him. They lived in a two room flat, built over a small warehouse. The furniture was of plain but serviceable hardwood, and several old weapons were the only adornments upon the wood plank walls. Although utilitarian in layout and sparse of decoration, the yellow glow of the large lamp on the table and the smells of onion and leather oils made it home to Taire. His father stood up from his chair and walked over to his son in the doorway. He smiled and tousled Taire's sandy blonde hair.

Taire looked up at his father. "Why are you home so early da? I thought you had evening post tonight in the castle." His voice was a slightly cracking tenor, a pleasant promise of the gentle, powerful voice he would grow into.

"Yes, I was up in the castle for a time, but my shift was cut short by the Captain. He wants me to accompany a caravan of goods heading down tomorrow morning, so he sent me home to rest up." His father removed his hand from Taire's head and looked his son in the eyes. He was pleased to find that he barely had to look down to meet the lad's eyes.

"I'll be going in deep this time, be gone two weeks, like as not." He waited to see how Taire would react. The last time he left on caravan duty, Taire had screamed and cried. Arn was proud to see that his son had matured. Only a slight tremble in Taire's lower lip betrayed his emotions to his father.

Seeing this, his father felt vindicated in the decision he had made. He reached out and put both of his hands on his son's shoulders. "This time, son, I think it's time you are on your own. I want you to stay here and take care of the house for me. Can you do that for me Taire?"

Taire felt both fearful of being alone and elated at his new status. His father was treating him like a man, and this was new territory for them both. Taire stood erect and met his father's eyes. "Yes, Sir, I can take care of the house while you are away."

Arn patted his son gently on the shoulders with both hands, and turned towards the small table on which dinner had been laid out. "That's fine, son. Now, let's eat, I brought home some of those meat pies that you seem to love so much."

They both sat down and ate their dinner in silence. The pies were made with genuine beef, Taire realized, rare and costly in the under city. As he broke through the flaky crust, steam swirled up towards the low ceiling, filling the room with the smell of the beef and onion. Arn mulled over his concerns about the upcoming trip while they ate. He had already made arrangements for a neighbor to look in on Taire from time to time and had filled the larder with dried goods. Taire knew how to cook and could take care of himself, but naturally Arn worried.

Taire on the other hand, was too busy devouring his favorite meal to worry.

After working together on Taire's schoolwork, they both went to bed early.

In the morning, Taire woke up early to watch his father get ready. He watched in fascination as his father donned his work clothes; a hardened leather jerkin, long leather leggings, black boots and his long sword, in its well-used leather scabbard.

Arn and his son gripped elbows in adult fashion, bringing another lump of pride to Taire's throat. Taire received from his father a small bag of copper to buy fresh food, along with the expected exhortation not to waste or loose the money. His father nodded silently and walked out the front door into the alleyway. He turned to face Taire, "Take care, son."

Taire remained silent, not trusting himself to maintain a semblance of maturity in front of his father if he tried to speak. He could not risk shattering the fragile bubble of adult behavior he and his father had created. His eyes burned with unshed tears, and his mind swirled between the fear of being alone, and the adventure of it.

The first week passed uneventfully, Taire splitting his time between school and lengthy visits to Trill's house. Trill visited the first day and tactfully asked Taire if he would mind giving an old man the comfort of some company. Although on the first day, Taire declined, he gladly accepted the on second and each subsequent day. Taire was glad for the company of the kind, if boring old man. Taire had few friends in school, as he was so much bigger and much quieter than the others his age. His father usually filled this gap in his life, and he never regretted the exchange. Now, with his father gone and an empty house to face, he found himself lonelier than he had ever been.

He filled this void in the company of Trill. He spent hours listening to fantastic stories of battles fought long ago. Taire wasn't sure if the old man had ever really fought in any battles, but preferred the stories to being alone, and knew enough to not challenge any of the information presented. He knew that the visits were just a pretense by the old man to fulfill an obligation to his father, but each of them kept the secret to themselves, protecting Taire's fragile dignity. Regardless of the circumstances, both parties enjoyed the relationship, and benefited from the short-term arrangement.

Towards the end of the second week, Taire began to get anxious for his father's return. He felt he had grown during his time alone, and was eager for his father to see his new maturity. Mostly though, Taire was lonely for his father's company and the comfort it provided. Each day after school he traveled the southern route to the central cavern; south through Barter Row, where the incoming trader's parked their wagons, and set up their stalls to display their wares. Taire rarely visited this section of caverns. His father preferred he stay away from the traders and the hawkers along the row. Their stalls boasted many bright fabrics and strange foodstuffs, weapons, housewares, and other treasures. Despite the lure of the array of goods, the sharp-faced hawkers were disconcerting to Taire, and he kept his distance.

All the way towards the end of the cavern, near Southtown (a newer subdivision of the city as a whole) was the heavily fortified exit into the depths of the under-earth. Each day he came here to ask about his father. Each day the guards informed him that his father's caravan was due back soon, telling him to be patient and come back the next day. Taire eagerly ran back to the guard station each day, with growing trepidation.

With the imagination of a boy not fully into his manhood, he envisioned the worst.

Finally, one day a full week past when the caravan was due, he returned to the guard post. He breathlessly greeted the guard on duty, a rather small and unimposing young fellow he had never seen before. "Sir, any word of the caravan that went out about three weeks ago, my father was one of the guards, and they are late returning . . ."

The guard, having heard about the boy from one of the many other gate guards Taire had pestered, interrupted Taire's rambling question. "As a matter of fact lad, I heard a rumor that two men from your father's caravan returned this morning. Neither one was your father understand, but they may have news of him. One of them is with the leech, but the other has returned to the upper barracks. I am off duty in a few minutes. If you can wait, I'll take you up to see the man. He should be able to tell you what happened to your dad."

For a moment, Taire pestered the man with questions about his father, about the injured man from his father's caravan, and about the other returned guard. The guard on duty, however, had not been present when the two caravan guards returned, and really didn't know anything. Taire paced the cavern restlessly, looking for some outlet to his nervous energy. He refused to allow his imagination to run away. Any number of things could have held up his father. It was not uncommon for a man injured during the journey to return with an escort, it did not mean his father had come to harm. He knew he would just have to wait and find out.

Finally, after an eternity of waiting, or about twenty minutes depending on whom you asked, a grim, older soldier relieved the guard from duty. The young guard called to Taire, who was sitting on a rock a short distance away. "Come on lad, I'll take you up to the barracks, and we'll find the man, so you can find out about your father." With a friendly slap between Taire's shoulders, he led the way, not looking back to see if the boy was keeping up. With a facade of bravery becoming a young man, Taire allowed the guard to lead him through the many halls and chambers of the city.

After a brisk walk of about a half-mile, they passed through the lower city levels up to the entrance to the barracks level. Taire's escort asked a few questions of another guard who was on post at the top of the ramp leading from the city into the military quarters. Taire loitered quietly in the background while the two men spoke. Apparently the guard discovered what he needed to know and began moving again, waving for Taire to follow. "Come on lad, I found out where he's at, lets go," the guard called over his shoulder, moving off at his business like pace.

Despite his preoccupation with finding about his fathers late return, Taire couldn't help but notice the peculiarities of the never before halls of the barracks section. The lighting was much brighter than elsewhere in the caverns, and the hallways were fashioned from smooth stone blocks and ran in long orderly runs and turned at clean ninety degree angles, as opposed to the almost haphazard placement of streets and alleyways of the lower caverns. Doors were evenly spaced, many with guards standing at post. Occasionally, through an open door, Taire saw stores of casks and crates of unknown materials stacked high to the ceiling. Without fail, these rooms boasted guards at the doors. Almost as an afterthought, Taire also noted the low carved ceilings. It was clear that the founders of the city had delved this level out of the solid rock, and he thought they must have found the caverns below later.

After a few more turns and long hallways, they arrived at a small barracks room. There was no guard at the door and Taire's escort knocked tersely and entered without awaiting a response. Taire looked about the hall one last time, took a deep breath and followed.

After being led into the room, Taire awkwardly awaited introductions. The young guard, seeing his hesitation shook himself lightly and spoke, "Faran, this is Taire, Arn's boy." After this brief introduction, he turned and left without further ado, leaving Taire to complete his business in private. Faran was reclining on a small military cot against the wall. He was out of uniform wearing only a warm pair of hose and patched stockings. There were about a dozen other empty cots in the room, all with a solitary trunk at their base for personal belongings.

Faran, Taire noted, was short, just over five feet, with a dark complexion, and nut-brown hair; the prototypical Barstolian. Taire shifted uncomfortable on his feet for a moment, unsure of how to ask the question that he was so desperately afraid to ask.

He was relieved of that problem as Faran stretched his arms and then stood up from his bunk to inspect his visitor. Standing, he was a good bit shorter than the younger Taire, but his lean form crisscrossed with scars made him appear somehow sinister and dangerous. The long scar across his forehead attracted Taire's attention involuntarily. It created a crease so deep, that Taire almost wanted to reach out and touch it. After only a brief moment, Faran forestalled further investigation of his battle marks by speaking. "So, it's Taire is it? Arn's boy? You're going to be big like your da, look a lot like him in fact." His voice was oddly soft and was completely at odds with his visage.

The compliment was almost lost on Taire, so absorbed was he on the question of his father. He fidgeted, unsure of what to do with his hands. He felt inadequate under the man's gaze; young, afraid, and unsure. He filled the pause in Faran's small talk by blurting out his question. "Sir, my father—is he dead, Sir?" It wasn't the question he intended to ask, it presented a blunt reality he wasn't prepared to accept.

Faran scowled, which made the scar on his forehead almost fold down over his eyebrows, and seemed to consider his answer for a moment. "Not a 'Sir', boy, just Faran will do. We leave the 'Sir' for the officers, and I don't much look like an officer or a gentleman do I?" The man fingered the scar on his head to emphasize the point. Taire wanted to scream at the man for not answering his question. Before he could ask again, Faran continued. "Well boy, let me tell you what happened, and you will have to make that decision for yourself. You see, we were guarding a train of raw materials down to Station Three, that's one of the deeper drak caves that we trade with you know. Everything was going by the book, no problems. 'Bout halfway there, we run into a minor cave in. The wagons could not pass, and the sergath were skittish, they can always sense unstable rock you know."

Taire had seen sergath many times in the caravan area. They were horse-sized lizards, with thick long bodies, short tails, and short muscular legs. They quickly replaced donkeys and oxen as beasts of burden for cavern trading missions due to their special affinity for the depths. They understood the underworld; they fed on its fungi and drank from the dank pools. They were slow, but untiring. It was news to Taire that they could sense potential cave-ins, however.

Faran continued, "we decided it would take too long to clear the debris, and that the balky sergath may not proceed anyhow even if we could move it all. We took what the Captain called a calculated risk. We had a rough map, and it showed a side passage that should have met with the main road a mile or so down. Not surprisingly, our map was wrong. Hell, outside of the marked passages we normally use, the rest of them seem change every time someone tries to map them. Damn frustrating it is. Anyhow, we traveled for almost a full day before we figured that we might be in trouble. Despite this, we decided to keep going as we had gone too far to turn back and still make the agreed upon delivery dates. The load had to be delivered, and we were at least traveling down, and south.

"Well, a few days later we found ourselves in wider passages, worn by heavy travel. It seemed we were on course to somewhere along the beaten path. It was only a half-mile before the passage opened into a large cavern, and we all knew what that meant. The cavern was filled with the large rocklike structures that the draks live in, although we did not see any about at first. Although it was not our destination, it seemed a safe assumption that we could get some help finding Station Three. We walked right out into the middle of their damned hive and started shouting, knowing that they always reacted quickly to unexpected visitors. Damn good thing we were with a caravan, I thought, as it is questionable how they would react to our being there otherwise. Anyhow, at first, nothing happened, but after a minute, we heard the loud clicking noise the draks make when they run. We looked to the left, where the sound was coming from just in time to see a large party of warriors enter the hive area. There wasn't a diplomat with them, or even an organizer, and they were headed right for us."

Taire remembered what his father had taught him: D'rakken marhe were hive creatures, creatures of instinct for the most part. The diplomats seemed to have the ability for independent thought, and localized command over the warriors and workers. Organizers seemed to be almost like antennae for the queen, they enforced her rule, and helped control the sometimes-fractious warriors.

"Well," continued Faran, "seeing the danger of uncontrolled draks, we began to retreat, taking cover behind the wagons, knowing an organizer or a diplomat would be close behind.

"Then they hit us without warning; a large group of degan surged out of another side passage. We were trapped between a raiding party of degan, and the defending draks, between the proverbial rock and a hard place if you follow my meaning." Faran gave Taire a half grin as he caught his breath before continuing.

Degan were a bipedal creature, rat-like in appearance Taire remembered. They were only a couple of feet tall, but relatively intelligent, and very ferocious. They ran in packs, and fed off anything they caught.

Faran, seeing Taire's lack of response at his cleverness, continued. "Anything in the cave that wasn't a drak was an enemy to the warrior draks and they attacked us as well as the degan. We found ourselves hard pressed from both sides. The Captain had myself and four other guards break for a side passage with the traders. Before we left, we saw the Captain fall, your father and four other men were retreating towards a small passage on the opposite side of the cavern from us, outnumbered five to one by draks.

"During our escape, we were harried by the degan, and only Dort and myself made it back. It was a long trip, running and fighting. Lucky to be alive, I am. We only had degan to deal with. But your father—well it would be a miracle boy." Faran looked pained at the memory, at the loss of friends in the depths.

Taire was speechless and numb with loss. Grief clenched his throat and tears burned in his eyes. His heart seemed to pause in his breast, as if he were unsure he could continue to live in the absence of his father. "Thank you Sir, I understand—I have to go." Taire fled the room before he lost his composure. He ran blindly through the military complex, until a guard chased him out to the ramp to the under-city. He ran home and cried through the night. He wanted his father back, but that was only the first of his problems and the beginning of his troubles.

Taire found the world an unfriendly place in the absence of his father, in the absence of money.

By the end of the week, the owner of the building evicted him after visiting to collect the rent and finding Taire alone and broke. All of the furnishings and personal belongings were held by the owner as what he called a 'penalty' for breaking the rental agreement. Taire was sure that this was unfair, but received a backhand for his protestations, and knew no one would support a lone young man over the landlord.

He found himself possessionless on the street. Even then, he did not fully understand the ramifications of his position. His situation had little to do with any understandable reality; he couldn't grasp its importance. Food and shelter were not something a child questioned; they just were. Taire began to learn just how wrong this assumption was. Neighbors and friends became strangers, unwilling to take on an extra mouth to feed. Without his father, he found himself without resources or support; even the doors of his school were closed to him. Torance was not known for the generosity of its inhabitants, it was a hard town filled with hard people, and none of them wanted to take the responsibility for someone else's child.

During the first nights he slept in the large park, hidden behind some shrubs. The temperature was steady and comfortable, but the hunger quickly became unbearable. Taire would have preferred to stay in the park, but none of the grasses were edible, he got sick trying several varieties during the second day, and he knew his only chance to find food was in the city streets, so he spent his days wandering the streets and alleys of the main level, looking for scraps of food in the rubbish bins. He found enough to eat to stay alive this way, but not enough to stop the painful grumbling in his midsection. Despite all of this, he tried to keep clean and be presentable. He knew that he could not be seen as a vagabond, or he would risk being pressed into excavation service in the drawven quarters. No amount of hunger would warrant risking that punishment; it was a lifelong sentence, and Taire's father had told him that not many lived long in the deadly mines.

He looked for work, but was too young for physical work or guard jobs, too uneducated for any skilled labor, and unwilling to work for those that hired young men as 'companions'. Even if he been qualified for any of the jobs, his efforts were only halfhearted, and he secretly waited for his father to come back and rescue him. At the end of the first week, his hunger finally led him to theft, the penalty for which was only a flogging. He was too big and awkward for a life of thievery, however, and was chased three blocks after his first and only attempt. Even after this, he still refused to beg, not willing to risk the mines.

Towards the end of the second week, hungry and desperate, he found himself at the small bridge that led to The Ruler's mansion in the common cavern. The mansion was a sprawling stone and timber structure separated from the rest of the cavern by a small but swift river. The building reminded him of dreams built with his father, and he found himself attracted to it like a moth to flame. Not really knowing why he was here, but seeing the mansion as the his last chance, he walked to the small bridge that spanned the brook, and was confronted by a large, armed guard.

The guard, a burly looking veteran who Taire had never seen before, looked at the tall boy standing in front of him with casual disdain. He waited a moment before determining that the boy was not going to go away before addressing him. "Move on boy, you got no business here."

Taire looked at the man with an intensity brought on by desperation. "Sir, I've come to offer my services to The Ruler. I am willing to do any work that needs done. I'm big for my age, and strong." *I don't want to be alone, I'm hungry and tired, please sir?* Taire managed to keep the last unspoken.

The guard considered him for a moment, considered the unspoken plea that was implicit in the boy's lean frame. After a moment, some part of him softened and he straightened his pike and stepped aside from the front of the bridge, allowing Taire access. "Go around to the back door and tell Myra I sent you. If work is to be had, she'll find it for you. Go lad." The guard waved Taire towards the indicated door. To Taire, it was like the opening of the gates of heaven. As Taire rushed past, the guard shook his head slowly and returned to his alert position.

It was one of the few kind things the dour guard had ever done. Had he known the results, he would never have considered it a kindness.

# FOUR

## THE RULER

Taire did indeed find work in The Rulers mansion. Myra, the woman the guard had sent him to, met him at the door. She was of indeterminate age, wearing her sandy hair in a tight bun. She wore a clean white apron over a worn homespun dress. She was pleasant to look at, although her mouth pinched at the corners. In all, Taire found her comforting.

"Hello, Ma'am. The guard at the bridge sent me," Taire said. "He said you could find work for me?"

The fact that he gained passage across the bridge attested to the honesty of his statement, and the women opened the door to allow him entry. "Come in then, lets find out what you may do to earn your keep." She looked him over carefully as he passed her into the large kitchen. She walked slowly over to a small wooden table and took a seat, motioning to Taire to do the same. His stomached lurched within as he caught the smells of fresh breads and various cooking spices.

"Well, you are well grown for a boy, although not so as to be able to do an honest days labor." Her voice was pleasant, if a bit abrupt, as if every word were bitten off. "It so happens," she continued in a businesslike fashion, "that I have been instructed to hire a boy, and I think you will suit quite well—once we clean you up a little that is. You're not afraid to work long and odd hours are you boy?" Taire shook his head to the negative. "Ever had the cough or the drooping sickness?" Negative again. "Not wanted by the guard?" Without waiting for a response this time, she went on. "Fine then, you might just do."

To Taire's immense relief and pleasure, Myra began to explain the daily duties of a personal page to The Ruler. He could not think of a more important or exciting job to have. It seemed his only duties were to attend the needs of The Ruler. The Ruler only spent a few days a week in his under-earth manor, and his duties, Myra told him, would be light. Taire felt that the job was important, even if it only paid room and board.

Better yet, while she talked she bustled about the kitchen, putting together a plate with bread, cheeses, and dried apples for Taire.

"Now boy," said Myra as she handed Taire the plate. "You must understand, if you take this job, you have to be here all of the time, no scampering about! The Ruler does not like to wait for his page so you must be here. You understand?"

Taire nodded in affirmation, too bemused to respond, and too busy eating the wonderful cheese and bread. Of course he didn't mind, he did not care if he ever left the mansion. It provided a home and structure and activity to fill the void his heart had become. He hoped it would provide him with a future, allow him to live until the pain went away and something mattered again.

In his bewilderment and excitement at having a home and food, he overlooked the lines of stress under Myra's eyes, the way she involuntarily flinched when she spoke of The Ruler. Nor did he notice the sorrow in her voice as she described his job duties to him. Every word was spoken like an apology.

During his first night in the manor, Myra cleaned and mended his clothing while giving further instructions regarding the workings of the household. He was told to sleep on a pallet in a small niche in the back of a large storage room just off the kitchen itself. The niche boasted a small straw pallet and a hanging lamp. One of the three walls was the heavy stone backside of the kitchen fireplace, and heat radiated into the room through the warm rocks.

Despite the promise of his first day, it wasn't long before Taire began to understand Myra's unspoken apology. The Ruler paid his first visit to his under-earth mansion the very next day. He examined his new servant with a trained eye. The frank look of appraisal he gave Taire made him feel strangely uncomfortable. Something about the man made his skin crawl. He remembered The Ruler as an imposing man, and he still seemed so, but in a more personal sense. He was intimidating, and frequently looked intently at his new servant at odd times with a disconcerting smile. His smile held no warmth or mirth; actually it terrified Taire.

He found his official job duties quite simple, to stand by The Ruler and be prepared to answer his every whim. Mostly he fetched things; papers, drinks, and any other thing he could think of. It seemed that this job just might be everything Myra had said it would be.

It wasn't long before he began to discover the meaning behind Myra's odd behavior when speaking of The Ruler. While carrying a cool drink The Ruler had requested, he stumbled on a lump in the rug and spilled a small amount of the red liquid on it. The Ruler stood and pointed a shaking finger at the small stain on the rug. "Do you have any IDEA how much that rug cost? How dare you be so clumsy, how dare you—don't you have any respect for my home, don't you—don't you . . ." The ruler seemed like he was going to go into an apoplectic fit, he was becoming incoherent with rage. His face was purple with anger, and veins stood out, pulsing in time with his rage, on his forehead.

Taire had never been the focus of such intent fury. Paralyzed with fear and confusion, he bent to the floor and mopped at the wet spot with the hem of his shirt. "I'm sorry Sir—I'm sorry—I'll clean it—I'm sorry, it was just an accident, I'll . . ." His jumbled apology was interrupted by a strong back swing of The Rulers hand. Taire sprawled to the floor. The Ruler, sputtering incoherently stepped over to him and lifted him by the arms until Taire was held erect in front of him. Taire was whimpering, tears running down his cheeks, over the dark welt developing there.

The Ruler shouted directly into his face, spraying him with

spit as he screamed. "Sorry . . . sorry? You little bastard, I'll teach you sorry." As he finished, he threw Taire from his grasp. Taire landed on his back, the wind knocked out of his lungs. He couldn't breathe or move.

"Wha, Wha," gasped Taire over and over trying to catch his breath.

The Ruler kicked him repeatedly in the legs and arms, now simply grunting with the effort. Seeing the beaten form on the carpet seemed to mollify the anger of The Ruler, transforming it into something more subtle, and more horrible.

When The Ruler finished beating Taire, he smiled down at the bruised, cowering form below him. It was a strange smile, a smile that contained a threat that the hurting boy could not identify. The Ruler did not seem oblivious to his pain; quite to the contrary, he seemed positively pleased by it.

The Ruler bent down next to Taire and gently stroked his bleeding forehead. "Now—I know you are sorry." He whispered the words in Taire's ear as he continued stroking his hair. His fingers tightened in Taire's hair, until it became painful. He forced Taire to look at his face.

A drop of sweat dripped from the trembling lip onto Taire's face.

"I'm sorry you made me do this," said The Ruler. "You must learn to be a good boy, I will teach you. You will learn to appreciate my home, and the lessons I teach you." He released his hold on Taire's head, allowing it to bounce on the floor. Taire was too shocked to register the pain his body felt. He was too afraid to respond to The Ruler. He just lay, bleeding, staring wide-eyed at The Ruler who rose and walked back to his desk.

Taire wiped the heavy drop of sweat from his cheek and kept scrubbing at the spot as if it burned. For several minutes he just lay there until Myra entered the room with a towel in hand. She stopped several feet away from Taire and looked to The Ruler, gently wringing the towel in her hands.

The Ruler gave an almost imperceptible nod, and Myra moved forward to mend to Taire's cuts and bruises. She did not say a word, and could not meet his eyes.

During the following two days while The Ruler rested in his manor, Taire painfully limped about his duties and learned to be careful. He made no mistakes, made no move that threatened to anger The Ruler. As long as he avoided upsetting him, The Ruler seemed content to only smile cruelly and say, "that's good boy, you learn quickly."

While The Ruler stayed in his home, Taire remained locked in his chambers with him at night, to be prepared to meet any of his masters needs. He slept on the floor by the door, as far from the bed as he was able. He served in silence, afraid of the reaction The Ruler may have to his voice or his words.

At the end of the third day, Taire was told by Myra that the master would be returning to the castle. He felt too much pain and uncertainty to feel joy at the thought of life without The Ruler. He was not sure he was capable of a real emotion like joy. The absence of pain was enough for now. It was not long before his satisfaction at The Ruler's upcoming departure turned sour.

Before leaving, The Ruler spoke to him. His voice was harsh and phlegmatic from heavy drinking. It matched his corpulent form, rasping from the depths of his depravity. "Boy, you don't seem to appreciate the opportunity I've given you. Sure, you learn to keep out of trouble, but you just don't appreciate what you have."

Taire stood with his eyes locked on the floor, carefully not responding. He had no idea of what The Ruler was leading up to. Seeing this lack of response, The Ruler continued. "You will learn to appreciate it—to appreciate me. You'll see. When I'm not here, you will have no life, understand, no life. No friends, no activities, nothing. You are MINE!"

So saying, he grabbed Taire's arm and dragged him across the floor to a small door across the room. Taire allowed himself to be dragged unresisting across the room. The Ruler opened the small door and thrust him inside. As The Ruler stood in the doorway for a moment looking at his him, Taire noticed the stout construction of the door, and the small slot at the base.

Finally The Ruler turned and slammed the door. The situation did not register on Taire until he heard a bolt shoot home on the other side of the door. He was imprisoned.

The closet was just over six feet to a side, constructed of tight fitting planks. The room had been emptied of all clothes, the sturdy shelves along the back wall empty. At the top of the shelves, about seven feet off of the floor, was a small barred window, allowing a small amount of light to filter in from the outside cavern. A small pot was provided for hygienic functions.

Despite the nature of his new home, it was still a home to Taire. Actually, he found the privacy comforting. Nothing could hurt him here, could it? During the first few days of his imprisonment, he explored the boundaries and rules of his existence. He was brought food twice a day. It was slid under the door quietly, and his attempts at calling for help from his server were met with silent indifference.

By the end of the second day, the vague satisfaction at being alone and safe was slowly being replaced by a need for human interaction. He had never truly been alone before, and he was beginning to find it unbearable. He was wrong in his thought that he couldn't be hurt here. Alone in the dim closet, he ached with loneliness. He climbed the shelves to peer out the window to find only a view of a small yard enclosed by the sloping rock walls of the side of the cavern. He realized he was looking out the back of the house towards the cavern wall.

Only a small amount of light traveled along the wall down into the small yard. He called for hours, vainly shouting at the immutable wall. His screaming, apparently, went unnoticed.

At times, he simple sat silently listening at the window. Once or twice he even thought he might have heard the lingering echo of a loud voice from the park, but he was never sure if it was real or imagined. It was not long before he gave up yelling and listening at the window.

During the third day he discovered the small hole on the lower back corner of the closet. He inspected the small opening and determined it was a knothole that had been enlarged by small teeth: A mouse hole. He lie silently near the hole, listening for the sounds of those that had made it. On occasion, like a gift to his lonely soul, he would capture a faint rustle of moving feet, and once or twice, he thought he saw a small face peer out at him, quickly darting away.

On the fifth day of his imprisonment, his exile from humanity ended.

The Ruler again returned to his manor and required his servant. Initially, the thrill at human interaction seemed to detract from the horror of his previous mistreatment. His memory of horror quickly renewed itself, however. This time, Taire was beat repeatedly. Each time, The Ruler would hold him up and shout, "Why don't you learn," or "don't you appreciate the life I've given you," or other equally pathetic excuses. He took pleasure in Taire's pain. Each time he would hit until he ran out of energy, and the tenderly instruct Taire in the error of his ways.

Taire developed a definition of evil, and a face to associate it with. He tasted despair to the depths of his soul.

After a brief stay of only two days, The Ruler again consigned Taire to his private hell of lonely despair and mind numbing isolation. He passed the time sitting on the opposite side of the closet from the mouse hole awaiting the visits of his furry savior. His small furry friend began to visit more frequently, and come farther out of its protective hole. Taire began to hold long, one-sided conversations in his dark closet. He spoke to the mouse of his life before The Ruler, before pain. He meticulously avoided talking of his present circumstances, instead fabricating stories of his fathers expected return and his rescue from The Ruler.

Taire began to leave crumbs just outside the small hole, eagerly awaiting the darting shape of the mouse grabbing the morsels. Over time, the curious rodent began to venture forth into the closet after carefully sniffing the air for signs of danger. At times, it would stand silently on his hind legs examining Taire for a brief moment before scurrying back into his hole.

Months passed by without notice, and Taire endured his cycle of privation and abuse. He endured in a world of fantasy revolving around the life of the mouse. He dreamt of its freedoms in the wondrous world within the walls.

Taire's body grew upon the nourishment given it, but his willpower withered. Soon, he became what his master wanted. His blank gaze and practiced servility satisfied The Rulers need for submission. Even when he made no mistakes, The Ruler occasionally beat him, explaining that he was responsible for Taire's 'education and upbringing'. Taire did not care any more.

Taire no longer felt his humiliation. From his world within the walls of the underground manor, he was oblivious to the privation and abuse of his body.

Taire became familiar to the mouse. Against the improbability, they formed a bond; came to know each other. The mouse would examine Taire's wounded form, black eyes shiny with what seemed to Taire to be compassion and understanding. It would stay and eat the crumbs he left for it. It would listen to his ramblings. It held his sanity together by its very existence. It provided a linchpin to his fading sense of self.

When the mouse left, he often found himself fantasizing that he could enter into the wonderful world tunnels and crawl spaces that the mouse inhabited. He imagined himself following his friend into his home, and escaping the torment of his life.

His need to escape was absolute. Purity of desire, coupled with a previously unknown talent, led to his salvation. One evening, shortly before The Ruler was expected to return, his friend again visited Taire. Its eyes burned like glossy black beacons in its furry face. Taire looked carefully into its eyes, and saw through into its mind and soul. There he found his answer, his hope, and his birthright.

# FIVE

## THE TORSCH

Morgan accepted the inclusion of Halnan as his Torsch with ill grace. He saw the quest as something personal, a risk that he shouldn't place upon anyone but himself. As the keeper of the oral histories, however, he knew better than any that the naming of a Torsch was a sacred right of those whose fates were intertwined with that of the Questor. His people had the right to protect the Quest by providing a second should he fail. It was the thought that they believed he might fail that rankled.

He viewed his life as a constant struggle to prove his worthiness to his people. They had rewarded his competence by naming him S'hapur. Now, they questioned his abilities by forcing him to include a second on his Quest. Morgan, in his confidence and complex loyalties, could not fathom the fact that his people cared for him. He would never understand that they sought only to provide companionship and assistance to their S'hapur. In the depths of his own self-doubt, the self-doubt that provided the balance that made him a truly great man, he did not understand that his people never for a moment doubted his ability to succeed.

On the morning of the departure, his personal page woke him early with a gentle shake. He sat on the edge of the bed for a moment, giving his body a moment to fully awaken. He stood and stretched luxuriantly, his body well rested and relaxed. In the pre-dawn gloom, he donned his leather breeks, and the hardened leather vest he selected to provide a measure of protection against unnatural hazards. Below the vest he wore a heavy woolen tunic to hold back the natural hazard posed by the cold of the high mountain air. The tunic was waterproof to provide comfort during the frequent highland drizzles and downpours. Over the vest, he wore a narrow sash designed with the Family tartan, a tight pattern of forest greens and ash grey. He slipped steel gauntlets over his hands to protect his wrists and hands, and quickly braided his hair into a long warriors braid. He slipped a short dagger into a boot, as well as a long one into a sheath on his belt. Finally, he buckled his sword onto his belt, its comforting weight resting along his leg, a constant reminder of the burden of responsibility he had freely undertaken.

He quickly ate the food that his page brought in on a tray, some apples, bread, and cheese, and washed it down with a cup of cider.

Feeling as ready as possible, he double checked his gear and stepped out of his pavilion into the brisk mountain air. The sun would soon rise over the mountain peaks to the east. Its rays already lighted the higher elevations of Northpeak and Westridge, making the heights glitter with the brilliance of diamonds in the sun. The beauty of the sun rising over the mountains always has a profound effect on Morgan. The mountains were ever changing, yet permanent, beautiful, yet deadly. He appreciated the contradictions, understood the complexity of nature, and enjoyed the challenges it provided.

Hundreds of his people had risen to see him off. They stood solemnly around the pavilion awaiting his emergence. Upon seeing him, heroic and dour in his fighting gear, they broke out in a ragged cheer. Morgan, little accustomed to pomp, assumed the look of one who had eaten something gone bad. His sour looks quickly quieted the crowds cheering, but not, apparently their goodwill toward the S'hapur and his charismatic Torsch.

Standing nearby, Halnan did a poor job of suppressing a grin at Morgan's discomfort. Morgan nodded once to his friend, and climbed into his steed's saddle. He selected Bran, his favorite battle horse, for the expedition. Bran was a huge brute of a beast, well trained and capable of fighting like a dervish. Like most of his kind, he was also strong enough to travel from dawn to dusk for days on end. Bran was bred to the mountains, and was sure-footed and intelligent. The grooms had brushed his chestnut coat to a gloss, and plaited his tail in glittering silver.

Halnan was outfitted for his role as tracker. He wore leathers much like those of Morgan, however he wore a bow across his shoulders and two long and sturdy knives at his waist instead of a sword. He was very tall for a Thulistan, taller even than Morgan, at a little over six feet tall, and also wider shouldered than Morgan. Despite his size, he moved quickly and soundlessly through the forests, and Morgan knew his help would be indispensable. As children, Halnan always beat Morgan at wrestling, but with a blade, none could match the S'hapur.

Halnan's hair was light brown and his eyes the typical hazel of the mountain people. He was quick to laughter, and anger, and had been a stout companion ever since Morgan's childhood. Morgan himself was the only man who could best Halnan in a test of strength or of arms. Together, they were a formidable party.

Halnan also rose into his saddle after tying the reigns of the packhorse to the back of his saddle. He rode over to Morgan and greeted him with a smile and a mock salute. "Good morning, S'hapur. Your humble Torsch requests his orders."

Morgan grinned. As usual, the effect was something between a grimace and a snarl. Halnan was one of the few people able to make him use those particular, almost forgotten muscles in his jaws. He retorted quietly to his friend with a look of feigned reproach. "I believe, my good Torsch, we should be off before my dignity suffers further from the sharpness of your wit. If you don't cease to prattle so in front of the others, I shall be forced to forget my humble nature, and command you beaten for your insolence to your exalted leader."

Halnan had not expected any response to his jibe in so public a place, and Morgan's response left him laughing uncontrollably for a moment, almost falling out of the saddle from the outburst. The assembled men and women looked at each other searching for some answer to Halnan's unexpected laughter.

Morgan took this all in stride, appearing unshakable and unbothered by his companion's apparent instability. He looked across those assembled and spoke a few carefully selected words to reassure them. "You have all placed your trust in me, and I will strive to be worthy. I have undertaken this Quest in answer to our families need, and will not return until the Quest is fulfilled."

He paused briefly, needing time to think of something more to say, to give some closure to his speech. He met each of the elders and battle leaders eyes for a moment. While still holding his councils gazes, he continued. "Care for the needs of the family, and do not worry for the fate of the Quest, I will succeed. Understand, I fully expect for things to be in good order when I return."

He turned his gaze outwards, his stomach twisting into a knot at the prolonged exposure to the crowd. "You must all continue to work hard to ensure the success of this community. Remember the honor of the family and the clan. Be well."

As loved for the conventional wisdom of his speeches as for the brevity, Morgan received loud shouts of approval and encouragement as he signaled to Halnan and rode slowly through the throng, Halnan and the packhorse close behind. As they rode from the village, Halnan waved at those who had come from their tents to watch them depart, and wish them well. Morgan was typically quiet, thoughts turned inward in contemplation of the days ahead.

They rode out through the northern end of the valley towards the high northern pass that would eventually lead them down into the deep valley to the north that the Long Wood filled. It was early in the autumn, and they knew that the high pass would be passable, although the temperatures would still be well below freezing at night, and the glaciers they would travel on would hide many fissures covered only by thin ice, and other hazards just as deadly.

For the first three days they traveled through the well-known but sparsely inhabited high vales of Northpeak. The weather held clear and cool except for the brief morning drizzles that were common to the northern highlands. They spoke briefly with some of the locals who recognized Morgan and asked of the oncoming danger of the d'rakken mahre. Morgan met all questions with a warning to move to the lower valleys and join the main body of the family for safety. Many brushed aside his concern, over-confident in their ability to survive by the harsh climate and fierce predators of the highlands. Others packed up and moved south, unwilling to risk family and friends to the unknown depredations of the d'rakken mahre.

Each night they found small settlements willing to take them in. They were fed and treated to such hospitality as the hard lifestyle of the mountains allowed. Most importantly, they gained information; stories from the north regarding the movements of the d'rakken mahre. On their third night, the last among the inhabited regions, they met up with a trapper just setting up camp for the evening in a small clearing. Upon casual inquiry he indicated that he had important information that travelers may be interested in.

The trapper was a gnarled, short man, wearing layers of poorly cured hides. Morgan and Halnan had smelled the furs even before seeing the man. His shaggy beard covered his face entirely, leaving only his mouth and gleaming dark eyes visible. Morgan sensed that behind the ragged exterior, the trapper hid a keen intellect. As with many traders, the man likely maintained his guise of simplicity to gain advantage in trade negotiations with the fur buyers in Billings.

The man's name was Kerny, and he invited Morgan and Halnan to share his camp for the night. The trapper provided them with a large dinner, and shared a flask of brandy as they enjoyed the warmth of the fire. After dinner, Morgan queried his host about the recent goings on around the mountains. Trappers were well known for covering large distances.

"Well," began the man, with his mouth still full of food, "it's been a while since I traveled deep into the mountains. Last winter I did very well you see—filled my storage shed with quality hides. Last spring I took the hides into Billings to trade them, and well— I sort of ended up staying in the city for about three months.

Drank and gambled all of my profits for the year. I'm just now returning to the mountains to begin trapping again, hoping to store away enough hides to pay my way through the winter."

Morgan, prone to impatience, interrupted the man. "So you are telling us that you have not even been in the mountains during the last three months? I was hoping to learn something of the d'rakken mahre, and their comings and goings. If your important information is not regarding the draks, what is it?"

Kerney smiled at Morgan's impatience, wiped some old food from his beard with a filthy furred sleeve, and answered. "Well, sorry I am if I have mislead you, but you did not specify that you wanted information regarding the draks. I do indeed have interesting information, though, to a man such as yourself who may know what to make of it. A poor trapper such as myself knows a good rumor when he hears it, but of course I couldn't tell you what it means." His mischievous grin left Morgan doubting that the man had any question as to the value, or the meaning of the information he was carefully withholding.

Morgan looked slowly at the man, trying to determine what he may want in exchange for his information. Halnan sat quietly, watching the entire exchange. After a moment, Morgan determined that the man wasn't pushing for any reward, but simply enjoying the verbal spar.

Morgan warmed up to the challenge. "Well, we are actually just simple folk, much like yourself. I don't possibly know what value anything you could have heard in the city would do for two soldiers seeking passage over the mountains to scout the forests beyond. The problem is, the evening is young, and I don't prefer to sit silently at camp for yet another night. Tell your tale if you will friend, and perhaps together we can determine it's importance."

"Soldiers eh?" Answered the old man. "Never seen soldiers with such fine weapons—well spoken too. Never mind that though, what's an old trapper know about soldiers? You could be battle leaders, or even S'hapur for all I know, although you'd be awful young for such honors."

Both Morgan and Halnan sat with stunned expressions on

their faces. Morgan assumed the man was bright, and realized he had clearly underestimated him. The man was obviously well informed, and had known all evening whom he had been hosting. "Well then," responded Morgan, "obviously you do understand what may be important information. I give in, good sir. Let us dispense with this gaming and discuss this information you have been withholding."

Kerny smiled and nodded. "Right then. In fact, you will surely find my rumor as interesting as any information regarding the draks. In fact, it's not just a rumor, but an established fact from a reputable source. It seems that Clans Kailison and Olbaric have issued a call to arms along the Barstol border."

Clan Olbaric, Morgan knew, was currently the clan of the Mal S'hapur-la, the leading clan of the Empire.

This fact made the information that much more disturbing to Morgan. Clan Olbaric inhabited the lands to the east of the Moghin Mountains that were adjacent to the Barstolian border, and had raided across the border for generations. Never before had they called to arms, though. That meant a call to all able-bodied men of fighting age from all families. Clan Kailison had long closely allied itself with the larger clan, and it was no surprise they would join in any action of Clan Olbaric. Even if the call did not extend any further, which was unlikely as at least two other clans, Wrastson, and Nemonson owed ancient blood debt to Clan Olbaric, the call to arms would mean as many as forty thousand fighting men collecting on the border.

This could only mean an impending attack by the Tulisian forces from Barstol. Morgan knew that if those forces were reinforced by one of the Tulisian armies from within Tulisia itself, Clan Olbaric would be forced to call upon all clans for levies to reinforce the border. This would then involve all fifteen clans, not just three. Even though many clans would only be able to send half of their fighting men, over one hundred thousand men could easily answer such a call. Morgan had a keen understanding of warfare and politics, and saw the long-range implications of such an act.

The Tulisians had spread themselves thin along many fronts

over the centuries, without ever fully completing any of their victories. Their military might was currently based on four armies of around fifty thousand men each. To the west, they had the First Army committed to the defense of the border by the Wild Wood. The border had been contested for centuries with the elves of the wood, which fought valiantly to regain ancestral forestlands that had been annexed by the Tulisians.

To the east, the Second Army was entrenched in up-keeping the two centuries old occupation of Tursys. Tursys had never surrendered, and was embroiled in an effort to throw off the yolk of their oppressors. It was rumored that a Tursysian army and naval force had been regrouping and preparing in secret on Maldin for the last decade. If they were able to overthrow the Tulisian occupation, they would again be free to rebuild the huge armada that had once controlled the Torlian and North Seas. This would create another front upon which Thulistan could be seriously threatened, as they had no navy. The fact was, Morgan mused, that the Tursysians posed a greater threat to Thulistan because no buffer nation existed between them as Barstol did between Tulisia and the lands of his empire. If Tursys ascended in power again, Thulistan would be at risk of losing its coastal lands, and access to the world trade markets.

To Tulisia's north, the Third Army lived in well-manned fortifications along the border of Thulistan in Barstol.

This left only the Fourth Army free for reinforcements. The Fourth had always been held in reserve in the Tulisian capital city of Cartiel. All three fronts had been relatively stable for generations, so the other units, the Fifth and Sixth Armies had been disbanded as unneeded expenses.

Morgan could not see the logic of an attack on the border by the Tulisians. They would have to call in the Fourth just to hold their own, and then probably call in additional troops from the first and second, weakening those fronts. This would inevitably trigger additional resistance from the elves to the west, the Tursysians to the west, or both. The entire idea was suicide to the Tulisian Empire. Morgan had an unsettling thought—what if the

Carstans were involved? The Carstans, closely allied with the Tulisian Empire, and often involved in their conquests, had never seriously threatened the southeastern border, and only the relatively weak Clan Larrs claimed the lands around Jocko's Corner, the only city in the southeast of Thulistan. The Carstans would be able to march into the Frost Steppes of central Thulistan before being seriously challenged.

Morgan knew that the clans could survive, that they would repel both armies if necessary, but there was one major unknown—the d'rakken mahre. They would play some role in this. It was possible that they had something to do with troop movements along the border. It was possible they had allied themselves somehow with the Tulisians, or Carstans—it didn't make sense, though. The Thulistan Empire could be ripped to shreds if it had to battle the formidable forces of Tulisia and Carstan, while dealing with the random depredations of the d'rakken mahre. No man would fight well knowing his family was in danger.

Morgan realized that it was a lot to extrapolate from such a small bit of information, but also felt deep down that he was accurate in his evaluation. Kerny patiently watched while he sat deep in thought, and finally spoke again.

"Judging by the time you just spent thinking, it appears that you see the long ranging effects this may have. Given the likely outcome, it does seem that I had some information that may be important to those seeking knowledge regarding the d'rakken mahre, doesn't it?"

Morgan absorbed this confirmation of his thoughts, and was again impressed by the depth of the man's perception. "Yes, indeed, you have provided me with valued information. Thank you. I think Halnan and I need to turn in for the night. I have much to think of."

So saying, he rose and moved to his bedroll, forestalling Halnan's unasked questions with a shake of his head. Morgan lay in his bedroll for hours thinking on the potentially far-reaching effects of the information garnered from the trapper.

In the morning, after a small breakfast, they broke camp and bade the trapper farewell. Morgan felt hurried; he knew that one small bit of information was little to speculate on, and was not enough to fully estimate the potential danger to the Empire. The danger to his family, clan, and the Empire were far greater than he had realized. He knew, now more than ever, that he must discover the meaning behind the emergence of the d'rakken mahre. Fortunately, armies moved slowly, and he would have a couple of months before the Tulisians could put enough men in place to begin the war. He would have to move quickly though; his search was likely to be a long one.

They rode at a brisk pace through the morning, Morgan's desire to move quickly burned as brightly as the sun overhead. He shared his thoughts regarding the Clan Olbaric call to arms with Halnan. Halnan, as a battle leader, understood the movement of troops and the details of war. He saw the dangers in the scenario that Morgan described, but failed to understand why he should care if Tursys regained power in their ancestral homeland, or if the elves flooded the west of Tulisia.

Later in the morning they ascended to the beginnings of the Northern Pass. The initial ascent twisted along a narrow shale path cut between the high crags. The horses had to move at a slow pace, placing feet carefully to avoid slipping on the constantly breaking sheets of shale. Thunder frequently rumbled through the high valley, echoing its warnings across the mountainside.

By the end of the first day, the horses were becoming skittish, both from the constant efforts to maintain footing, as well as the combined sounds of the harsh, whistling winds and the rumbling thunder.

They made camp in a shallow cave, hoping to gain some measure of protection from the bitter, howling winds. The horses trembled from exhaustion and nerves. Halnan built a large cheery fire and worked to lighten Morgan's mood by reminiscing about shared childhood memories. "Remember when we wanted to see how well wool burned?" He paused until he saw that he had Morgan's attention. "We lit that big shaggy ram's coat on fire: the beast startled as I recall and ran off through the pasture towards the lake. A running ball of screaming flame, he was. You know, some of the elders still believe it was a vengeful daemon come to burn down the village. I remember the confused look on the shepherd's face as he brought the ram into the village the next day to have the healer look at it. Quarantined the poor beast for a month, thinking it had the pox or something, being inexplicably half bald as it was. God's, I'm just glad the beast had the sense to find the lake, would have felt terrible if it had been badly hurt."

They both laughed at the story, finding strength in the depth, and breadth of their friendship. They proceeded for some time to take turns telling stories of the adventures of youth.

The warmth of the fire and companionship worked its magic, and both men slept deeply, awaking refreshed and ready to continue the ascent towards the unknown.

Before noon they reached the end of the shale covered crags, and entered into a heavily wooded valley. Morgan let out a long, low whistle of relief while patting Bran on the neck.

"Well now, this is a nice change." Halnan voiced his pleasure at escaping the narrow shale cleft. He slapped his roan's flank, setting it and the packhorse into a trot into the woods.

Morgan wondered at the behavior of his friend. He lightly kicked Bran forward and followed his exuberant friend at a statelier pace.

About an hour later he caught up with Halnan. To his surprise, and pleasure, Halnan had started a fire and was cooking a small creature of some sort on a spit over the flames. He had been busy it seemed. Bemused, and slightly impressed by his friend's competence at hunting, and more importantly, cooking, he lowered himself from Bran and walked over to the fire.

The meat cooking over the fire smelled wonderful. "Is this some poor creature that died of fright when it saw your ugly visage tromping through the forest on that great shaggy beast of yours?"

Halnan, who had been busy preparing a broth for the meat, turned towards Morgan, considering a response. Lacking anything witty to say, he simply responded, "would you like to apologize for that last comment, or would you prefer to catch and cook your own lunch?"

Morgan bowed deeply to his friend in mock submission. "My most humble apologies. Never should I call your magnificent horse a shaggy beast. I truly regret any harm to his pride, or any lasting damage to his confidence."

Halnan sat with his mouth open, muttering, "you are an uncouth savage, but I am pledged to your service. Sit, and eat. At least it will keep you quiet."

The meal was very tasty, Morgan admitted, although he never gathered the courage to ask what they were eating. It was hot, and tender so who cared? They spent almost an hour eating and resting, while the horses contentedly cropped moss and the stubborn grasses that grew in the high mountains.

After lunch, feeling light hearted and well fed; they trotted on through the mountain forest. They had forgotten the pressures of their journey for a time, and traveled purely for the pleasure of the wind in their hair, and the company of true friends. Late in the afternoon, their peaceful reverie was rudely interrupted, and their Quest was almost brought to careless ruin.

The horses were silently trotting through the soft loam of the forest, while their riders spoke cheerfully about matters both great and small. Neither noticed the soft mounds of freshly turned earth that were becoming more frequent in the soft loam between the trees. The trees had become increasingly dense, hemming them in on both sides. The horses slowed down to a slow walk in the encroaching gloom of the early evening.

In the twilight, they did not notice the fallen tree crossing the path until they were nearly upon it. Morgan dismounted his horse to inspect the tree, and see if any easy path presented itself around it. Just as he prepared to call for Halnan to get a saw from the packhorse, Bran screamed in fury and fear.

He turned and saw Bran rearing up, hopping backwards on his hind legs. Before the great horse, the earth opened up and was pouring forth a wriggling stream of bloated white creatures, two to three feet long, with long claws. They appeared much like white pigs with short legs and claws. Morgan instantly recognized them as ska, the flesh eating diggers common to the forestlands. Ska rarely attacked armed men or horses though, preferring carrion or wounded beasts more easily overcome.

Halnan's horse was also rearing up, and he was struggling to maintain his seat. He couldn't allow his horse to turn and flee, however. As easy as it was to outrun ska on a horse, Morgan was unable to get to his horse, separated by the pit swarming with the vile creatures. A half of a dozen ska began to claw towards Morgan at an alarmingly quick rate, while many others continued towards Bran, seeking to sink claws into the flesh of his hind legs.

Bran had other ideas, however, and was fighting effectively against those that came within kicking or stomping distance. Halnan, having controlled his mount, dismounted and tied his horse and the packhorse to trees a short distance away. He quickly strung his bow and began to fire arrows into the ska wriggling out of the pit. Each arrow found its mark and the bone chilling screams of the wounded and dying ska filled the forest.

Meanwhile, Morgan was hard-pressed. His sword was like a living presence in his hand, expertly cutting down through the ska that had reached almost to his legs. Their hide was remarkably tough, and any cut not angled correctly deflected harmlessly. Despite this, he was confident in his ability to handle the half a dozen or so that were coming at him from the pit. Halnan's arrows seemed to be able to halt any further ska from emerging to attack him, but Halnan could not risk shooting those near to him, afraid of misfiring in the twilight.

Morgan's confidence was temporarily shaken, however, as he felt a burning in his left hamstring. He turned, and fell off balance as he saw the ska attached firmly to his leg by its short, sharp teeth. Morgan realized it had tunneled underneath and behind him to catch him by surprise. As he fell backwards, he wind milled his arms, trying to regain his balance, and in doing so, dropped his sword. As he fell backwards into the pit filled with a score of ska, he curled into a ball, reaching for the dagger at his waist.

A mound of fleshy bodies broke his fall into the pit, and his sudden backwards movement dislodged the ska from his leg. For a moment, his loathing and fear lent him strength and he fought valiantly with his dagger, killing or badly wounding a handful of ska. He was raked by claws and bitten by teeth, though his leathers protected him from serious harm for the time being. For a moment, he believed he would prevail. He heard Halnan calling to him and knew help was coming.

He felt a shifting of the earth underneath him, and felt the ground begin to give way. The earth opened again, dirt crumbling away into some deeper pit or cave. As Morgan struggled to control his fall, he caught a brief glimpse of Halnan at the edge of the pit, holding a long knife in each hand, shouting a war cry. He looked invincible, like some vengeful demon. Then he struck the bottom, and his head bounced off of a hard object. Morgan's last thought was of disappointment in himself. Before he could further contemplate the errors he had made, a dark fog rolled in through his consciousness and all was dark and silent.

# SIX

## LESSONS IN HUMILITY

The dark and silence were abruptly interrupted with the muffled sounds of battle. Nearby, he could hear the muted sounds of scuffling feet as well as other, less identifiable noises. After a moment, Morgan's battered consciousness began to register the import of the sounds. He forced open his eyes and found himself in the semi-dark of the cavern he had fallen into. A dozen paces away, in a brighter area directly under the opening to the sky above, Halnan stood, covered in dirt and blood, kicking at one of the few remaining ska. White, bloated bodies surrounded him, some writhing in their death throes, others clearly dead, their motionless bodies lying in pools of gore and blood.

As Morgan scuttled backwards from a dead ska near his feet, his elbow bumped into something small and solid. He reached for the item and found it to be the dagger he had been drawing as he fell. As he grasped onto the dagger he lurched to his knees. The walls of the cavern spun around him, his vision swimming.

Halnan bent low and plunged one long knife deep into the last remaining ska. The creature curled into a ball and in its dying throws sought to bite Halnan's hand. He quickly released the knife and stepped away from the twitching creature. With his single remaining long knife in hand, he looked about for his next foe. All of the ska were dead, however. Scattered about him were the bodies of almost two-dozen of the diggers. During his scan of the area, he caught sight of Morgan struggling to his knees. Halnan let out a sigh of relief. He had not been sure that Morgan had survived the fall.

He called to Morgan. "Morgan, I'm glad to see you moving." He reached down and grasped the knife protruding from the now dead ska and pulled it free. He wiped the gore from both blades on the hide of the ska and stepped over it towards Morgan.

Morgan forced himself to his feet. "Ho, Halnan, well fought it appears, I'm sorry that . . ." his greeting was interrupted by a sudden bout of light-headedness. He wiped his forehead with the back of his hand. As he lowered his hand, he noticed that it was covered with blood.

Halnan almost reached his now standing friend when he saw the blood running down across his face. The blood ran freely and a sizable puddle pooled on the floor where Morgan had lain. Morgan looked him briefly in the eyes. As he began to topple backwards, his shock found voice. "Damn—hurt—by a ska!"

With a look of profound disbelief, he lost consciousness and crumpled to the floor.

When Morgan next opened his eyes, the light of dawn was angling across the mountain glade. He was lying on his bedroll, his pack supporting his head. As the fog lifted fully from his mind, the pain began to register. It pulsed from his forehead through his entire body. Drums pounded in his ears.

He closed his eyes to the pain. After a time, the drumming in his ears receded enough to concentrate. Not yet willing to risk again opening his eyes, Morgan opened his other senses to his surroundings. Birds chirped in the woods nearby, and the horses whuffed quietly. As his senses became more acute, he could also hear the gentle tink of metal striking metal.

The last sound confused him at first, but then, his other senses answered the mystery. The fresh mountain breeze carried the faint odor of cooking stew. The smell filled his nostrils and set his mouth to watering. Morgan slowly brought a hand up to shade his eyes, and risked opening them again. The light brought less pain this time, and his headache was continuing to recede.

He slowly turned his head toward the smell and saw Halnan stirring a pot hanging over a small campfire. The movement brought another wave of pain, and black spots swam across his vision. This time, however, he did not lose consciousness.

"Hello, again," he croaked through parched lips.

Halnan looked up from his cooking and saw that his friend had again regained consciousness. He reached behind himself and grabbed his canteen, stood, and stepped over to Morgan. After pouring a small amount of water on Morgan's lips, he carefully checked the bandage wrapped around his forehead. The wound was clean, dry, and healing well.

Satisfied with Morgan's recovery, Halnan smiled and sat down next to him. "You took a nasty fall. Your head hit a sharp stone. You've lost a lot of blood, but you'll be fine in a day or two. I am sorry to say that the stone didn't survive the impact, though."

"Hmmmph," was the only response to Halnan's clever wit that Morgan could manage.

"Good comeback, friend. Anyhow, you'll need some food to get your strength back. Just lie back and I'll feed you some broth." With a gentleness surprising in one so large and brusque, Halnan fed and cared for his oldest friend.

By late the next day, under Halnan's careful ministrations, Morgan felt ready to stand and take a brief walk about the camp. As he made his attempt at standing, however, he felt as weak as a child, and decided another nights rest might be in order.

Sitting by the fire that night, Morgan looked at Halnan with newfound respect. He had always known his friend to be a competent warrior, a man of great humor, and one possessed of a congenial disposition. He had not, however, realized the depth of character Halnan possessed. Halnan was showing himself as a caring and dedicated man, with a gentle nature.

His gratitude compelled him to broach the subject with his friend. "Halnan, I—um—well there is something I need to tell you." For a man who preferred silence to words in most cases, this was going to be extraordinarily hard. "You see, when this began, I really did not want you along. You have always been a boon companion—but that was always in fun and battle. You see; I have always thought of you as, well—sort of foolish. I'm sorry I believed that of you. Anyhow, the point is, I was wrong. You saved my life and nursed me back to health. For this, I am grateful. Um—thank you."

Halnan waited through the awkward speech with a half grin on his face. He was aware that Morgan had always seen him as immature. In fact, he went out of his way to have fun in Morgan's presence. Morgan was a bit stiff, to say the least, and Halnan provided some balance for his friend. He saw it as his duty to his best friend, and his S'hapur.

At the end of Morgan's speech, he responded in a carefully selected flippant tone. "Well, it was either save and care for you, or bury you and complete the Quest on my own. To be honest, I don't want the responsibility of the Quest, and the ground is too damn hard for digging a good grave. Saving you seemed easier, that's all. Sorry about the misunderstanding, but it was a pretty speech. Next time, save it for the ladies. I can't stand to see you all touchy feely. It gives me the creeps."

Feeling that he had confused Morgan enough for one night, he lay back on his pack and closed his eyes.

Morgan sat open mouthed, staring at his friend. Halnan's speech reaffirmed his previous thoughts regarding his maturity. He fell asleep slowly, disappointed in his friend. He had hoped Halnan was finally growing up.

Morgan was sound asleep later that night when Halnan opened his eyes, crept over, and checked his bandage and washed his forehead with gentle fingers.

The next morning, after a hearty breakfast, they continued their journey. A small storm had blown through during the night, dumping rain on the camp leaving the two men cold, wet, and stiff. In addition, Morgan was still weak, but all in all, he felt much better. The long gash on his forehead was healing well and was only lightly wrapped in a bandage to keep it clean. The morning air was brisk, and getting brisker as they climb higher into the mountain.

By mid-day, the forest began to thin, and patches of ice and snow became frequent in the shadowed areas. By the afternoon, the forest was replaced by scrub and increasingly large snow and ice fields. Morgan pulled up his horse. "This is it, Halnan; from here we enter into the pass proper. We will be a full day in the snow before we begin our descent. I think we should camp here, and make the crossing in the morning."

Halnan turned in his saddle. "Aye. That's a good idea. I'll unpack the tent, so you don't freeze off anything important. I don't want to incur the wrath of your future bride, if you get my meaning." With an impertinent wink, he slid off of his horse and moved to the packhorse.

Instead of responding to his friends baiting, Morgan smiled. He couldn't help think that perhaps his friend was just fine the way he was. He slid slowly out of the saddle, and sat heavily on the ground while Halnan set up camp. He was tired and sore, and was glad for his friend's service.

The next morning found the two riding slowly through the mountain pass. The horses' hooves sent sprays of ice at each impact with the ground. From the high pass they could see for miles both to the north and the south. To the south were the forests and patches of lighter green that signified the grasslands of their homes. To the north, they could see the endless deep green of the Long Wood. Patches of dark clouds, like heavy winter wool, churned along the skyline below them to the east, moving away from their current position. The persistent metallic rumbles of thunder echoed from the lower hills.

Throughout the afternoon they rode. By early evening they were beginning to head downwards, out of the pass. By nightfall, they were again in the comforting confines of the forests, where they made camp in a glade surrounded by tall redwoods.

The next day, about mid-day, they were well into the highlands of Long Wood. Just as they were preparing to stop for lunch, they were surprised by a shout from the slope just above them. "Ho, travelers, what news from the south?"

Startled by the unexpected intrusion, they searched quickly about for the source. Morgan turned his horse uphill and trotted off a short distance to find the man who had called. He found two men, one a miner and the other a guard by appearances, along with their burrow, a few hundred paces up the hill. The miner waved emphatically as they sighted each other, the guard scowled and unlimbered a large crossbow.

Seeing the threatening gesture of the guard, Morgan reigned in his horse and held up his hands. "Peace travelers. I am Morgan of Family Partikson, Clan Piksanie."

The miner, a burly, dirty Thulistan, turned to the guard and pushed the crossbow down towards the ground, muttering something Morgan could not hear. He looked back at Morgan. "Sorry, friend. I've traded with men of family Piksanie—honorable folk. Glad to meet you!"

The miner continued towards Morgan, and the guard followed, after slapping the burro into motion. By this time, Halnan and the packhorse arrived to join the party. The miner joined them and waved toward the guard. "Names' Targ. This lummox," he indicated the huge guard accompanying him, "who was so ready to skewer you, is my dimwit son Bart. Bart works off the expenses of his upbringing by guarding for me. He's as strong as a bear, and about as smart. Say hello, Bart."

The guard, who stood a head taller and twice as broad as either Morgan or Halnan, turned his blank stare to Morgan. "Hello, Bart." His voice was the even monotone of a trained mimic.

Targ rolled his eyes and slapped Bart good-naturedly on the shoulders, smiling at him. He looked back to Morgan. "See my point? Who's your friend?"

Halnan nodded to the man. "The name is Halnan. Good to meet you. And you too," he indicated Bart, who responded with a huge, gap toothed smile.

Morgan and Halnan dismounted. Morgan walked over to the miner and gripped arms with him. "My friend and I are traveling north, into the forest. Any signs of danger; morkai, or draks?"

The miner dug around in his matted hair, scratching at his scalp for a moment before answering. "Well, I don't go too far into the woods, but I have spoken with some that have come from the woods recently. Word is, the draks have disappeared. Three weeks ago, they were wandering all around the lowlands. Now, they have all but disappeared. The morkai have begun to move back towards the lowlands from the mountains. They all moved out of the lower forests to avoid the draks you know."

The news about the morkai was interesting, and accounted for encountering two during his last scouting mission. The news about the d'rakken mahre was disconcerting. He had an unshakable feeling that there was something going on with them that was going to have long-range effects. The oldest tales shared by S'hapur gave hints of an unknown purpose of the d'rakken mahre. Morgan understood that the d'rakken mahre were connected in some way to the k'aram mahre. The histories tied the two inseparably together, although the nature of the connection had never been defined.

He sang quietly a snippet of an ancient tale named 'K'aram mahre'.

> "Varsnya gifted life eternal,
> heed the power of the call.
> Many lives to learn the wisdom,
> to in the end redeem them all."

Bart, who had removed a shoe and had been intently picking at his feet, looked up briefly to see what the singing was about. As soon as the singing ended, he went back to work on the foul job. The miner smacked at his sons hand to keep him from eating something he had dislodged, and gave Morgan a confused look. "What's that all about son?"

Morgan shook his head. "Sorry, just part of an old song I was thinking about. It's nothing really." It was something though. He believed it held the key to the d'rakken mahre. Now, he thought, was not the time to discuss it, however, and the miner certainly was not the one to discuss it with. He determined to talk it over with Halnan when they were alone.

After sharing lunch with the man and his son, and sharing trivial information, they waved good-bye and moved on.

By that evening, they were well into the lowlands of the forest. At camp, Morgan broached the subject of the song. "Did you hear the words of the song earlier?"

Halnan leaned forward from his seat on the other side of the fire, the light glinting in his eyes, giving him a shrewd look. "Aye, I myself was thinking about the song a few time in recent days."

Morgan was surprised at the revelation. Halnan had possibly outthought him, made the connection first. Worst, he hadn't even bothered to mention it. "You mean you . . ."

Halnan interrupted. "Yes, Halnan the foolish thought of the connection already. Something is happening with the d'rakken mahre, and more importantly, it's something foreordained by the Gods."

Morgan was pleased with his friend. "None of it really makes sense, but the line 'many lives to learn the wisdom', seems to have some bearing here. I know you've heard the stories of the k'aram mahre. Do you think the d'rakken mahre and the k'aram mahre are somehow one and the same?"

Halnan shrugged his shoulders and leaned back again. "Aye, I do, although I can't say how it came to be or what it means, nor could I give any proof to back my belief. The question you mean to ask though, is that if it means that they are coming to the surface to take on another of the 'many lives', isn't it?"

Again, Morgan was shocked at his friend's perception, when he chose to exercise it. "Very good, my surprising friend. That is indeed the interpretation I have been rolling about in my head. If it is a correct guess, then we have an even greater problem on our hands. D'rakken mahre as an enemy are one problem, d'rakken mahre as the God gifted saviors of redemption are another matter entirely. How can simple men such as us determine what course to take in such times?"

"Why that's the easiest question of them all—simple men go to sleep, and leave the decisions to the leaders. Have fun S'hapur." Halnan put his pack under his head and closed his eyes against Morgan's angry glare.

During the next few days, while they searched fruitlessly through the forest, Morgan spent many hours working on the riddle of the d'rakken mahre. They saw signs and heard stories of the d'rakken mahre, but none indicating recent activity. By the end of the week, they came to the decision that the d'rakken mahre had moved on to pursue their unknown purpose elsewhere, seemingly back under the earth, or to another hidden location. Both agree that they needed more information on the history of the d'rakken mahre. The only place where they could think of to get such information was far south, in the ancient libraries in the city of Parnan, in Desil. Parnan was the world capitol of learning and boasted many ancient libraries and learning centers.

Both knew the trek would be long and difficult. Crossing the Barstol border presented a number of problems in itself with troops amassing along it. Nonetheless, information was the key, and there was no other place in the world to get it.


The trip back up into the mountains began with a heavy rain that began abruptly shortly after they left camp. The noisy sloshing of the horse's hooves was interrupted in the early afternoon by loud crashing noises out in the forest to their left.

Halnan, who was riding in the lead, reigned in at the sound. "Ho, Morgan, only one thing makes that much noise in the woods. You can be sure it knows where we are and is heading this way by now." As he spoke, he slid off of the horse and un-slung his longbow, pulling a bowstring from an oiled sack within his pouch. He cringed at the thought of ruining a good string in the damp air. Upon again hearing a loud crack of a sapling or large branch breaking, Halnan quickly overcame any remorse over the loss.

Morgan also climbed off of his horse. Even the best-trained warhorse needed room to be effective, and the dense forest was not terrain suitable for fighting from horseback. He drew his long sword and moved forward to join Halnan. The crashing in the forest continued just out of sight, circling slightly off to the right.

They smelled the morkai before they saw it. An odor like sour milk and rotten flesh permeated the area. "Gods, what a smell!" Halnan was covering his nose with his sleeve.

Morgan, who had experienced morkai twice before, was somewhat more prepared for the stink. "Aye, that's how they hunt. The stink kills the forest animals and they just lumber about, pick up the bodies and eat them."

Halnan chuckled at the rare jest from his friend. His laughter stopped as he caught his first sight of the morkai. The creatures white fur was matted with filth, making it a dirty grey color. It was manlike in form, with massive arms and a bear like head. The creature stood over nine feet tall.

As the morkai made visual contact, it paused. Its mind worked slowly as it examined the edibility of its intended prey. Seeing armed men, it turned to a nearby tree and broke off part of a large limb to use as a club.

Halnan took advantage of the pause to fire two arrows in quick succession. The first arrow lodged deeply in the creature's chest, and the second in its shoulder. The morkai bellowed a hoot of rage and began to move forward.

"Try to put a few more arrows in that thing to slow it down. Be quick, it'll be on us soon." Morgan was unruffled, his voice even.

Halnan did not need the urgings of his friend; he had already knocked another arrow and taken aim. He fired, and the third arrow struck its leg. The morkai howled again and paused long enough to pluck the arrow from its leg. Blood spurted from the open wound. The creature seemed enraged by the blood, and again lumbered forward, at an even faster pace.

Not anticipating the burst of speed, Halnan was forced to rush his final shot. He aimed at the creature's head, hoping to do some real damage. The arrow flew wide and only grazed the side of its head, just over its ear.

As Halnan dropped his bow and drew his long knives, Morgan called to him. "Don't bother aiming for the head in the future, arrows just bounce off—mostly bone." Morgan stepped forward to take the initial charge of the morkai.

Morgan stood steady, his sword poised for defense or offense. The morkai, however, surprised him by bowling directly into him at full speed instead of stopping to engage. There was no defense for such a tactic, and he was knocked temporarily senseless to the wet ground a few feet away.

The enraged morkai moved directly for the source of its injuries. Halnan was prepared for the charge. He rolled under the swing of the club. His roll carried him directly in front of the morkai where he came up and planted one of his long knives into the creature's belly. Hoping the wound would prove fatal; he managed a brief twist of the blade before releasing it. Halnan dropped and rolled away to avoid being caught in the death throws of the morkai.

Halnan came out of his roll a few feet away. The morkai stopped to look down at the knife sticking out of its gut. It looked surprised, eyes flicking back and forth from the knife and Halnan, only slowly making the connection. Morgan, meanwhile, climbed slowly to his feet, trying to recover his wits.

Morgan called to Halnan. "What are you doing just standing there?"

Halnan turned towards Morgan to see what his shouting was about. He interrupted Morgan. "It's safe to get up now, I've taken care of . . ." he in turn was interrupted by a loud sound from behind him.

Halnan barely had time to turn back towards the dying morkai before he realized the beast wasn't quite dead. The morkai had decided the knife wasn't worth worrying about and was tired of playing with its prey. By the time Halnan realized his mistake, the morkai was already in the process of swinging its club.

Halnan just had time to duck directly under the swing that would have crushed his head. Before he could rise, a hairy foot lashed out. The morkai's kick connected with his leg. He distinctly heard his leg snap under the impact as he was lifted off of the ground by the force of the impact. His brief flight ended in a bone jarring impact with a large tree. He slumped down to the ground, waiting for the inevitable crushing blow of the club to finish the battle.

The blow never came, however. The morkai's advance was halted by a loud war cry from behind it. It turned to find Morgan standing, sword at the ready.

The morkai turned to face this new threat. Morgan moved in slowly, circling with his sword held ready. The morkai, spurred by the success of its previous charge, again ran directly at him. This time, however, Morgan was ready for the tactic. He ducked under and away from the charge, making a roundhouse cut with the sword. The sword cleaved cleanly through the creatures hamstring.

Suddenly finding itself unable to stay upright, the morkai fell forward, crashing into a rotting stump. It quickly turned on the ground and pulled itself to its knees. Morgan circled, looking for an angle of attack while the morkai tried to rise to its feet. On the second attempt, it fell hard, losing its grip on the club.

Morgan stepped in while the creature was fully grounded. He made a strait lunge and buried the tip of the sword into the morkai's neck. Before the morkai could retaliate, he pulled away. As his sword slid free, blood gushed from the neck wound.

Morgan moved away, knowing the creature could not rise, and would bleed to death soon. The morkai, confused by its inability to rise, thrashed about for a few minutes, speeding the loss of blood from its neck and gut. The thrashing broke off the arrows that had been sticking out of its chest and arm. After a minute, it weakened too much to move. It weakly tugged the knife free from its gut and flung it at Morgan, but the blade fell short. Finally, the morkai just clawed uselessly at the ground for a few minutes, convulsed mightily, and finally lay still in a pool of blood and rainwater.

Morgan knew better than to turn his back on the creature until he was sure. He tentatively poked the beast a few times with the tip of his sword, balanced on the balls of his feet, ready to jump away should the need arise. The morkai, however, was dead. He turned, picked up Halnan's knife and walked over to his injured friend.

Halnan lay against the tree, panting shallowly, holding his ribs. "Never saw such a thing," he gasped. "Beast should lay down and die when you plant a long blade in its gut."

Morgan smiled thinly. "Should have warned you. Morkai are too stupid to know when they are dead. Sorry. How are you?" He knelt down in front of Halnan.

Halnan looked up. "Thanks for the warning, I'll try to remember next time—leg's broken bad, some ribs too, I think. Can't move at all and it hurts like hell." The pain was clear in his voice and his glazed eyes.

"We'll have to get you home. You'll be laid up for a month or two. For the time being, I'm going to have to set and splint this leg. Ribs will heal on their own—but it's going to hurt when you breathe deeply." Morgan stood and searched for two stout branches to use as a splint, and went to the packhorse to retrieve some cloth to tie the splint with. The rain had died to a light mist and the sky was clearing. The clouds swiftly blew away, leaving the ground steaming in the sunlight.

"Morgan, while you are up, could you get something from my saddlebag." He waited until Morgan finished collecting the cloth and walked over to his horse. "On the left side you'll find a small black vial. Bring it please."

Morgan dug through the saddlebag without question and found the vial. It was a small vial stoppered with a cork. Inside was a viscous black fluid, the consistency of hot pitch. He returned to Halnan with the splinting supplies and the vial.

"What is this vile looking potion?" He held out the item to Halnan.

"It was given to me by a kindly Barmaid in Billings—she was concerned about my . . . well-being. She said a small sip would give my body rest, make me able to—ah—recover more quickly from certain exertions, like sleeping for a week she said. I held onto it, thinking it may come in useful. Maybe its restorative properties will help in other ways. Set the damned leg, and then give me the potion." He lay back flushed and panting from the pain.

Morgan sat in front of Halnan and gave him a wood chip to bite down on. "Hold steady, friend, I'll make this quick." Before he finished the sentence, he pulled the leg strait out, with all of his strength. He felt the bone slip into place, and released the pressure. Halnan was panting in quick shallow gasps. Morgan quickly tied the splint to immobilize the leg.

After he was satisfied with his work, he pulled the cork from the vial and helped Halnan drink the contents. The fluid smelled awful, like rotted vegetation, and Halnan gagged on it. Morgan smiled. "Judging by the smell, I bet that really tastes horrid. For your sake, I hope this isn't a fake. The smell alone may kill you."

"Gods, it's bad. It burned all of the way down, and my entire gut is on fire. I think perhaps I should have only taken the small sip the Barmaid recommended. I feel—sort of . . ." before he could finish, his head dropped onto his shoulder and he was unconscious.

Morgan sniffed the vial again and frowned. He hoped the potion wasn't dangerous in large quantities. He checked Halnan's pulse and found it strong, and his breathing was deep and regular. He set camp and lay Halnan comfortably in his bedroll. With great effort, he dragged the morkai off into the forest, where its smell would not bother them. In his rush to get back to Halnan, he never even thought of skinning it.

Halnan slept soundly for almost two full days before rousing. Morgan heard his groaning and came over in time to see his friend begin to awaken. He was relieved to see Halnan return to consciousness. He had already determined that the potion was having a positive effect, the mottled bruises around his broken ribs had receded to a soft yellow, and his breathing had eased. There was no way to determine the progress of the leg, however.

Halnan opened his eyes and saw his friend nearby. "Mmm. That was a nice nap. Gods I'm hungry, how long did I sleep?"

"That love potion of yours put you to sleep for almost two full days."

Halnan's eyes widened at the news. "Two days—well, I guess I do feel better, though. Maybe the potion worked, my breathing seems a might easier."

"Yes, you do seem better. I was a little concerned about how that nasty drink would affect you. Drinking a months worth of an untried love potion—I was afraid for the virtue of the horses—had to keep a close eye on you. Anyhow, how's the leg?"

Halnan poked and prodded at the leg for a moment, wincing slightly. "Well now, it's tender, but feels more sound. I would hazard a guess that it is knitting nicely."

Morgan bent to inspect the leg. "Yes, it is more sound. You may be able to ride now, but it still needs time before you can walk."

Halnan smiled. "Well then, if I can ride, I can continue on the Quest. It can heal in the saddle. Never rode with only one working leg, it should be interesting . . ."

"Wait just a minute, you are going home! You will just slow things down."

"You can't stop me from following you, which I will if you try to leave me. Just a waste of time on your part, time you need to get to Desil. Now, help me up into my saddle." Halnan pulled himself upright on the tree, and stood on one leg, smiling widely.

Morgan's protestations were useless. Shortly, they were on horseback, cantering through the forest, eating breakfast while riding. Desil was indeed a long ride, thought Morgan, even longer with such a nuisance along for the ride. He rode on with a smile creasing his face. Gods he thought, all of this smiling is likely to strain muscles in my face. Secretly, he was truly glad for Halnan's company. He had changed from this prolonged association with Halnan; he knew he laughed more frequently than he had since assuming the role of S'hapur. The change felt good, and he was as happy as he remembered being.

# SEVEN

## SMALL WORLD

At first Taire couldn't tell what changed. He looked around his small prison, and to his astonishment it seemed as if the walls had pulled away. His vision was distorted in the periphery, making it appear he was looking at the world through his father's best beer mugs. He could not even make out the ceiling in the gloom. Looking down, the floor was clear with a crystal clarity that he had never experienced. He could see every grain of the wood, every imperfection.

His mind barely registered the cool hardness of the floor on his feet, or the overwhelming smell of the breadcrumbs left on his plate. Everything was as it should be, until he sensed the movement behind him. With lightening quick instincts he jumped and turned, seeking to flee.

As he landed, he discovered it was not something dangerous that startled him, but the mouse. For a moment they stood and looked each other over. After a moment, Taire's whiskers quivered in recognition and greetings. Whiskers? Taire knew he didn't have whiskers. He raised his paws to his face to stroke the clean skin that he knew to be there. Paws? Not only did his body seem to have changed, he also began to register his earlier perceptual information. The room had grown huge, or he had become small. His eyes didn't work right; they were made for seeing things closely, not at a distance. He could smell breadcrumbs!

Realization dawned like a new day. As he realized what he had become, and strangely wasn't afraid. He was past fear, taught to disregard fear by his cruel master. In fact, this was what he had dreamed of. Although he didn't trust in dreams any longer, he couldn't help feeling elation at what his transformation meant. He could now escape. He had fulfilled his dream. The impossibility of what he had done escaped him. The danger and consequences were irrelevant. His overwhelming thought was that The Ruler would not touch him again! The thought repeated itself through his mind until he began to understand its importance. His transformation meant an end to his torment. In the body of a mouse, Taire found the courage of the lion. He found the will to live, to take action, to save himself.

Through all of this, the mouse patiently waited, unperturbed by Taire's transformation. It sat comfortably on its hind legs, watching with glittering eyes. The intent behind the gaze was imponderable to Taire. Despite his shape, he retained his human intellect and understandings. He also sensed something more. Underlying his humanity was the soul of a mouse, the urge to flee, to feed, to mate? Instinct.

Into his rambling thoughts intruded a small voice, "greetings man cub, I am Piffer. I wondered when you would recognize the power within you. I am glad you have freed your soul from that tormented flesh. This is better. Feed and let us run."

The speech was an interesting combination of high-pitched noises and body language, and yet Taire understood it clearly. Without knowing how, he responded to the lure of freedom, and responded to Piffer, his friend. "Yes, let's run. I'm not hungry. Show me where to go, take me away from here. Please."

Without further ado, Piffer turned tail and sped away. For a moment, Taire could not make the adjustment to his four feet, could not coordinate his movements. He stood looking at his feet, unsure of what to do with them. He became concerned that Piffer would lose him. As soon as he thought about something besides his coordination, he began to move. His body took over, doing what it yearned to do—to run.

Even though Piffer outpaced him, he realized he could smell the trail. He could follow that smell as clearly as any markings. He rushed through the large hole in the wall, seeing the individual gnaw marks where Piffer or others had widened the hole. As he entered into the space between the walls, he discovered the functionality of his vision. It was dark, but he could see clearly. His vision was meant to encompass small areas only. It was something like looking through a type of fish-eye lens. Objects close by were crystal clear, to the sides they became fuzzy. Despite the fuzziness, he realized his peripheral vision extended evenly to his sides, up and down, giving a wide viewing range. Clarity wasn't important to the periphery. Mice lived in tunnels, and their vision was well adapted to this fact, adapted to survival, and early warning of danger from any angle.

The space between the walls was narrow, the wooden planking carefully caulked with a white substance to keep out drafts. It was warm and cozy. It seemed to be everything he had envisioned.

Taire ran along to what would have been the front corner of his cell, and turned the corner following the smell of Piffer. He traveled along the inner walls of The Rulers bedroom until he came to a junction where a number of rooms must have come together. He could feel vibrations in the floor coming from one of the nearby rooms as someone walked by. He could smell the food prepared in a nearby kitchen. The instinct to run away from the vibration of moving feet was almost overwhelming.

He paused for a moment to absorb the intricate detailing of his new world before resuming his trek. Piffer crossed over a low stud and climbed down through a hole in the floorboards to a lower level. Taire traveled along a diagonal beam between two walls down to the floor of a lower level of the manor. The walls were of cruder material, and it was cooler as he descended. Obviously, Piffer lived in a basement of some sort, safely away from the human inhabitants of the house.

As he reached the bottom of the beam, Piffer's scent became nearly overwhelming. He turned a corner and found himself in a comfortable sized, (for a mouse), room lined with paper and wood shreddings. Piffer had made his home in a small wooden box attached to the wall supporting one of the pipes used to drain water from the structure above. The water draining through the pipe must have been warm most of the time, as the room seemed to be significantly warmer than the outside passage had been.

Piffer patiently awaited Taire's arrival, lying comfortably in his nest, cleaning the fur on his head by licking his forefeet and stroking them over his ears. After a moment he completed his grooming and looked up at Taire. "For a man cub you run well. This is my nest. My mate was killed above while feeding, and my cubs live in other places throughout the house with their families. Welcome into my home. Here I rest and contemplate what I have learned. I study the men above, and learn of their habits."

Piffer examined Taire for a moment closely, as if trying to determine the importance of his association to humanity. His eyes held a balance of intelligence and concern. He looked at Taire with more intelligence and perception than Taire had previously believed possible from a rodent. Piffer, it seemed, was a scholar among the mouse world, perhaps having a wisdom of sorts. At the moment, he seemed to be weighing Taire's soul.

Apparently satisfied, he continued along his previous train of thought. "You, however, are unlike other men. When I look at you, I don't understand what I see. When in man shape, your soul cried for release. Now, in a form like my own, I see you do not fully belong here either. You fit in, but you don't belong. There is incongruity in your body and soul, and the shape you take on won't heal it. I can see the wound upon your soul. I have seen what the large man did to you. I would invite you to stay with me and heal should you wish it, man cub."

Taire did indeed wish it. He was, however, conflicted. He had developed an almost instinctive distrust of kindness, and more confusing yet, the mouse in front of him seemed to care about him. It was difficult to accept anyone being kind without wanting something from him. But not Piffer he thought, possibly mice lacked the human capacity for cruelty. This was an acceptable belief for Taire, and he was able to formulate a response based on it. "Yes,

I would like to stay here, if it is no trouble. Also, my name is Taire if you please."

Piffer did not answer, but just sat quietly looking at the boy. Taire was looking back at Piffer. As his senses adjusted to his form, and its nuances, he realized the mouse was old. His whiskers sagged and his fur had lost much of its luster. Piffer spoke to him with the wisdom and sincerity that often come from age. Piffer reminded him painfully of his father. For a moment, Taire wept inwardly. All of his losses, all of his pain, and all of his humiliation poured forth after having been bottled up for months.

For a time, it seemed like his emotions would overwhelm his fragile balance. He could not reconcile his previous life with what had happened more recently. He didn't deserve his fate. The unfairness struck him almost senseless. Mice, however, lack the means to externally express these emotions. Despite this, Piffer seemed to understand. He moved from his nest and comforted Taire with the warmth of his physical presence.

After a time, it worked. Taire found himself, and remembered the ability to survive. He allowed himself to be led to the nest, where Piffer encouraged him to rest. "Sleep man-cub Taire, rest in safety and comfort." Then, in rodent fashion Piffer nestled into the nest next to Taire. For a moment, Taire was uncomfortable with the physical nearness, but he sensed nothing but kindness from the elderly mouse and relaxed. Before he fell asleep, he looked carefully at Piffer. In a moment of rare and almost forgotten emotion he spoke to Piffer. "Thank you. You have been a good friend. I would have died . . ." it took him a minute to continue "and please, my name is just Taire. I don't want to remember being a human right now. Just Taire please."

Having released a great burden he dropped off to a deep and dreamless sleep. Piffer lie awake for a long time afterwards, struggling with the pain he felt from his young friend.

During the next few days, Taire learned about the secrets of his small world from Piffer.

Piffer showed him around the inner spaces of the manor house, and introduced him to its other four legged denizens within the walls. Taire found most of these other mice to be uncommunicative and simple compared to the talkative and friendly Piffer.

He learned from Piffer how to find food in the pantry and kitchen while avoiding human and feline dangers. Together, they traveled, slept, and discussed human and mouse behavior. Taire learned again to trust and care for another being. They formed a bond that transcended the differences in their backgrounds.

After a week and a half, Taire began to fill the emptiness in his soul with his relationship with Piffer. Old fears began to fade away in the newness of his life as a mouse. Taire began to lose his sense of humanity, releasing himself to the growing instincts within him. In many situations, he responded to his environment on pure instinct, without any cognitive awareness of his actions. At quiet times at Piffer's side at night, he would contemplate this change. Every time he thought about it, however, he decided it was for the best. He was happy.

Despite this, Piffer had reservations regarding Taire's behavior. Although he said nothing to Taire, he had the strongest sense that Taire did not belong in his small world inside the walls. The closer he and Taire became, the more sure he was that they did not belong together.

During the first month of Taire's stay, Piffer avoided any mention of, or contact with The Ruler. He knew that The Ruler had visited many times during the month, and had beaten the rest of the household staff believing that they had assisted in Taire's apparent escape. He believed that Taire was too unstable to handle seeing his tormentor. Taire's shedding of his humanity led him to change his mind, however.

The Ruler returned to his underground manor, and Piffer heard that he had acquired a new page. On the second evening of The Rulers visit, another mouse by the name of Silver came to the den and spoke briefly with Piffer, privately, away from Taire. After Silver left, Piffer stood for a moment looking at Taire, his black eyes gleaming thoughtfully. After a moment, having come to a decision, he turned and exited the den, calling to Taire as he left. "There is something you must see Taire, follow me, and remain silent."

Taire felt confused by Piffer's behavior. For the previous few days his friend had become reticent, almost somber. Piffer constantly turned their conversation towards Taire's previous life. Taire rebuffed all efforts to open up the subject, and remained confused by the change in Piffer. When Silver came and spoke to Piffer, he could see the weighted gaze Piffer fixed upon him. Although he could not understand what it was going on, he felt the change in Piffer, and was worried about what it meant. Despite this, he followed Piffer from the den without question. He followed him because he couldn't bear to be alone. He followed because he lacked the independent will to refuse.

Piffer led him up through well-known passages to the level of The Ruler's private quarters. Taire barely flinched as they passed the small hole leading into his previous prison. Piffer stopped to examine Taire's reaction to the memory of his incarceration. Seeing Taire's near indifference at the memory, he felt sure of the path he was undertaking.

Piffer took off at a run again, this time along a path Taire had never been on. They went around the rear wall of the house to a small crack in the outside wall. Piffer pushed his head through the hole to the outside, sniffing the air for any danger. After a long minute, he squeezed through the hole and dropped to the hard earth below. Taire followed after a brief safety check of his own.

They were in a small yard of dirt and stone that occupied the space between the manor house and the outer edge of the cavern. They ran along the foundation of the house, partially concealed by mushrooms and other detritus thrown from the house. At one point, Taire paused, overwhelmed by the desire to feed on some grain that Piffer had run past. Before he could finish the first grain, he saw Piffer looking at him with a mixture of impatience and concern.

Taire shook his whiskers in consternation and dropped the half eaten grain. He couldn't understand what could be so important that they could not stop to feed. "It is grain, food, we should not pass it up. Feed with me."

Piffer understood the instinct to feed, but also understood how to control his instincts. He felt concerned at Taire's lack of restraint. "Remember who you are Taire, now is not the time to feed. Follow, and remain silent." The command in his tone was irrefutable. Taire dropped the grain half eaten, trying to understand what Piffer's rebuke had meant. This understanding, however, was beyond his current state of mind. Again they ran.

At the opposite end of the house from where they began, the rock wall again closed in towards the house. At this point Piffer paused near a broken gutter downspout, as if trying to determine the best course of action. After sniffing around for a brief moment, he circled carefully around the jagged open end of the gutter downspout. After his second circuit, he made some determination and entered into the downspout.

Taire followed and climbed up the downspout after Piffer, becoming increasingly disturbed by the silent, harried pace set by his friend. The climb was nearly vertical, with only small chips of rust and debris to cling to. After some time of scrambling upwards, they reached the top and exited into the open roof gutter. Piffer led him up to the peek of the buildings roof and paused for a moment while Taire caught up.

Taire's poor eyesight did not allow him to see much, even in the relatively bright light of the cavern. The space in front of him opened up a fuzzy haze of light and dark. His mind's eye filled in the details with remarkable clarity. His almost forgotten humanity surged forth memories of the grass, fungi-forests, the river, and the farm plots. He remembered his father, but only with the blurred indeterminacy of a dream.

He found himself temporarily lost in a painful reverie of human feelings and understandings; love, hate, pain, pleasure? The feelings only lasted a short moment before his rodent self began to re-assert itself. The sounds coming from the distance in the cavern, the bright light, the unfamiliar smells all conspired against his timid rodent soul. He panicked, and ran for cover.

Taire fled down the roof to where the eaves of a low gable met with the roof of the main structure. Within the darkness of the eaves he found safety. He sat silently, his heart pounding out its fear and confusion in the comfortable small space. He huddled, panting a litany against his fear, "This is my home, I belong with Piffer . . . this is my home, I belong with Piffer . . ."

Into his fright came solace. Piffer nudged up against him in the cramped space, lending him comfort and courage. Piffer's nose twitched in a frenzy of concern for his young charge. Piffer's voice broke through Taire's muttering. "Do not fear your past, it is part of you. Do not lie to yourself about what you are. There is kindness in that world too, this you must remember." Piffer's calming voice and nearness allowed him to regain enough of his self to control the beating of his heart, to allow some of his remaining humanity to temper his flight instincts, and to absorb the meaning of the words.

Seeing that his charge had regained self control, Piffer again ventured forth across the roof without a word of explanation. Still compelled by Piffer's unknown determination, and somewhat less afraid of what Piffer may intend to show him, Taire followed.

They ran along the base of the gable-like structure Taire had concealed himself under until they came to a small knothole below a large window. Piffer passed through the hole quickly without pausing. Taire, for some reason, paused at the hole. Something felt wrong, as if a known, but forgotten nightmare lay inside. He flattened his ears against his head, and with a twitch of his tail climbed through the small hole.

Inside of the knothole was a narrow sill below the large window. The window and sill were part of the high gable they had entered through. In front and below them was a large, private chamber at the top of the house. The chamber was richly appointed with rugs and tapestries. In the middle of the room was a large table with a dozen chairs around it. Torches evenly spaced along the walls brightly illuminated the room.

Although his eyesight was poor, Taire could determine using his other senses that there were humans below at the table. He looked at Piffer next to him to determine some indication of why Piffer brought him here. Piffer only looked sadly at him and moved to block the exit to the roof.

As he first heard the voice of The Ruler, the voice of his nightmares, he understood why Piffer blocked his exit. Below him, at the head of the table, sat The Ruler. The part of him that remembered being a human boy cried out in fear and anguish. Behind him, Piffer nudged him forward, onto a support beam. Numbly, he inched a short distance out onto the beam until he was almost directly over the table, where even his weak eyesight could make out the scene below him.

He was beyond shock or caring when he determined that the other figures sitting at the table were large, black, insect like creatures, with chitinous armor. They had long limbs with claw-like appendages for both feet and hands. Their heads were also black, with the mandibles of an insect as well as long antennae.

Taire remained uncaring of the affairs of the humans and d'rakken mahre below him, at least until Piffer brought to his attention the small figure cowering near The Ruler. It was a ragged, terrified boy; Taire could smell the fear emanating from the child. The boy, who could not have been over ten, seemed unfazed by the presence of the d'rakken mahre, but was staring fixedly in horror at The Ruler, his hand twitching compulsively at his sides. Taire could smell the loathing and fear emanating from the child.

As he examined the boy, he remembered what he had been trying to forget. He remembered his humanity. He knew he could not forget what he had been, what he was. The pain was a part of him, and had to be remembered also, to give meaning to the pleasure. His current form was an escape, and Piffer had helped heal and bring him back to himself. As he realized this, it struck him that what he was seeing below did not make sense.

D'rakken mahre did not just come to dinner. As if awaking from a deep refreshing sleep, Taire found himself with a renewed sense of curiosity and desire. He had to know why creatures that would so carelessly kill his father and other men would docilely sit at the table with The Ruler. He also knew he had to help the small boy that had assumed his fate. He felt responsible, his flight had brought on this boy's captivity. Taire understood the nature of the servitude the boy suffered. It turned his stomach to watery fear and loathing.

Piffer seeing Taire's deep involvement in watching the scene below slowly backed off of the beam back towards the knothole exit. He left quietly, returning to his den, leaving Taire alone to rediscover himself and develop a sense of purpose.

Taire hardly noticed the exit of his friend, so intent upon the scene below him that he was completely unaware of the world around him.

At the table, a d'rakken mahre that Taire assumed to be a diplomat spoke to The Ruler in its sibilant voice. Each word sounded like a hiss, the vowels soft and the consonants watery. "Human, we wish egress to the lands above your city. Our scouts roam the mountains, unable to find suitable passage to the south. It is our understanding that your city opens to a valley with open flat lands to the south. We must have access to this valley. It must be soon. What recompense will you require?"

Taire had obviously entered into the middle of the conversation, just at the crucial point. He had heard the stories of the d'rakken mahre to the north.

The Ruler interrupted his thoughts with his corpulent phlegmatic voice. "Recompense, eh? What you ask is nearly impossible. I can't just allow your entire people to march through the city. The people would riot in fear. Why should I even consider such a proposal?"

The question was of great interest to Taire also. Why did the d'rakken mahre seek 'egress' to the upper world? What was it to the south that they desired?

The other d'rakken mahre around the table were apparently warriors or organizers. In reaction to the diplomat's consternation at The Rulers response, they tensed, moving forward in seats, partially rising. At a gesture from the diplomat, they quieted back into their seats, again becoming as motionless as obsidian statues.

The diplomat spoke again. "Please do not confuse what I ask. We will exit the underworld, we must. No other path presents itself to us. We ask not if we may travel through your city, but what recompense you will require for our use of your passageways to the surface." The creature crossed its long clawed hands in front of it, a look of infinite patience or indifference on its face.

The Ruler was not pleased, however. He stood up, knocking his chair over backwards. His face was purple with consternation. "How dare you explain to me that my permission is not required to exit through my city. In case you have not noticed, this city is a fortress. A fortress guarded by an army of thousands. And THEY ARE MINE!" His rage and belligerence mounted towards a level of physical confrontation. Four guards stepped out of recesses towards the far end of the room with swords drawn.

Taire was holding his breath, hoping fervently The Ruler would make an error that would force the d'rakken mahre to kill him. It would provide an answer to one of his wishes in life. It would make the world a better place in a small way.

The d'rakken mahre diplomat, however, remained composed, diffusing the tension. After a moment, the guards sheathed weapons and withdrew.

The diplomat continued as if The Ruler had not threatened him. "Your thousands mean nothing. Our tens of thousands will prevail should you challenge us. Now, tell me, what payment will suffice for our passage?"

The Ruler remained standing, ruddy cheeks puffing in indignation. "What payment!?" He paused and suddenly became reasonable. "Fine then, gemstones will suffice. You will bring me two large chest filled with cut gemstones to pay for your passage. I will have payment before your horde shows up at the doorstep. This will show your good intentions. Furthermore, you will pass along marked passages only, leaving the city and people alone. Any stragglers will be destroyed. Do you understand? These are my terms, MY ONLY TERMS!"

Taire was both disappointed at The Rulers survival of the confrontation, as well as relieved for the rest of the city's inhabitants. Belatedly he realized that he had been neglecting the thousands of lives that hung in the balance of the negotiations unfolding below him.

The diplomat chirped for a moment to one of its companions

at the table, an organizer to judge by the longer antennae. The organizer silenced and sat silently, head bowed for a moment. Then it lifted its head and chirped back to the diplomat.

The diplomat nodded once in acknowledgment, then looked back to The Ruler. "Done. You will have your stones in one month. The hives will follow two weeks later."

So saying, the d'rakken mahre rose as one, and left the chamber through the rear exit, leaving a bemused and only slightly mollified Ruler.

After a few minutes, The Ruler and his guards also left, leaving Taire alone in the rafters, fearing the outcome of the meeting he had witnessed, and more personally, fearing for the young boy who followed The Ruler from the room.

# EIGHT

## BITTER PARTINGS

Taire returned slowly to Piffer's den, carefully retracing his way back. He was scared. He was scared of the d'rakken mahre, scared of The Ruler, and scared of the decision he must make, or had already made. Mostly though, he was scared of being a human again.

He found Piffer in his den. The elder mouse looked at Taire, an implicit apology in his bright eyes. "I am sorry for having to remind you, for having to show you that. I understand your pain . . ." he was unable to continue.

Taire felt Piffer's pain also. Not the pain for a boy who had to relive terrible memories, but the pain of an old mouse who had lived alone too long. Piffer suffered the pain of remembering love just in time to realize it had to be given up. Taire was speechless. He also had come to love Piffer, for the friendship and stability he provided as well as for companionship that transcended the bounds of species. Piffer had a kind soul, and had done much to heal the damage done a young, hurting boy.

Eventually, Piffer continued. "You must go now. I have come to care for you as if you were my own, and because of this, I can't let you stay. I was correct when I said you do not belong here. You are not a mouse. Perhaps you are not fully human, but it is the form upon which your soul has centered. You may know many forms, and may even discover one that truly fits. Sadly, I will never know the answer. I do know, however, that you have great deeds before you."

Taire finally found the ability to speak. "But how can I leave you? I know that I can't stay here any longer, but won't you come with me?" His voice was a whisper of hope and longing.

Piffer's whiskers twitched for a moment. "No, I can't come with you. I am old, and furthermore, in case you haven't noticed, I am a mouse. My old heart could not take being exposed, out among the humans. Besides, you must learn about yourself, I cannot teach you any more than I already have.

"Now, you must relearn what it is to be human. Come." Without transition, Piffer darted out of his den.

Taire followed him down onto the floor of the rarely used basement. He found Piffer sitting quietly along the far wall by the steep staircase leading to the kitchens. Taire could smell the presence of others. He paused in the middle of the floor and was able to make out a dozen or so other mice collected along the floorboards along the walls. All of the visitors sat quietly, sniffing for signs of danger, whiskers twitching in anticipation.

Piffer's eyes gleamed blackly in the twilight of the basement. "There is much information we have to share with you before you leave us. Taire, these are my children, I would have you meet them, and they you."

Each of the assembled rodents slowly approached Taire in turn. Some spoke to him, telling him secrets of the house, where to find food, supplies, and weapons. Others were more reticent, and simply approached to look at their fathers adopted cub. Finally, Piffer again approached.

"Taire, I wanted all of my family to know you. You will always be known amongst my children as family. Now it is time: you must change back. You must learn to change forms at will or you will not be able to make your escape. Remember your father, remember the happy times. Make your body remember its humanity." Piffer backed away, returning to the deeper shadows of the floorboards.

Taire sat quietly, trying to remember what it felt like to be human. He understood the need, but was unable to remember how. After a few minutes elapsed, he was ready to quit in frustration. He simply did not know how to change; the mechanism was beyond him.

Then, he received a gift from his dead father. For a moment he could see his fathers face and hear his fathers voice in his head. When he was a young boy after first having come to Torance, he had asked his father why he was a guard. He was afraid for his father, afraid of losing him, and had wanted to know why he risked himself to protect people he didn't even know. His father had sat him down on a table so he could speak with him eye to eye.

"Son, not all people can protect themselves. The young, elderly, and disabled need others to ensure their safety. In addition to this, there are other dangers in the world that need to be met. Somebody has to do this, to hold the lawless of society at bay so that everyone can live at peace. This city can only be a good place to live while there are those willing to make some sacrifices to keep it so. That is my job. I take risks because it is a duty I have, a duty of honor as well as an obligation to those who are less able. A man must commit himself to such good as he is able, do you understand?"

At the time, Taire had only understood that his father was a heroic, loving figure: larger than life. Now, however, he saw the words in a different light. His father had taught him two important lessons. He taught his son the meaning of duty and obligation. More importantly, he had given his son a lesson in humanity. His father's words provided the framework he required to understand his humanity. His father had gifted him with an example, and the desire.

The change was instant. Only the change in perspective provided proof of his success. Taire looked down at his body and was surprised to find himself fully dressed, as he was when he changed. His body seemed unfamiliar to him: big and ungainly. He looked at his hands, and rubbed them over his now smooth face. His eyes were slow in adjusting to the dim light. As they did, he was surprised by the acuity of his vision. He peered slowly around the room, noticing that the assembled mice had fled, unable to shed their instinctive fear of man.

For a moment he felt very alone amongst the crates, casks, and clutter of the basement. Then he realized he was not alone; one mouse remained. Piffer sat unmoving in the deep shadows of the floorboards near the staircase. Taire moved slowly towards him, noticing the agitated twitching of his friend's whiskers. He knew Piffer was instinctively afraid, and it hurt him that his friend should be afraid of him. He knelt a few feet away from Piffer, and nodded his thanks to his friend, tears springing unheeded to his eyes.

Piffer overcame his fear and came forward, touching his furry nose briefly to Taire's lowered hand, and looked up. His black eyes were dull. Then he darted off along the wall and disappeared into a pile of crates.

Taire sat and cried softy for a moment, feeling as if he had lost his father again. He knew he would not see Piffer again in this life. He did not sink into despair, however. He remembered his father's words. He remembered that he had a duty to humanity, and it was time to begin making payment for his debts.

He slowly made his way up the stairs and listened at the door. There was no sound coming from the kitchen, so he opened the door a crack to peer in. The room was dark except for one small wall lamp. He entered and, using the information passed on to him by one of Piffer's children, located a burlap sack and filled it with cheeses, bread, and a flask of water.

He had been told where to find everything he required for his trip, and he traveled through the house, carefully and quietly, occasionally shifting to mouse form to pass unseen to collect the items. He never noticed the small black eyes peering out of hidden spaces marking his progress. Piffer was proud of his man-cub as he secretly watched his progress, but wouldn't interfere.

Taire found that, like his clothing, everything he carried in human form traveled with him in mouse form. It was a handy trick of magic, and although he didn't understand it, he appreciated it. While traveling about the house, he was able to collect a backpack, new shoes and leathers, a serviceable dagger on a belt sheath, and various other items he may need. Having collected everything he felt he would need, he switched to mouse form and traveled quickly to The Rulers bedchambers.

Thankfully, The Ruler was not present. He changed back to human form and quickly unlocked the door to the closet in which he knew his successor would be locked away. Inside, huddled to the rear, he found a terrified young boy. As he walked into the closet, the boy flinched away, huddling deeper into a corner, making quiet sobbing noises.

Taire knelt down quietly by the boy and put his hand on a shivering shoulder. He was nearly overcome with pity for the boy, and anger at The Ruler for his cruel perversions. The boy, unused to such gentle treatment, raised his head slightly and peered over his hunched shoulder to see who had come into his cell.

Taire spoke in an even, quiet voice. "It's all right. I'm going to take you out of here. Do you hear me? Stand up. We are going to leave. You can get away from here for good, but you have got to stand up quietly and come with me."

The child, bruised and mentally battered did not understand. He was, however, used to following commands. He stood slowly, wild eyes focusing on nothing in particular. As Taire led him from the closet, he followed quietly, walking with a painful limp. In the light of the room, Taire was shocked at what he saw. After the meeting with the d'rakken mahre, the boy must have been beaten severely. The Ruler had apparently vented his anger and left back to the upper castle shortly after. The boy's eyes were nearly swollen closed, and his scalp was bleeding in several places.

Taire and the boy moved slowly through the seemingly empty house. The boy moved mechanically, his eyes vacant, his spirit seemingly destroyed, or hidden deep down where the depredations of The Ruler couldn't touch it. They climbed through a window near the front door and slumped down into the shadows. Crawling low along the front of the house, they moved until they reached the far edge of the building and paused. They were only fifty paces away from the bridge, their only path to the safety of the city. On the bridge, however, stood a very alert sentry, his pike resting on the stone cobbles of the bridge.

Before Taire had a chance to develop a plan to avoid or distract the guard, the boy jumped to his feet and began to run towards the guard, screaming incoherently at the top of his lungs. Taire was unable to stop him. Not knowing what else to do, he crouched and ran after the boy as far as the shadows would allow him. At the edge of the shadows, still about twenty paces from the bridge, he paused, transfixed by the scene unfolding before him.

The boy's screams alerted the guard, who turned and lowered his pike against the unknown threat. As the boy burst from the shadow in a rage of savage screams, the guard dropped to one knee and leveled his pike into a defensive position. Before he could determine the source of the horrible cries, the boy ran forth and met the pike head on. Taire watched in terrified fascination as the pike head emerged from the boys arched back.

At the last moment, just as his pike entered the boy's body, the guard realized his error. He fell back, releasing his pike with a shout of alarm and warning—but too late. As he lay on his back on the stone of the bridge, holding himself up on his elbows, the boy stood for a moment, held up by the long butt of the pike, blood gurgling from his mouth.

Taire's frozen moment was broken as the guard leaned back on his elbows staring incoherently at the boy. He jumped from the shadows and ran towards the bridge, vowing to make the boy's sacrifice worthwhile. The guard, in his shock did not even see him until he was making his first steps onto the short, steeply arched bridge. Taire ran quickly across the bridge, unhindered by the guard. As he passed the boy, the image engraved itself in his mind. The boy lay half on his side, the pike holding him in a semi-upright position. His eyes were open and bright, even in death. His bloody mouth was locked in a smile. The boy made the only escape he could manage, and the slow chuckling of the stream under the bridge mimicked his death rattle.

Leaping over the guard, Taire reached the open cavern, and turned south towards the less inhabited areas. As he raced through the nighttime twilight of the cavern, he understood his father's commitment; he understood why those that could defend themselves had to champion those less able. With bitter bile in his throat he ran southward, away from danger, away from death and terror. He ran in blind panic towards an unknown future.

He ran blindly for a moment and then found himself at the far northern end of the cavern, in the park he had visited so frequently with his father. He ran past the livestock pens that hemmed in the park to the south: large pens housing cattle, chickens, sheep, pigs and horses. The horses whuffed quietly at the disturbance as he slowed to creep by closely avoiding the newer houses that had been built in the open cavern known as Southtown. Southtown had developed as another sub-city of Torance as Northtown, where he had grown up with his father, had filled up. Knowing guards frequented the market area at night, he traveled through a large fenced vegetable garden to behind the shacks, to the east of the market area. A dog barked briefly as he passed close to the farmhouse and quickly quieted as he passed over the southern fence at a full run.

Panting heavily from the extended run, Taire passed the storage sheds of the caravaneers and cut over to the east wall towards the large mining office that blocked the entrance into the mines. He paused at the mining office to catch his breath and listen for pursuit. He could hear no noise except for the distant tapping of the picks and hammers of the sleepless dwarves, searching for iron and gems in the long mine tunnels behind the office building that served to keep intruders out, and the solitary dwarves in. No one in the city ever spoke of having met a dwarf, and it was rumored that The Ruler held them in the city against their will to do his bidding.

From his vantage point, he could see the dim lantern light glowing a hundred paces away from the caravan entrance into the underworld. He knew there would be guards posted there who would question a lone boy traveling at this time of night, so he continued at a slower, more cautious pace, close to the eastern wall. As he approached Southtown, he could hear the sounds of men making merry in the common room of the Lamp Lighter, one of Southtown's more popular drinking establishments. Southtown was loud and less orderly than the neatly laid out Northtown. His father had always forbidden him to visit the disreputable neighborhood, so Taire knew little of it. To the east of Southtown's one hundred or so buildings, dwarven miners were slowly excavating another cavern. For a moment, he considered hiding in the excavation area, or using the ramp along the Northeast edge of Northtown to ascend to the upper levels of the under-city, where he was less likely to be recognized.

Taire, however, was not prepared to meet with other humans yet, or willing to risk an encounter with dwarves working in the excavation. He steered away from the noisy two storied buildings of Southtown and the ramp to the even more populated upper levels, cutting back east across the cavern towards the caravan area. There were very few caravaneers tents present, it seemed, but he gave the few scattered tents a wide berth to be safe.

After a brief sprint across the open space near the caravan area, he reached his destination. Ahead was the low fence that marked the entrance into the large side cavern in which the community tended a large forest of the giant edible mushrooms that were one of the staples of the city's dwellers diet.

The side cavern had a narrow entrance, guarded by a low fence, mainly to keep out stray sergath, which were fed the more common and less tasty giant fungi that were grown about the cavern. Taire climbed the fence and quietly crept past the farmer's darkened household. Behind the house, a narrow cave opened up into a nearly circular cavern with a diameter of nearly a hundred paces. The entire space glowed gently green, dimly illuminated by the slimes and fungi that grew along the walls.

The forest had a dreamlike appearance; huge mushrooms sprouted up to ten feet, the caps spreading as wide as thirty feet on some. The mushrooms were of varying heights, creating a cramped feeling in the cavern. The cavern floor was a soft, moldy loam, in which the mushroom thrived. In the center of the cavern, was a pool, about twenty feet across. The silence of the cavern was broken by the occasional drip of water from the high ceiling into the pool.

Taire approached the pool and bent down to take a drink. As he dip his face to the water, he noticed a glowing from deep within the pool. As he dipped his head and drank deeply, he noticed the glow under the water brighten, and grow in size, as if coming closer to the waters surface.

Alarmed, he jumped away from the water, his short blond hair dripping onto his face. The water in the pool seemed to swirl lightly on its own. The brightness below the waterline increased, as did the turbulence on the surface. Taire became afraid and ran from the pool, deep into the mushroom forest. It was warm and humid in the cavern. He cut a large portion of mushroom from a stalk and ate it slowly, formulating a terrible but necessary idea in his mind. Slowly, as thoughts of killing The Ruler filled his head, he slid away into sleep beneath the protective cap of one of the smaller mushrooms. He slept with a smile on his face. He was dreaming of his father, and his father approved of his son's plans.

# NINE

## DANGEROUS PLANS

Taire awoke rested and surer of himself. The shock of the previous evening had not been erased, but carefully cataloged and stored in his memories; another strike against The Ruler, he thought. He was awakened by the noise of the farmer and his sons harvesting a large mushroom some distance away. He scuttled away from the noise, not wanting to be caught trespassing on the farmers property. When he reached the wall of the circular cavern he followed it away from the farmer towards the exit into the main cavern, where, during the artificial light of day he could blend into the bustle of daily activities.

He was able to successfully sneak past the farmer's house, the smells of a home cooked breakfast wafting out through its open windows. The smell evoked visions of family, of the type of home he would have picked for his father and himself had his mother lived. With his mind filled with impossible dreams, Taire jogged across the cavern. He ran slowly enough not to attract attention, heading for the ramp towards the upper caverns. The ramps were always busy, people and carts jostling for position up the narrow passages. Taire found himself hard pressed to wind his way past the morning crush of carts and people.

The upper cavern of Torance had originally been the only occupied part of the caverns. Even with the recent additions, it was still overcrowded and dirty. Taire had visited the upper cavern enough to know the general layout. At the top of the ramp, he found himself on Wailing Way, a wide street running east to west most of the distance of the cavern. The cavern itself, he knew, had been excavated in a rectangle, about two-thirds of a mile east/west and around one-half mile north/south. The cavern was only about twenty feet high, and all of the buildings were built from the floor to the ceiling of the cavern to best utilize the space available. Only occasional pillars of stone remained to support the ceiling, it almost looked like the roof was supported by the rows of buildings. The city was a maze of large and small streets, all dimly lit by evenly spaced lamps affixed to the sides of the buildings.

Fortunately, Taire knew where in this great tangle of streets he was going. His father had brought him with him many times on his shopping trips to the upper caverns. Taire traveled west along Wailing way until, almost at the far end of town, it narrowed into a small street. At its end the street convoluted into a number of ninety degree turns through an area filled with taverns, wine shops, and one large inn. Finally, the passage turned northward; a small sign marked the street as Whispering Way.

Whispering Way was little more than two hundred feet in length, and narrow. It was heavily traveled though, with its own small ramp to the lower levels making it a popular route for those on foot who wished to avoid the carts that used the larger ramps. Taire jostled his way through the crowd, pleased to discover that his body had grown during the previous months. He was taller than many of those around him, possibly six feet already, and beginning to widen in the shoulders. Although still clumsy and gangly, he knew he would be a large man like his father. It was a pleasing thought as he worked his way through the crowd, partially by dodging, and partially by pushing.

A short way up the street he found the doorway he sought. A crude sign above the door showed a picture of two crossed swords. It read 'Rufold's Weapons'. Taire's father had exclusively shopped at Rufold's, and had brought him along on one of his visits several years ago. He doubted that he would be recognized by the man, and knew him to be fair.

Taire reached into his pocket and pulled out the small coin purse he had stolen from The Rulers mansion. He confidently opened the door and stepped into the traders shop.

The shop itself was a large rectangular building with shelves along the sidewalls, and a long counter along the back wall. Behind the counter was a steep stairway leading up the living quarters of the trader and his family. On the side shelves rested an assortment of ordinary weapons:, daggers, maces, various sized swords, and hammers. On the long shelves behind the counter, however, were the more expensive and well-made items.

At the sound of the door opening, the shopkeeper, Rufold, looked up from what he was doing behind the counter. "Hello lad, what needs you?" The shopkeeper was a huge man, close to seven feet tall. He was fair skinned, with blond hair. He spoke with the unmistakable deep voice and harsh accent of a Carstan. It sounded like he was talking with his mouth full of food and had to spit out each word. It was clear that Carstans did not put much emphasis on education or speaking skills.

It seemed that wherever weapons were found, there would be a Carstan about. Their trade was war, and they loved the tools of their trade.

"Well, Sir," Taire spoke as he approached the counter, "I have some money my father gave me for my birthday. He says a man should have a man's weapon."

Rufold seemed to heartily approve of this statement. By the time Taire reached the counter, he had already begun bustling about behind the counter grabbing items. Taire stood for a minute at the counter before the man returned with an armload of weaponry. The excited shopkeeper dumped the load on the counter in front of Taire.

"Good, lad, very good. Now here are some manly weapons. You need perhaps a good long sword? Boring, but serviceable."

He held up a well-polished long sword for Taire to examine. Taire shook his head. "No, sir, what I really want is . . ."

Before he could finish, the man interrupted. "Of course, Rufold understand. You're needing a real man's weapon." He sorted quickly through the pile and produced a huge battle-axe, double bladed and wicked looking. It looked imponderably heavy and dangerous. The shopkeeper held it aloft, in his outstretched hand as if it had no weight at all. "This is better, yes? It can split a man like a melon, even in armor." His smile stretched from ear to ear.

Taire found the man's exuberance amusing, if a bit disconcerting. He couldn't help but picture the results of Rufold hitting a man in armor with the axe—the result would be quite predictable, and quite devastating to the victim. His biggest problems was, though, that he knew what he wanted, but was trapped by his own story. "Yes, it is wonderful. Any man would be proud to bear such a weapon. But . . . I sort of had my heart set on a handbow." Handbows were small but powerful crossbow that could be wielded single handedly, and were an effective weapon in enclosed spaces.

Rufold dropped the battle-axe to the counter, a look of distaste on his face. "But, it is not a man's weapon. These are weapons fit for a brave young man. Why you seeking a cowards weapon such as the handbow?"

"Well, I just want it for a back-up you see. I already have a sword, and my dad thought I should be prepared to handle any circumstance . . . I wouldn't use it except in defense." His response seemed lame, even to his own ears, but it was the best he could do on the fly.

Rufold shook his head. "Well, if you say you wouldn't shoot a man with it unless he tried cheating first . . ." he walked to a small box on the shelf behind him as he spoke, and removed the desired weapon.

Cheating? How can one cheat in a fight to the death? Taire couldn't help but think that Carstans were contrary people.

Meanwhile, Rufold returned to the counter and set the handbow down with something like disdain. The weapon was made from sturdy oak and steel, and included a brace of bolts. "It will cost you eight golds. Done?"

Taire counted the golds from the pouch, almost emptying it in the process. He set them on the counter and held his hand over them. "Include a leather bag to carry it, and done."

Rufold nodded in agreement. "Good idea. You should hide such a thing, so others don't think you a coward." He handed Taire a small leather pouch he produced from behind the counter and took the golds from the counter.

Taire took the handbow, put it in the bag, and tied it onto his belt. "Thank you, sir."

The shopkeeper was no longer paying attention, however. He was busy replacing the weapons onto the shelves, lovingly dusting each one before moving on to the next.

Taire exited the shop and hurried through the late morning crowds towards the main ramp up to the castle. With thoughts of murder on his mind, he walked north through a number of twists and turns until he saw the street sign for Silver Way under a flickering corner lamp. Silver way was a major highway, running east/west, and ending at a large open courtyard. To the east of the courtyard, a large ramp led upwards towards the military barracks. Taire remembered a day, some months ago when he had traveled up this very ramp to discover the fate of his father.

A guard stood to each side of the ramp directing traffic up and down the ramp. Taire walked quickly by the guards, his eyes downcast. For a few terrified heartbeats, he was afraid one of the guards might have recognized him. He knew by now that the guard from the bridge would have passed his description, and the city guard would be looking to take him for questioning. The moment passed, though, and a man who had overturned his cart at the base of the ramp caught the guard's attention. In the ensuing commotion, Taire made good his escape.

The ramp led to another large open room, with many passages leading away, all guarded. The largest of the passages was the second ramp, leading to the surface. He had only been to the surface once, that day years ago when his father brought him to see The Ruler. The guards on the ramp were only concerned with those coming down from the surface, very few were heading up, and those that were, passed unnoticed. He slipped up the ramp close behind a small merchants wagon, and wondered at the heat he felt from above.

Some minutes later, shielding his sensitive eyes from the brightness, Taire found himself standing in the large marshaling area of the castle, sweating lightly in the late autumn heat. He stood blinking for a time, feeling as if he was being suffocated by the openness. He felt so open, so unprotected. It reminded him of how it felt to be a mouse, in the middle of a bright room. His eyes darted about searching for an escape from the openness.

To his left, under the walls of the inner castle, stood a ramshackle collection of shacks used by traders on the weekly market day. Careless of the attention he might attract, he ran quickly to one of the now empty shacks and climbed over the counter. He hid in the shadowed coolness under the counter until his heart returned to its normal pace.

Knowing that there would be very alert guards at the entrance to the inner castle, he knew that such an entry would be impossible. While Taire waited for the cool darkness of evening he examined the vine-covered rock of the castle wall behind him. As it darkened outside, he heard the voices of the city guards shutting the gates, and clearing the last of the travelers from the bailey, moving them down into the depths of the city. The sounds of the night were unfamiliar. Something chirped loudly from the far side of the traders shack, and Taire was too scared to find out what it was. In addition to this, the feel of the wind, as well as the noise it made whistling through the patched roof seemed alien and unnatural to one accustomed to the stillness and silence of life underground.

Finally, sure that everyone had moved indoors for the night, Taire stood and looked around. The bailey was uninhabited. Countless stars twinkled in the night sky. It was beautiful and magical to Taire. He was surprised to find tears in his eyes, seeing the glory of the heavens at night for the first time. At night, he thought, the surface had some beauty, and some comfort.

He looked around, embarrassed, even though no one was about, wiping his eyes with his sleeve. Turning, he looked at the imposing inner castle wall. The wall stood over forty feet tall, ivy tendrils spreading widely across its surface. Taire pulled at the ivy. A long strand broke off in his hand. Too weak to climb, he thought. Then again, it wouldn't be too weak for a mouse, would it?

Taire was too scared, and too determined to spend time evaluating the wisdom of his course. Again he glanced about to ensure the area was uninhabited. With a surge of desire and will, he changed into the other form his body had so recently inhabited. From his new vantage point, the vines were as large as trees, and the root-like tendrils sticking out from the body of the vine made it as easy to climb as a ladder. He scrambled up the vine for an endless time with the agility of a natural climber. Near the very top of the castle, where he assumed The Ruler would chose to reside, he searched for a while along the vine before discovering a small opening in the wall where the mortar had broken away.

He wriggled into the crack and worked his way through the fissure a seemingly great distance before arriving at the inside wall. He poked his head partially out into the space beyond the hole and sensed nothing dangerous.

He dropped carefully down to the stone floor, and found himself in a long corridor, lit dimly by widely spaced torches held in wall sconces. He felt a vague sense of unease, although he could not distinguish the source.

Taire scampered quickly down the long corridor, moving close to the outside castle wall. After a distance, he came to a wide opening that led into a large chamber. Taire thought it likely to be a tower storeroom. There was a smell of humans in the place. Although there were none currently in occupancy, it was clear that it had been visited recently and frequently.

Again Taire felt the sense of danger, more immediate this time. He sniffed and looked about. Sensing nothing of the cause, he darted across the opening and continued along the long corridor hugging the outside of the castle, trusting his instincts to guard against danger.

Those instincts saved Taire's life.

He paused briefly to investigate a small crack in the wall. As he prepared to move on, a sudden sense of terror overwhelmed him. Even before he could react to the sensation, a howling ball of furry terror leapt at him from the shadows of the opposite side of the corridor. With a fluid, lightning fast motion, the feline threat struck him with a paw and sent him bouncing off of the wall.

Content to toy with its meal, the cat sat and watched Taire for a moment. Taire was bleeding from the cat's claws and sat in breathless terror against the wall. The instinct to flee was overwhelming. Ignoring his wounds, Taire ran for the crack in the wall he had been near. He did not know how deep it went, or to where, but hoped it would suffice to protect against the cats deadly claws.

The cat sat placidly until Taire had almost reached the wall, and then reached casually out with a paw, claws extended, and trapped him against the floor.

He was helpless. His heart nearly burst from its exertions, and from his fear or what must come next. The cat did not choose to eat him, or even kill him yet. Instead, he was released and batted lightly away from the wall again. Badly scratched, and even more frightened, Taire lay motionless. He retained enough of his human awareness to know at what game the cat play. As he lay as still as death, the smell of the cat filling his nostrils, Taire searched for an escape.

Seeing no way to out wait or outrun the cat, Taire did the only thing that the cat would not anticipate or understand; he gathered himself and attacked.

The absurdity of the situation was lost on the cat, which had never had a mouse charge directly at it, squeaking loudly. It sat mesmerized by the sight, right up until the moment the mouse bit it soundly on the paw.

Screaming indignantly, the cat leapt high into the air, giving Taire free access to the crack in the wall. With barely suppressed terror and exuberance, Taire jumped forward and entered into the hole.

After only a short distance he found himself in a large room on the other side of the wall. The room was dark, and smelled of must and disuse. Briefly, he could hear the cat claw about the insides of the crack searching for its missing dinner. With a plaintive yowl, the cat ceased its attempts.

Taire began a quick search of the room, darting about looking for an exit. The room was lined with unused bunks; apparently an auxiliary barracks of some sort. Finding no other exit, he moved towards the door that led back into the corridor he had just left. The door was open only a crack, and light was streaming in from a torch in the corridor. As Taire approach the door, his senses warned him of the danger awaiting him outside.

At approximately the same time he sensed the cat, the cat sensed him. It hissed cruelly and its paw shot under the door, claws extended, grabbing for Taire's soft flesh. Fortunately, Taire was too far away. He scampered back a few more feet to be sure. The cat was clawing and pushing at the door, and the door creaked open a notch. Seeing its success, the cat redoubled its efforts.

Taire knew that there was no escape, and he also knew the cat would soon be in the room. At first he could only think of escape. Then, in a moment of self-awareness, tinged with embarrassment and anger, Taire remembered what and who he was.

The cat required only a matter of minutes to push the door far enough to enter. It did so, yowling and hissing its consternation at its chosen prey's ability to elude it so far. Into the room it burst full of hate and hunger. It met its prey, but not on the terms it expected.

Taire looked down at the feline, who was looking back at him, a look of profound confusion on its furry face. With some small sense of malice, Taire took the opportunity to jump directly in front of the cat, waving his arms and yelling. "Yaa, scat you mangy beast."

The sight was too much for the cat. It yelped briefly and ran at top speed for the door, its hackles raised in fear. In its haste, it misjudged its exit, and ran headfirst into the door. It fell back stunned, shook its head slowly, and exited more carefully, if not more slowly.

Feeling satisfied, and just a little guilty, Taire walked to the door and exited into the corridor. In the torchlight, he could see that the scratches the cat had given him were still present in his human form. He had a long gash in his left arm, and a smaller one on his left leg. Neither bled too badly, and both seemed clean, so he made two simple bandages from some cloth from his pack and moved on.

Taire moved slowly down the corridor, alert for signs of guards, but finding none. At the end of the corridor, he found another large tower room, this one empty, except for a stair leading down. To one end of the chamber was a closed wooden door.

He listened at the door for a moment, and then, hearing nothing, slowly opened it. Inside was only darkness, and a musty odor. He looked quickly about, and then grabbed a torch to investigate the room. He worried that the missing torch might arouse suspicion if a guard were to make rounds, but decided to risk it.

This room, like the first he had entered was a disused barracks room. It held nothing of interest except another door to the rear. Taire quietly moved to the rear of the room and opened the door.

As the door opened, the torchlight was reflected back manifold from shiny objects inside. Taire eagerly stepped inside to discover the source of the reflections.

The room was an armory of some sort. On the walls hung various bits of armor, all carefully polished and oiled against rust. Tables were stacked with weapons, mostly swords of varying length and heft. Taire closed the door, and placed his torch in a wall sconce. The contents of the room held him in an almost magical trance for a moment. He walked around the room, fingering blades and trying on pieces of armor. He pictured himself as a great warrior, a hero adored by the masses.

He found a highly reflective shield and looked at himself. He donned heavy chain armor and a conical helm. In the reflection, he could see that the helm was slipping forward on his head, and the chain mail rode high on his too tall frame. Feeling foolish, he removed the armor.

Remembering his mission, Taire more carefully selected a leather vest and breeks, along with a short sword and a matching sheath to hang on his belt. Finally, after a long search, he found a common infantry helmet, with a slightly bent nose guard, that fit well enough to stay upright on his head.

Feeling as well armed and armored as possible, Taire took his torch from the sconce and made his way back to the descending stairs in the tower room.

He cautiously crept down the first few steps to the landing. At the landing, he peered carefully around the corner, down into the room below. Smoke from the many torches in the room and corridor ran along the ceiling to vent through openings in the outer wall. A guard stood attentively at the entrance of the tower room.

The guard faced out towards the corridor, his back to Taire. Taire fingered the bag in which he had stored his hand-bow. Although he greatly desired the death of The Ruler, he squirmed at the thought of killing an innocent guard. The guard probably had family of his own, perhaps a son. No, he thought, he would not stoop to murder, he would risk orphaning another child.

Even though he would not kill the man he knew he had to get past him. With a steadying deep breath he pulled his sword from its sheath and quietly snuck up behind the man. Almost gently he rapped the man on the back of the head with his sword hilt. The result was predictable, and the man slumped gracefully to the floor.

Taire looked at the sword in his hand, surprised at the ease at which he knocked the man senseless. He was afraid of the power his body held, afraid of using the power to kill, afraid of the responsibility his strength carried with it. Sheathing the sword, he knelt down and checked to ensure the man was alive. The guard was breathing deeply and evenly. Feeling deep guilt, he dragged the guard back into the tower room and laid him gently underneath the stairs.

Taire knew he was truly committed now.

The guard would be found soon and the search would

commence. Although he had the means to hide from any search, The Ruler would be alerted to an intruder, and be more heavily guarded. His chances would be lost.

With haste only barely tempered by caution, Taire moved down the corridor searching for steps to the lower level, to where he now believed he would have his best chance at finding The Ruler. He found a stairwell almost immediately. As he crept down the stairs, alert for guards, Taire began to hear a quiet, melodic chanting. He recognized the priestly chants of late evening services, and followed the sound downwards.

Taire followed the melodic sound along a corridor until he reached a corner, from where he felt he was almost on top of the sound. He took a look around the corner and saw that it led out onto a high balcony. The balcony was protected by a low wall, and extended thirty or more paces to an area of balcony seating; currently the entire area was empty.

He crept out onto the balcony on all fours for a distance and risked a peak over the balustrade. Below he saw a large chapel only partially filled with worshipers for the evening prayers to Varsnya, the Last God of Creation. With the sound of the melodic chants masking the sounds of his movements, Taire crept along the balcony to the empty seating area to get a better look.

The seating area sloped slightly, allowing all seats an unobstructed view. Taire hid behind a chair and watched the ceremony below. A priest walked out onto the raised dais at the front of the chapel, swinging a censure on a short chain. Smoke swirled about him like a blue/grey snake.

As the last of the worshippers arrived, the priest motioned for all to be seated. The chanting stopped on cue. As everyone was seated, Taire was afforded a better view of those assembled below. In the front row, seated amongst a number of guards, was the familiar head of The Ruler.

His heart in his throat, Taire crept along the balustrade, back towards the entry, nearer The Ruler seated below. When he reached the end of the balcony, where it met the corridor he entered, he was almost directly over The Ruler.

He felt his cheeks heat as his heart eagerly pounded blood through his body. An unfamiliar emotion welled up from within the depths of his soul: hatred. He had never hated before he met The Ruler, but now he knew both hate and loathing. He loosened the strings on the bag holding his hand-bow.

His fingers fumbled with the strings, and with the pouch itself before he finally managed to remove the hand-bow. His heart was laboring in his chest and his hands were slippery with sweat. As he leveled the small bow, taking aim, he saw how badly his hands were shaking. The bow waved erratically in his shaking grip, making an accurate shot impossible.

He took one deep breath, then another. From deep inside, from the center of his hatred, from the memory of a boy lying dead on a stone bridge below, he found a sense of calm. With steady hands, he looked through the site until The Ruler was centered within it.

In a frozen moment, a moment of complete awareness of himself and his surroundings, Taire tensed his finger and fired the bolt. The hand-bow recoiled slightly in his hand as the bolt released.

Within the bubble of awareness in which Taire existed, he watched the flight of the bolt as it traveled through space. He had taken aim at The Rulers head, and the bolt appeared to have released true.

Below, only a split second after Taire had shot the bolt, the guard next to The Ruler bumped lightly into him. The bump moved The Ruler a few inches to the side just as the bolt struck. The bolt tore through his ear and cheek, tearing off much of the ear, and part of the cheek. In a spray of blood, The Ruler fell forward into the pew in front of him.

Above, Taire watched in disbelief as The Ruler avoided death by a freak accident. He began to reach for another bolt as the first shouts erupted from below. Arrows followed the screams, and Taire dropped the hand-bow and fled the balcony.

He tasted bitter failure as he ran for his life.

# TEN

## OUT OF THE FRYING PAN . . .

Taire ran heedlessly along his previous path, fleeing the shouts of his pursuers. He knew it would only be a matter of minutes before the pursuit organized and cut off all avenues of escape. He ran up the stairs and down the hall towards the room in which he had left the unconscious guard. He slowed briefly as he round the corner, worried that the guard may have come to, or worse, been discovered. The room was clear, however, and the soft sound of snoring attested the guards continuing unconsciousness. Taire's helmet slipped down onto his nose, and he took a moment to remove it and drop it to the floor. He also removed the sword and sheath, which consistently tried to trip him while he ran.

The shouts of the pursuers neared, and Taire forced himself into panicked motion again. He leapt up the last flight of stairs three at a time. As he ran along the dim corridors of the topmost level of the castle, he pushed open each door he passed, hoping to set off the pursuit.

As he round the last corner before he reached the spot he had entered, he interrupted the cat in its hunt. With a terrified yowl, the cat leapt up and tore down the hall, away from him. Despite the dire straits he was in, he couldn't suppress a smile as he thought about the cat. Payback is hell, he thought.

Halfway down the corridor, he stopped at the spot of the small crack in the wall he had entered through. The sounds of pursuit had receded. The guards chasing Taire were confident that he was trapped, and began a room-by-room search to ensure their prey could not double back and escape.

With a surge of will, he changed to his smaller form, and with a flick of his tail disappeared into the crack in the stone wall.

The only witness to his act was the cat. It cowered behind a tapestry a short distance down the corridor. With its tail twitching in agitation, it began to consider a change in diet.

It was only a matter of minutes before Taire found his way back to the shack in which he had concealed himself only a few hours earlier. Staying in his rodent form, he found a small patch of dead leaves in which to sleep and nestled in for the night. The distant sounds of guards searching the castle kept him awake for some time.

Later during the night, Taire's sleep was interrupted by a nearby shout. Near to panic, he squirmed deeper into the ivy leaves. The light of a torch passed just outside of the shack, casting the helmeted shadows of two guards on the castle wall. One of the guards paused long enough to ensure no one was hiding in the shack.

The remainder of the night passed with the echoed shouts of the guards calling to each other across the courtyard, the smoke from their many torches adding a hazy dream-like quality to the night.

The vendor arrived at his booth with the early morning crowds, setting out his wares for display along the front counter. He was whistling softly as he worked, glad that it was market day. He paused for a moment from his labor, hearing a strange noise behind him. His whistling abruptly stopped. He turned slowly, the hairs on the back of his neck standing.

His heart paused in his chest as his peripheral vision picked up a large figure against the ivy of the castle wall. He jumped backwards, hands outstretched to fend off the shadowed figure.

Taire jumped forward, towards the man, palms facing outwards. "Sir, I wont hurt you. I'm sorry—I was just leaving—excuse me." He inched past the man, who was stammering in fear. Seeing that the man was not going to call out, he jumped the counter and melted into the morning traffic.

Behind the counter, the vendor looked from the castle wall to the receding back of the large young man who had frightened him so. He couldn't figure out how the young man had gotten behind him, or why his hair was filled with dead ivy leaves. "Hmmmp," he whispered to himself, "suppose I really would rather not know." With now forced cheerfulness, he again began to whistle and put out his wares.

Taire walked along with the crowd towards the exit from the castle, which led out into Talon Valley. At the exit, he was held up in a shuffling crowd of merchants and townsmen. At the head of the crowd, six guards were searching all wagons, and questioning each person seeking egress from the castle. On the inner wall of the tunnel leading out of the castle, Taire could see a large parchment, with a drawing roughly resembling him.

The guards watched closely as everyone filed by the drawing; asking them if they had seen the subject. Taire began to back away from the tunnel, realizing there was no chance of escape through the gate. As he shoulder his way through the crowd, back towards the entrance to the under-city, he held his head down, trying to control the sense of panic that threatened to overwhelm him.

Every face seemed unfriendly, a threat to his safety. With much bumping and jostling, Taire worked his way back to the entrance to the under-city. There, he found only one guard, and quickly slipped by as the guard searched a merchant's wagon.

At the landing of the first ramp, he was again stopped in a crowd. There were two guards more carefully checking those passing down the second ramp, and a half dozen or so other guards lounging about the large chamber. Taire realized he might have trapped himself. Seeing no other alternative, he continued with the crowd, the metallic tang of fear in his mouth.

As he reached the front of the crowd, a guard stepped in front of him. "Name and business lad." The soldier spoke in an authoritative monotone.

Thinking quickly, Taire lied. "Rolf, sir. I'm working for my Da, as a guard. He's a trader. He went on ahead of me while I looked around the market. I—um, need to catch up sir. Excuse me." He tried to squeeze past the guard.

"Hold, just a minute." The guard grabbed his arm, and called to the guard on the other side of the ramp. "Jons, let me see that drawing the Sergeant brought this morning."

Taire looked at the other guard, as he reached into a pouch at his waist, and then back to the guard holding him. His heart threatened to burst from its exertions, and sweat began to bead on his forehead. "Sir—I really have to get going. My Da will blister me if . . ." he broke off his lie, realizing he was in deep trouble. With a surge of strength brought on by panic, he knocked the guard's hand away and leapt down the passage, throwing aside anyone in his path.

"Jons, get after him!" The guards shout echoed down the ramp, but Taire was already well ahead of his pursuit, running for his life. At the bottom of the ramp he slowed and melded into the crowds on the streets. In the familiar streets of the city, Taire felt more comfortable of his ability to elude pursuit. Moving quickly, but not enough so to attract attention, he headed for the last ramp, that to the lowest level of the city.

Without mishap, he reached his home section of the city. He carefully made his way southward until he was near the caravan area, where he found an unlocked, empty storage shed. After insuring no one was about, he slipped into the shed and hid behind a stack of empty crates. The exertions of the day and night had left him tired and emotionally drained. It was only minutes before he was sleeping deeply.

He awoke refreshed later that afternoon. He climbed some crates to look out a high window to view the area around the shed. Nothing outside indicated that the search had reached him yet.

The fact was not consoling, however. He knew he was trapped in the lower city now, and that the guards would search very thoroughly now that they knew roughly where he was. He had to escape, and the under-earth presented the only possibility; and of course it was heavily guarded.

A gentle snorting from below the window interrupted his contemplation. A sergath wandered over near the building and began sniffing the wood, checking for anything edible. Not finding anything, it lumbered away, back towards the cavern wall. The ponderous beast gave Taire an idea.

---

Bert worked for one of the wealthier caravaneers of the city. The caravan master had instructed him to load up the sergath in the yard, for a trading run to Station Two. During the last few days, virtually all of the traders had packed up and left on deep trading runs. Rumors were spreading that the d'rakken mahre were calling for increased shipments of certain types of goods, and paying any price asked for the goods. The lure of easy money had everyone scrambling for profits.

The five sergath in the yard were the only ones his master had not already sent traveling into the depths. He whistled to the sergath and they came to the entrance of the yard on command. He fed each beast a small bit of dried fungus that he pulled from a small pouch at his waist. As the long tongue pulled the morsel from his hand, he affectionately pat each beast on the head, evoking a rumbling hum of pleasure.

The first beast he saddled for the caravan master to ride. Then he began to tie the loads on the other four beasts. After he finished with the second load, he noticed something odd. He looked to the saddled beast and then the loaded ones. "One," he pointed at the sergath he had saddled, "two, three," he pointed in turn to the two he had loaded, "four—uh—seven, nine." He finished by counting the unloaded beasts. He shook his head, something was wrong with the count, there was supposed to be five, the boss had told him that.

Bert scratched his chin, perplexed with the advanced math. "Nine? That's—um two too many." He mumbled to himself, confused. He began his count again. "One, two, three, four," he paused, thinking deeply. "Seven—FIVE!" He finished very pleased with himself for working the problem out. "Knew there was five," he muttered as he resumed packing the beasts.

At the caravan exit to the under-earth, the caravan was thoroughly searched by a dozen attentive guards. Every pack was opened, and every guard was examined and questioned. Finding everything in order, the guards allowed the caravan to pass through both the inner, and the outer sets of portcullis, into the descent to the underworld.

Bert watched the caravan go, slightly concerned about one of the sergath. It seemed to keep stumbling, tripping on its feet. He had checked its feet and legs and found it sound, but it stumbled like a soldier leaving a taproom. As the caravan passed into the darkness, the beast seamed to be doing better, and only stumbled once more before lumbering out of sight into the depths.

"Probably ate some bad fungus." Bert shook his head as he walked back towards his home.

Taire was just figuring out how to move with an even gait as he passed into the unlighted depths beyond the last portcullis. Every other guard carried a torch, creating a dim, flickering light that threw their shadows on the far walls of the cavern. Taire, however, found that his eyes adjusted very well to the decrease in light, and he could see clearly in the gloom.

The cavern varied in width and height, sloping ever downwards. Taire found his new form uniquely able to travel on the sloping, uneven surface of the cavern. His wide toes found a sure grip on the cracked surface, and the great muscles of his legs worked tirelessly. Swinging his ponderous head to the side, he found that he could see the variations of the heat in the stone of the cavern. He could smell the water in the waterskin of the guard nearest him. All in all, Taire found this form remarkably well suited to life under the earth.

During the next four days the caravan plodded downwards into the depths, and Taire awaited a chance to escape. On the third day, the caravan turned off of the large passage in which they had been traveling into a much smaller side passage. Taire listened carefully to two guards talking about the change in course. A recruit was questioning the grizzled veteran near him. "Why're we turning into such a small cavern Bogs?"

Bogs, a veteran of hundreds of trips chuckled at the boys concern. "Well, lad, that large passage leads to Station One. That's the most common caravan destination cause it's the largest of the drak cities; the queen lives there." He paused his narration long enough to spit. "Station Two now, it's much smaller, but also closer. We will be there in a day or so now. The problem is, this damned passage is tight. Going to get hot too, there's a few spots where it's as hot as the nine hells together."

"If Station Two is so small, why are we going there instead of a larger drak city?"

Bogs scratched his stubbled chin. "Because stupid, every other caravan has already been to Station One, it's likely picked clean by now. Boss thought we should try one of the less populated cities to find a fresh market. draks have been buying up all sorts of goods during the last month—business is good."

The small passage was indeed hot, Taire could see the veins of heat running through the stones in places. He enjoyed the heat though; his cold-blooded body dealt well with the warmth, and he found his body responding positively to the change, his muscles loosening and his energy increasing.

That night they camped in a small side cavern. Taire and the other sergath munched on the small fungi that grew along the rear of the cavern. He kept his mind busy thinking of other things than the green scum he was eating, afraid he would be ill if he paid attention to what he was doing. In this form, however, he couldn't help admitting that it really didn't taste all that bad.

Water ran freely down the wall, and Taire could smell the underground river many feet behind the wall from which the water escaped. It flowed sluggishly along a slimy path on the rocky cavern floor until it disappeared into a large sinkhole on the opposite side of the cavern.

Late in the evening, after the sergath were hobbled and all but the first shift of guards were asleep; Taire decided it was time to leave. He was afraid that the d'rakken mahre would discover his ruse, and believed he had to escape before reaching Station Two. The sergath near him had all lain down with their large legs splayed out to the sides. Their breath wheezed through large nostril slits.

The packs had been unloaded for the night, providing the freedom of movement that Taire required. He quickly changed to mouse form to escape the hobble. As soon as the change occurred, he scampered away at full speed, hoping to avoid being caught up in the falling hobble. His change had one effect he had not anticipated. Nearby, one of the sergath turned a half lidded eye his way, its nostrils open and sniffing deeply.

Searching his memory of the sergath mentality, he discovered a fact that had previously eluded him, and realized his error too late. The sergath shot to its feet, and surged towards the one treat it enjoyed more than the fungi that grew in the caverns. Fortunately for the fleeing Taire, the hobble tripped the beast and it fell heavily, landing a few feet short. Unfortunately, the noise it made awoke the rest of the camp.

Unwilling to risk being trampled or eaten: Taire changed back to sergath form before the guards were able to come near with torches. He rushed with all of the speed his enormous bulk allowed towards the sinkhole.

"Ware the sergath!" A loud voice shouted. "One's loose. Someone get a rope before the beast hurts itself."

Shouts erupted all around the cavern as Taire rambled towards the sinkhole. A guard rushed towards him with a length of rope in his hands, and leapt onto his back. Taire writhed for a moment trying to throw the man off as he attempted to tie a loop around his neck. The knot was complete before he figured out how to dislodge the rider. He dropped to his side and began to roll. The guard shouted and jumped away to avoid being crushed.

Taire rolled back to his feet and continued towards the sinkhole.

Shortly before he made it, he felt the rope tighten around his thick neck. Twisting his head backwards to look over his neck, he found that the guard had picked up the rope, and another guard had joined him in his efforts to anchor the line.

"Damned beast thought it was smart! Hold it steady. Someone get the damned hobble back on it!"

Taire decided not to wait for this to happen, however. With a surge of strength, he pulled the two men off of their feet; one lost his grip altogether and fell hard on the stone floor. The second man, the original guard that had looped the rope around his neck, held firm as Taire dragged him along the cavern floor. Taire reached the sinkhole and plunged in. His footing was sure and he easily scaled down the nearly vertical climb. The guard released the rope, deciding that he had no desire to fall into a deep pit presently occupied by a crazed sergath.

The sinkhole opened into a small horizontal passage after a short downwards crawl. Taire paused in the entrance to the small passage, water trickling between his toes. The floor of the deep passage was moist and covered with a thick olive colored slime. Taire's infrared vision showed him that a thinner coating of the viscous slime covered the walls and ceiling of the passage as well.

A dim light flicked down from above. The guards stood looking down into the sinkhole, torches held low to give light. "Damn," muttered the caravan master, "hard to replace a trained sergath. Redistribute the load into the other sergath. Come on now, its gone men, lets get some rest."

The voices and the light faded away as the men moved back to their camp. Taire shuffled a short distance down the passage and found a dry shelf of rock. He changed quickly to human form to release the rope from around his neck. In human form, the darkness was complete and terrifying, and the smell of slime and moisture nauseating. He quickly pulled the rope off of his neck and changed back to sergath form, in which the cavern seemed a very comfortable place. He lay down on the shelf of rock, and dropped off to sleep.

Some time later, he awoke to the low plunking sound of dripping water. He drank deeply from the small stream, and grazed the slime on the walls until he felt full. It was still an act of concentration to keep his mind from straying to human thoughts of revulsion at what he was eating, but again he managed. He sniffed the air deeply, searching for signs of some solid food, but could not catch wind of any nearby prey. Feeling as ready as possible, he traveled off into the depths of the earth, hoping to find a safe passage to the surface. He knew he couldn't return to the trade routes and risk being recaptured, so he had to find his own route through the uncharted subterranean labyrinths.

In some places, the small passage barely allowed his large body egress through its twists and turns, but always the passage continued. Taire moved along its subterranean undulations with the steady gait of his strong sergath body. He learned how to follow the heat signs in the stone towards caverns that would provide food, and he learned that he had an unfailing sense of direction.

Taire traveled for nearly a week through scores of miles of tunnels. He moved ever eastwards, and slowly upwards, always following the cooler rock towards the surface. He knew that he was possibly above ground level, moving into the caverns that honeycombed the Moghin Mountains. On the sixth day, a welcome aroma interrupted his journey. The smell of live food filled his senses.

Taire's sergath instincts caused him to become stone still in the passage, sniffing deeply to locate the source of the smell. He knew that the smell meant food, but could not accurately identify what sort of food. He waited quietly as the smell intensified, coming nearer.

A chittering echoed off of the close walls of the cavern. Taire was able to determine that the sound was coming from a group of degan sahre, the bipedal rodent-like creatures; the same creatures that had inadvertently brought about his father's death. His senses were telling him that they were a favored prey of the sergath. Weeks of eating slime, mold, and fungi, had lessened his aversion to the sergath's appetite. In addition to this, other more personal emotions caused him to feel little compassion for the creatures. Mostly though, Taire thought, it was the only solid food available, and he was hungry. He allowed his mind to fade away into the hunting instincts buried within the mind of the form he inhabited.

Taire backed his bulk as far as possible into a shallow alcove to await the oncoming creatures. By the sound they made, he believed it to be a pack of fewer than a dozen; an easily manageable number, and a good-sized lunch. As the first degan sahre round the corner, Taire lunged forward and caught it in his jaws. He bit down lightly to ensure the creature would live, but not escape, and let it fall to the ground.

He burst around the corner into the unsuspecting pack. Charging through the pack, Taire used the weight of his body to wound a number of degan sahre, catching another in his jaw before he finished the pass. After passing completely through the pack, he turned on his tail and examined the scene before him. The pack scattered, leaving five wounded trying to crawl away. Seeing ample food available, Taire paused to straiten the twitching body in his jaws, lifted his head and gulped it down. Sergath did not chew their meat; they swallowed whole.

Moving towards the wounded degan sahre, his attention rapt upon the upcoming meal, Taire was surprised when a small stone struck him on the head, near his left eye. He raised his head to find three degan throwing stones at him. A natural and aggressive predator, the sergath took off after the additional prey. As he lurched down the passage, Taire's intellect began to intrude. It didn't make sense for degan sahre to attack a sergath. With his keen senses, they could not lose him, nor could they defeat him in a battle of might. They could, however, outsmart a sergath.

Taire stopped cold in his tracks. It slowly sank into his sergath mentality that degan sahre also fed upon sergath when they could catch it, and to do so, they must have some tricks available to them. He stopped, watching several degan sahre a mere dozen paces ahead of him. They also paused. The degan sahre began to throw stones again, but the small stones couldn't harm Taire, and he had his instincts under control. He sat still while he contemplated the actions of the degan sahre.

The degan sahre became frantic, moving closer and trying to enrage the sergath. Taire looked around to see what they were up to. Sniffing deeply, he discovered another group of degan, above him and just ahead in the passage. He couldn't spot them however. Continuing to sniff, he discovered a gentle flow of cool air in the part of the passage he was in that he hadn't noticed when passing through earlier. Following the scent, he discovered that it came from above also.

Unsure of what the degan sahre were up to, Taire decided to attempt springing the trap. He let out a long hiss and surged forward. As soon as he moved a couple of paces, he turned on his tail and leapt away from the taunting degan. He barely avoided the large boulder that came crashing down from above.

Above, the remaining degan sahre chittered angrily for a moment and then disappeared down a high passage that had previously been mostly blocked by the stone they had pushed. The three on the other side of the boulder had already disappeared down the passage. Instead of pursuing, Taire turned back to the wounded and dead degan sahre and finished feeding.

After eating, Taire sniffed for signs of danger, and finding none, decided to rest where he was. His bloated body required that he find the warmest spot available and rest while it digested the several whole degan inside of it. Before sleeping, he stopped to ponder events. He barely remembered being the afraid and helpless boy he had been with The Ruler, nor the ignorant happy child he had been with his father. In his sergath form, much like in mouse form, he relied on instincts to survive, instincts that were enhanced by a human intellect. In his sergath form, however, he lacked the guidance of Piffer, or any other kind being to help him remember himself.

Although he retained his sense of humanity, he had lost his childhood, lost the ability to feel joy. Any emotion other than resolution, determination, and hate seemed too remote to grasp onto. Taire felt empty—devoid of value or meaning. The information he carried regarding the d'rakken mahre was important, even crucial to those on the surface, but he had come by it only through happenstance. It had nothing to do with him; it gave him no value or meaning. It did, however, give him a purpose, and this was enough for now.

With a mental sigh, he slid off into sleep. He had resolved the dilemma the same way he always did. Ultimately, he knew he must survive to give value to the lives that had touched him: Piffer, the boy, and his father. The value of his life was yet to be measured, for now, just living was enough.

Well fed and rested, Taire moved at a strong pace during the following days. He moved steadily up, into colder and colder passages, further and further from the deeper passages of the underworld.

It was the third day after the encounter with the degan sahre that Taire had his first experience with a dwarf.

For the past hour a gentle tinking had been ringing through the passage. The sound drew him along the passage, slowly, smelling the air deeply to identify the source of the sound. All he could sense was stone and some water. The sound was near enough that he should be able to smell something, he thought. He paused to consider. He thought the sound resembled the sound made by the hammers of the dwarves in the mines at home, the problem was, he could not smell anything alive nearby.

With the significant stealth his body could achieve, he moved down the final few paces of the passage before it turned a blind corner. From somewhere just around the corner the rhythmic tapping continued ceaselessly, very nearby now.

Just before rounding the corner, he paused to try once more to identify the source of the sound. He could sense the source of the tapping was very near to the corner, but still could not smell anything other than the normal odors of the passages. The impossible nature of the situation struck Taire. It went against everything he had learned about his sergath form, he should know what it was, and how many there were by now.

He was beginning to become truly frightened. The only theory he could devise was that he had run across a ghost. He had heard tales of lonely ghosts wandering the tunnels of the deep and dark places of the world, but had never heard of a ghost using tools.

He gathered his courage and turned the corner. He found a long low chamber dimly lit from glowing crystals along the roof of the cavern. The walls were smoothed multicolored stone, chiseled into intricate patterns and shapes. The patterns seemed to have a meaning just beyond his ability to grasp. The walls had been worked to show off the natural beauty of the stone and minerals itself. In sections, the stone had been worked around a natural vein of gold or other precious metal. One long vein of gold in particular had been left intact, a glittering snake of beauty unearthed at seemingly random points along the wall.

The effect was magical. Here Taire thought, in the depths of the earth, a type of perfection had been achieved. The chamber was a work of art in progress, a canvas upon which a new order of artistry had been created. The wonder of the scene almost caused him to miss the figure toiling at the far end of the chamber. It stopped its chipping and stood looking at Taire.

It certainly isn't a ghost, thought Taire, edging nearer. He sensed nothing dangerous about the way the creature sat looking at him, in fact he felt compelled to approach the docile humanoid. As he approached, he saw that the creature was a dwarf. He thought it strange that the odor of the dwarf mingled seamlessly into the odor of the rock and earth of the cavern.

The dwarf stood about four feet tall and appeared as if it were made from grey/brown stone. Its features were like a crude parody of a human: nose, eyes, ears, and mouth all blunt and seeming almost unfinished on the hairless head. Judging by the smell, Taire judged that it was possibly just what it appeared to be, animate stone. It was immensely broad of shoulder, and Taire guessed that it must easily weigh several hundred pounds.

"Graatzck kzarnad." The creature's voice sounded like stones rolling down a slate hill. It motioned to Taire, waving for him to approach.

Taire did so, approaching within reach of the dwarf. As he reached what seemed to be the rear of the cavern, he saw that a small passage wound away around a corner just off to the side of where the dwarf was working. He could see that the dwarf had been slowly unearthing a gem, working the stone around it to expose it to the cavern, further enhancing its beauty.

"Graatzck traziir, rskinag." The dwarf touched its hand to its head and bowed slightly.

Taire did not understand the dwarf, or why it would be speaking to a sergath. It seemed to be waiting for him to respond. Unsure of the ways of dwarves, (he had heard they were odd creatures, difficult for humans to understand) he tilted his head back and met the creatures' eyes. They were like round pieces of obsidian, all black, glittering lightly in the glowing light of the cavern. They were alien, conveying neither intelligence nor warmth.

The eyes frightened him, and he pulled back a short distance, hissing deeply. The dwarf stepped forward. "Nsk, nsk," it said, dropping its pick to the floor. "Graatzsk, nsk." The dwarf continued to come forward and raised one thick-fingered hand, palm out, towards him. In an attempt at a gentle voice it continued. "Graatzsk nsk, ne kre reszki."

Taire looked closely at the approaching hand. It looked like an unfinished sculpture, the fingers too thick and short, and the palms only roughly chiseled. The dwarf seemed peaceful, and Taire stood still while it placed its hand upon his reptilian head. With its hard, cold hand in place, the dwarf leaned forward until its eyes were only inches from his Taire's.

Taire began to feel a disconcerting tingle at the point of contact with the dwarf's hand. Its eyes seemed to fill his vision, and he sank into the depths of their obsidian purity. His mind floated freely for an unknown time, lost in the timeless depths of the dwarf's eyes. After a journey of indeterminate length, he again regained his senses.

Things seemed different. The dwarf stepped back and stood examining him, its arms at its sides. Looking at the dwarf, Taire sensed a feeling of age about it; he knew he was looking at a being thousands of years old, although how he got the knowledge he couldn't say. As his body slowly began to get messages through to his mind, he recognized he was no longer in sergath form, the messages were all wrong.

He did not remember changing, and couldn't imagine achieving the act without conscious thought and effort. Without looking, he knew what form his body had taken. No creature other than a dwarf could possibly feel the very breath and pulse of the earth the way he now was. The life of the rock underneath him nourished his soul and strength pulsed into him from the bare rock under him. For a moment, Taire connected with the great consciousness of the earth. In that moment, he understood the fleeting nature of humans, and life itself on the world: all life but that of her dwarves who would live as long as the earth itself existed.

The entire ascendance of man only filled the space between deep breaths of mother earth—she had little interest in human affairs. He could sense the love the earth held for her dwarves, her children, however. He revised his estimate of the age of the dwarf before him from thousands to scores of thousands of years. This was a creature that may have spent the last ten thousand years developing the beauty of this cavern alone. Such was the existence of dwarves.

Taire's reverie was broken by the dwarf's harsh speech. "Shepherd, you are welcome. The All Mother has awaited your coming and acknowledges your existence by gifting you with the form of Her children."

None of what the dwarf had said made sense, except perhaps the part about being gifted this form by the All Mother, whom he understood to be the life of the earth itself. It would, at least explain how he could have changed involuntarily to a new form.

"Thank you—but my name is Taire, I don't know anything about a 'shepherd'. If you changed me, can I change back, or have you really changed me?"

"Shepherd is your destiny, not a name. It is good to know your name. Greetings Taire. The form you have now is but temporary, as it must be. You are the Shepherd, you have your own form." The dwarf paused to let the importance of its statement sink in. "I was selected to await and prepare for your arrival by the All Mother. She acknowledges you through my labors.

"Long have I labored, since long before the humans came to the lands above. Behold my gift—the Song of the Shepherd." The dwarf opened its arms wide to encompass the entire cavern.

Taire turned, following the gesture. His mind filled with

wonder at what he saw. Before he had seen beauty, now he saw the flowing verses of the earth's song, carefully uncovered for his viewing. He was overwhelmed. To his Dwarven senses, it sang as bravely and tunefully as a minstrel on festival day. He could feel the meaning but not translate it to words. The meaning was far beyond the ability of mere mortal words to convey.

The song was about him, although he did not understand why. It spoke of great deeds, love, sacrifice, and a long journey of discovery and salvation. Most importantly, it spoke of friendship. The beauty and meaning of the song softened something hard inside of him. His grief welled up within him, but was blocked by his dwarven form.

The dwarf moved to him and almost gently touched his arm. "The pleasure was in the crafting. How else could the All Mother express her gladness at your arrival? I can say no more of your destiny than I have in the song. Now you must go. You will find that I have given you the memory of the way to the surface. A bleak, barren place it is, but you must go. Glad I would be to meet again. This is where I will be, it has been my task, and the song must continue, as does your task. It is my belief that you must change back to human form. It is more aptly created to express the feelings within you."

Taire did, for the first time in many days, change back to human form, and sat crying for a long time. His shoulders shook with suppressed grief, terror, and rage. By the time he finished crying, he felt purged of the pain, empty and ready to start over. There was beauty in the world, and he had a purpose that he was compelled to discover, a purpose important enough to inspire the dwarf to such extravagant labors.

Without changing form, he fearlessly walked through twisting, dark tunnels in the domain of the All Mother. He now saw the stone as comforting and alive, not cold and dangerous.

Within a few hours, Taire emerged from the womb of the All Mother into a gentle forest on the lower slopes of a mountainside. He sat near the low cave from which he emerged, blinking, eyes watering from the unaccustomed brightness, reborn into the world in more way than one.

# ELEVEN

## MEETINGS

Morgan and Halnan had been riding for almost two weeks. Although fall had begun and colorful leaves adorned the trees, the weather held mild and dry. During the first few days they had ridden very slowly, only traveling for about three or four hours a day due to Halnan's recuperating leg. Halnan's leg and ribs continued to heal quickly under the influence of the potion, and their traveling pace picked up each day until the end of the first week when only a slight stiffness in his gait betrayed any sign of an injury.

Instead of again crossing the mountains, they had followed the Long Wood valley to the Southwest. On the fourth day of travel, they had camped a day near Long Lake, a lake of such size that it took a man on horse two days to travel its length. Its waters were a crystal blue, and a man on its surface could see the bottom even at depths of over a hundred feet. At camp Morgan commented, "It's said by story tellers that fish that can swallow a man whole swim in the unknown depths of the lake. How about a swim friend Halnan? I'm sure you would be safe, nothing alive would eat something that smells like you do."

"Thanks, but no. I think my leg still needs to heal some before I attempt to out swim the finned beasts of this inland ocean you call a lake. By the way Morgan, why don't you check your reflection in the lake before you insult me further. The way you look, you give credence to the stories of man being descended from lower beasts."

Although Morgan did not answer Halnan's insult, the next morning, he was clean-shaven and washed. He also refused to respond to the wry grin Halnan gave him upon seeing his clean visage.

The second week of their trip took them mostly westward, winding their way through a long, high valley that roughly separated the upper Rhunne Mountains that enclosed the Long Wood to the north, and the lower Rhunne Mountains, the south side of which was home to the families of Clan Picksanie.

This long, deep valley eventually gave way to wide grasslands known only as The Steppes in the lore of the Thulistan's. The Steppes were cold and harsh for eight months a year, only giving way to a brief spring and summer during which the rocky soil was covered in grasses and wildflowers. Even during this time, harsh winds blew from the Blayse Ocean to the west. They found the days cool, and the nights bitter cold. This harsh and unpredictable climate kept even the hardy Thulistans from populating the wide-open lands. Instead, they had opted to live in the ample and more predictable spaces east of the mountains.

Their brief journey on The Steppes only lasted two lonely days. Hardy wild flowers still covered much of the endless flatlands, and clung stubbornly to the rough sides of the cliffs and clefts that broke the otherwise serene landscape. It was a land of secrets and silence. Through it, the two rode silently in deference to its mysteries and ghosts.

Mid day on the second day they approached the Rhunne Gap, the gateway to southern and eastern Thulistan. The Gap lay between the Moghin Mountains to the south, and the furthest southward peeks of the Rhunne Mountains to the north.

The Gap itself was only a mile wide; a flat ride through high grasslands, the opposing mountain ranges to the north and south standing as silent sentinels, rugged cliffs rising from each side of the Gap. Morgan had been worried about traveling through the Rhunne Gap for the past several days. "Have you ever heard the tales told about the Rhunne Gap?" He broached the subject with Halnan.

Halnan thought a moment before responding. "Only tales told by drunken adventurers in the taverns of Billings." Billings was the closest city in the Empire to the Rhunne Gap, a journey of only two days travel on a good horse. "If everything they say is true, the gap is populated by spirits and monsters that protect the secrets of The Steppes. The only problem with that theory is—well, we've just spent two days on The Steppes and I haven't seen any secrets worth protecting. Sort of puts a damper on the spirits and monster theory."

Morgan nodded. "You have a point there—but something just doesn't feel right. There are stories about the Rhunne Gap, other than those told by drunkards. The last S'hapur told me once that not all of the Clans of Thulistan completed the journey across the ice from the great northern continent. It is said that one clan; Clan Moncall, was separated by shifting ice. It is said by the wise that perhaps they did not all perish, but the great ice flow eventually allowed egress to the northern lands of The Steppes. Not knowing where the rest of the clans had gone, and feeling bitter by their abandonment, they chose to live in the harsh tundra's of The Steppes. Here it is rumored that they await a sign from Varsnya to again rejoin the clans and take their place of greatness as redress for the millennia of hardship."

"After traveling The Steppes, it is clear that no sign exists as to whether they did in fact reach land again, but it is as if I can feel restless spirits in this place. It gives me the chills . . ."

The words carried softly into the wind. Morgan let the thought trail off into silence, cocking his head to the side, listening to the sound of the wind.

Halnan interrupted the silence. "Do you think . . . ?"

"Shh," Morgan cut off Halnan's response abruptly. Halnan looked crossly at his friend for a moment, wondering what the problem was. Morgan continued his careful listening to the whistling of the wind, turning Bran in a slow circle, inspecting the surrounding grasslands. Finally he stopped his inspection, facing west, back towards the Steppes.

"Show yourselves." He shouted suddenly into the swaying tall grass. "I am Morgan, S'hapur of Family Partikson, Clan Piksanie. If your intentions are honest, step forward and proclaim yourselves. Else ways, beware, I undertake a Quest, and will broach no delays."

Halnan was looking at him with a bemused expression, unsure of why his friend was shouting to the empty grass. His expression changed to surprise and then wonder as human forms emerged from the tall grasses all around them.

All around them men were emerging from the grass, wearing leathers dyed in patterns of green and browns. Their heads were covered with light brown hoods worn down low. All carried short bows, held at the ready, but not in a menacing manner. Directly in front of Morgan stood the largest group, consisting of perhaps a dozen men. From this group a man stood forth. He slowly pulled back his hood. Morgan could hear a faint hiss of surprise from Halnan. The man's face was thoroughly tattooed, in various shades of greens and gold, in circular and curved patterns. His head was shaved and tattooed in the same patterns and colors as his face.

Upon closer inspection, Morgan could see that the tight fitting leathers along with the low hoods allowed the men to blend seamlessly among the tall stalks of grass. Both he and Halnan glanced around the nearby grasses, wondering how many more men may lie concealed therein. Already, fully twenty men had arisen from the grass.

The man who had stepped forward communicated quickly with the others with a series of hand signals. A half a dozen melted back into the grasses in various directions. The rest began to remove their hoods and unstring bows. Each face was covered with heavy tattoo patterns, much alike, but uniquely different from the leader who first stepped forward. The colors were the same, but patterns and mixtures as different as the faces they adorned.

The leader stepped forward again, coming within a few feet of Morgan sitting atop Bran. He looked up and met Morgan's eyes for a long moment. "It is said in the prophesies of the Indebted that a Tarcha," Morgan recognized the term as an ancient Thulistan word for leader, "would come to show us the way to redemption.

The Tarcha, it is said, can see what the land has hidden for centuries, and can hear our voices and thoughts in the wind." He dropped his gaze to the ground and carefully lowered himself prostrate amongst the grasses. The surrounding men followed suit. "I am Norin, S'hapur of Family Caully, the last surviving family of Clan Moncall, the Indebted. I greet the fulfillment of the prophecy, I greet the Tarcha."

Morgan sat quietly, grappling with the impossibility of what he was seeing and hearing. It was not possible that he could be the prophesied leader spoken of by these men, and yet, how could he turn away from the remnants of the missing clan. Before him were a people missing from the Empire for several millenia, people who added a distinct chord to the song of the Thulistan's. Prophecy or no, could he allow these people to remain any longer away from the homeland they had been denied for so long?

Halnan, as usual, was a little less in control of his emotions. He sat astride his horse with his mouth wide open, speechless for once.

"Please arise Norin, honored S'hapur." Morgan lowered himself slowly from Bran to stand before the slowly rising man. "I would be honored to lead your family back into the Empire. As I explained, I am on Quest, and cannot tarry long from my chosen path, but Billings is not too great a detour. From there I could ensure your being taken directly to Terney where you can again see the Tartan of your clan displayed among those of the Empire. It has been, I am sure, much too long absent. I do not fully understand this prophecy of which you speak, but please call me Morgan."

Norin stood quietly awaiting the end of Morgan's speech. The men surrounding Morgan and Halnan began to rise and slowly move towards their leader. Norin gently touched his hand (which Morgan noted was also tattooed) to his forehead, his fingers lightly brushing his brow. "Tarcha-Morgan, you misunderstand my statement regarding the prophecy, and your part in it." Morgan cringed at Norin's misunderstanding about his name, but let it go. "We are the Indebted. It is not our time to re-enter the Empire of Thulistan, this we could have done any time on our own. Our solitude is not yet ended. We have yet a debt to pay Varsnya, the price of our salvation from the flows of ice. There is much for us to speak of, but now is not the time to discuss the debts of Clan Moncall and the repayment thereof.

"What you must understand, though, is that you are the Tarcha, and we are prophesied to follow you in aid to your Quest. Long have we awaited the fulfillment of our debt. In service to your Quest, we will absolve it." Norin looked closely at Halnan for the first time. He walked over to where Halnan sat astride his horse and bowed lightly, repeating the hand gesture to the brow. "Greetings—I would know your name."

Halnan gathered himself while the two spoke and replied evenly. "I am Halnan, Torsch of the Quest, a battle leader of Family Partikson, and friend of your 'Tarcha'. It is a—unique experience to meet you honored S'hapur."

Norin stare intently at Halnan for another silent moment before speaking. "Halnan, you are not of the prophecy. You are not the Shepherd that is prophesied to accompany the Tarcha." He abruptly turned from Halnan back to Morgan. Halnan frowned, caught between confusion and affront at the words of the strange S'hapur. "Tarcha, not all parts of the prophecy are in place, this," he indicated Halnan, "is not the Shepherd."

Halnan interjected, "My pardon for being the wrong..."

Morgan cut him off. "Halnan, I am sure that no affront is intended. There is much here that we do not yet understand about these people and their prophecy. S'hapur Norin, I do not understand your words. I have accepted without question your statements, for your existence proves that there are powers in action beyond my previous understanding, but as to my companion, the Quest would have already ended in my death had he not accompanied me. He has earned his place, perhaps this other is yet to come."

Norin looked to Halnan again. "I am sorry for my unseemly speech, it was a great surprise to find the Tarcha of the prophecy, and I never considered that you may not be the Shepherd. It was disconcerting. By the words of the Tarcha, however, I believe that you are necessary. The prophecy, it seems did not tell all. Varsnya loves surprises it seems."

Halnan relaxed in his saddle, accepting the apology with some semblance of good grace. "No harm done," he bitterly half muttered to himself.

Later that evening they rested near a cheery campfire in a hastily set, but well-ordered camp, eating the last of a large meal provided by the Caully men. Norin dispatched most of the men on various missions of which he had not yet spoken to Morgan or Halnan about. Only three men and Norin remained.

Norin had been slowly giving the history of Clan Moncall to Morgan and Halnan in broken bits while eating. After finishing his meal, he came to the portion of their history where they broke away from the rest of the Empire. He spoke with the smoothly metered cadence of a well-trained S'hapur.

"When the ice began to break apart, the families of Clan Caully, the last to take to the ice, found themselves sundered from the rest of our peoples. The majority of three families were lost In the initial shifting and sinking of the ice. Those that remain swore to the tartan of one of the remaining families and the Clan endured.

"The titanic ice flow upon which they traveled moved slowly, and months passed before they came within sight of land. Most of another family had been wiped out from starvation and exposure, as well as a significant number of members of the remaining two families. The surviving remnants of each decimated family again were allowed to swear to the tartan of one of the remaining families if they so chose.

"Most swore to Family Caully, which seemed to have faired well in the catastrophe, and in fact was growing, not shrinking in size. The two remaining families determined that they were drawing no closer to land, and decided to leave the ice flow and make for the mainland, far to the southwest of where the other Thulistans had arrived. The freezing waters took most of the rest of family Montal (the second of the remaining families), and again the people of family Caully survived almost unscathed, and their numbers were swollen by the addition of the last members of Family Montal.

"It was on the unknown frozen shores upon which they had landed that the prophecy was written. The S'hapur had taken a fever and was ranting. In the middle of the ranting, the prophecy was spoken. The words contained such power that all of those nearby knew them for prophecy and remembered them carefully. There died Family Caully and Clan Moncall, and was born the Indebted of Varsnya."

Norin paused and drank deeply from a wine skin that Morgan passed to him. After a moment to decide how to proceed, he continued. "The prophecy offered a path for our people, and an explanation for our survival when all others perished. We adapted to the harsh lands of The Steppes, learning to harvest grains and hunt its endless wilds. We learned to live in harmony with the harsh land, becoming its equal in determination. We held onto some of our Thulistan heritage and Clan practices, adapting them to our new lives."

Morgan interrupted. "What are the meanings of the tattoos your people bear?"

"They are our tartan, as it were. As I said, we adapted. We lived in isolation, hiding from the world. We protected ourselves and ensured that our secrets were maintained, as the prophecy demanded. Instead of lose our tartan altogether, as wearing a tartan was—inconvenient in these lands, we integrated the patterns and colors into the tattoos, which are part of our camouflage in these lands. We have honed our bodies and minds, preparing for the trials that we knew awaited us. Only through the prophecy will our people be allowed to re-enter the society we were torn away from.

"So we have lived for these many centuries, the ghosts of The Steppes, keeping ourselves ready to fulfill the prophecy. Now it has come, and we are ready."

Halnan, who had been silently watching and listening spoke up. "How can you be sure Morgan is the Tarcha prophesied, and what is it we are to do?"

Norin thought for a moment before answering. "I know because Varsnya touched my mind with the knowledge. The prophecy could not go unanswered because of the shortsightedness of man. There is no doubt. As to what we are to do—well the prophecy does not go beyond the meeting of the Tarcha and the Shepherd. Our path from here is in the hands of the Tarcha—your hands." He nodded to Morgan. "We will pay the debt through this service, whatever may come, Varsnya only knows. If you were to tell me of your Quest, perhaps we may better understand this purpose.

Morgan discussed his story, Halnan filling in details now and then. At the conclusion of his story, the fire had burned to embers. Norin listened intently, without interrupting until Morgan ended his narration. "I am only sure of one thing. The d'rakken mahre are tied in with the k'aram mahre in some way, and the k'aram mahre are the last creation of Varsnya. It is clear that all of our purposes are intertwined in some way.

Morgan agreed that something beyond his understanding was going on, and that he, Halnan, and apparently Norin all had a part to play. He could not, however, bring himself to believe he was a predestined Leader of the lost Clan. Also, he was unsure of the 'shepherd' spoken of by Norin. These thoughts, however, he kept to himself.

"Well, come what may," said Morgan. "We must continue the quest, and if you will not re-enter the Empire, what will your people do? We travel to Desil, and the border between Barstol and here is amassed with troops. Your people cannot follow where we go."

"I have already foreseen this problem," responded Norin evenly. "I believe I see the purpose of our people. Should I be wrong, Varsnya forgive me, then it is the doom of my people, but it is the time for action. It is my decision to make, and I have made it. I shall travel with you to your destination, as I believe is my destiny."

Norin paused for a long moment, uninterrupted by Morgan or Halnan. His men sat alertly, awaiting word of what they were to do. They appeared eager to fulfill their promise, to pay their debt. Only then could they live their own lives free of the prophecy.

"As for the men of Clan Moncall, they have other duties,"

Norin spoke at last. The d'rakken mahre have gone to ground again it seems, but not for long I am sure. Your story has convinced me that they will arise soon, to their unknown purpose. To my people I lay the charge of awaiting the rising of the d'rakken mahre. We will find them and ward them, as well as ward others from them."

Morgan looked from Halnan to Norin. "Yes, it is indeed a fair purpose to what you put your people. There were many problems with the d'rakken mahre and many people were killed. It is my belief that these problems can be averted with your peoples help. Until we discover the purpose of the d'rakken mahre, we cannot allow them to war with our people."

Norin nodded to one of his men. "You have heard Nuorn, alert the Clan. We will not settle again until our journey is completed. Seek the d'rakken mahre and provide escort. Follow, guard and ward. You know our path, send a messenger if the d'rakken mahre are found." He turned his attention back to Morgan. "Now, let us rest this night, tomorrow the prophecy begins its fulfillment."

As he spoke, his men packed their cooking utensils into their pouches and without a word jogged off into the evening. To Halnan they seemed over-eager for the fulfillment of their prophecy, and that perhaps no price would be too great for the repayment of their ancient debt. He knew the dangers of fanaticism, but held his tongue. These people had lived under the harshest of circumstances for centuries. Their intensity was startling, but unsurprising.

Morgan, on the other hand, understood dedication to purpose. Their drive to fulfill the prophecy was very similar to his drive to fulfill his potential. The only difference was in degree.

There was little need for further conversation, and Halnan and Morgan unrolled their bedrolls and slept near the fire. Norin, who carried no bedroll, wandered away from the fire into the darkness to sleep.

The next morning dawned brightly, only a few scattered wisps of clouds marring the clean blue skyline. Halnan woke Morgan after he roasted a brace of rabbits over the fire. Halnan had found the rabbits near the fire; he assumed Norin left them. Of Norin, however, there was no sign.

After eating breakfast, they cleared all traces of the camp and mounted their horses. "Should we wait for him," Halnan asked.

"No," answered Morgan, "I think not. He has chosen to accompany us, and I have a feeling he will catch up to us, or we will catch up to him, either way, I doubt he will be easy to shake. Let's get going; we have a long trip ahead." He nudged Bran into motion. With a sigh, Halnan followed on his mount, trotting into the tall grasses, heading southwest.

Taire had spent the entire previous day making his way down the rocky slopes of what he assumed to be the northern Moghin Mountains. After reaching the gentle slopes at the base of the mountains, he spent a miserable night in the chill mountain air, sleeping fitfully in short naps only to awake with chattering teeth. Taire had never actually experienced cold before, and the clothing he brought from Torance did not offer appropriate protection.

After the ordeal of the previous months, he felt strangely empty. It was not so much that he felt disconsolate or worthless as he had previously felt, but empty in the sense that he could feel a need to find himself, discover what he was. As the sun rose to cast its rays upon his shivering body, he rose from his resting place to continue his journey into the unknown world.

The outside held no terror for him any longer. Taire had known terror, and found nothing threatening in the trees around him, or the vast blue canopy of sky above him. He looked up in wonder at the dawn sky, wispy blue clouds scuttled across the blue canvas while the sun slowly rose into the heavens. Steam rose from the moisture on the ground, ghostlike in appearance. These things were all magical to Taire, the riot of colors nearly overloading his senses, and yet he drank them in as if he were starved for such sensory input.

As he stumbled down the gentle slopes he found the trees thinning further, making way to heavy grasses and bright late summer flowers. He could see the grasses get progressively taller up ahead, to well over his head. His stomach rumbled violently. His hunger was becoming acute, and yet he was unsure of what was safe to eat. He thought that he may be able to eat the leaves or grasses in sergath form, but his sergath form was clearly unsuited for daylight, and may attract attention. Even worse, he was afraid something would eat him if he took mouse form. Despite this, he became more and more tempted to take one of these forms to aid his search for food.

By noon the sun shone warmly overhead as Taire traveled away from the forested hills of the mountains. He quieted his stomach by nibbling at some grasses, and was waiting to see if he would become sick. Between stomach grumbles a foreign sound intruded. A low thudding sound came from the north, slowly growing louder. The tall grass obscured the view into the distance, hiding the source of the noise from Taire. His heart began to beat loudly in his chest and he stood poised for flight. Looking around he saw the futility of flight on the flat lands; instead he mastered his fear and stood his ground as the sound neared, resigned to meet whatever fate provided.


Shortly into their ride, the sun only a few hand spans above the horizon, Morgan and Halnan were joined by Norin. He jogged out of the grasses from the east and nodded greetings without breaking stride. Morgan nodded back. "Thank you for the breakfast. We have saved some of the meat, are you hungry?"

Still pacing the trotting horses, he answered. "Thank you Tarcha, but no. I have eaten. Let us continue." His voice was even and he showed no effects from the long run.

Halnan watched him run for a few moments before commenting. "Friend, perhaps you would like to ride one of our pack mounts, or do you have a mount somewhere ahead? Time is pressing."

Norin smiled slowly at Halnan. "What need have I, one of the Indebted, of a horse? Fear not for our progress, your horses will not outpace me, or any of my people."

Halnan looked incredulously at Norin, and even Morgan looked skeptical. Seeing his smooth stride, and his calm appearance while keeping pace with two trotting horses, Halnan shrugged his shoulders. "As you wish friend, we'll see how you feel in a half hour."

A half hour passed, and another and yet Norin still paced silently along beside the horses. The three traveled in silence until shortly before noon when Norin interrupted the silence. He tapped Halnan lightly on the leg with a spear to get his attention. "Ware the Tarcha, I sense something ahead." Without explanation, he surprised Halnan with a burst of speed, leaving the horses well behind. After only a brief moment, he disappeared into the tall grasses ahead, visible only as parting grass from the higher vantage of horseback. Soon even this telltale sign was lost as Norin passed out of sight in the gently rolling grasslands.

"What was that all about?" Morgan asked, still peering ahead.

Halnan waited a moment before answering, loosening one of his long knives in its sheath. "Our traveling companion just warned me to guard you, and ran off ahead because he 'sensed' something." Halnan look into the distance again. "Did you see how quickly he left us behind? He's been running for hours, and he just left us behind like we were holding *him* back!"

"I think our friend may be loaded with surprises. In the meantime, I think we should pay heed to his concern. Keep your weapon ready, and listen carefully. In this grass, sound is likely to be our first sign of any danger."

They rode in silence for a quarter of an hour, leading the horses through a gentle fold between two low hills. As the crease opened into wide grasslands, Morgan whistled quietly to get Halnan's attention. As Halnan look his way, he pointed toward a spot in the distance, ahead and to the east. There they could see that the grass was bent away from someone or something. They slowed their pace, riding warily until they were able to make out the sight of a tall spear standing like a beacon above the grass.

Recognizing Norin's hunting spear, or that of one of his people, they relaxed slightly, and increased their pace to cover the remaining distance. As they approach the small clearing they first recognized the form of Norin, standing with his back facing them, holding his spear on his shoulder. As they veered out and around Norin, another form became evident.

A man sat a short distance in front of Norin, resting in the grass, and eating.

As they arrived, Morgan and Halnan dismounted to discover whom Norin had found in the seemingly empty grasslands. Norin stood facing his ward with a satisfied smile on his face. Upon closer inspection, it was clear that the man on the ground was perhaps more boy than man, despite his size. He looked up without concern as Morgan approached, but continued to eat the food he had apparently been given by Norin.

For a moment, the strangeness of the scene kept both Morgan and Halnan silent. Norin and the boy seemed content to remain quiet also. Finally, Halnan broke the silence. "Would one of you two explain what's going on?"

The boy, finishing his food, stood up and stepped away from the seemingly belligerent Halnan. Both men were surprised by the size of the boy, who stood a half a head taller than either of them. The boy looked from Halnan to Morgan, finally settling on the latter. "I don't understand either. Ask him." He pointed at Norin, flushing slightly from his discomfort at being around armed men, who all seemed either hostile or crazy.

Morgan and Halnan both turned to Norin, who still stood passively, smiling broadly. "Well," began Halnan, "don't just stand there grinning like a sailor in a brothel. Explain!"

Norin turned from Halnan to Morgan, still not speaking. Halnan moved to get back into his line of sight. "Have you gone daft on us? I would like . . ."

Morgan stopped his speech with a hand on this shoulder. He knew better than to allow Halnan to fall prey to Norin's baiting. Despite this, he was more than a little annoyed himself with the smug S'hapur. "All right, that's enough." He turned his attention to Norin. "You seem to be hoarding some great secret or jest. Let's have it now. Who is the lad, and why are you so damned pleased with yourself?"

"Greetings Tarcha. The prophecy comes one step nearer completion on this day. This 'lad' as you call him is one that you have been destined to meet. Tarcha, I introduce you to the Shepherd." With a nod, he indicated the boy standing uncomfortably a few feet away.

Morgan looked carefully at the lad, who was uncomfortably looking back at him. The boy spoke first. "Greetings Sir, ah Tarcha is it? It seems your crazy friend here expected me. He popped up out of the grass and made me wait for you. He greeted me as the 'Shepherd', and this is not the first time I have been called so. I don't understand what it means, or why we have to meet. He would not explain anything to me. My name, by the way is Taire."

The voice was that of a man newly come into his manhood, deep and gentle. Morgan revised his estimate of the boy-faced man before him. Taire seemed to be taking things in stride; in fact he seemed to have his wits more about him than either Halnan or himself.

"Well met indeed, Taire. My name is Morgan, not Tarcha. That's a title he," he indicated Norin, "bestowed upon me. This is Halnan." He slapped Halnan on the shoulder, getting his attention. Halnan had been standing staring at Norin with a sour look.

Halnan stepped forward. "Uh, hello Taire, sorry for seeming so rude, our traveling companion seems to delight in surprises."

Taire suppressed a small grin. "Yes, I have noticed that also. I am indeed pleased to meet you also Halnan." He was in fact, pleased to meet some potential traveling companions less intimidating than the tattooed spearman. Norin provided food, for which he was thankful, but he seemed to know something no one else knew, and refused to share it. It was intimidating in a way, and more than a little annoying. Morgan seemed quiet, not quite brooding, but thoughtful. It was clear he was a man of importance, one who others follow. Halnan, on the other hand seemed both more and less dangerous. He was clearly a warrior, but expressed himself freely, and had a ready smile on his face.

Halnan gripped Taire's hand enthusiastically, smiling at the clarity of the lad's expression. "Well Taire, we have a lot to talk about it seems. I know you just ate, but it is lunchtime according to my stomach. Perhaps you could join us for some hot food and explain your presence alone in the grasses? Of course you are welcome to continue on your own, but I would consider it a personal favor if you stayed long enough to explain a few things. If you go, I have to try to get this painted peacock to explain, and he is not a great conversationalist."

Taire chuckled at Halnan's description of Norin. He quickly suppressed his laughter and smile as Norin turned his sour glance from Halnan to him.

Morgan interjected into the conversation. "All right, both of you behave." He looked at Norin and Halnan in turn. "I think lunch is a great idea. As a matter of fact, Halnan, let's make camp for the day, I have a feeling we have a lot to discuss with this young man."

Not only did Taire feel surprisingly comfortable with these men, he discovered the dried meat that Norin had provided had only dulled his hunger. At the mention of hot food, his stomach rumbled back to life, making its needs plain to everyone within hearing distance.

"Well," laughed Halnan, "I'll take that as a yes?"

"I am a bit hungry," admitted Taire. "And I believe you are right, your friend greeted me as the 'Shepherd', which is a title given me by another recently. I think we may all benefit from comparing notes."

Morgan, impressed by the young man's maturity, simply nodded his approval and turned to help Halnan set up the camp.

# TWELVE

## THE ADVANTAGE OF FRIENDS

Taire sat quietly off to the side of the small clearing, watching the two men set up the camp with practiced ease. Norin, the dangerous looking hunter had gone off in search of game.

He noticed the way that Halnan, for all of his bluster, worked quickly and with diligence. Halnan was open and friendly in a way that put him at ease. Morgan, on the other hand, disconcerted him. He found that the seemingly taciturn warrior intensified the emptiness that had developed within him. His meeting with the dwarf had helped him to abate his grief and terror. Purging his grief was not the whole answer however. Seeing the calm balance and leadership of Morgan reminded Taire poignantly of his father, and these memories were met with a vague sense of anger and unhappiness. This was what caused the unease at Morgan's presence. Something about Morgan inspired more commitment that he was prepared to make. He would have to care about something again. The intensity of Morgan's gaze would accept no less than total honesty, integrity, and commitment.

Morgan divided his attention between helping set up camp (which Halnan needed little help with anyway), and examining the young man who so recently joined their expedition. Although the lad was tall and well grown, there was nothing about him that would distinguish him as someone he was fated by prophecy to meet. He noticed how Taire stayed away from him and Halnan, sitting at the outside edge of the clearing.

He noticed that the young man occasionally looked up to watch them setting up camp. Whenever their eyes met, Taire would quickly look away, as if he were afraid of what Morgan might see behind his gaze. Morgan considered the appearance of the young man. It was clear from his bearing that Taire had been through enough hardships to become inured to fear of physical danger. Perhaps, Morgan thought, there are other dangers that Taire sought to avoid.

Before either individual could investigate their thoughts more deeply, Norin trotted into the camp carrying the limp carcass of a small deer over his shoulder. He stopped near the fire and dropped the deer onto the ground before Halnan's feet. "This needs to be gutted." As always, Norin appeared unaffected by his running, evidently running carrying a forty plus pound deer did not constitute a true exertion to the man.

Halnan looked from the deer up to the tattooed face of Norin. "Pardon, but I set camp; clean your own deer." His annoyance at Norin's assumed authority was clear.

For a long moment, Halnan sat still, looking from the deer, to Norin and back again. Finally he determined that the man had no intention of moving the deer or cleaning it. He looked to Morgan. "Perhaps you, the precious Tarcha could explain to him that I am not a servant!"

Norin turned to Morgan awaiting his response. Morgan scowled slightly, tired of being caught in the middle of their petty squabbles. "Just clean the thing so we can eat, and quit being so difficult," he snapped irritably.

Norin turned back to Halnan with a small smile of victory. Halnan rose to his feet, sputtering with anger. Seeing no support from the two S'hapur, he turned to Taire who watch quietly watching the scene. "Can you believe this? Treated like a servant!" He grabbed the deer by its hind legs and began to carry it away from the camp to gut it. A smiling Taire rose and walked after him to help.

After they cleared the camp, Morgan looked to Norin. "And you, quit being so damned smug and aloof. If you continue to anger him, he is going to kill you, and I am going to let him do it just so he will shut up about the whole thing!" The tight anger of his voice smothered the smile from Norin's face.

Taken aback by the Tarcha's rebuke, Norin turned and followed after Taire and Halnan to offer assistance.

Dinner passed quietly, no-one willing to broach the subject of Taire and his journey until after they were done eating. Throughout the meal, Halnan looked somewhat perplexed, glancing towards Norin. Taire ate heartily, wishing only to prolong the moment before Morgan began to speak directly with him. Morgan barely tasted his food, trying to interpret the silence of those about him. He hoped to gain a key piece in the puzzle from Taire, but sensed the hesitancy of the young man.

Finally, dinner was completed and uncomplaining, Halnan began to gather dishes and clean up. Sensing the unavoidable, Taire sat still, eyes locked on the fire, awaiting with mixed feelings Morgan's first question.

He did not have to wait long.

Morgan watched as Halnan busied himself about the camp, and Norin stood without pretense and came closer to the fire to better take part in the questioning. Taire, he saw, was sitting quietly, etching circular patterns in the dirt with his finger, trying to hide his nervousness. Norin showed his impatience by leaning forward and clearing his throat, preparing to begin the conversation.

"So, friend Taire," Morgan interjected before Norin could begin. Morgan ignored the cross look he was given by Norin. "It seems clear that you have some part in the prophecy of Norin and his people. It just so happens that I, to my discomfort, also have some role in this prophecy. Together, perhaps we can piece together how it is we are to serve this prophecy, and how it all fits, if at all, into my Quest. I think that first I should tell you something of my Quest, and of Norin's prophecy. Then you can better judge what you would like to tell us of how you ended up with the title of 'Shepherd', and came to be wandering the grasslands."

Hearing that he was to be given a reprieve in his questioning, Taire relaxed visibly, which was precisely Morgan's purpose. Norin, on the other hand, was displeased with Morgan's stalling tactic. He wanted answers to fill in the gaps in the prophecy; he ached for the answers, for the answers to his service.

Sensing Norin's frustration, Morgan sought to hold off interruptions from the eager leader of Clan Moncall. "Norin, perhaps you should begin by sharing your prophecy with Taire so that he can better understand the title you have given him."

The wind taken from his sail, Norin looked quickly from Taire, to Morgan and back again. "It would be my honor to share the prophecy with the Shepherd, so that he may better fulfill his role within it, and perhaps make more clear to all what the fulfillment of the prophecy is to entail."

His duty to the prophecy had quickly overridden his eagerness, and educating Taire in the precepts of the prophecy was an important task to which he fell with a will.

He recounted the prophecy to Taire, along with his interpretations of its possible meanings. Taire listened carefully and patiently to the entire tale, thinking deeply on what he was hearing, and trying to tie in what he had already learned and guessed from his meeting with the dwarf. Still, he could not understand his role, what the Shepherd was to do, or why he was assigned the title.

As Norin's tale drew to a close, Morgan rose and moved over towards Taire. He sat down near the fire and motioned for Taire to come nearer. Feeling comfortable that the men were not going to begin hurling questions at him, Taire rose and moved gratefully nearer the fire. As the evening progressed, the air had become chill, and Taire was shivering lightly.

A few minutes previously, Halnan had rejoined the camp after finishing cleaning and packing the cooking utensils. He was holding a skin of wine, which he opened and took a long pull. "Warm fire and good wine help pass a cold night." He passed the skin to Norin, who took a small sip and passed it silently on to Morgan.

Morgan took the skin and took several small sips, looking at his two companions as if seeking the best course to move on. Finally he shrugged his shoulders and passed the skin to Taire. "It helps to bring the words out lad, have a shot and pass it back."

Taire, surprised at being included, took the flask uncertainly. He looked around at the assembled men and, seeing Halnan's broad smile, took his first drink of wine. The taste was musty, but fruity and lightly sweet. He took another drink, unsure of whether he liked the beverage or not. Deciding he liked it, he downed several gulps.

Seeing Taire's reaction, Halnan laughed out loud, Morgan chuckled, and even Norin smiled. Taire smiled, unsure of the source of the men's mirth, and passed the skin back to Morgan. Strangely, his face felt warm, warmer than the fire accounted for. Within minutes he felt his body relax, and felt almost willing to talk about the experiences of the past months.

Despite this, Morgan forestalled any speech on Taire's part by beginning his story, the story of the d'rakken mahre and the Quest he had undertaken. His story, in its entirety took over an hour to tell. Halnan occasionally interjected information, or corrections to the story. Halnan, Norin, and Morgan continued to take occasional drinks from the skin (Halnan, sitting in-between the other two, drank every time the skin passed through his hands, in effect allowing him to drink twice as much as the other two without seeming to). They allowed Taire to take several more small sips, warning him against overdoing it, but wanting the young man comfortable and relaxed.

Taire was very much relaxed, and rather content. He felt a sudden sense of warmth and friendship for the three men surrounding him. Surprisingly, even Norin seemed like a friendly fellow in his present state of mind. His wits were still about him, however, and he listened to every part of Morgan's tale with interest. Most importantly, Morgan's information regarding the d'rakken mahre helped him put something together that he had been working on. The final pieces of the puzzle of the d'rakken mahre seemed to be falling into place in his well-lubricated mind.

Looking for some clarification, he asked the first question that came to mind. To the group in general he asked, "many times you have spoken of Varsnya and the d'rakken mahre in a way that seems to hint at some connection. What is the connection?"

Morgan smiled, and Norin nodded. Even Halnan noted the quickness with which Taire arrived at the potentially crucial question.

"Honored S'hapur Norin, would you instruct our young friend on the histories of creation?" Morgan asked.

Norin looked into the fire for a moment, recalling the story using the tricks of memorization and recall used by S'hapur to accurately recall the histories without change over the centuries. After a moment, he cleared his throat and leaned forward towards Taire, his eyes glittering in the firelight.

"In the beginning of all things," he began in a smooth monotone, "was only the void. Into this emptiness came the three Gods of creation: Tular, Varsnya, and Talvar. The Gods found the universe to be an empty place, lacking beauty. This lack, they found, reflected within themselves, and they found this to be unbearable.

"As their consciousness grew, they sought to overcome the emptiness of their souls. First the Gods created light, symbolic of their goodness. Into this light, the Gods placed a world. This world, they named Numorin, or 'first place' and covered it with water, for water was to serve as the basis of life. The world lacked shape and character to interest to the Gods however, and so did they cause the stone to rise up and form the lands of the world, the land of Tulisia being the first among these lands and the favorite.

"Onto Tulisia they planted great forests and gardens to enhance the beauty of the land. The Gods were eager to continue creating, and did not wish to tend the gardens of their creations. Therefore they gave unto the trees the ability to generate their own caretakers. And so did the trees giving of their life forces, give birth to the elves, the caretakers of the forest. Because each forest needed special care, so were the elves different to serve the trees of which they were created to serve. The Gods were pleased by this, and gave to the elves the ability to nurture and guide the forests, and help the trees to continue the propagation of the elven species.

"Then, seeing the joy of the life in the forests and in the living things, the Gods found that the hills and mountains seemed lifeless and devoid of joy in comparison. No thing should exist so lacking in knowledge of its being as the stone did, so the Gods breathed magic and memory into the very heart of the earth, giving it a slow life of its own. The stone used then used its magic, as had the forest. Through this power came into existence the dwarves, created to tend and shape the stone so that its beauty should not pale by the beauty of the living forest, but enhance it.

"The dwarves flourished deep within the earth. They tended the stone, adding beauty to the dark places of the world. They delved deeply, bringing forth the treasures that the Gods had placed therein.

"Again the Gods were pleased as balance was achieved.

"Then the Gods did rest and watch the life of their first world. To their dismay, they again found a great lack in their creation. On Tulisia, the dwarves and elves lived joyously within their environments, performing the tasks they were set forth to perform. Their lives were simple and their society lacked the ability to grow beyond the narrow confines of their purpose. The world lacked the ability to grow and change. To correct this shortcoming, the Gods did create the races of man. Of great variety were the races of man created, and spread across the continents of the world.

"Of these races, the Thulistans were held above the rest. The Gods gifted the Thulistans with longer life spans than those of other men and with a lust for life that was unmatched. The Thulistans, however, lived apart from the other peoples of the world, living in isolation upon a great northern continent. The rest of the world's peoples spread throughout the world, and gave names to the previously unpopulated places. All of these races gave joy to the Gods, but none so much as the Thulistans, who were their best creation, that which they loved most dearly.

"Believing their work to be done, Talvar and Tular left Numorin to make other worlds and continue to fill the void within themselves. Varsnya, who cared deeply for her first creation resisted the almost overwhelming urge to continue onto new creations, stayed to further nurture and watch over what had been wrought. For many millennia the peoples flourished on earth, but soon they began to expand throughout the world and encounter one another. From these encounters emerged a new capacity from the races of mankind—the capacity for war.

"Not understanding how such a thing could happen to her peoples, Varsnya sought to discover a way by which she could save her creations from each other. Knowing that she could not undo what had been wrought, Varsnya gave birth to one last being. Working alone, Varsnya put forth all of her will and much of her very being into this creation. The result of these efforts was an incredible winged humanoid known as the karam mahre. The karam mahre did not mingle with the other races, but held themselves aloof, pursuing their unknown purpose in the skies of Numorin.

"Varsnya's power was greatly reduced by the act of their making, and her last overt act upon the world was to give these histories to the Thulistans, her favored peoples. Although the purpose of the karam mahre was not given as part of these histories, the Thulistans revered the karam mahre and their unknown lofty purpose.

"As the peoples of Numorin came together on the continent of Tulisia and made war upon each other, the Thulistans, also new to the continent, found themselves beset from many sides. During this period of strife and warfare, the clans of Thulistan became savage in their fight for survival, and fought amongst themselves as often as against the outsiders that began to encroach upon their lands. Eventually the Thulistans emerged from this dark period, embracing their fellow clansmen and remembering their histories, but they found that the karam mahre had disappeared from the skies forever. Believing that the loss of the karam mahre was somehow linked to their digression into savagery, as if a punishment by the Gods, the Thulistans vowed to uphold the wishes of Varsnya, to cherish the histories given them and seek not the lands of other men. Since this time, the recitation of the oral histories has been our greatest gift, and our continued fulfillment of Varsnya's wishes. The oral traditions say nothing more of the karam mahre."

Norin ended his recitation slowly, reluctant to finish the tale. Upon its completion, his shoulders sagged lightly and he looked to Morgan.

Morgan listened intently to the story, reciting it word for word in his mind as Norin spoke it. He smiled at Norin's tattooed face and nodded. "Well told, S'hapur. Truly have the S'hapur's of the lost Clan Moncall held to the oral traditions."

Norin smiled at the compliment. He feared that Morgan would find his knowledge or abilities lacking. It was a great relief to know that the generations of S'hapur of Family Caully, and Clan Moncall had been diligent and true to their studies.

Meanwhile, Taire sat quietly, oblivious to the by-play between the two men. He contemplated slowly the history as told by Norin. Speaking the thought as it formulated in his mind, Taire looked towards the other men. "If the karam mahre were known to have gone into the earth—and no one has heard of them or about them for thousands of years, it stands to reason they are gone, doesn't it?"

Morgan nodded his agreement. Halnan, anticipating a revelation of some sort from the young man, began to pay closer attention, and Norin listened closely.

"Well," continued Taire. "If they are gone, then it seems they must have either warred with the d'rakken mahre and been defeated, or something else happened." Morgan leaned in as if he were going to interrupt. "But," continued Taire forestalling any interruption, "that doesn't make sense based on the histories. If Varsnya created the karam mahre as some sort of answer to the war-like nature of men, then surely they would not attack another society in such a way?"

"Taire, wha . . ." Norin began and was quickly cut off by the slightly drunk, very talkative young man.

"Even more odd is the fact that the d'rakken mahre are not mentioned in the histories," continued Taire, now rambling freely. The rest of the men then gave up interruptions and gave Taire's wine loosened tongue free reign.

"The only thing that makes sense to me is . . ." Norin and Morgan leaned in closely in anticipation of Taire's conclusion. Halnan, smiled to himself, casually leaning back near the fire, taking another sip of wine. Taire tilted his head slightly in thought, his pause hanging heavily throughout the camp.

"Well," Taire again let his next thought hang a moment. "Well—then the karam mahre didn't attack the d'rakken mahre, but somehow are the same thing. They went under ground and changed for some reason."

Morgan was shocked that Taire was able to make the same deduction that he had been chewing on for weeks. The young man was obviously gifted with strong reasoning skills. Norin still sat unmoving, awaiting further input from Taire, while Halnan simply sat smiling and drinking.

To everyone's surprise, it was Halnan who spoke next. "Very good friend Taire, you have just deduced the theory that we were so pleased with ourselves for developing after weeks of thinking over the problem, and after having known these histories all of our lives. Since you're so good at this, we will let you continue. Why are they coming back to the surface then? More importantly, how do you and Morgan fit into this prophecy of Norin's, and why should we care anyway?"

Taire looked at Halnan for a moment, speechless with the immensity of what he had been asked to reveal.

Morgan intervened to give him a moment to consider. "That is a big order you ask of our young friend, Halnan. Taire, you know of our story, and it is indeed time to hear yours. You and I are linked to the prophecy of Clan Moncall, and Clan Moncall is linked to the search for the d'rakken mahre—to my Quest. It is all tied together, somehow you see. The pieces of the puzzle are almost all in place, but you haven't shown us your pieces yet. This is important, Taire, please help us."

Taire was still somewhat giddy from the wine, but was quickly sobering with the thought of dredging up the painful memories of his past few months. "All right, I understand. I think I can help you; I do indeed know something of the d'rakken mahre and their plans. It is part of a long story, one that I suppose I must tell. Then perhaps you can help me deduce what my role as 'Shepherd' is to be."

Taire story began slowly, the memories carefully buried and difficult to dredge up. The three men around him listened carefully, making no noise or other distractions that may stop the reluctant storyteller. Norin listened with detached indifference to the story of the child's hardships. Morgan contained his emotions as he always had, understanding the young man's pain but unable to show his compassion. Halnan sat with tears running down his cheeks by the time Taire reached the separation from Piffer (whom he only described as a 'friend' who helped him), and the death of the young servant boy. The proud warrior wept unabashedly, shedding tears of sorrow for the boy. The tears glistened in the firelight, dropping from his chin into the hardened soil of the earth.

Taire's story passed slowly with many pauses. It was all the more poignant for Taire's inability to express the grief and terror of his own tale. He spoke in a detached tone, as if he could not truly yet grapple with the reality of his own pain and experiences. Regardless of the passing of terror, anger, and hatred, Taire had not yet truly purged himself of the grief held in his heart.

He told the entire story, only withholding one piece of information. He did not tell the men about his discovery of his shape changing ability. He created plausible lies to explain details like how he escaped the closet and survived under the earth. Taire was afraid, afraid they would misunderstand his abilities and cast him out.

Even while telling of the plans of the d'rakken mahre, there was no interruption of Taire's narration. The information Taire imparted, although the original intent of the story, had become temporarily meaningless in the face of such pain and suffering.

When Taire finished his telling, he hung his chin low onto his chest. He sat breathing deeply, unmoving. Norin, unsure of what to say or do, simply sat still, watching Morgan, awaiting some cue. Morgan was equally at a loss. Nothing in his life prepared him to deal with this type of pain. The simple pain of a warrior was one thing, but what Taire had experienced: the loss of his father, privation, abuse, and the survival in the darkness of the underworld alone, these were types of pain beyond his ability to cope with.

Halnan, however, understood Taire. Although his life had never included pain such as this young man had experienced, he was better able to cope with his own emotions that were evoked by the story than the other two men were. Following a drive stronger than conscious thought, he stood and walked over to Taire. He stood over Taire and reached down to him.

Taire looked up. Something about the tears streaming down Halnan's face caused a wall to crumble within him.

Taire stood slowly to meet Halnan's eyes. Halnan reached out and embraced the young man, to help Taire make contact with his pain, to understand and share it with another who cared. At first, Taire stiffened in his grasp. Gradually, by degrees, he relaxed into the embrace, and soon found himself weeping uncontrollably. The two men stood that way for some time, oblivious to the two spectators. Norin was embarrassed and confused by the unmanly display. Morgan felt, for the first time in his life, a true sense of inadequacy. He wished he were able to help in the healing of the brave young man.

As Taire released his hurt, and began to acknowledge it instead of hide it, Morgan underwent a change also. After a time, he came over to Taire and Halnan and put one hand on each man's shoulder, sharing in the comfort and purging of the pain.

No words were spoken, and no one wanted to continue the topic of the d'rakken mahre that night. Morgan, Halnan, and Taire went to sleep near the fire within reach of the fires comforting reach. Norin walked a distance away from the others, an unreadable expression on his face, without a word of explanation. He set up his own small camp and slept away from the others, separated by more than the short distance. Morgan, waking in the middle of the night looked around the camp. Seeing Norin sleeping many paces away, Morgan felt sorry for the man, sorry for the time, distance, and destiny that had truly separated his people long before this night. Morgan sighed and fell back to sleep.

The next morning, gshortly before dawn, Norin gently roused Morgan. Morgan awoke to find the tattooed man kneeling low over him. "I must return to my people to tell them where the d'rakken mahre will arise."

Morgan blinked several times and wiped his hand across his face. "But we do not know where the d'rakken mahre will be going to, nor have we decided on a proper course of action. You must stay at least until after we have all spoken again—I can awake the others now if you wish."

"No," cut in Norin abruptly. "It does not matter where the d'rakken mahre go. I know where they will arise, and I will lead my people there. We will ward the d'rakken and warn the peoples of their coming. I understand my purpose and my part in the prophecy and your Quest. It is your job to understand the d'rakken mahre, you are the Tarcha, and Taire is the Shepherd. You will learn what you need to know, and will then lead my people in the repayment of our debt."

"How can you be so sure? What if you are wrong—it just seems that we should discuss this further. We have time, it will be weeks before the d'rakken mahre are to arise into the Talon Valley."

Norin reached out to Morgan, putting his hand on the shoulder of the sitting man. "I am sure. Varsnya spoke to me in my dreams and I was made to understand my role, and much of your and Taire's role. You are the Tarcha, and my people will follow you when you fully understand your course of action. Taire is the Shepherd, and the d'rakken mahre, I believe, will come to be his flock. He must come to this understanding on his own, though, when he is ready. Now I must go to fulfill my role. Varsnya be with you friend Morgan, Tarcha of Clan Moncall."

Morgan was left sitting open mouthed, lacking any response to the revelations Norin had spoken of. The man was clearly beyond him, and above his right to pass judgment upon. We watched as

Norin jogged quickly off into the pre-dawn gloom, his purpose as strong as his stride. Morgan respected the man, appreciated the clarity of purpose that Norin enjoyed. Yet, the man lacked joy and peace. Morgan understood what that loss meant. He looked over at the sleeping Halnan and smiled. He went back to sleep for the final hour of darkness, glad for the interference of his friend throughout his life.

# THIRTEEN

## AWKWARD SITUATIONS

Sometime shortly after sunrise, Morgan was shaken awake for a second time. Having slept fitfully during the last hour, his eyes snapped open to find Halnan squat over him, a concerned look on his face. "Morgan, Norin is missing. He left during the night."

Morgan stretched lightly and crawled out from under his blanket. He quickly tightened his braid and pulled on his breaks and shirt. "Yes, I know."

Halnan, thrown off by his friend's answer frowned heavily. "What do you mean you know—if you knew he was leaving, why didn't you wake us, or stop him—why didn't you . . . ?"

Morgan cut off his friends rambling admonishments. "You needed your sleep, and there was nothing you could have done. Why don't you wake Taire while I bring up the fire. We'll talk about it during breakfast."

Halnan turned and walked away grumbling. "Sure, why bother informing the mere mortals—why do I bother—damned prophesies and Quests—I just want a beer and a barmaid!"

Morgan chuckled softly at his friend's temper, knowing he had successfully baited the man. He placed some fresh wood on the fire and stirred the embers until the new wood caught fire.

During breakfast, Morgan explained the circumstances of Norin's leaving, but did not go into the details of his role as Tarcha, or Taire's as the Shepherd. Halnan's indomitable humor brought him through his sour mood quickly, and Taire actually seemed relieved by Norin's absence.

Taire was indeed relieved by Norin's departure. Norin scared him. Although Norin had shown him nothing but respect, the tattooed man's dark demeanor intimidated him. He was relieved that he would not be questioned by Norin, glad that he would not have to open himself up the his scrutiny. He looked over to Halnan and then Morgan and smiled. "So, Sir Tarcha, where is it we will be honored to go under your divine guidance." He managed to spit the entire thing out just as Halnan had recommended, without laughing.

Morgan looked in surprise at Taire. "Wha—You've been talking to Halnan too much—he put you up to that, didn't he?" He then turned a sour glance to Halnan, whose face was twisting in its efforts to suppress laughter. Morgan sputtered, "you—you horrid, terrible—I will get even with you for this—I—I." Further speech was impossible for Morgan who could no longer keep up his bluster. He began to laugh hysterically, rolling on his bedroll, holding his belly.

Taire had at first been afraid that Halnan's advice had gotten him in trouble as Morgan blustered and stammered. Soon however, he began laughing at Morgan's antics, and at Halnan's hysteria. Many minutes went by before any of the three could control themselves enough to speak again. As Morgan explained that they would go south to Desil to search the libraries for information regarding the d'rakken mahre, each of the men would still occasionally break into an uncontrollable fit of laughter.

"It seems to me," Halnan spoke, "that the best way to avoid the armies would be to travel near the coast through the Welkwood." The dense forest seemed like the perfect place to avoid enemy troops. "Surely there will be some patrols by both armies, but the dense undergrowth should allow us to avoid them. Once we are across the border, we can cut due south through the relatively uninhabited coastal forests."

Morgan nodded in agreement. "True, and it should only be two or three days to the Desil border, where we can again travel upon the roads and make directly for Parnan, the capitol city."

Taire, knowing little of the world and its countries or politics voiced a concern. "If we get to Desil, wouldn't it still be dangerous to travel on the roads? Won't the road be used by soldiers heading north from Tulisia?"

"Yes, you are right about that," answered Morgan. "There will indeed be soldiers. They will not be a concern, however. Desil, though it is thought of as part of the Tulisian Empire, is a more like a neutral country, in which peace will be held regardless of outside war. No one will risk breaking the peace of Desil for fear of retributions by the Central Bank. The Bank holds power over even the most powerful of nations."

Taire had heard of banks, but found it amazing that a moneylender could hold power over entire governments. Nevertheless, he trusted Morgan's word.

They prepared the packhorse for Taire to ride, and showed him the rudiments of riding. Taire found the docile beast easy to ride and had little problem keeping up with his friends.

For the next two days they traveled southeast, cutting towards the border and the Welkwood, which was nestled in the far southeast of Thulistan, stretching for over a hundred miles across the Barstol border, almost to the border of Desil itself. They passed many groups of clansmen armed for war, heading southward. Most wore the tartans of Clans Olbaric or Kailison. A few groups, however, consisted of men from Clan Nemonson. This concerned Morgan greatly. Although he suspected that Clan Nemonson would be brought into the fray as payment of old blood debt to Clan Olbaric, he had hoped the conflict would be contained to the original two clans. He was at least glad that Clan Wrastson had seemingly thus far avoided inclusion in the call to arms.

Nonetheless, he knew that Clan Nemonson would add close to ten thousand additional fighting men to the massed force along the border. This would likely drive the Tulisian Generals to call in further reinforcements. Ultimately, this could mean as many as one hundred thousand Tulisian troops along the border instead of the current fifty thousand. If this came about, Morgan knew, all clans would be called upon.

Haunted by thoughts of Thulistan's warriors dying wholesale along the border, Morgan increased the pace at which his small band traveled.

Late the next day they arrived at the outskirts of the Welkwood. The tall evergreens of the forest mixed freely with now russet and yellow ash and alder trees. The trees cramped in upon each other, fighting for space. The ground was covered in newly fallen leaves and the soft loam of years of fallen needles. Adding to the chaos of the forest, thick groupings of rhododendron and creeping vines filled the spaces between the trees.

"There isn't any room to move in there, it's a solid wall." Taire looked in shock at the forest through which they were to travel for most of the next week. It was a tangled, dark, menacing place; full of unnamed dangers, and Taire did not want to enter within its clutches.

Halnan looked to Taire. "Don't worry lad, the forest is dark and close, but the worst we are like to encounter is elves, or perhaps ska." After saying the last, he looked at Morgan who was frowning slightly. "If we travel carefully, we should be able to avoid their snares."

Morgan loosened his sword in its sheath. "Can you defend yourself, should there be trouble?" The question was directed at Taire.

Taire reached into his pack and pulled out his dagger in its sheath. The weapon was only about eight inches long, and seemed silly in comparison to Morgan's sword, or Halnan's twin long knives. He shrugged. He put the dagger away, thinking of the sergath form he knew so well, or the dwarven form. "Well, I suppose if it comes to it I'll manage."

Neither Morgan nor Halnan understood Taire's subtle smile as he put the dagger away. If the lad said he could protect himself, then so be it. Slowly, they rode into the dark, dense forest, ducking to avoid the grasping branches.

The first day passed uneventfully as they made their way towards the Thulistan/Barstol border. At one point, in the middle of the day, Taire was looking off into the midday gloom of the forest, feeling that he was being watched. He didn't sense any ill intent, however, so kept the feeling to himself. Sunlight only rarely reached the forest floor through the heavy canopy of leaves and needles overhead. The hooves of the horses made little noise in the thick loam of the forest floor.

Continually throughout the day, Taire looked off into the forest, sensing something at the edge of his vision, just beyond his ability to see. The silent forest imposed its will upon them, and no one chose to speak. That night at camp, Morgan first broke the silence.

"I'll set camp. Halnan, do you suppose you and that bow of yours could locate some dinner for us?"

Halnan smiled. "Assuredly most revered S'hapur. As always your Torsch is pleased to serve." He winked at Taire, turned, and walked quietly from the camp, stringing his bow.

Taire, feeling like a useless piece of luggage, looked around for something to do. "I'll get some wood for the fire," he finally offered.

Morgan considered the offer for a moment. Taire obviously wanted to help, to take part as an equal in the camp. It should be safe enough with Halnan hunting the woods nearby. Nothing could come within a quarter mile of the camp without being detected by the stealthy hunter. He nodded his assent. "Thank you, Taire. We will indeed need a few armloads of wood. Try not to make too much noise, Halnan will be greatly put out if you scare off his game."

Taire walked just out of sight of the camp and began to gather the abundant wood scattered about the forest floor. He had just about finished collecting his first load when a slight noise alerted him to something nearby. Believing that Halnan had found him, he turned, prepared to greet his friend.

The words died on his lips, and he noisily dropped the bundle of wood as he caught sight of the elf standing nearby. He knew it had to be an elf. It was just over four feet tall and slight of build, with angular features and telltale pointed ears. Its skin was greenish-brown, and textured like the bark of a forest pine. The creature was not dressed, but showed no overt characteristics of being either male or female. As Taire stare at the creature, he had a sense that the distinction did not apply.

The elf looked around and sniffed the air. Its head swiveled almost completely around on its neck, causing Taire to shudder involuntarily. It was clear that this was a truly alien creature. It movements and actions were smoothly deliberate. It stepped forward, its legs seeming to bend fluidly along their entire length rather than at a knee like a human.

As the elf approached, Taire felt wonder, not fear. He watched its approach and knew that he should call to Morgan or Halnan, and yet chose not to. Moving slowly and cautiously the elf approached until it was directly in front of him, its diminutive form coming only to his chest.

The elf reached branch-like arms up and placed its thin gentle-fingered hands on Taire's shoulders. With surprising strength, it pulled him down onto his knees, where he could see eye to eye with the creature. The elf's eyes were a luminous green; round with a diamond shaped iris, much like those of a cat. Taire blinked as the creature held his eyes for a long moment, its lidless eyes fixed upon him in a steady unwavering gaze.

"Mans come forest. Mans bring war, fire." The voice was a sibilant, soft whisper, like the wind through the leaves. It cocked its head inquisitively. "Shepherd leads mans away?"

Taire listened to the quiet voice, moved by its potency, the potency of the trees and living things of the forest. He did not understand how the creature knew what he was, and knew he could not lead the men away from the forest, or the war they sought to pursue. He knelt there, shaking his head in denial.

The elf met his eyes. "Looks, see my eyes. See my soul, Shepherd. Understand?"

Looking deeply into its eyes, Taire found that portion of its being, its soul, that he uniquely understood. He saw the creature, and understood that he could borrow its form at need. He nodded to the elf. "Yes, I see. Thank you for your gift."

The elf nodded once slowly. "It is good. Now understand. Mans must leave. Shepherd make mans leave—follow. See." It reached up and pulled Taire's head down until their foreheads touched.

Taire's mind exploded with visions. He saw flashes of what was and what was to be. He saw a thin boy running alone through the darkness of the central cavern in Torance. He saw the grey muzzle of a mouse, whiskers twitching. He saw his father, a dying boy impaled by a pike, and finally The Ruler. He saw it all in a flash. Many of the visions, he did not at first understand. He saw a host of d'rakken mahre moving through forested hills. He saw men fighting d'rakken mahre and fighting each other. He saw Norin, or someone like him. He saw himself, walking amongst the horrid forms of d'rakken mahre!

The elf released him and stepped back. Taire was numb from the visions, from their power, pain, and promise. The elf looked him once more in the eyes. "The Shepherd must show the way. The mans will follow. It must be. Lead well, the mans must survive that which is to come. Peace Shepherd."

As the elf finished its farewell, Morgan called out, "Taire, where are you with that wood? Halnan's back and dinner's awaiting!"

The shout jolted Taire back to full awareness of his surroundings. As the first word of Morgan's call rung through the forest, the elf turned and fled into the trees. It moved with lightning quickness, almost beyond the ability of the eye to follow. Taire shook his head, collected the armload of wood and returned to the camp trying to make sense of the words and visions the elf had imparted on him.

Upon reaching the camp, he found that Halnan had already started a fire with a small amount of wood he had collected near the camp and had already put two large rabbits on spits to cook. Halnan took the wood that Taire carried, and seeing the queer look on the lad's face, held back his recrimination for his tardiness.

"What's the matter Taire? You look as if you've seen a ghost, as pale as you are." Halnan spoke casually as he put the wood on the fire, building it up further.

Taire considered for a minute. He kept much from these two men. He knew he would have to tell them about the elf, and that he would have to let them know about his shapechanging. Unsure of how to begin, he simply blurted it out. "I'm sorry. I just met an elf."

Morgan's head shot up to look at the young man, and the laughter died on Halnan's lips as he saw the serious look on Taire's face.

Morgan, always composed, responded first. "Taire, perhaps you could tell us of this meeting—why you didn't call for us?"

Taire held up his hand to forestall any further admonishments. "Wait—you don't understand. It did not harm me, it spoke to me, explained some things. Let me start from the beginning."

Taire told the missing portions of his previous tale; of his discovery of his abilities. He told of Piffer and of being a sergath. He explained his time as a dwarf, and finally, the words and visions of the elf. Halnan and even Morgan sat in shock at the story. They had known that there were gaps in the lad's story, but assumed it was memory loss from the trauma or some such. As Taire told of his abilities, many things began to make sense.

The story of the elf, its instructions and the visions it imparted on Taire were nothing short of amazing to Morgan. "If I understand this aright," he spoke hesitantly as if still working out the thought. "The Elf showed you moving amongst a host of d'rakken mahre. It seems to me that the elf was showing you leading the d'rakken mahre somewhere, and thereby causing the armies to leave this area; to attack the d'rakken mahre presumably."

Taire nodded in agreement with Morgan's understanding. "There is more to it, though. It seemed to me that the elf was trying to explain that the men's following the d'rakken mahre was a lucky, if helpful coincidence, not the purpose. I was leading them somewhere. Somewhere where they are seeking to go, somewhere that it is important to all of us that they make it too—I don't know for sure, but that's how it seemed to me."

"For every answer, more questions," mused Halnan. "It's a dangerous flock you are to lead, Taire. Somehow, none of this surprises me though."

Morgan raised his eyebrows at his friends boast.

"Well, the part about changing shapes was a mild shocker, but it's the fact that that the d'rakken mahre are the key to everything that doesn't surprise me. The Quest, the Prophecy, and the words of dwarves and elves; all have pointed to us being involved in the fate of the d'rakken mahre. That's all I meant," he finished somewhat lamely.

"Well, we have plenty of time to discuss it. It is all the more clear that we need information about the d'rakken mahre. We must know where they are going before anyone can consider leading them; especially if we are to do so with two armies in pursuit. Varsnya loves heroes and fools. History will tell which we are to be. Now, tell us more of this ability to change forms, how does it work?"

Taire explained in detail everything he could remember about each of his forms and how he achieved it. It was a tremendous relief to let everything out. Even more to his relief, Morgan and Halnan seemed unbothered by his abilities; in fact they seemed impressed.

"That may prove more than just handy during our journey," said Halnan. "So far, you have been a mouse, a sergath, and a dwarf. In addition to this, the elf showed you how to become an elf also?" Taire nodded in agreement. "That's fantastic. Can you do anything you want?"

Taire shrugged. "I really don't know. So far—well so far I have been able to change when I really needed to and I had the other form to study and learn. Up until now I really never thought of it as something I wanted to do, or as a gift. Assuming this is going to be important, let me try something."

Taire stood up and walked over to his horse, the placid mare was chomping contentedly on some scrub grass. Morgan and Halnan watched, understanding what he was going to try. He walked slowly around the horse, and looked deeply into its big brown eyes. After a moment, a feeling deep inside him told him he had seen the horse, seen its essence.

Taire concentrated and felt something within him trigger. Without transition, he felt different, felt his perspective change drastically. He could smell the grass below him and was tempted to lower his head and chomp some. The impulse was interrupted by a heavy nudge from behind him.

Taire swung his head to find the mare nuzzling his hindquarters. She looked up at him, brown eyes glazed over with bovine stupidity. She moved up, pulling her body close to his and rested her neck up and over his.

"Mate," the mare spoke plaintively. "Mate—make foal for me?"

Taire pulled away from the advances of the simple-minded creature, becoming uncomfortable with the subject matter. The mare turned her hindquarters his way and leaned forward on slightly splayed front legs, presenting herself for him.

"Make foal now." She turned her head to look at him.

Taire concentrated and quickly turned back to human form. He saw the mare give a slight jump at his change, looking at him for a moment before forgetting what she had been doing. The stupid beast went back to cropping the grass.

His examination of the mare was interrupted by the sound of the uncontrolled laughter of Halnan and Morgan. He saw the two men holding their bellies, bent over in uncontrolled fits of mirth. With a red face he walked over to the men.

Halnan spoke first to the embarrassed young man. "Well . . ." he was having trouble speaking, and was obviously working to contain his laughter. "I guess that was a successful experiment. Perhaps you could explain to those of us burdened with the limited understanding of men, what was the mare doing with you?"

Morgan also contained his laughter, awaiting the lad's answer.

"She—well I—there are things that horses do differently. I—um think she liked me." Taire gave up in exasperation, understanding what the horse had wanted, but not really the mechanics of how it all worked.

Morgan was the first to respond. "She . . . liked you." He turned to Halnan. "Would that every maid we met 'liked us' so!" The two again fell to uncontrolled fits of laughter, leaving Taire embarrassed and more than a little confused.

As they ate, Morgan questioned Taire regarding some details

regarding his shapechanging. Taire welcomed the questions, and found that by answering them he was better able to deal with his unique gift. Morgan also helped Taire to see some of the possible benefits of his ability. By the end of the evening, he felt better than he had since his ordeal had begun. The two men he traveled with were true friends who seemed to care about him, friends that appreciated him for what he was, despite the fact that he was not even sure himself what he was.

The next morning found the camp blanketed in a thick damp fog. Taire arose shivering from his moist blankets to find that the fire had died down to popping embers. Morgan and Halnan were already awake, and offered him a portion of dried meat and some bread for breakfast. He packed up his bedroll and helped to clean up the small camp before departing.

The thick fog obscured anything more than a few yards to either side, the tree boles nearest them were only visible from the ground up to about fifteen feet above ground where the fog cut them off like a low ceiling. The horses' hooves made no noise, muffled both by the damp ground and the thick fog that seemed to enclose sounds as well as the sunlight.

Around mid-day, Morgan whistled low and motioned Halnan and Taire to silence with a slicing hand motion across his throat. The other two men listened for a moment before they heard a faint clinking sound. The sound gradually grew, and multiplied into a number of rattles and clangs. The sound came from the south and passed them by within a hundred feet of where they sat, patting their horses and keeping still. Morgan counted the sounds of what he believed to be a dozen or so war horses, fully armored passing by when a piercing whistle blew from nearby, just off to the northeast. A brief trill answered it from the passing horsemen, who were almost directly west of Morgan and his party. The jangling of the horses began to come closer, as the men cut across to the call of their scout.

Halnan acted quickly, dropping silently from his horse and

stringing his bow. He looked to Morgan and pointed from his eye to the direction that the whistle had come from, indicating that he was going to see where the scout was, and ensure his friends did not come upon Morgan and Taire. He knocked an arrow and carefully moved off into the fog. Taire was nervous, not knowing who the men were and what would happen if they were discovered. Despite this, he wisely remained silent, awaiting Halnan's return. Over the next few minutes, they heard several sounds that could only be the twang of Halnan's longbow, followed by loud shouts of alarm. The nearby horsemen charged towards the sound, turning slightly away from Morgan and Taire.

Morgan, looking concerned, took advantage of the noise to ride over to Taire and whispered to him, "Hurry now, let's take advantage of the covering noise."

Before Taire could ask about leaving Halnan behind, Morgan cantered off into the gloom, heading south, leading Halnan's. With a brief glance backwards, Taire followed.

Halnan quickly located the scout and was surprised to discover he was a Tulisian scout, not a Thulistan. They were well inside Thulistan and it was disconcerting to know that the Tulisians had penetrated into Thulistan without resistance. He shrugged it off, realizing that only small parties could traverse the woods, and that they would be met with firm resistance when they tried to exit the wood.

He traveled around the scout and to the north. Taking aim, he fired an arrow at the man, striking him in the leg. The scout shouted in pain and alarm. "Attack, we are attacked from the north! Help!"

Hearing the loud rumble and clanking of the armored horses advancing through the heavy forest, Halnan ran north into the fog, pausing occasionally to fire a blind shot towards the oncoming horsemen. Twice he heard shouts of pain attesting to the accuracy of his blind shots.

The thick undergrowth and close trees allowed him to stay comfortably ahead of the horses of his pursuers. After about an hour of running Halnan had left the pursuit far behind in the fog. He found a large branch to wipe clear his trail and began to travel south again, circling wide around where the horsemen should be. He used the fir branch to cover his tracks quickly for a short while, until he found a dry, stony streambed to travel in. He knew the scout would not be doing much tracking for a while, but was unwilling to take any chances of leading the party back to his friends. It took him four hours at a fast jog to again catch up with Morgan and Taire, who had slowed to a walk, allowing him a chance to catch up.

Morgan turned his horse at the sound and drew his sword, motioning Taire to stay behind him. As Halnan's shape materialized from the gloom, he smiled and sheathed his sword. "Welcome back friend. By the sounds, I assume those were unfriendly troops nearby?"

Halnan stood with his hands on his hips, breathing deeply, trying to catch his breath. "Indeed," he gasped. "Tulisian heavy horse. About a dozen." His sentences were short, interrupted by heavy breathing. "Wounded the scout. Two others also, I think. Made a lot of noise. If we have any hunters in the woods, they should by on them by now."

Morgan smiled, and Taire frowned. Taire did not like the thought of being mistakenly shot by a hunter who may not stop to ask them who they were.

Seeing Taire's apparent distress, Halnan motioned to him to get his attention. "Don't worry Taire, Morgan and I have been very careful to avoid the attention of any hunters. I would say that by now, anyhow, we are nearing the border and under more threat by Tulisian patrols than by Thulistan hunters."

Taire, for some reason, did not seem to gather any confidence from the statement. Halnan shrugged his shoulders. "Well, they are only Tulisians. Nothing to worry about here in the forest," he mumbled only half to himself.

Twice more during the next two days they heard far off sounds of armed men passing through the forest. The clinking of their armor rang loudly in the silent forest, allowing the small party to easily avoid them, using the persistent coastal fog to help them remain undetected.

They were well into Barstol, and would reach the end of the forest the next day, leaving only a short trip to the Desil border. So far their luck had held remarkably. They camped in a small clearing that night and awoke to a clearing sky the next morning. The fog thinned to gentle wisps wrapped around the tops of the trees, and even these vestiges were quickly burning off in the morning sun as they broke camp.

As the morning progressed, the three rode into the thinning forest, enjoying the warmth of the sunlight. It was here, far from home, and out of the protective clutches of the fog and deep forest that their luck ran out.

# FOURTEEN

## FOR THE GLORY OF GOD

After departing Morgan and Taire, Norin ran throughout the morning, his long legs devouring the distance. During the long run, his mind wandered freely, contemplating all that he had heard. He knew that his task was to protect the people from the d'rakken mahre, and vise versa. He now knew where the d'rakken mahre would arise from the earth.

His people had long awaited this moment, and would not fail in their duty. There was no going back, and no room for failure. Going back meant disgrace, and failure would mean the extermination of the last of Clan Moncall. He and his warriors would dance on the razor's edge, between the d'rakken mahre and the armies of the world if needed. Norin smiled a cryptic smile at the thought, finding that it appealed to him. It was a fitting return from the dead for Clan Moncall; a fitting repayment of the debt to Varsnya.

Norin ran throughout that day, and the next. Moving rapidly northward at his distance-devouring pace, he passed through the Rhunne Gap into the harsh lands his people called home. No guard met him as would have a week sooner. There was no longer any need to protect the gap, no further need to maintain their secret. The men of Clan Moncall would be moving north towards where the d'rakken mahre were believed to be, and Norin knew he must quickly overcome them. With a burst of determination, he increased his speed.

During the next two days Norin moved northward into the blustery winds of the steppes at a pace most horses would be unable to sustain. He ran for Varsnya, the Tarcha, Clan Moncall, and lastly for himself.

Although no one would ever tell the tale, Norin's feat of endurance would live forever in the memory of the Gods. He traveled on foot for four days and covered as much ground as had Morgan and Halnan in over eight days on horseback.

Towards the end of the fourth day he was passing the great lake that marked the beginning of Long Wood. Beside the lake he found the men of Clan Moncall. They were camped in the verge of the woods, in tents of greenery and canvas that few would notice, even at close range.

He slowed his pace after a mile or so; still passing large clusters of tents and finally warmed down to a slow walk. After a few moments he was approached by one of his battle leaders, a hardened and scarred man named Gurdon.

Gurdon nodded in deference to his leader. "Welcome honored S'hapur. The gathering has begun and the Clan is moving toward our goal." His voice was a neutral monotone, as if he were speaking a ritualistic phrase.

"You have done well Battle Leader," responded Norin. "Indeed, many have gathered and you have followed the path I set you upon. It is fortunate I met with you so soon, however, for Varsnya has shown me the true path to absolution of our debt, and you are traveling in the wrong direction."

From any other man, Gurdon would have searched for signs of humor in the statement. From Norin, the statement could only mean that something tremendous had happened.

"In the morning," continued Norin, "we shall travel south, along the western side of the Moghin Mountains to their southern end. There we will find the beginning of Talon Valley. At the northern apex of this valley the d'rakken mahre will arise. The Clan must reach this place within two weeks. Send out runners tonight to spread the word to those still gathering and following. The entire Clan must serve to absolve the debt."

Gurdon simply saluted and turned away to do the bidding of their leader. There was no questioning Norin, no questioning the will of Varsnya. He had a long night ahead of him.

Norin, satisfied that Gurdon would do his bidding, turned and jogged a few miles southeast, up into the rocky slopes of the mountains. He made camp and rested the remainder of the night alone.

He awoke before dawn and climbed to a narrow promontory that overlooked the southern end of the lake, and the lands around him. Below him, along the shores of the lake, the clan gathered to hear the words of Gurdon and the other battle leaders.

Norin smiled as he estimated the number of men gathered below. Over fifteen thousand finely trained and conditioned hunters stood ready to follow the commands of their leader, and the Tarcha. Norin knew that he could expect to collect close to ten thousand more men during the trip south. Every able-bodied man in Clan Moncall would answer his call.

It would be his twenty five thousand guarding uncounted d'rakken mahre against several hundred thousand other Thulistans and Tulisians. "A fair fight," he whispered to the wind as he turned and ran down to join his army.

# FIFTEEN

## THE MEEK SHALL INHERIT

Morgan, Halnan, and Taire finally made their way out of the forest to enter into Barstol proper. Barstol was a bleak country, sparsely wooded, and mostly covered in mud from the near constant drizzle. The people of Barstol were few and demoralized. They lived in squalid villages, scratching an existence from the mud and from the one resource that existed in surplus in Barstol; pigs. The people were a sorry few, beyond even caring that their country had been decimated and then annexed by the Tulisians. In all, Barstol was a dead country whose inhabitants tried in vain to feed off of its corpse.

Taire had been uneasy all afternoon. He could not put a name to his ill ease, but knew something was going to go wrong. They passed from the thick forest into the more open lands of southeastern Barstol and then rode at a quick pace under the sunny late autumn sky.

They paused to eat lunch in a small hollow protected by a thicket of blackberry bushes on three sides. The small fire put up a thin wisp of smoke that trailed up into the breeze and was quickly dispersed.

Halnan and Morgan had been talking quietly for some time. Still feeling uneasy, Taire was listening to the wind and looking into the distance. After a moment, he turned his attention back to Morgan and Halnan.

Halnan looked up from the conversation with Morgan. "We should reach Desil about midday tomorrow," he said to Taire, answering the unasked question while picking at his teeth with a twig.

Morgan looked off to the south through the open side of the thicket. "I'd rather ride through the night and cross the border today. I'm uneasy about Barstol; it's too quiet. What are you thinking Taire?"

Taire had only been paying partial attention to the conversation and caught himself staring at the smoke rising into the sky. "Wha— Oh, well—I don't like it here. I'm all for riding for as long as it takes to get out of this place. It seems dead and gives me the chills."

Taire looked over at Halnan who was chuckling. "What are you laughing about? If you like it here so much, you stay, I just want to leave!"

Halnan was still laughing as he responded. "I'm sorry Taire, It's not you I'm laughing at—well not just you. It's just that you and Morgan are so alike sometimes. We have been free from trouble for the last few days and all you two do is complain about your 'feelings'. As far as I'm concerned, you should save your feelings for the ladies."

The sour look Morgan turned on Halnan was an even match for the one Taire gave him.

The silence that followed, while Taire and Morgan brooded over Halnan's ribbing was broken by the distant sound of a horn.

Morgan and Halnan jumped to their feet. "Get the fire," hissed Morgan. Halnan quickly buried the fire with dirt while Morgan packed up their belongings. They then pushed their way through the thicket to look to the north. Taire finished packing the cooking utensils before following the two.

The brambles pulled at his clothes as he forced his way to the front of the thicket where Morgan and Halnan squat quietly. As he neared them, another horn sounded to the west, louder, closer.

Halnan began climbing back through the brambles. "Damn, coming in from two sides. We've got to get moving south, and quickly. If we move now, we may be able to slip through the noose."

"Move Taire," hissed Morgan as he followed Halnan. "We may yet lose them. The trees will give us some cover until they are right upon us."

They mounted the horses quickly and exited the thicket on its open south end and began trotting southward. Halnan, seeing Taire's 'I told you so' look, shrugged sheepishly. "Don't even say it," he said.

Morgan, riding to the far left of the three, turned to his companions. "Taire, you will have to forgive Halnan, he represses his feelings. Causes him to miss the cues his body gives him in these situations. From what I hear, it sometimes causes him to be over enthusiastic with some of his many wenches too. I've heard, that on occasion, the party is sometimes over before . . ."

"That's not true," interrupted Halnan. "If I find out who began those rumors—well I'll—I'll—Oh you'll pay for this Morgan!"

Morgan turned his horse and kicked it into a full gallop. He raced southward, his concern over pursuit temporarily overridden by a deep feeling of satisfaction. Halnan spurred his mount on, following Morgan, sputtering and fuming all the while. Taire, last of the group, rode on with his ears hot with embarrassment. In addition to this, he again had that slight feeling of confusion that came upon him whenever the two joked about women.

As they rode, the sounds of horns from the north became more distant as their fresh mounts out paced the tired mounts of their pursuers. To the southwest, however, the horns became progressively louder.

"They can't be too far away," shouted Taire.

"Just keep riding," replied Halnan.

Further conversation was broken off as the riders concentrated on staying on their horses as they entered into a small copse of trees. Trees whipped by to either side for several minutes and then they broke once more into an open field. In the distance both ahead and to the west of them, the sun glittered off of shiny moving objects.

Taire saw Morgan stand in his stirrups for a moment. He sat back down and pulled up his horse. Halnan followed suit, as did the shocked Taire.

"It's no use running," he shouted at Halnan and Taire. "Let's ride back to the copse and try to make a defense. They are in front and to the west. With the sea to the east and those behind us, we are caught. I count ten men between the two groups."

The riders were approaching at an alarming rate. They had clearly spotted their quarry and were beginning to converge towards the three riders. Taire was the first to begin to move. He turned his horse and kicked it into a rapid gallop for the nearby copse of trees through which they had so recently passed.

Halnan waved to Morgan and yelled, "you next, I'll follow as soon as I am certain you and Taire will make it ahead of pursuit. I'll ensure you have time to set up a defense—go, now!" Not bothering to watch Morgan follow his order, he began to string his bow with practiced speed and competence.

Morgan rode at full speed into the copse and pulled his horse up when he sighted Taire, sitting fretfully on his horse. "Taire, get off your horse and get it out of here!"

Taire quickly complied, sliding off of his mount and slapping its flank hard enough to startle it. The horse ran off through the copse, closely followed by Bran, Morgan's steed.

"Don't worry, if we live, they will be nearby. If not, they will be well cared for by their new owners." Morgan spoke as he prepared himself, unsheathing his sword and looking about for the most defensible position. It only took him a moment to reach a decision. "Move over to that ring of oaks and be ready to defend yourself. The trees will force them to either dismount, or ride in blind through the low branches. Move!"

Taire ran towards the roughly ring shaped group of trees, seeing the sensibility of Morgan's selection. In the middle of the ring was a large, low stump; the charred remnant of some monstrous oak that had evidently burned down to a lonely stump. Taire ran to the stump and quickly hid behind it, crouching low. Shortly behind him, Morgan arrived and placed himself carefully behind a large tree bole, ready to attack from his place of concealment.

A crashing sound of breaking branches caused Morgan to stiffen, bringing his sword high for a stroke. The sound was followed by several other vague sounds and then the rapid tattoo of running feet on the brittle leaves. Morgan knew that the lone footsteps must belong to Halnan, and yet barely was able to withhold a killing stroke, as a blurred form broke into the ring of trees at a full run.

Halnan watched Taire and Morgan flee while the men approached. There were ten of them, armed for battle, shorts words raised and shields positioned. He carefully fired two arrows at the approaching men. The first struck true, piercing through the rider's neck, knocking him backwards off of his horse to land limply behind the still moving beast. The second arrow struck a horse in the chest. Its front legs crumpled under it causing its hindquarters to come up and over. Halnan flinched at the results. If the rider survived being thrown and then rolled over by the dead horse, Halnan thought, he would most certainly not be in any condition to fight.

Suddenly, he realized he was about to be overrun. He turned his horse and kicked it brutally into a full gallop. His bow lay on the ground behind him discarded. He knew he would have no further opportunity to use it and chose to save time by discarding it for now.

As soon as he entered fully into the copse of oak and ash, he jumped from his still moving horse. The unaccustomed motion caused the horse to startle and redouble its running efforts. Halnan hit the ground, rolled and came to his feet at a full run. He quickly scanned the area, and seeing the circle of oak, made for it. As he entered the ring of trees, he made out Morgan form in his peripheral vision. To avoid a potentially deadly error in judgment by his friend, he let his feet come out from under him.

His slide took him under any potential sword strokes. He then kicked and pushed himself up, coming to his feet and drawing his twin long knives in the same motion. "Glad to see you, Morgan," he panted with a smile. "Get ready, eight bad guys will be joining us shortly."

Morgan barely had time to register the meaning of the last statement before the sound of horses coming into the copse commanded his full attention.

# SIXTEEN

## RISE TO GLORY

Davan 'av Carpea, Marshal General of the First Tulisian Army was not having a very good day. His post for the last ten years had been along the border of Tulisia and the Wild Wood, defending against the incursions of the elves of the wood. He had chosen this post ten years past for its constant struggles, and the opportunities that they provided. Davan had been very successful and over the years had moved quickly through the ranks, both due to feats of personal bravery and skill, as well as demonstrations of his natural leadership ability.

Two years ago he had achieved the position of marshal general of the First Army, the most seasoned of Tulisia's fighting forces. His command consisted of fifty thousand fighting men spread along one hundred miles of border. In addition to this, one battle group each was sent to the far southern forts of Far Post and Torcoth Keep along the coast.

With no small pride in his accomplishments, Davan mentally recapped the promotions of the past ten years. As the son of a rich Desilian family, he received a position as a commissioned officer at the early age of eighteen. He started as a sergeant of a squad of fifty men in the Fourth Army, posted in Cartiel. By his own request, and to his parents' dismay, he requested a posting at one of the border forts. Within the week he was shipped off to man the wooded palisades of the western border.

While serving a post at Torcoth Keep, the battle group he was serving in (First Battle Group, Seventh Division, Second Host, First Army) was attacked by pirates, or more likely Tursys raiders flying pirate colors. Of the five squads at the keep, three were destroyed before retreating within the Keep itself. The Knight Captain of the battle group was killed, and the only other remaining officer was a weak willed Barstolian sergeant.

Davan took charge and held the Keep against the unusual siege for thirty-four days on minimal rations. On the thirty-fifth day the Second Battle Group, Seventh Division, reinforced by the Fourth Battle Group (which had been stationed just fifty miles north at Far Post) arrived and drove the pirates back to the sea. Davan led his men forth to assist in the attack and personally killed the leader of the siege force.

Two and a half weeks later, he returned to West Post. Two days following this, amidst a chorus of cheers, he was formally promoted to Knight Captain of the First Battle Group, filling the position vacated by the death of his previous commander, and increasing his command to two hundred and fifty men.

Less than two years following this, a late night raid by several hundred elves against West Post itself offered another opportunity for the young Knight Captain, who was patrolling with one of his squads.

Davan formed an orderly retreat against a superior force, and alerted the rest of his battle group in time to repel the attack with only two casualties.

Again his men cheered loudly as he received his promotion. He was more than pleased to be a general, a leader of a division of a thousand men.

Due to his superior tactical and fighting skills, he received another promotion three years later after the death of the marshal of the Fourth Host. With ten thousand men at his disposal, he felt very powerful, and most pleased with himself.

After all of this, it was no surprise when, six months later, after the Marshal General of the First Army retired, Davan was selected to replace him. Davan 'av Carpea at twenty-eight, was the youngest marshal general in the history of the Tulisian army.

As if this fact wasn't enough to cause his ego to swell, Davan was every bit as good as his position would indicate, and he knew it. At close to six and a half feet tall, he was a giant among Desilians. His was lean and strong, and lightening quick with his saber, a light weapon only used by fools or experts. Davan was no fool.

His features were chiseled and his waxed mustache swept below his chin to either side of his mouth, curling up at its ends. His skin was a light bronze, hair jet black, and eyes a penetrating green. Davan truly was a striking figure. He was, of course, very aware of this fact.

Despite all of this, today had not been a good day. Dawn found Davan walking a portion of the palisade, a wall structure formed by sharpened fir trees that had been extended to the north and south over the decades, and now stretched in broken segments for almost fifty miles. The palisade formed the last line of defense against any marauders that were able to cross the river from the Wild Wood.

Davan knew that he could hold the river and palisade against any force of up to twice the size of his host of fifty thousand. While he was here, the border would be secure. In addition to pride in service, Davan lived like royalty. A marshal general answered only to the Emperor himself, and the Emperor had never called on the rustic western border forts. He was, in effect, ruler of his own empire. Davan greatly enjoyed this fact.

It was true that the Emperor had never called on the western border, but the Imperial Offices did send occasional documents through the courier system; recalls of officers back to the city, official reports of Army movements, etc. During his morning tour, a courier had arrived with one such package.

He retired to his private quarters to review the information contained within the sealed pouch. The courier pouch was sealed under the Emperors own seal. Tampering with this seal was a death warrant to anyone other than to whom it was addressed.

With a sense of impending doom, Davan cracked the seal and opened the pouch. Never before had he received any missives sealed under the Emperors seal. As such, it did not come from the offices of the Emperor, but the Emperor himself!

He pulled the single long sheet of paper from the pouch and flattened it onto the table in front of him. From within his desk he pulled out the appropriate template and began to translate.

Davan 'av Carpea, Marshal General, First Army of the Tulisian Empire.

Dictated by His Majesty Ulsath II, Emperor of all Tulisian lands, Commander of all Tulisian Armies

Marshal General Davan:

>As stated in previous missives from the Imperial Offices, a massive deployment of enemy soldiers has begun along the Thulistan border. The size of this deployment has exceeded original estimates. It is Our determination and that of Our staff, that this border can no longer be considered stable, or safely under Tulisian control.
>
>It is therefore, by the Our royal order that you are to, at first opportunity and no later than two weeks following receipt of these orders, select two Hosts from the First Army to bolster the forces existing at the Thulistan border. You are to travel at forced march north to Rache, upon Blayse Bay, where you will rendezvous with a fleet dispatched from Epsat. This fleet will convey you along the Talon River to its fork in the Moghin Hills. From here your men will have ten days to travel the remaining distance to the Thulistan border.
>
>At current troop build up levels, your arrival within one month should provide additional forces to hold the border until the slower heavy units from the Fourth Army can arrive, along with several hosts from the Second which require time to safely pull out of Tursys.
>
>It is my added pleasure to hereby name you Field Commander of the Thulistan Campaign. Until the

campaign is successfully completed, or at such time as We personally assume command, you have full power over all forces upon the field. These orders have been copied to all marshals, and marshal generals.

You are ordered to hold the border, and keep the enemy troops in place. While your forces of over one hundred thousand soldiers holds the attention of the Thulistans, a mounted Carstan army will drive through the sparsely inhabited lands of eastern Thulistan and come up against the rear of their border Host.

At this time you are to drive across the border and crush the Thulistans against the Carstan army, which is expected to number in excess of thirty thousand heavily armored, mounted knights. At our best estimates, Thulistan can field no more than seventy five thousand fighting men, giving you a two to one advantage, as well as the natural advantages of training and superior tactics.

Thulistan is to be under Tulisian rule before the first heavy snows of winter.

Outside of these general guidelines, all decisions as to tactics are left to you and the staff you select.

Long has the Empire awaited this opportunity. Upon your victory, many shall be rewarded, yourself above all. The Tulisian lands of Thulistan will require a regent. Varsnya be with you.

It was an opportunity surpassing any Davan had ever hoped for. It was finally time to tame the northern wilds, and to end the border raids of the savage Thulistans. He knew full well that, at odds of two to one he would destroy any enemy quickly and with few losses.

Despite this, Davan had a very bad feeling about all of this.

Later that same day, Davan called his five marshals to his quarters to discuss the orders. He waited until all of the assembled men read the orders.

"So, men—which two hosts should be granted the honors?"

Each of the assembled men stepped forward at attention, the military equivalent of volunteering. Davan paced by each man, silently considering his qualifications. There would be no pleading or arguing. Their job was to volunteer; his was to select.

After a moment he nodded to himself and looked to his men. "At ease men, I've made my decision." Each man relaxed his shoulders and stepped back a pace. "There is not one of you who does not deserve this honor, but honor is in duty, and for those staying behind, duty remains. Holding the border with just over half of the force will require double shifting the men while still maintaining battle readiness, it is a great burden. This honor I will give to the First, the Third, and the Fifth Hosts. The Second and Fourth Hosts will accompany me."

Not a flicker of emotion was shown by any of the assembled men. Davan had chosen and that was all there was to it. It was true that no Host was truly more able than the others. In this case, it was a matter of loyalty. As a previous member of the First, and Marshal of the Fourth, Davan could expect an exceptionally high level of morale and a certain fanaticism that would be a benefit in the campaign. As Field Commander, he would need a solid base of support. Half of his officers would immediately be parceled out to other divisions and battle groups in trade, spreading his loyalty base even further.

"Marshal Alvir will assume the position of Field Marshal General Pro Tem in my absence. Marshal's Carcho and Linsar, begin to bring in your men. Plan with Marshals Troas and Ominat to ensure the border is protected during your pull out. The men must be marshaled and ready for forced march within one week. See to provisions for a four-week march. That is all. Marshal Alvir, would you stay for a moment please."

The men saluted fist over heart, turned in unison on their heels, and exited the room, leaving Davan alone with Marshal Alvir. Alvir was an old campaigner, in his late fifties. He was well known and respected as a stern and experienced officer.

Despite his age, Alvir was firm and completely capable of

defending himself in personal combat. For the most part, one look from his deep grey eyes was enough to cause most men to avoid confrontation. His hair was mostly grey, as was his short-cropped beard. His face was marked with many deep scars from his long years of combat experience. He awaited Davan's pleasure impassively.

"Alvir," began Davan, carefully selecting his words. "I selected you for both your experience, and your practicality. You have proven most loyal to the men and myself over the years. There is something I must tell you regarding my orders."

Alvir responded simply by raising his eyebrows.

"It is my belief that your command will be under tremendous pressures while I am gone. Call it a hunch, but I believe you will be attacked by the elves shortly after my leaving." Davan watched for a moment, and seeing no response continued. "Do you understand what I am saying?"

"Yes, sir." Responded Alvir.

"Do you understand what this may mean?"

"Yes, sir." Alvir showed no emotion or concern. At least he continued this time. "Sir, should they attack, we will hold. The men are veterans and worthy. I will hold your post until you return. Elf scum don't frighten us."

"That is all to the good, Alvir, but there is something more to this—something I can't put my finger on. Danger is afoot and blood will be shed. It is not the elves alone I fear, though you should not underestimate them. I fear that too many things are happening at once; that the Emperor is overextending. The balance in the world is tenuous; we stand atop a warbling plate. Let us hope we are not dumped."

He had said more than intended. He had practically challenged the wisdom of the Emperor! A sentence of death could be imposed for what he had just spoken. And yet, Alvir stood patiently, awaiting further orders.

Davan sighed. "That is all, Marshal Alvir. Meet with the others to ensure preparations are going apace."

Alvir saluted. "Aye, Sir." He turned crisply and left the room. It was odd, he thought, that the Marshal General should show such doubts. Odd or not, he was the Marshal General, and Alvir just an old campaigner with a job to do. War waits on no man, he thought as he went about his business.

It took only four days to pull in the outlying divisions of the Fourth that were currently assigned to Mid Point Fort and the surrounding lands to the south. The majority of the First Host was currently in the field to the north, and would hold their ground as they were relieved by troops from the Fifth Host. Instead of traveling south, they would wait for the remainder of the First, and the Fourth to come to them. In the meantime they prepared the supplies for the journey.

Due to this planning, the men were marching within six days, and reached the Blayse Bay three days before the fleet. This allowed the troops to rest and prepare for the upcoming campaign.

Two weeks later, a full week ahead of schedule, Davan 'av Carpea and his two Hosts disembarked in the gentle Moghin Hills. The Admiral of the Blayse fleet personally came to see Davan off.

"The Gods themselves speed you on your way Marshal General. Never before had the wind held so steady and strong on this stretch of river. Shall your campaign succeed as quickly and surely!"

Davan looked at the Admiral, a small Desilian wearing the White coat of an Admiral in the Tulisian Navy. The man looked dangerous, more like a pirate than an officer. "Varsnya speed you, Admiral. Thank you for your rapid conveyance."

Despite the early hour, Davan ordered camp set, to allow the men to start fresh in the morning. Far to the east, unbeknownst to Davan, three men who invaded the land he was to protect were about to engage in a fight for their lives. Even further away, to the north, a host of grim, heavily tattooed Thulistans were approaching the border—ready for war, and prepared to die if necessary.

# SEVENTEEN

## THE BREATH OF DRAGONS

Morgan quickly turned from Halnan back towards the gap between the trees through which he had crashed. The rider paused a short distance away and was checking the tracks on the ground to determine Halnan's whereabouts. The horses' tracks led off in one direction, but the riders in another. Confused, he looked up and examined the direction of the horses' tracks, and then Halnan's. Seeing the tight ring of trees and the excellent defensive ring it would offer, the tracker came to a decision.

"He's in here men! Jort, Sul, circle north to cut off his escape." As he finished shouting, he unsheathed his sword and leapt back atop his mount. As he did so, the first of the following five riders entered into the copse behind him. Confident in his abilities to take the fleeing man at two to one odds, he spurred his mount forward yelling to his comrade. "He's in there, watch for his partners!"

Halnan, not wanting to lose the advantage of surprise, jumped out into the open space in front of the gap, where the approaching riders could see him. With a dramatic flair that Morgan never suspected he had, he looked back over his shoulder, and in an anguished tone yelled, "I'll hold them masters, flee for your lives!"

With their final question answered regarding the other two men accompanying their prey, the first two soldiers blindly rode into the ring of trees, eyes on Halnan.

The scout, whose horse had fallen a pace behind his comrades, barely had time to register the flash of steel from behind a near tree. The first horse, its legs cut out from under it, crumpled in a heap. Its rider died instantly in the fall, his spine snapped.

The scout pulled his horse hard left, away from the crumpled body of his partner's horse, away from the deadly steel of the mysterious attacker. Holding his steed's reigns, he slid from the saddle and used his horse to physically shield him from would be attackers while the rest of his party had a moment to arrive.

Morgan jumped out to ensure the rider was dead, and finding him very much so, began to move towards the far side of the glade, where the second rider waited. Halnan, both blades at the ready advanced towards the rider from the other side.

Morgan and Halnan were so involved in dealing with the second rider that they were almost too late responding to the abrupt entrance of the other four riders from the south. A shouted warning from Taire saved them.

Taire crouched low behind the stump, peering carefully over the top, watching the action beyond. The ease with which his friends utilized their violent arts surprised him, although he wasn't frightened by their abilities. He winced as the horse went down and thought he heard a snapping sound as the rider's chest met the ground, and his lower body was forced up and over by the momentum of the horse.

As he watched Halnan and Morgan advance on the second rider, he caught a flash of metal in the sun to the south. Knowing the rest of the riders had arrived, and seeing that his friends had not seen or heard the approaching horses, Taire shouted a wordless exclamation of warning.

Further away from the entrance, Halnan had a brief moment to prepare himself before two mounted men set upon him. Morgan, reacting by instinct dove forward pulling a dagger from his boot. He rolled under his original opponent's horse and came to his feet, putting the full strength of his upward thrust into planting his dagger in his opponent's gut.

His force threw the scout, wide eyed with surprise, backwards off of his horse. He hit the ground before he even realized he was going to shortly be dead.

Morgan, using the horse as a shield as his opponent had, pulled his sword just in time to defend against the first sword stroke of his next opponent.

Taire's viewing was interrupted by a sound from behind him. He turned and heard voices from just beyond the ring of trees. The two soldiers that had circled north were arriving on foot, carefully approaching the ring of trees, hoping to achieve a measure of surprise.

Taire's heart was pounding in his throat. He knew that Morgan and Halnan were hard pressed by their opponents. The enemy soldiers dismounted to attack, taking a more cautious approach than their now dead fellows. It seemed clear to Taire that the approaching two men would surely turn the tide quickly in the enclosed space. Without conscious thought, he did the only thing he could to protect himself. The last thing he remembered was an image of the biggest, angriest sergath he had ever seen.

Morgan was holding his own with his two assailants. He had nicked both men multiple times, although he had not managed to get in a serious cut on either man. He was sure that it was only a matter of time before one of his opponents made a mistake and he could safely dispatch him. He was confident that a single opponent would then prove little difficulty.

Halnan, however, was hard pressed, and lightly bleeding from several shallow wounds. His long knives flashed in protective sweeps about him, but the heavy sword blows reigning down upon him by his opponents were beginning to tire him as well as press the luck that he had so far held on to.

It was clear that their opponents were skilled warriors, not common soldier types. Seeing Halnan's position, Morgan began to consider a risky rolling maneuver to cut down one of his opponents. If successful, he could sooner lend aid to his slowly failing friend. If anticipated, the two soldiers would cut him to shreds. He began to position the two men into a position from which he could launch his attack, when a shriek from the northern side of the copse of trees caught a portion of his attention.

Morgan stepped back a pace, looking to see if the cry had come from Taire, whom he knew was hidden near that end of the small clearing.

What he saw there shocked him, almost causing him to miss a parry that would have cost him his head.

One foot on the stump behind which Taire hid, a great reptilian beast stood looming over the field of combat. The creature was almost twice the size of a large steer, but low to the ground on stumpy legs ending in large toed feet. Its skin was brownish grey, and looked like heavy, dry leather. Its head was somewhat snakelike, but more squared and powerful. The body ended in an awkward looking stubby tail.

It only took Morgan a moment to realize that the creature across the glade from him was Taire. Seeing his opportunity, he jumped back, away from the men he was engaged in with a terrified yelp, looking over the men's shoulders.

Expecting to find his two companions coming from behind to help, one of the men turned partially back towards where Taire was poised. "About time you got . . ." the rest of the sentence died on his lips as he saw a sergath for the first time in his life.

Completely forgetting Morgan, he turned and began to back away from Taire muttering to his partner. "Dragon—big—angry dragon!" Taire timed a long, loud hiss perfectly with the statement, and the man was running. His departure was prematurely stopped by the point of Morgan's sword.

His partner, as well as two men facing Halnan, was more careful. Having seen Taire in his sergath form, they began to back up towards each other for protection. Taire rose up on his hind legs and lunged forward. He struck the ground only a few paces from the three, his weight causing leaves to fall from the trees as he impacted on the ground.

This was too much for the men, who lost all sense of reason and bolted in three separate directions. Halnan was too weary and injured to give chase, and Morgan too concerned about his friend. Giving chase was not necessary, however, the fleeing men had no desire to turn back and face the angry 'dragon' in the glade, and they continued running for quite a while.

Morgan put aside his interest in the form Taire had taken and took several quick strides to see to Halnan's wounds.

Halnan dropped to one knee and was leaning forward panting heavily. One of his blades lay on the ground, and the other was still pushed point first into the soil, providing support for his weary arm. As Morgan reached his side, he looked up with a forced smile. "I think I need some sparring practice. Those two were only moments from finishing me. I used to be able to defend against three in sparring practice with my men. The Tulisian army must be more formidable than I ever imagined if their soldiers are so well trained."

Discovering that his friend had only received several shallow, if bloody scratches, Morgan let out a sigh of relief. "Don't feel so bad, I was hard pressed too. Anyhow, those were not regular soldiers. I recognized the tabards—that was a detachment of the Border Hunters, the elite pride of the Fourth Army." The few hundred men that composed the Border Hunters were selected from the finest warriors in the Tulisian Empire. They were trained to meet the raids of the Thulistans, and used as shock troops during times of conflict.

"Come on—get up." Morgan reached out a hand to help Halnan to his feet. "We'll have to scrub the dirt out of that head cut, as well as the long one on your arm."

Morgan, having begun to turn away to go after the horses, missed the grimace Halnan turned his way.

As he completed his turn, he again caught sight of Taire's reptilian form, watching them from across the glade. He walked over to Taire, closely followed by a slightly hesitant Halnan.

Approaching Taire closely, Morgan could not help being impressed. The creature was huge, and quite frightening. They saucer-sized eyes caught his attention. Deep within the eyes he could sense Taire's presence. There was intelligence hidden behind those watery black eyes.

Halnan, having overcome his reluctance was running his hands down the creature's flanks, moving towards the head. As he reached the head, Taire turned it up and almost over, on an angle impossible to anything except a reptile, to gaze at him. The large slitted nostrils opened and slowly inhaled, smelling Halnan. A moment later, the mouth opened slightly as he exhaled.

"Wooo—Taire, your breath is really bad. What could you possibly eat that could smell so bad?" The words were accompanied by an act of pantomime, as Halnan made greatly exaggerated motions of waving one hand in front of his face, while pinching his nose between his thumb and forefinger of the other.

Taire backpedaled a step and changed back to human form. The transition was instant. His cheeks were hot with embarrassment as he cupped a hand over his mouth and checked his breath. "I don't smell anything—I didn't know . . ."

Morgan cut short his embarrassment by punching Halnan in the ribs to stop his pantomime. The blow was met with an exclamation of shock from Halnan. Morgan ignored him and spoke to Taire. "Don't worry about it Taire. That was amazing, what sort of creature was that?"

Struggling not to laugh at the simple method by which Morgan had utilized to silence his friend, Taire answered. "It—well we call them sergath, they are used as beasts of burden in the underworld. I just imagined the biggest and meanest ones I could, and—well it seemed to work. I really didn't know about its—I mean my, breath. The last time I was in sergath form, I ate a lot of fungus, as well as a few degan sahre, which are these rat-like two legged creatures. I suppose that when I change forms I end up the way I was last when I was in that form, so now you know what it smells like when you mix degan sahre and fungus. It's really gross when I think about it now, but in that form it seems really normal . . ."

Halnan cut off the long-winded explanation, feeling a little bit sickened by the description of Taire's diet as a sergath. "It's all right, I forgive you for you dietary indiscretions as a sergath. I was just kidding, really. Would you have—well would a sergath want to eat people?"

Taire barked a laugh at Halnan's obvious concern. "No, sergath are highly domesticated, and even those living in the wild eat only small prey and other more disgusting stuff. They are generally terrified of humans until domesticated. I don't have that particular problem, and I can usually control the instincts of the form I take, unless I stay in the form for too long. If I had to, I could have attacked, but I really don't want to hurt anybody. I'm just glad they ran." Taire was, if fact, unsure of what he would have done if the men had not run.

Halnan, wiping blood from his brow, added wryly, "Can't argue with that logic."

"Well, we can talk about this later. Right now, Halnan has wounds needing to be cleaned." Morgan's tone brooked no arguments, and they went off to collect the horses.

A short while later, they found the horses, which had run only as far as the end of the copse of trees where they had collected around Bran, who looked prepared to protect the others. Using water and fresh rags from the saddlebags, Morgan cleaned Halnan's wounds, and was relieved to see that they were both shallow and clean.

Having learned the danger in overconfidence, they again began their southward journey. This time, Halnan rode far out in the lead, scouting for enemy soldiers. Morgan rode to the rear looking for pursuit. In the middle, Taire looked constantly back and forth, ensuring the men were still within visual range.

# EIGHTEEN

## BROKEN MINDS, BROKEN PLANS

Tension was pervasive in Torance; an almost palpable presence. The last caravan had returned from the depths several days past, bringing with it rumors to chill the blood.

It was said within the city that the d'rakken mahre were coming. Some rumors stated that The Ruler had sold out the populace of Torance to the d'rakken mahre, and that they were to all end up as slaves. Other rumors told of the d'rakken mahre forming an alliance with The Ruler to carve out an empire on the surface world. Regardless of the rumor, the fact was the inhabitants of Torance were uncertain of their future. This uncertainty brought near panic throughout the populace.

The Ruler, sitting comfortably in the sitting room of his under-earth manor, was only marginally aware of the tension in his city. Next to his seat set several chests, one opened. Within the chest glittered countless scores of precious stones, diamonds, emeralds, rubies and others. The Ruler rubbed his hands compulsively as he contemplated the glittering stones.

The wealth appealed to him, but it was not enough. With the stones, he could rule an empire. Despite this, he felt that he was losing what he required most; control.

It all started when he lost that damned boy! The boy had shown potential to be one of the best he had ever owned, and he had just disappeared. The Ruler had beaten the entire staff to get the truth of the boy's disappearance to no avail. Something changed from that point. He had loved that boy, needed him, and the child had run away without so much as a thank you!

Then along came the d'rakken mahre, telling him that they wanted to use his city as a gateway to the surface. The wealth in the chests in front of him only just began to make up for what his city was going to lose in trade in its future. Torance would die as a city without the trade from the under-earth, and The Ruler knew it. Within a decade, his city would no longer exist.

Then, as if he hadn't had a bad enough month, his new boy managed to escape with unknown help, only to die squirming on a guard's pike. The news of a battered dead boy on the bridge to the mansion had gotten out, and he had since been unable to acquire another boy! It seemed like every time he went out in public now, everyone looked at him in a strange, accusatory way. Some even shouted disparaging remarks, although always from the safety of a crowd or shuttered window. This behavior is what bothered him the most. Their taunts echoed in the silence of the room; his emotions seethed with the pain of their lack of gratitude.

Rubbing the deep, puckered, semi-healed wound that was healing slowly along his cheek, and fingering the scabbed area that used to be his ear, The Ruler vowed he would not let it end like this. He would not watch his city die while the thankless citizens plotted behind his back, seeking his death. Wincing from the pain caused by the intense rubbing on his cheek, he came to a decision. The Ruler set a course for his revenge and immediately committed to it.

Silently cursing the lack of a page, he stood up and bellowed. "Guard!"

A bare moment later, the door guard entered the room and came to attention. The intensity of the glare that The Ruler directed at him set his heart pounding. The Ruler stood breathing deeply for a moment, fighting for self-control. The guard was afraid! Why would the guard be afraid if he wasn't plotting against him? The Ruler smiled at the guard, and moved his corpulent form across the room towards the man. The smile did nothing to decrease the ice in his glare.

Without ever taking his eyes off of the guard, he slowly sauntered across the room. Slowly, so as not to tip off the guard, he reached behind his back and removed a slim stiletto from its sheath in his belt at his back. "Guard, what is your name?"

The guard, sensing that The Ruler was unbalanced, involuntarily winced at the harshness in his voice. Only his years of training kept him from bolting for the door. "Sir, my name is Ghalar." His voice only trembled slightly.

Arriving directly in front of the guard, The Ruler paused, looking deeply into the man's eyes. "Well—Ghalar is it? Ghalar, I have a message I want you to carry. Pay attention closely. The message is this—"

With a swift motion, he swung his hand around and planted eight inches of stiletto in the guard's chest. The blade passed easily through the links of the guard's chain armor. The guard slumped to the floor, blood bubbling on his lips, and a profound look of surprise on his face. As he slid along the wall, his mouth worked as if trying to speak, but all that came out was a "Hwa, hwa," sound accompanied by coughed up flecks of blood.

The Ruler kneeled down in front of the dying man, taking his face in his hands, turning his head up so he could make eye contact. "Yes, the message is this—anyone who dares challenge me, who dares plot against me—will die. Tell them in Hell! If they don't know why they died, tell them! I am not stupid, I will not be fooled by the pathetic plots of those who owe their lives to me!"

The Ruler was shaking violently in his rage and madness. He released the dying man's face and stood up, slowly regaining control. After a moment, he again knelt. Seeing pain and awareness in the guards' eyes he reached down and pulled the knife from the bloody chest. The guard gave a convulsive heave as the blade came free. "Tell them, Ghalar, that I killed them all. I want them to know." He examined the blade, touching the blood with his finger. He licked the blood from his finger and looked at the guard.

The man was breathing shallowly, his eyes closed. The Ruler patted the man on the head. The guard opened his eyes slowly and forced them to focus. His focus was somewhere beyond The

Ruler. With effort, he coughed the bloody foam from his mouth and began to speak. The soft words sounded as if they were coming from deep within the dying man, they had a liquid quality. "Var . . . ," he paused and coughed for a moment. "Varsnya take me." His voice became stronger, clearer. "Forgive this man—he knows not . . ."

With a swift motion, The Ruler ended the man's speech with a long cut through the neck. The man died then, in a swift gush of bright blood. The Ruler could not believe the gall of the man. No one made excuses for him. The guard was the one who needed forgiveness, forgiveness for his traitorous deeds. The Ruler once again lost control, and began to stab repeatedly into the unmoving body.

After spending his energy, hate and fear, the ruler stood up, leaving the blade planted in the man's neck. He looked down at himself. He was covered in blood and gore. Then he looked at the hacked body on the floor. The guard's body was a bloody mess, but it was the face, not the body that disturbed him. The man's face was locked into restful smile.

The Ruler backed away, wiping his hands on his equally bloody coat. He ran to the wall and pulled down a tapestry and began to scrub wildly at the blood covering his body. For a time he twist and turn within the tapestry, coating it with gore and blood. Then he frantically unwrapped himself and dropped it to the floor. His hair stood on end, held up by drying blood. Streaks of gore were drying on his face and arms. He looked like death and insanity personified, standing with eyes bulging, and breath escaping in ragged pants.

He could not escape that smile. "Wha—What—What—What are you smiling about! You are dead! I am alive, alive you see! Don't you get it? I won! I am still alive!"

He ran across the room to the smiling man and lifted him by the head. With adrenaline enhance strength, he lifted the man until the dead, smiling face was equal to his. The Rulers arms quivered with effort as he looked at the man. "Tell me what it is! You kept a secret, and I must know it! You will not die until you have told me, you must not!"

Finally, his strength, and his sanity, completely gave out. He crumpled to the floor on top of the dead man. He rolled around the floor, holding onto the messy corpse for a time, shouting incoherently, and finally passed out from exertion.

Later, Myra, who had first discovered the gruesome scene, led the two guards and Tupar, the guard captain, into the room. The Ruler lay on the floor holding onto the dead man. His eyes were unfocussed and he babbled endlessly. "They all know—took it to Hell with him—Ha, I will not kill the next one—got to know, secrets—secrets—kill them first—I am alive—alive—d'rakken mahre will do it—Ha, ha, to Hell." The diatribe went on endlessly.

The scene spoke for itself. Tupar decided quickly that this decision was out of his league and cleared the room. Outside the door, he ordered the two men to allow no to enter the room, unless accompanied by him, and quickly departed to the barracks level to seek help.

Myra went back to do her job with a smile on her face. No one even noticed the blood on her foot from where she had kicked The Ruler. Her foot ached, but she felt deeply satisfied and safe for the first time in years.

Later that day, after secretly spiriting The Ruler to a secure prison cell in the southern guard complex, near the entrance to the under-earth, a small group of military leaders discussed the future of Torance.

They met in the room of the Caravan Guard. The three hundred men that comprised the permanent caravan guard were all under full alert. All entrances and exits, both to the under-earth, and to the main cavern, were sealed and heavily guarded.

The assembled men included Ardra, the General of the Lower Troops, Tisen, Allin, Urnat, and Howat, his most trusted Majors. Additionally in attendance were Garteth, the Captain of the Southern Complex, and finally Tupar, the Captain of the Manor

Guard, who had clearly shown his discretion in his handling of the situation thus far.

The meeting was held secretly, and the complex was locked under the ruse of a direct order from The Ruler. Ardra was confident in the loyalty of the men surrounding him, but realized that these men only commanded about half of Torance's militia. Another thousand men were quartered in the castle above, and the hand picked of The Ruler led these men, and they would likely remain loyal to the wishes of The Ruler.

They plotted no less than the complete takeover of Torance. Ardra was present at the meeting with the d'rakken mahre, and knew what his orders had been. The Ruler had never intended to allow passage to the d'rakken mahre. His plan had been to take the wealth offered, and then force the d'rakken mahre to find another way to the surface. Despite the words of the d'rakken mahre liaison, he believed they meant to destroy his city to recover the jewels they had paid for passage.

Ardra knew that this would lead to the complete destruction of Torance. He knew the power of the d'rakken mahre, and knew that the defenses of Torance would barely slow them down.

"Garteth," he began by addressing the Captain of the southern complex, who was the key to the entire operation. "You more than any of us knows the futility of resisting the d'rakken mahre. I propose we go along with the original agreement made with the d'rakken mahre. Your duty is to ensure that the portcullis is opened by the time the d'rakken mahre arrive, and clear the path to the main ramp. The civilians must not be allowed to panic and do anything foolish."

Garteth, a seasoned, competent soldier simply nodded. He had his orders, and would find a way to follow them. His loyalty was to the military structure within the city, and Ardra was the general. A change of orders posed little difficulty.

Tisen, one of Ardra's newest majors, interrupted, "Sir, if I may?"

Ardra nodded assent.

"Well, Sir," began Tisen, "I am sure that Garteth's men will follow orders, but what if someone decides to talk? If the castle troops discover what we are doing—" he let the implied threat hang for a moment. "How can we assure secrecy? We are all dead men if they find us out!"

Howat, one of Ardra's oldest and most seasoned majors grumped in response. "Hmp, get a grip man. The men need not know anything. They will do what their officers tell them, and you know who tells those officers what to do! Military men do not question orders . . . if they do you execute them on the spot! Now, the only ones that need know are those in this room, as well as several other carefully selected captains."

Ardra smiled at the grizzled older man. "Indeed, Howat, the men are not a concern. Our concern is executing this coupe in such a way as to avoid panic and bloodshed in the city. Our problems will begin once the d'rakken mahre have entered the city. At that point there will be no keeping a secret of it. The castle troops will seek to close the upper cavern exits to the topside and then retreat to the safety of the castle while the d'rakken mahre destroy us for betraying them. This is our biggest challenge.

"Howat, this is where you and your command come in. You will be stationed in the bailey with two hundred men, under the guise of training. As soon as we sight the draks, I will send two runners. When a runner reaches you, you are to clear the guards at the upper exit to the surface, as well as secure the main gate to the castle. You personally will lead your men into the inner castle. You are to take and hold the gate-room. If you can hold them, the castle forces will not be able to come against us, or bar the way against the draks.

"Not only must you hold, but enough men must survive to open the gates once the draks have left. Then the battle begins for control of the city. Hopefully the heart will be out of them and we can take the inner castle with little resistance."

Howat pondered his role for a moment. "It will be a close thing, Sir. I estimate that two hundred men can hold for about two hours, no more. Once fatigue sets in, they will cut us down like winter wheat. Don't keep us waiting."

"Two hours should be enough. Just be sure you make it."

"Aye, Sir. Two hours, my word on it." Howat had given his word, and he would make it two hours. He guessed he would open the gate alone, or with his last few men, but he would make it two hours.

"Tisen," Ardra continued, "you will secure the path for the draks to travel upon, and keep the civilians away. Take them up the Southtown ramp, it's the largest and keeps us away from city streets. Once to the main level, take them up Twilight way to the Dark Court ramp. From there it's just a short trip to the bailey without any more civilian involvement."

Tisen, looking nervous and unsure, nodded his assent.

"Now, finally, Allin and Urnat. You two must control the city. If civilians panic and attack the draks, they will be slaughtered in response. They will protect themselves with single minded and devastating effectiveness. This we must avoid! First, I want your troops to backup Tisen's along the selected passage, and second I want them spread out throughout the city in double patrols. I want them to reassure the citizens, and if necessary control them. Have the men prepared for riot situations. Shields and clubs only, understand?"

Both men nodded.

"In addition to this, I want you to bring the owner of every private guard company, as well as every hunter, mercenary, and retired soldier to these quarters. I want them bought using the jewels in those chests." He indicated the two chests that had been brought from The Rulers quarters. "Buy their services at regular rates, and promise quadruple pay for their silence. Also promise a large bonus upon successful storming of the castle. Once the gates are opened, they are going to be our shock troops. They will suffer losses, but that's why we will be making them such rich men. Understood?"

The two officers both nodded again; there were no questions. What they undertook was a life or death struggle. A general's job was to set goals, and his officers were to achieve these goals through superior execution. Of course there were no questions.

They had a fighting chance, which was better than they had had before this coup began. It was enough.

# NINETEEN

## WINDS OF WAR

Davan's booted feet crunched through the light frost that covered the dying brown grasses that grew sparsely on the large knoll his pavilion occupied. A heavy fog covered the entire area surrounding the Moghin Hills during the night, generating the first frost of the season. As the sun rose into the sky, warming the air towards what promised to be a crisp, bright fall day, the fog dissipated until only thin tendrils remained snaking along the lowest points between the hills.

Upon arrival the previous day, Davan had met with his officers and begun their integration with those already upon the field. Camped in the shallow valley near the hill he had set up command on, the main camp of his army was stirring itself into readiness for the day. From his vantage point, it was much like watching a nest of ants that had been stirred with a stick.

Close to fifty thousand troops were encamped in the immediate area surrounding the hill, half from the long encamped Third Army, and the rest from Davan's First, as well as small segments of the Second, and the Fourth.

The vast majority of the troops from the Second and Fourth had been sent out in division strength to support the scattered divisions of the Third securing the near two hundred miles of the Thulistan border. The total count of divisions in the field had reached fifty-two by the end of the previous day. The Emperors own Engineering Division from the Fourth Army was the last division to trudge in during the late hours of the night.

Davan walked the perimeter of the hill, the three marshals he had held back in camp standing at attention, awaiting his orders. They were, he knew, all solid officers—veterans. He sent the two more recently promoted marshals to the field to help ease the integration of new divisions into the Third Army. After a prolonged ten minutes of walking and contemplating, he paused in front of his marshals.

"Marshal Owans," he addressed the Marshal of the Second Host, First Army, the only one of his own marshals he kept nearby. "You will see to the assignments of the Engineering Division. I would like them broken down by field battle engineer group. I want the twenty groups to advance to the border and begin fortifications at five-mile intervals running from the border of the Welkwood to the western edge of the Moghin Hills. Tell them they have ten days to complete the fortifications, using all available troops as labor.

"I want log palisades, bordered by trenches, as well as sturdy forts to utilize as fall back positions. Understood?"

"Aye, Sir," Marshal Owens clicked his heels smartly, saluting fist over heart. "Sir, I will send them with general orders for the marshals on the field, instructing them to assist in the construction, and then to hold the forts until further orders."

"Excuse me," interrupted Yith, a shrewd greying marshal of many seasons along the Barstol border. "Perhaps we should double up the divisions on the field, so that each fortification can be held by a full division, while its active partner division patrols the assigned segment of border in battle group patrols."

Yith looked at the other four men about him, and upon seeing agreement on their faces continued. "It only makes sense, utilizing the palisades as a central location to billet the men between patrols. This way, we fully utilize fully forty divisions, leaving only the remaining fifteen to twenty divisions on the way from the Second and Fourth to support our main thrust, as well as lend additional support to the far west. Even though it's nearly unthinkable that they would attack from there, it pays to cover all bets."

Davan compressed his thin lips into a grim smile. He approved of forthright suggestions from his chief officers. The short and grizzled Yith surprised him. Behind the puckered face, one eye glazed from an unfortunate knife wound, was a keen mind, able to grasp tactics on a grand scale.

"Excellent, Marshal Yith. Marshal Owens, see that the orders are written. Write them under my name as Field Commander, and co-sign them under the seal of the Third Army.

"Marshal Horath," he addressed the third and final man accompanying him on the hill. Horath was a fighting man, still young and fierce, the perfect man to lead a force into battle. "I want you to personally take a squad of hunters for protection and locate Marshal General Kratch. He is traveling with the Third Division, Fourth Host currently. You should find him near the Welkwood. He has been trying to keep the wood free from trespassers. Personally pass on a copy of the orders, as well as my personal instructions to take command of the border fortifications."

Davan knew that Marshal General Kratch was avoiding him. A copy of the orders placing him in charge should have arrived over a week before. Just under a week ago, he was told, the Marshal General had left to tour with an outward-bound division, considering the imminent warfare, this was borderline mutiny. Davan was not about to show concern over his wayward second in command. To the contrary, he intended to act as if the Marshal Generals absence was part of his plan. He would deal with the man after the campaign, and until then, Kratch would be kept very busy.

Peering northward, Davan rubbed his chin. "Yith—how many men do the Thulistans have massed along the border?"

"Sir, our scouts have been very busy trying to answer just that question. The fact is, they move around so quickly, and travel in such differing sized groups, it is near impossible to say."

"Best estimate?" Davan had assumed that Yith would have an

accurate count if such were possible. The fact that no clear estimate was available was disconcerting.

"Well—best estimates range from twenty to over one hundred thousand. Depends which scout you ask. My estimate—over a hundred thousand, Sir."

Davan swallowed his surprise, keeping his visage outwardly calm. He was led to believe that the Thulistans could not field so many. If Yith were correct, which Davan did not doubt, then the Tulisian forces were in for a battle of even odds, in weather that favored the enemy, on the enemy's soil. This was not going to be a good day.

"Sir," continued Yith. "It may get worse. I've traveled in Thulistan extensively in years past. They have challenged my host many times, and that was with only one or two families raiding across the border. The fact is; I believe that we may soon be up against many entire clans, possibly all of them."

Yith scratched his head slowly, thinking over the rest of his thought. "That means, Sir, there could be as many as a hundred thousand more coming. I have suggested many times to the Emperor, may he live forever, that he greatly underestimates the size of the Thulistan population. They live widely spread, and do not have many large cities, but I believe that they can field an army of over three hundred thousand, if all clans were to come together in a common cause."

"Are you saying," began Davan slowly, "that our massing along the border may be just such a cause?"

"If we were to cross over, Sir—yes, it would. But not, I'm thinking if we stay put. They are a prickly lot Sir, a lot of positioning from clan to clan. It seems likely to me, that if this is something brought on only by a few clans, the others may stay out of it until they determine what action we take."

Horath, incensed by such talk to cowardice, could hold his tongue no longer. "Yith, if you haven't the stomach for a fight, then go camp with the whores and other women, and leave the fighting to men! Do not, however, use these fantastic, ridiculous premonitions of doom to protect your precious hide. If you want out, retire! The Marshal General would never allow . . ." realizing where his tirade had led, Horath quickly became very silent.

Yith listened calmly to Horath. Davan understood the particular brand of fanaticism the army bred into men like Horath. In many ways, he shared Horath's beliefs in the superiority of the Tulisian armies. He was not, however, foolish enough to underestimate the importance, and legitimacy, of Yith's opinions and information.

Forestalling any further infighting, Davan made a curt gesture with his hand. "That will be enough, gentlemen. Horath, you have your orders, and will carry them out. Thank you. I have my orders also, and will carry them out. To do so, I require all information, and opinions, so that I may formulate the best strategy to achieve our goals."

Horath sniffed and turned crisply on his heals, after making only a minimal effort at a salute.

"Marshal Yith—that will be all. You have your orders."

Yith stood for a moment, watching the Horath's retreating back. Before the pause caused Davan to again address him, he smiled and made a crisp hand over heart salute. "Aye, Sir. It will be done as you say." Without further word, he turned and marched away, a slight limp adding to his aura of toughness.

As soon as the others were out of earshot, Owans cleared his throat loudly.

"Speak freely Owans. As always, I trust and value your insight."

"Horath worries me, Sir. He is not a tactician, and not really happy with the change in command. Are you sure sending him to the Marshal General was a good idea?"

"The Marshal General has already stated his allegiances. He has ruled his own empire up here for many years, and will not accept me as commander. Although I have the support to bring him into the fold, it would cause excessive friction. If the men are to fight, I can't have them do it with that sort of uncertainty on their minds. Horath and Marshal General Kratch will join forces to the east. Kratch will bring in the Fourth Host under his command, and Horath will likely collect up the vast majority of the Second Host on his way east."

"But, Sir..."

"No—listen Owans. The fact is I do believe Yith. Nonetheless, I am under orders to take Thulistan with our forces, regardless of circumstances. I believe our only hope is to meet directly with the Carstans before we engage the Thulistans.

"Kratch, and his twenty thousand will take an offensive stance on the eastern borderlands, pulling a large portion of the Thulistans towards him. With Horath goading his ego on, they will advance within the week, expecting to force our hand into a flanking maneuver. Unfortunately, he is going to be on his own."

Owans eyes widened at the last statement. "Sir, you can't possibly mean to allow twenty thousand men to die?"

"The penalty for mutiny is death Owans. In their death, they will serve a purpose. We will not move to protect them. The Thulistans will see that we are staying put, and leave only enough force nearby to ensure we don't surprise them in a flanking maneuver. At that point we will gather in the remaining three Hosts and move directly North at full march. They will not be prepared to stop us from moving north, away from where we should be going.

"We pull them along behind us as they seek to stop us from reaching Terney, the capitol city. We should meet up with the Carstans long before then, and then we can turn and crush them against the remains of the Fourth and Second Hosts, as well as the two hosts we will leave behind in the new fortifications. If the Carstans have done their job there will be no large forces ready to attack from our rear."

Owans, smiling broadly, finished the thought for Davan. "We will have destroyed near to half of their forces, even at Yith's worst estimate, with the loss of only two Hosts! Is it a safe guess that we will then dig in, and hold the fortifications until spring, after sending word of a stunning victory, despite surprising enemy strength? Is it further safe to assume that the Emperor, pleased with our progress, despite not completing our goal, will send additional troops in the spring—enough to allow us to finish the job?"

"Very good Owans. In the spring, we can march, spirits high, with as many as a hundred and fifty thousand troops. The Emperor will have to strip the outlying areas bare, but will risk it. By then, the Fifth and Sixth may even have been reformed to support the stable fronts to east and west, allowing more veterans to our campaign. Time is short, Owans. Send the appropriate orders."

"Sir!" Owans saluted smartly, eyes gleaming. Davan 'av Carpea always won, and this would be his greatest victory.

The rest of the world, however, did not share Owans' enthusiasm, or Davan's plans.

Far to the south, the few remaining officers of the First Host, First Army were hard pressed to maintain any sense of order in their southward retreat.

During the late hours of the night, the log palisades had been breached in numerous locations. Entire squads were annihilated by tens of thousands of invading elves pouring over and through the palisade. West Point itself received little or no warning as the host of elves fell upon it. The fort was systematically destroyed through magic's never before seen by men. Logs burst into splinters at the touch of the elves, and great long vines crept through small chinks in stone walls, growing until the walls themselves were torn down by their tendrils.

Of those inside, only very few escaped the carnage brought about by the elves. The elves themselves were terrible foes. They fought silently, and without weapons. Elves simply overwhelmed foes with numbers, swarmed over them and tore them apart with gleaming teeth and unbelievably strong hands and arms.

The main thrust of the attack had been from the north, where the Wild Wood encroached nearest the log palisade. Many of the squads that had been assigned the southern patrols, had seen the smoke arising from the north, and hastily returned to West Point. Some were caught in the battle and destroyed, and others escaped southward. Those that escaped met with others returning to the fort, and collected them up after describing the hopelessness of the situation at the fort.

The fleeing remnants of the First Host numbered less than two thousand by the time they reached Mid Point and joined the bulk of the Third Army. Between the eight thousand dead from the First Host, and the numerous patrols of the Fifth Host, who had been on rotation to the far southern forts, as well as providing additional patrols along the central regions, over ten thousand were assuredly dead. Others were scattered to the north and east.

Marshal Alvir, who was last seen upon the walls at West Point, was undeniably dead, and the whereabouts of Marshal Troas, who had been touring the northern reaches of the log palisade, was unknown.

Marshal Ominat assumed command of the remnants of the First and Fifth Hosts and began to reinforce Mid Point Fort. The fort was protected by the waters of Lake Mid Point, and was many miles from the Wild Wood, but overconfidence had already cost the First army a full Host or more.

With those men still coming in, as well as those that could be pulled from Far Post and Torcoth Keep, Ominat would have fifteen thousand men at best to recapture West Point. At any costs, he knew West Point must be retaken. West Point was the key to the Tulisian Empires Western border. If not retaken, the elves would be free to move eastward into the vast farmlands that occupied western Tulisia. These farmlands fed much of the Empire, and boasted thousands upon thousands of homesteads.

Unfortunately for these farmers, their farms were on lands that, several centuries ago had been forested and inhabited by elves.

Unbeknownst to Ominat, West Point no longer existed. It, along with about fifteen miles of the log palisade, had already been dismantled and burned, clearing the way for new stands of tree plantings. Already, thousands of elves had left their labors on the log palisades to begin moving westward to retake the rest of their lands.

Ominat, having estimated that a minimum of fifty thousand elves, possibly many more, had poured out of the Wild Wood, wisely decided to call for reinforcements from the Fourth Army in Cartiel before beginning his counter campaign.

In a long bay on the Southeastern coast of Maldin, thousands of carpenters and boat wrights were finishing the final ships of the great fleet upon which they had labored for three years. The moderately populated agricultural island provided a perfect base for the rebuilding of the Tursysian Navy, and a marshaling point for the Tursysian Freedom Force.

The people of Maldin had not resisted the Tulisian invasion that had taken themselves and Tursys under the Tulisian yolk. Viewed as a strategically unimportant location with no natural resources to speak of, they were mostly left alone by the Tulisian Army. They only concession they had been forced to make was a monthly tithing of crops to feed the Tulisian forces on Tursys.

Over recent decades, the tithing began to rankle the proud, hard working farmers of Maldin. Although they had no desire to form an army of their own, they had been more than eager to harbor the growing Freedom Force of Tursys. The Nobles of Maldin, now numbering very few, were all distantly related to the Royalty of Tursys and were deeply dedicated to their cause. All of these factors sent much of the young population of Maldin flocking to the camps of the resistance forces, seeking glory. The fair skinned men of Maldin tended to be very large and solidly built, and made perfect recruits for the Tursysian Army.

During the building of this fleet, carefully placed enclaves of 'pirates' along the far reaches of the Tulisian Archipelago kept the prying eyes of the Tulisian fleet too busy to discover their actions. The armada consisted of over six hundred vessels of all shapes and purposes. The Tursysian Freedom Force consisted of over fifteen thousand sailors, and over twenty thousand soldiers.

Together, with the forces in place on Tursys itself, lying secretly in wait for the pre-ordained signal, they would outnumber the occupying Second Army. This, along with the fact they would have the advantage of surprise in their fight for freedom and country, gave them great confidence in their chances of success.

One man, a carpenter named Prat, had disappeared during the early hours of the morning. Prat had spent over a year scouting about Maldin before discovering the enclave of the Tursysian movement. After being captured by a patrol of outriders, it had taken him another four months to be allowed to leave the prison camp and be taken to the secret naval base to serve in building the fleet.

Two years ago, hundreds of Tulisian spies had been sent to Maldin to investigate the rumors of the formation of a resistance army. Prat had discovered, to his surprise, that only five of these men had made it into the camp itself. The previous night, one of the men had overheard a conversation between two Tursysian army officers. They spoke of deploying troops to the fleet within one month's time for the invasion. During the early hours before dawn, Prat and his four companions commandeered a small sloop rigged for speed and slipped away from the base.

He and the others would reach Odsel, a large city on the eastern coast of Tursys, within a week. From there they could inform the Marshal General of the Second Tulisian Army of the impending invasion. Their message would arrive in time for reinforcements to be called in from the Tulisian mainland.

In a small tent, within sight of the newly built invasion fleet, Tuvor, the Commander of the Tursysian Army met with Larin the Admiral of the newly rebuilt navy.

"They have left the camp." Tuvor, a short bulky man, spoke in brief, terse sentences. His gaze could bring any man into line, and he ruled his army with an iron fist.

"Can we assume, then, that the false information has been passed on, or did they simply flee before being caught?" Larin was as smooth as Tuvor was rugged. Dressed in the blue admiral's uniform with the red sash at his waist, the small Tursysian carried himself like a born leader.

Larin was, in fact the known leader of the Resistance Movement. He was the middle of the King of Tursys' three sons. The Tursysian royalty had been allowed to continue as a puppet government over the centuries. Larin had been secreted out of the capital city of Kapson at birth. None but the top officers in the Freedom Force knew Larin's true identity. Larin knew that the royal family would be executed as soon as his forces approached the capital city of Kapson.

He was prepared to achieve restitution for this act. He was prepared to make the Tulisian army pay for every death they had brought about during the centuries old occupation. Papers secreted in the royal palace would prove his identity in the event that the entire royal family was destroyed, and he would lead his country in its retribution against Tulisia.

Tuvor's gruff speech interrupted his reverie. "The first one to enter the camp, the cook, 'overheard' two of my officers discussing plans. They will expect us in about a month after the spies arrive in Kapson. Their arrival in Kapson will provide the long awaited signal for my troops secreted across the land. Word will pass like wildfire, and our arrival will begin the scouring of all Tulisian scum from Tursys!"

The underground network within Tursys would not miss the return of the Tulisian spies. The network had eyes and ears well placed within all of the major cities and Tulisian military installations. The Tulisians would find themselves fighting against Tens of thousands of armed and trained resistance fighters, as well as the newly assembled army of the Freedom Force itself.

"Very good, my friend, very good. I will pass orders; the fleet is to sail in one week. Will your men be able to deploy in time?"

"The Army is ready, and will be deployed on their assigned ships on time. Tursys will again be ours within the month. With the population of Maldin behind us, they will never dare threaten again!"

Long had Tethir, the King of Elindar awaited an opportunity to recapture the lush southern lands of Carstan. At one time, Carstan and Elindar had existed as one country under the name of Carstan. The people of Carstan were numerous, living in a feudal society centered around the many castles that the Carstans were so fond of. They were warlike and fierce people, with a deep love of weapons and combat.

Even before the Tulisians had come, there had been a split among the royal family regarding matters of governance.

Elindar, the eldest son of the king, resisted many of his policies of his father. Finding a lack of support among the family, he left the royal court at Doroth and traveled to the east, where dwelt many nobles that supported his position. There, he pulled together the many lords and landowners supporting him, and formed the country that would later be known as Elindar, named after its founder.

A century later, the Carstan welcomed the Tulisians. The two countries formed an alliance, with Carstan providing many of the arms and armor utilized by the Tulisian army; superior weaponry that helped the Tulisians conquer much of the known world. The Royal family of Carstan became very rich, and the population of the country continued to grow.

Elindar continued its struggles with Carstan during the following centuries; a Carstan backed by the military might of Tulisia. Sieges were held for decades at a time, and the tides of warfare ebbed and flowed. Slowly, however, the Tulisian backed Carstan was depopulating Elindar. Carstan had more soldiers, more military training, and more money. Elindar could barely feed itself.

Therefore, when Tethir heard of an Army of near thirty thousand Carstan mounted knights heading toward the Thulistan border, he decided to risk all in an effort to save his country from slow strangulation. Thus far, Tulisia had not directly interfered with matters of war between the two countries, and Tethir suspected that they cared little, as long as they got their weapons and tithes from Carstan.

It was well known that Carstan had stripped itself of nearly one third of its knights to support the Tulisian invasion of Thulistan. Although the remaining knights and mercenaries could easily hold the country against serious invasion, the sparsely populated southern tip of Carstan would be ripe for the taking. These lands were separated from the main portion of the country by a long spur of hills and mountainous country. The southern lands were primarily farmlands, and also boasted a deep-water port, something that Elindar lacked. Although Sorst, the capitol of Elindar was a port city, it was a shallow port, at the end of a bay controlled by a long stretch of Carstan coast. Very few ships came to Sorst.

Tethir sent royal orders to all of the knightly orders, as well as the lords of all manors and castles. The orders required that each lord and all knightly orders send half of their active knights to Sorst, where they would meet with the bulk of the Elindarian army, over twenty five thousand men at arms. With an army of over forty thousand, he would sweep through the southern lands of Carstan like a scythe through grass. Come spring, Elindar would occupy one third of Carstan's land, and Carstan would be hard pressed to re-take the lands after he fortified the hills against them. Their battles with Thulistan would prove more than enough to keep them busy.

If things went well, and with a little recruiting of mercenaries from the Free Cities, Tethir would hold. If not, death in battle was preferable to the slow economic and military strangulation they now suffered.


Before the Carstanian army entered into Thulistan, a scout arrived with reports of large-scale movements of knights within Elindar. Fearing collusion between the Thulistans and the Elindarians, the commander of the Carstan force determined that it would be wise to leave a force of knights to guard against the Elindarian knights and eliminate the threat. It seemed a prudent move, and one relatively safe. The Thulistans were little threat. With the combined might of the hundred thousand Tulisians and twenty thousand mounted Carstanian knights (the knights being the more dangerous opponents in his opinion), they would be crushed just as quickly as they would with thirty thousand mounted knights. Like swatting flies with a sword, he thought.

Orders were given and the Knights of Saint Hespah, ten

thousand strong turned to await the oncoming Knights of Elindar. They would pull in soldiers and knights from Napsin and Doroth to the south and hold the border with over forty thousand men, easily enough once fortifications were in place.

Meanwhile, thousands of knights and soldiers moved to the agreed upon marshaling grounds in southern Elindar, far away from the awaiting Carstanian army.

In Thulistan, Nemsith, the Mal S'hapur-la called upon all S'hapur-la to attend him in Terney. The call had gone out quickly and the response was just as quick. Within several weeks, all fifteen S'hapur-la were in attendance. Nemsith, having come from Clan Olbaric, fully knew the dangers of the Tulisian buildup. Clan Olbaric had made a general call to arms, and many of the assembled men had seen many of their younger warriors, hot blooded and eager to prove themselves, flock to the call.

Nemsith, however, was most concerned with the Eastern border. Should Tulisia advance to the west, Carstan, their longtime allies would not be far behind in the east. This could prove most dangerous to the relatively small Clan Larrs who held the long stable border.

Within two days, the diverse, independent clans of the Thulistan Empire developed a plan to work together to hold their borders against all foreign forces. Clan Larrs would be reinforced with men from their northern neighbors' clans Traagson, McKallinson, and Clan Trakarie from the Tulan Hills. These clans had lost few men to Olbaric's call to arms, and together would provide over thirty thousand mounted warriors to the border, enough to hold, or at least drastically slow an army of any size until reinforcements could be called if necessary. Of the remaining clans, most had been greatly depopulated by the call to arms, and the Mal S'hapur-la would not require any clan to go under half strength. Clans' Driskarie and Grathson who inhabited the lands near Terney, in the Frost Steppes, would hold back much of their forces to move either west or east as needed. In addition to this, they would guard against the possibility of a Naval attack on Terney itself (considered very unlikely with the oncoming winter).

Prepared to hold their borders against the entire world if necessary, the Mal S'hapur-la of Thulistan sent all of the S'hapur-la proudly back to their people, prepared to once again hold back the tides of war. Nemsith knew that the Tulisians had surprised Thulistan centuries ago in an attempt at conquest. After a bitter, long fight they had been repelled, and wounded deeply enough not to try again; until now. This time, he vowed, they would meet a prepared enemy, and would learn a lesson they would never forget.

# TWENTY

## THE HAPPY WIDOWER

After two days of hard riding, all the while avoiding Tulisian patrols, Taire, Morgan, and Halnan crossed the border into Desil. The weather had been cold and damp, great grey clouds loomed overhead, blocking the sun completely from view. Once across the border they began to travel on the main road, which ran from Terney in Thulistan, all the way to Parnan and eventually into Tulisia itself.

In Desil, truce held, and the three riders were able to ride amongst troops of Tulisians moving northward without fear of molestation. Hostile words were exchanged, primarily between Halnan and most of the passing Tulisian riders, but no further actions were taken. In Desil, economic power was the potent glue that held together the fragile truce, even during wartime.

This continued for two more days as they made quick progress along the stone paved road. Late during the second day, the tall spires of Parnan became visible as the party crested a long low incline.

"What's that?!" Upon seeing the gleaming towers in the distance, Taire stood high in his stirrups, shielding his eyes with his hand. Excitement was evident in his voice.

Halnan laughed at Taire's juvenile enthusiasm, glad to see signs of joy in the young man. "That, my sheltered young friend is Parnan, one of the oldest, the largest, and most certainly the richest cities in the world."

Morgan, who also had been peering ahead added, "as a matter of fact, those glittering white and gold towers you see are the ancient Towers of Learning, they form the foundation of the University of Ancient Learning. It was the first, and is still the largest of the educational centers in Parnan."

Taire, who barely even listened to Morgan's speech, lightly kicked his horse into a canter, forcing Morgan and Halnan to increase pace to keep up. "How old Halnan? How big? And how rich?"

"Hold up, Taire. One question at a time please! Morgan is the better historian, so perhaps he could answer best. It gives him a chance to earn his S'hapur's pay every now and again."

Taire stopped his peering into the distance for a minute to look over at Morgan. "You mean S'hapur is a job? I thought it was just a title, something you got from your father or something. How much does it pay?"

Morgan glared at the smiling Halnan. "Taire, S'hapur is not just a family title, it is an honor bestowed by—oh, never mind, I guess it doesn't really matter right now does it?" He turned away from Halnan, unable to bear his victorious smile. "Anyhow, to answer your question, Parnan is over three thousand years old by most accounts, the oldest city outside of Cartiel in Tulisia, and Kapson on Tursys.

"The city grew up around the University of Ancient Learning, which was built by the early colonists from Tursys who sought to create a society based on education and the arts. Parnan grew up around the university, and soon other universities were founded: The University of the Arts, the University of Philosophical Pursuits, and finally, about five hundred years ago, the University of Commerce and Trade. The University of Commerce and Trade was formed as a result of the explosion of Desil's banking industry, which actually provided the money that led to Desil's growth as an independent country, and eventually its complete control of the worlds economy."

Morgan, pausing to catch a breath, discovered that Taire and Halnan had ridden ahead out of earshot. He had been so caught up in his storytelling that he hadn't noticed the two breaking away. With a huff of irritation, he kicked Bran into a full gallop to quickly cover the distance between them.

As he caught up to the other two, he slowed pace to equal theirs. "Excuse me, gentlemen, but I was in the middle of answering Taire's question. Why did you ride off?"

Halnan was stony faced, but Taire, who responded to Morgan's question looked sheepish. "Well—I wanted to know about the city, it looks so magnificent! But—well—I just wanted to know three simple things—I was afraid that you were about to start explaining the building process of the city itself, and..."

Morgan interrupted, "That will be enough Taire." He turned his stern gaze to Halnan. "You have been a very bad influence on Taire. I try to give a little important history to enrich the visit for the lad and you—oh, never mind" he finished dispiritedly.

Halnan, still maintaining a straight face, sat with eyebrows raised at Morgan's failed explanation.

Halnan's expression proved too much for Morgan. He sputtered for a few moments before he began to chuckle lightly to himself. "Yes, yes—you are right. It was boring drivel, not at all something that our young friend would want to hear. All right, here it is Taire. As I said, it is older than the dirt itself. The city; the capital of Desil, is also one of its three major cities. It is believed to house over two hundred thousand, mostly bankers and scholars. Finally, Parnan is richer than you could ever believe. It is said that those towers are plated with gold, and the people are paid a stipend simply for being residents of the city. No one lacks for food, shelter, or four horse carriages in Parnan."

Taire turned in his saddle to face Morgan. "Thank you. I am sorry I was rude before, but I've never dreamed of anything like it, and I was eager to see it. Maybe later you can tell me the rest?"

"Oh please, could you?" Halnan mimicked. He could not miss the opportunity to play on Taire's enthusiasm.

For what seemed to Morgan like the hundredth time since dawn, he found himself scowling at Halnan. "Shut up," he muttered.

"Snappy comeback," returned Halnan.

Morgan's scowl turned into a chuckle again. Someday, he would figure out how to get the best of Halnan in a verbal exchange.

As they approached the city, many other tall towers and exotic domes came into view. The buildings were enameled in all of the colors of the rainbow, as well as plated with copper, silver, or gold in some cases. As they came within several miles of the city, crowds had begun to thicken on the streets; traders bringing wares to the city, would be scholars seeking admittance to the various universities, and business men traveling to the holy Mecca of world commerce.

Taire's head turned side to side as he gawked at the people, and the city ahead. The noise of the passer's by drowned out any attempts at conversation.

By the time they reached the gate, they were wedged in near shoulder-to-shoulder crowds, consisting primarily of carts of foods and dry goods going to market. Taire's gawking was briefly interrupted as he struggled to maintain position near his two companions in the milling masses.

At the gate, a half a dozen guards watched impassively as the crowds jostled past, apparently not concerned with the comings and goings of the traders, bankers, and others entering the city. As they pass under the high arch formed by the gate, Halnan shouted over the din to Morgan. "Look northward!" He waited until Morgan looked to the north and saw the oncoming darkened line of an approaching rainstorm before continuing. "It's coming on quick, and looks to be a gully washer. Let's get to an inn, and quickly!"

Morgan grunted agreement, and Taire simply followed the two, watching the downpour move closer, obscuring the landscape in sheets of water.

The rainstorm came on quickly, and the only warning they had before they were drenched in its deluge was a faint hissing noise as the rain pelted the dry streets close behind them. They were all thoroughly soaked by the time they located suitable lodging.

They selected an inn called the Happy Widower. A large sign, brightly painted and swinging lightly in the winds, depicted a man, wearing black, kicking his heals near a tall tombstone. The inn itself was a long two-story building, with a large stable outside. As Morgan climbed down from his horse, a thin young man came out from the stables and took the reigns of his horse. "A silver a day for all three, Sir." His teeth were chattering in the cold.

"That will be fine. Taire, will you help this lad stable the horses, and be sure they get wiped dry and brushed?"

Taire, hair dripping into his face, looked sullen at the thought of having to wait longer before drying off and warming before a fire. "Sure, I'll be in in a bit."

Halnan dismounted laughing gruffly. "Don't grumble like a child, Taire! The quicker you get going, the quicker you'll be warm and dry!"

With a look halfway between consternation, and embarrassment, Taire took the reigns from Halnan and followed the stable hand into the stables leading his mount and Halnan's.

The stables were warm and dry, with a musty odor of horse and hay. The effect was comforting. The stable hand had already found three open stalls together and was busy wiping off Bran in the first stall. "Bring them over here," he waved to Taire. "By the way, my name is Karrel. What's your name?"

Taire turned towards the boy and noticed for the first time that they were of very similar age. Karrel looked to be fifteen or sixteen years old, although he was much smaller than Taire's lanky six feet. "Nice to meet you Karrel, I'm Taire."

"Well Taire, why don't you take off your wet cloak, and we'll get these horses wiped down quick-like. Who are the two men you travel with? Is one of them your Da?"

Taire tossed his dripping cloak over a low beam on the side of the stall and noticed that it was steaming in the warmth of the stable. He took up a blanket and began to wipe down Halnan's horse first. "They are Morgan and Halnan, the one with the fierce eyes is Morgan. Neither is my Da, they are just good friends who

I share a common goal with. We have only been traveling together for a little under a month."

"If neither one is your Da, then did you run away to go adventuring? They both look to be fierce warriors, but you, well, you're big and all—but you just don't look like an adventurer if you don't mind my saying."

Taire moved on to his own mount, and Karrel began brushing Bran down. Taire thought a moment about what would be safe to say to the other young man. Although he had just met him, Taire liked the youth. Karrel had an open, honest face. He was typically Desilian, small boned and dark of complexion. Taire realized that Karrel was the first person his own age he had spoken to since trying to save the boy at The Rulers mansion.

Karrel worked industriously with his brush for a few minutes before looking to see it Taire was going to respond to his question. Although he was young, he was a sensitive young man, and saw the pain in Taire's vacant gaze. Taire was simply standing, bush in hand, unmoving next to his horse. The horse whuffed lightly and was nuzzling his shoulder with its muzzle, but Taire was not responding. "Hey, Taire," he spoke tentatively.

Taire shook himself as if startled.

"I'm sorry, I didn't mean to pry where I don't belong. It's not often I get to talk to someone my own age—at least I think you are, even though your as big as a horse—but anyhow, my Da always told me that I talk too much and ask too many questions. I am sorry though."

Taire smiled slightly and began to brush. He was still very wet, but beginning to warm up. "No, it's not anything you said, I was just remembering someone. It seems like such a long time ago, and he was just a kid, younger than you or I by a bit. He—well—something terrible happened to him. Anyways, like I said, it was a long time ago." Taire wanted to change the subject. "You spoke of your Da, is he the innkeeper?"

Now, it was Karrel's turn to frown, if ever so slightly. "No, my Da died two years ago and my mother left with a merchant instead of having to take care of me. Since then I have worked here in the stables for Rialthi, the innkeeper."

Taire looked at the young man in the stall next to him. He felt a sudden sense of camaraderie for the other youth. In Karrel, he had found someone whom he could talk to, someone who had experienced pain similar to his own. "I'm sorry, Karrel. You asked earlier why I would be with men like Morgan and Halnan—well, the answer is that my father and mother are both dead, my Da died earlier this year. I have no family, and Morgan and Halnan are the only friends I have. They have been very kind, despite their frightening demeanor. Morgan is kind of serious most of the time, but Halnan is sometimes quite the clown, actually."

Taire realized for the first time how much the two men had come to mean to him. He also was warming up to Karrel, and it felt great to be talking to someone his own age.

"It sounds like your lucky to have such friends, Taire. Rialthi is a goodly man, but not a friend, and I have little time to make other friends. I can't complain though: I eat, sleep here in the stables, and even make a copper now and again."

Taire looked around the stables. "Where do you sleep?"

Karrel dropped the brush, having more or less finished and bounded off in a rush of adolescent energy. "Follow me, I'll show you!"

Taire grinned and tossed the brush aside. He followed Karrel up a steep ladder into the loft. He climbed over the stacks of hay bales, ducking low to avoid hitting his head on the roof beams. Back in the far corner of the low ceilinged loft, a stack of hay bails formed a rough wall with a small doorway, over which a blanket hung. Taire pushed aside the blanket and stepped inside.

The room was over ten feet to a side and swept clear of hay. Up against the wall, under a small window was a small cot. In addition to this, the room had an old washstand, two chairs, and a small but solid table. A small lantern hung from the low ceiling, its flickering light casting ever-changing shadows across the room. The room was warm and relatively well furnished. It was obvious that the innkeeper was a kind man, and he took good care of Karrel.

"Wow, Karrel, this is a great room—and all to yourself?"

Karrel grinned broadly at the statement. "Yup, I even get to eat in the common room when it's not too busy—maybe I can eat at your table tonight and meet your friends? Anyhow, I even got a window to look out, come here and see. That's how I knew you and your party arrived, that way I don't have to get wet waiting for customers!"

Taire looked through the window down towards the entrance to the inn. He agreed it was a great setup, and a friendship was born. The two began to talk of many things great and small; Taire avoided talk of his quest, or anything involving Morgan and Halnan.

After about a half an hour, a loud voice interrupted their conversation. "Taire, where are you!" Taire jumped and rushed to the ladder, peering downwards with Karrel. The voice called out again, this time angrily. "Taire, I hear you up there—get down here! You haven't even brushed my horse!"

Taire climbed down the ladder, and Karrel simply jumped down, rolling lightly in the straw on the floor and coming to his feet. Karrel spoke first. "I am sorry sir, that is my job, and I will complete it right away!" He squeezed past Morgan and took up the brush and began to work diligently.

Taire stood at the base of the ladder, his face red. He knew Morgan would soon begin a stern lecture about his responsibilities.

Morgan, grim faced, walked over to Taire. He had surmised that the two young men had been up fooling about in the loft, and although he had at first been angry, quickly cooled down after seeing the sheepish look on the worried lad's face. Remembering his and Halnan's antics during their youth, he approached the squirming Taire. "Taire, Halnan and I have changed and warmed by the fires, while you have been out here doing—whatever you have been doing, while you should have been tending the horses. Now, dinner is about ready, why don't you go in and change."

Finally, he smiled at Taire and grasped his shoulder. "It must be nice to talk to someone your own age. Why don't you go get your cloak and ask your friend to join us for dinner?"

Taire smiled, and Karrel, who was listening carefully while

working, let out an involuntary whoop of relief and joy. Taire grabbed his cloak and ran for the inn after telling Karrel to meet them in fifteen minutes for dinner.

Under Morgan's watchful eye, Karrel finished his work with a will. Morgan stayed until the brushing was done and even helped the lad feed the horses. He tipped Karrel a silver. Karrel took the coin, his eyes wide with wonder. He had never held a silver before. It was more than he usually collected in a month. He slipped the coin into a small pouch in his coat and followed Morgan back through the rain to the inn.

Taire quickly changed, and was already seated next to Halnan at a small table near the fire when Morgan returned with Karrel in tow. The common room was large, boasting over a dozen small tables as well as several long tables; sturdy benches to each side. The storm had filled the room with travelers and merchants. Barmaids shouldered through the room with foaming mugs and steaming platters with practiced ease.

They ordered roast mutton for four, along with several hot loaves, and a plate of greens. Halnan ordered two mugs of ale for Morgan and himself, and Taire ordered cider, despite Halnan's offer of ale. Taire remembered how he felt after the last time he drank an alcoholic beverage, and was not eager to repeat the process.

Karrel, following close behind Morgan, protested as he saw the crowd. "Excuse me, Sir, but I can't join you when the room is so crowded. I have to eat in the kitchens—no disrespect to you, but that's the rules."

Morgan turned to Karrel. "Tonight, you are a guest of Halnan and myself. Halnan has already ordered for us all. Paying customers sit at tables, not in the kitchen."

With a grateful smile, Karrel joined Taire at the table, and thoroughly enjoyed shouting to the barmaids for refills of his mug, and more gravy for his mutton. The barmaids, scowling at him the whole while, complied only due to the generous tips given by Morgan. All in all, it was an enjoyable evening for all involved, and it was late before Karrel retired to his room, taking Taire with him; despite the rather expensive room Morgan had already paid for. Morgan and Halnan retired to their respective rooms, tired and content. They had both enjoyed watching the two youths enjoy each other's company. It brought up memories of their own youthful friendship, and easily justified the expense.

The next morning dawned brisk and clear, the storm having passed on to the south. Morgan awoke early and sent Halnan to the stable to fetch Taire. They saddled their horses with help from Karrel and prepared to leave for the University. Karrel and Taire stood off to the side, whispering furiously.

"Taire, it's time to get going." Halnan interrupted the whispered conversation of the two young men.

The whispering stopped and Taire turned to face Halnan and Morgan. "I know, but we—I mean—I was just thinking. Wouldn't this be easier if we had a guide, someone who knows the city? It just so happens that Karrel has already been granted the day off, and was willing to help us, free of cost!"

Morgan looked up with a smile from the job of checking his tack. "Free of cost, you say? Well, how could we pass up on such a bargain, although I am willing to wager that this will cost me at least the price of lunch!" He pretended to ponder for a moment. "Well, despite the cost of feeding you young brutes, it seems a fair deal. Lets be off then, Taire, you and Karrel can ride double."

It was only a short ride of about a dozen blocks to the outbuildings of the University of Ancient Learning. Karrel informed them that these buildings were primarily a smattering of private libraries, domiciles for the servants and lower staff members, as well as dormitories for the undergraduate students. These buildings were only slightly nicer than the surrounding homes, shops, and restaurants.

As they approached the five towers that comprised the center of the university; Karrel's running commentary turned to the towers themselves. "The four outer towers were built at the four points of the compass, with the fifth, the tallest, in the center. The center tower was built first, and is known as the Tower of Ancient Learning. It houses the Great Library, as well as providing housing space for the most senior tenured professors of the university. The other four towers are where the classes take place, and where the lesser professors live. Each outer tower has its own smaller library devoted to the material studied within the tower.

"Each tower represents a school of thought within the University itself. Starting from the tower with the blue and gold gilt roof—that's the western tower by the way—the schools are as follows, the School of Evolutional Patterns, the School of Random Happenings is the red and gold, the School of Cyclical Histories with the white and gold, and finally the School of Theological Guidance with the green and gold.

"As I understand it, each school represents a theory of how history and humans interact, although I couldn't explain what it all means. History is history, isn't it?"

Halnan nodded at Karl's commentary. "You know a lot about the university Karl, where'd you come by such knowledge?"

Karl shrugged. "Everyone knows at least that much if they live in the city. They teach it in school."

Each of the outer towers stood over two hundred feet tall, topped with conical roofs, colored with gold gilt, mixed with the color of the school. The central tower stood near to three hundred feet tall, and was topped in gold mixed with patterns of the colors from all of the schools. They were all broad based, growing like toadstools to their conical peaks.

Morgan, unaware of his non-sequiter, answered Karl's previous question. "I think history is history, but it's the interpretation, and the conclusions it leads us to that are changeable. Anyhow, let's avoid all of these interpretations altogether and head for the central building. The library is the best chance we have to learn what we need."

Karrel turned in his saddle towards Morgan. "And that is?" As soon as he said it, Karrel realized it was an over-bold question. Taire had made it clear that their business was not to be discussed. He turned back in the saddle away from the glowering Morgan.

Morgan decided it was better to address the situation, rather than ignore it. He rode up close and caught Karrel's eye. "It is something we will discuss in private, perhaps. But only if I believe you know when to hold your tongue. It is Taire's life at risk as well as Halnan's and my own."

Karrel swallowed. He had not realized that he had involved himself in a life and death situation of any sort. He resolved to keep quiet and mind his own business.

After a short time, they approached the entrance into the University proper. Trees lined the space from tower to tower, tall cypress growing closely together created a hedge of sorts. The lane on which they rode passed through the middle of the hedge, opening up to a huge open plaza.

All but Karrel gawked at the huge cobblestone plaza that occupied the space between the four outer towers. The plaza was a giant square of smooth cobblestones, with carefully tended gardens and trees interspersed throughout the square. Each garden had several benches and tables, almost all occupied by men in robes of blue, red, white or green. In many, a professor, marked by a golden sash around the robe, lectured to eager students; in others, students debated theory or studied ancient scrolls in the pleasant afternoon sun.

The overall effect was peaceful and almost magical as the robed men went about the business of learning.

The plaza itself declined slightly towards the central tower. At the bottom of the shallow bowl arose the massive bulk of the library, perhaps fifty feet taller than it had originally appeared due to its placement at the bottom of the decline.

Very few visitors were to be seen in the bowl, and more than a few robed men looked askance at the rough looking warriors and their two young companions.

It took about five minutes to reach the library, where Morgan quickly dismounted, handing his reigns to Halnan. "Stay here with Karrel. Taire will come in with me, and we will speak to a librarian regarding our problem. We may be a while, so don't get worried."

Without further bidding, Taire dismounted, leaving Karrel alone on the horse. He followed Morgan, who was already moving purposefully towards the high arched entrance to the tower.

Just inside the entrance they found a large square foyer with many doors along the side walls, as well as one large door, marked 'Reference' directly ahead. It was for this door that Morgan moved, with Taire in tow.

The door led to a corridor with a high vaulted ceiling. Tapestries and art decorated the walls, and bright lanterns cast a warm glow throughout the passage. After about fifty feet, the corridor opened into a large square chamber, which, Morgan surmised, occupied the center of the tower. The chamber itself was about twenty feet across with spiral staircases evenly spaced around its outer rim. These staircases led to a series of balconies lined with high shelves of books.

Taire craned his neck, counting the balconies. He could see men in robes of all colors moving about the various balconies. There were ten levels of balconies, each about ten feet deep, with bookcases radiating out from the outer wall like spokes on a square wheel, packed closely together. While Taire counted the bookcases on the first level, Morgan moved to the small central booth in the middle of the room to speak to the librarian.

After a few minutes of whispering, Morgan turned and walked quietly over to Taire, who was still staring upwards, nodding to himself as he counted shelves. Morgan tapped him on the shoulder to get his attention. Before Morgan could speak, Taire blurted excitedly, "There are ten balconies, and each one has thirty five book shelves. Each shelf looks to be ten feet high and almost that long. With that many shelves, there must be—well—tens of thousands of books here!"

Taire's outburst was met with several loud shushes from around the central floor.

Morgan couldn't help but smile. He remembered the fascination the young had in counting things, and could imagine the impact that the library was having on Taire. With a hushed voice he explained, "Taire, in a library, you have to be quiet! Anyhow, you are right, there are tens of thousands of books. That alone would be difficult, but the librarian just explained to me that this is just the reference section. All of these books are simply the reference library. He said that these books are used to narrow down the search on a topic, so we would know where to look for the actual books we need."

Taire's eyes widen in surprise. In a over-exaggerated whisper he began, "you mean . . ."

"Yes Taire, this is only a tiny fraction of the library. Many of the chambers surrounding this central chamber, the twenty full levels above this, as well as ten huge catacombs below are all filled with books. The assistant librarian at the counter explained to me that there are over two million books currently on file in the library. He was able to tell me that there was a reference section dealing with Thulistan early history, that may help narrow our search. Other than that, he explained that the stacks of texts written on Thulistan and its histories could be found in the seventh depth, one of the lower catacombs he explained. There are supposedly over ten thousand books there, and only a small portion are even cataloged."

Taire shook his head. "I guess we better use the reference section then?"

"A fine idea. This is going to prove very time consuming, I think."

The two, with directions from several Assistant Librarians, climbed several staircases and searched for several minutes before finding the reference section labeled 'Thulistan'. Within this section, they searched through several sub-sections, such as ancient history, clan history, political structure, and many, many others before settling on legends and mythology. Within this section there were only ten reference books.

"Pick a book," began Morgan skeptically. "Let me know if you find anything about d'rakken mahre, or k'aram mahre. For that matter, let me know if anything looks helpful."

Taire selected the book labeled 'A-C', and began to peruse it. Within the book were names of other books, accompanied by brief descriptions, the author's name, when the book was written, and a reference number to help locate the tome in the stacks.

During the next few hours, Morgan worked through four books, and Taire three. Taire was in the middle of the H's, and was reading carefully all the titles named 'History of . . .' Although he could not find any titles that appeared helpful, he did notice that many of the titles were written within the last fifty years, by the same author.

"Morgan," he said to get the other man's attention.

Morgan looked up from his book, blinked several times and knuckled his eyes. "Did you find something?"

"No—well maybe, depending on what you mean by 'find something', it's just that I was going through the section of titles beginning with the word History. None of them gives any real information as to whether it is what we want or not, but it seemed promising. There are several hundred titles though, and that alone could take more time than we have to peruse. Anyhow," he forestalled Morgan's impatience, "what struck me as interesting is that one author wrote over fifty of these books. Some were written seventy or more years ago, and a few as recently as fifteen years ago."

Morgan blinked again, not quite following. "So what is your point, Taire?"

In exasperation, Taire blurted loudly, "My point is, what if someone around here was his student, or something? They might help us weed through what he wrote!" At the last, he was nearly shouting. He blushed, looking around to see if anyone was about to shush him. Fortunately, no one else was nearby, and his outburst went mostly unnoticed.

"Taire, that is an excellent point! Thank you. Now, what is the name, so we can ask the librarian!"

The author's name was Mugwort 'na Krispin P.H.D. Armed with this information, they climbed back down to the librarian's desk.

The librarian, annoyed with their ignorance, explained. "Obviously, the P.H.D. indicates that the author is a past scholar of this school," (a fact that neither Taire or Morgan was aware of, as neither had any experience with educational titles). "As such," the pinch faced little librarian continued, "information regarding him and any protégés he may have had can be found in the Education section of the reference library, subheading Students, or possibly even Staff. Now, try to think of your own answers in the future before bothering me. I am a busy man, and the reference library is set up so that even ignorant, uneducated louts such as yourselves can figure it out!"

Morgan, hand on dagger hilt, leaned in towards the man until his face was only inches away from that of the diminutive librarian. In a quiet, menacing voice he spoke. "Perhaps, friend, you need to find the section on courtesy. If not, then look up something on pain. That way, you will understand what you are feeling next time you speak so to me. Thank you for your assistance."

Morgan turned and walked away, never noticing that the small man was trying in vain to cover the wet spot on the front of his robe. Red-faced, he stood, covering his front with a large book, and walked quickly towards a side door. Trying to hide his shame, he exited to a small private chamber where he proceeded to have a small nervous breakdown.

A half an hour later, Morgan and Taire emerged triumphantly from the library. They found Halnan and Karrel relaxing on a bench and eating fruit they had purchased from a nearby vendor. The horses contentedly munched on a low shrubbery nearby, much to the consternation of a nearby gardener, who seemed afraid to mention the fact to the large warrior and his friend.

Halnan noticed their arrival first. "Ho, Morgan and Taire. Did you find your book and get your answer?"

Taire and Morgan exchanged a look that neither Karrel nor Halnan understood before Morgan answered.

"Halnan, we have some information that may help, though finding a book with the answers was perhaps a bit—shall we say—optimistic. Anyhow, it appears that a man named Mugwort was a professor here up until about fifty years ago, and has written many texts regarding ancient history in Thulistan, some as recently as fifteen years ago."

"All right," began Halnan, "so now we go talk to a dead guy?"

"The book says he is not dead! Or at least wasn't five years ago when the reference book was last updated." Taire's excitement had been mounting ever since he found the name, and he couldn't wait any longer without voicing his enthusiasm. He saw the look that Halnan was giving him and continued. "He would just be—well, really old," he finished lamely.

"As a matter of fact," added Morgan, "according to the book, he would be over one hundred and forty years old."

"Like I said," remarked Halnan, "we go find the dead guy."

Taire and Morgan mounted up. Morgan waited for Halnan to do the same, and for Karrel to climb up behind Taire. "Either way," continued Morgan, "we have an address of a private residence. Although he should be dead by now, whoever lives there would likely know something of Mugwort, and perhaps lead us to a student who knows of his studies. It's our best shot. Either way, we won't know until we try!"

Halnan, however, was convinced that they were about to embark on a wild goose chase, wasting precious time. Scowling his displeasure, he reluctantly followed his friends as they rode off into the city.

# TWENTY-ONE

## A MOMENT'S CLARITY

After only getting lost three times under Karrel's 'expert' guidance, they found the address listed in the reference book. The building was on the outskirts of the University properties, many blocks away from the towers. It was a long, low stone building with a high black iron fence surrounding it. The grounds were in disarray; overgrown with weeds and creeping vines, which also covered most of the building itself.

The front gate hung askew on one hinge, allowing the four to squeeze through after dismounting and tying the horses to the fence itself. They walked on cracked flagstones to a well worn, but still solid, wooden door. Morgan pulled a frayed cord near the door. In the distance behind the door, they could hear a dull clanging of a loud doorbell.

After several minutes of waiting, Taire and Karrel wandered off a few feet and began to chat quietly. Morgan paced within the tight confines of the doorway, and Halnan drummed his fingers on the stone wall, his patience at an end.

"This is a waste of time!" Halnan barked, turning to face Morgan. "I say we either search the books, or head back to meet with Norin and the d'rakken mahre! But I will not wait for a ghost to answer this door any longer!" He turned crisply and began to walk back towards the gate, pushing through the surprised Taire and Karrel.

Before the bewildered Morgan could respond, a soft grating sound caught his attention. He looked at the door from which the sound came, and after a quick scan, saw that a small panel had slid open at about waist level. He knelt slowly down and carefully peered into the hand sized opening. At first he could only make out darkness behind the panel, and then, the opening of an eye broke the darkness.

Morgan jumped back in alarm, and then moved slowly forward again. Taire and Karrel moved forward to see what had captured Morgan's attention, while Halnan squeezed through the gate oblivious to it all.

"Hello, who's there?" asked Morgan gently, as he met the blinking eye at the small portal.

"Hey, unfair! That is my question to ask. Who are you? Did Heechee send you?" The voice was thin and high, cracking from time to time. There was more than a hint of insanity in the voice.

Morgan waved Taire and Karrel over. Halnan, seeing that something was going on back at the door, turned from his horse and again passed back through the gate.

When the party was fully assembled in view of the small opening, Morgan made introductions. "My name is Morgan, and this is Taire, Halnan, and Karrel." He pointed to each in turn. "We are here in hopes of getting information regarding a Mugwort 'na Krispin, the author. I know nothing of any Heechee, though."

"Mugwort," responded the voice, "you seek Mugwort? What could two Thulistans, a Desilian and a—where is the big lad from? Anyhow, what could you want from Mugwort, except to spy for Heechee? Tell him to rot!"

The small portal slammed shut.

Halnan stepped forward and slammed his fist on the door. "Sir—open up! As my friend Morgan said; we need to speak to this Mugwort! If you be he, or if you know of him, please let us in. The d'rakken mahre are marching and we must know what they are about, so we can protect our . . ." Halnan cut himself off as he realized what he had just shouted.

Morgan looked pained at his friend's indiscretion, and Karrel looked from Morgan to Halnan in horror. "The d'rakken mahre? You mean the devils of the legends walk the earth, and you think you can to stop them—I—are you nuts—I knew you were involved in some trouble, but this is too much—I'm sorry Taire, but I'll keep my skin a while longer!"

All three had turned from the door to look at the raving Karrel, who upon finishing, turned and ran, leaving his friend and the two older men.

Before anyone could speak, the noise of the door opening behind them caught their attention. As one, they turned towards the slowly opening door. From within the widening gap of door could be heard grunts of effort as the man tried to force the rusty hinges to work. Halnan leaned in and lent assistance to the effort and the door came open the rest of the way more easily.

Within the dim light inside the doorway stood the smallest, oldest man any of them had ever seen. He was stooped and shriveled, standing barely over five feet tall. His skin clung tightly to his bones, and his head was adorned by a few long wisps of white hair that hung down over his shoulders. He had two teeth that they could see, and his nose was long and narrow. Despite all of this, his eyes shone brightly.

The animated skeleton looked carefully up at them. "D'rakken mahre you say? Walking the earth? Oh my, I shall have to write of this—indeed—but my hands, my poor hands can't hold the pen so well any more." The insanity crept in and out of his voice as he cackled on. "Are you sure you were not sent by Heechee, using a lie to gain admittance—he has always wanted to get at my original research."

"Old man," began Halnan impatiently. "We are not . . ."

Morgan cut off Halnan with a hand on the shoulder. "Mugwort, you are Mugwort aren't you?"

The old man clapped his hands. "Of course I am. Who else could I be? Trying to fool me, I see. Well it won't work, I am Mugwort no matter what you say!" He seemed to suddenly realize he was ranting and clapping and seemed to come to himself for a minute. "Yes, well, come with me to my study. It's warmer there, helps my old bones. Follow, and tell me what you know of the d'rakken mahre. Talk quickly now, I'll remember, but the mind comes and goes now. Old, I'm too old, but still have much to do, history goes on, and my studies never end. Talk . . . talk. Come on!"

Mugwort began a rapid shuffle away from the open door, which Halnan pulled shut before following. As they walked, Morgan, along with input from Taire and Halnan began to explain in quick, brief sentences the news regarding the d'rakken mahre. As this was their single best chance to learn about the d'rakken mahre, they left nothing out, political or personal.

After reaching the study, a large room cluttered with shelves and tables stacked with books, they continued their narration. For about an hour they shared all, and finally, near when they were done, Mugwort seemed to lose control. "Enough, enough already! Why do you gab on so? I never knew Heechee employed such long-winded spies! If you are here to spy, then do it, Heechee will never understand my data however, he will have to make his own observations, do his own interviews. My history of Thulistan will be the only complete and accurate text on the subject, not his!"

The old man shuffled over to a table and patted a huge, incomplete manuscript. It was easily a thousand pages, and still in the works it seemed.

Taire suddenly remembered something from the reference books he had read. "Wait a minute. Heechee is Miran Heechee, the author of a book called the Historical Treatise on Sheep Herding in Thulistan. I remember seeing his name and thinking what a stupid thing to write about." Taire looked quickly at the aged scholar to see if any offense had been taken, and, seeing the old man contentedly talking to himself, continued. "Anyhow, as I recall, he died about thirty years ago."

Halnan chuckled to himself for a moment while Morgan tried to get Mugwort's attention by shaking his shoulder lightly.

Morgan spoke softly, "Excuse me, Mugwort, but Heechee is dead—do you understand? Did you hear what Taire said? We obviously don't work for him. We just want to find out some history about the d'rakken mahre so we can better understand where they are going—please, you are our only hope!"

Morgan's plea seemed to bring Mugwort out of his reverie. He shook his head slightly and looked at Morgan. "Yes, well of course Heechee is dead—just the sort of thing he would do to stop me, make me slow down in my work. It won't work though! No, no, as long as he is dead, I will work twice as hard, so that when he is alive again, I will be done with my text, and there will be nothing he can do about it! Ha, old Mugwort won't grow complacent just because Heechee decided to be dead."

Morgan turned to Halnan and Taire and shrugged his shoulders. "Gentlemen, I think we are at a dead end here. Let's try rifling through that manuscript, maybe there will be something of interest in it." He patted Mugwort gently on the shoulder as he walked by him to the large manuscript on the table.

Halnan began to shuffle about the room, looking at the various shelves and tables while Morgan flipped through the unfinished text. Mugwort watched their movements with a fascinated gaze. Taire, feeling very sorry for the kindly, if confused old man, stepped nearer and attempted to engage the man in some sort of conversation.

"Hello, Sir, are you all right? I mean—I know that you don't understand all of this, but I hope you aren't in pain or anything. You seem like a really nice person, I am sorry this is all so confusing to you. In the library, I saw all of the titles of books you have written, and it is obvious you were—um, are I mean, a very intelligent man. We hoped to learn so much! I know it doesn't effect you anymore, but my life seems so wrapped up in all of this, and I had so hoped . . ."

Taire didn't notice the sudden clarity of Mugwort's gaze; as he looked at the young man, so kindly speaking to an old, confused man. Mugwort understood more than he had let on, and in truth, didn't want to get involved. He was tired, and wanted to rest. Rest helped restore clarity, and allowed him to work. He couldn't ignore the plea for help from this earnest young man, however. He knew of the old prophecies, and believed he understood the role that these men were to play.

"Taire." His voice, although cracking and thin, held something potent that caught Taire's attention, as well as that of the other two men in the room. "Many things have been forgotten, but I remember."

Taire excitedly jumped in. "Can you tell me about . . . ?"

"Wait," the old voice almost wailed, "let me finish!" Mugwort paused and composed himself, as if preparing for a great expenditure of energy. After a deep breath, he continued. "You are the Shepherd." He pointed a bony finger at Taire. "You must do what it is a shepherd does. Your flock must be led to reach its destination. Remember, it is not the sheep you must protect, though, but the wolves as it were."

Mugwort paused for a moment, his arms and legs twitching violently. His tightly closed eyes bled tears as he fought for control of his rebellious body. After a moment, he opened his eyes, and his limbs almost ceased their twitching. Taire looked concerned, and Morgan was on the verge of giving the man assistance. They waited, afraid of breaking the fragile balance that Mugwort's mind fought to retain.

"Yes, remember who is the danger." The voice was weak. "Finally, you must determine where they go. They are an evolutionary being, I know this much. The k'aram mahre went into the earth and—changed. Now I believe that they arise again as the d'rakken mahre. They must change again. 'Many lives to learn the wisdom, to in the end redeem us all' says a line in an old poem. Another life begins, and the world badly needs redemption."

Mugwort lifted his hands and embraced Taire's face within his shaking palms. "Please understand. I must go now. Heechee is always watching, and I can't stop my work. Perhaps I should have collaborated my work with him—perhaps I still will. Yes, I miss working with Heechee. It has been a long time since we spoke, a very long time."

The old man dropped his hands and turned away from Taire. He took several slow steps to a low, faded sofa, where he carefully reclined and closed his eyes.

Inexplicably, Taire felt a tear run down his cheek for the old man and his pain. He stepped forward towards Mugwort, but was held by Halnan's restraining hand. Morgan stepped over and stooped in front of the reclining figure. He brought his cheek close to the face, and felt the neck for a pulse.

Taire pulled Halnan's hand from his shoulder. "Is he going to be all right? Did we over-tax him?"

Morgan stood up and walked over to Taire, putting his arm around his shoulders and moving him towards the entry hall. "He is resting Taire. He needed a rest. Let's leave him to rest peacefully." He turned his head to Halnan as he led Taire out of the room and shook his head gently. Halnan waited for them to leave the room, and gently placed a rough blanket over the still form. He could think of no better place for Mugwort than in his study. Resolving to have someone come back to attend to the body after they got to the inn, away from Taire's attention, he stood and followed his friends.

The ride to the inn was made in silence, each man holding to his own thoughts.

Upon returning to the Happy Widower, Morgan requested dinner be served in a private dining room for himself and his two companions. Morgan and Halnan returned to their rooms to bathe and change, and Taire went off in search of Karrel.

By the appointed time for dinner, Morgan and Halnan had enjoyed long, warm baths, and were feeling more prepared to broach the subject of the revelations brought out by Mugwort. Taire, on the other hand, arrived in the private room looking rather crestfallen; he had searched the stables and asked around for Karrel, only to find that the young man had returned, and then left again without leaving any clues to his whereabouts.

Morgan sat deep in thought at the table, and took no notice as Taire sat. The room they were dining in was a small private chamber off of the main dining area. The chamber was mostly filled with the table itself, which could sit six comfortably, and a large fireplace that crackled merrily at the end of the room opposite the door.

Halnan, who was sitting sipping a mug of ale, was the first to speak. "Were you able to speak with Karrel, Taire?"

Taire looked up at Halnan slowly. "No—he hasn't been around all day. He must hate me for not telling him what we are involved in." Taire sounded dejected.

"Well, I wouldn't worry too much, Taire. He has to return sometime before bedtime. I am sure you can explain things to him, and apologize for the fact we couldn't explain everything. He seems a good lad. He'll understand, I am sure."

Although Taire wasn't so sure, he managed a feeble smile. "Yeah, I hope so."

Taire did feel a little bit better. Even if Karrel did not speak to him, Halnan's words showed friendship towards him and reminded him how thankful he was for the companionship of the two men. He turned towards Morgan, at the far end of the table, and found that Morgan was sitting forward over the table, chin on hands, staring intently at him. Taire pulled back in his chair, away from the intensity of the gaze.

"Why are you looking at me like that? Did I do something wrong?"

Morgan dropped his hands from under his chin and rested on his elbows. "Taire, I have been thinking about what Mugwort said. Have you given it any thought?"

Taire considered for a moment before answering. "No, I haven't really had time, with looking for Karrel and all. I didn't pay all that much attention to what he said, it was kind of scary with him holding my head and staring into my eyes. I am sorry it was such a waste of time, I thought it was a good idea when I thought of it."

"Taire," interrupted Halnan, after wiping foam from his lips, "think about what the old man said."

Taire, looking a little confused, tried to remember. "Well, he talked about my being the Shepherd, which I already knew, but still don't understand—he also talked about my flock, and wolves, and something about the d'rakken mahre. He was so confused, it really seemed a lot of nonsense."

Morgan spoke. "No, Taire, Halnan asked you to think, not remember. Mugwort explained almost everything, and you missed it all!"

Taire was embarrassed and a little bit angry at the statement, but wisely held his tongue as Morgan continued.

"He told you to do what you as a shepherd are to do, then he explained what your flock is to be; the d'rakken mahre. Don't you see Taire, this supports the visions that the elf gave you!"

Morgan paused while this sank in, watching Taire's reaction. Taire went a little bit white as he absorbed the information. He was a bright young man, and many things clicked in his mind as soon as Morgan had made the statement. Despite the obvious logic, the thought terrified and repulsed Taire.

"Surely you don't think—there is no way I am getting anywhere near those horrible creatures! He meant something else surely, there has to be another interpretation, doesn't there?"

Halnan sipped his ale quietly, and Morgan waited for Taire to work past his panic.

Taire was afraid, but saw the truth in the words, and after a moment began to think again. "That's what he meant about protecting the wolves from the sheep; I am supposed to protect the people from my flock, the d'rakken mahre. That's impossible though! Why would I want to anyway—as far as I am concerned, they can all die—they killed my father!"

Morgan responded in a quiet voice. "No, Taire. There is much about the d'rakken mahre that Halnan and I have figured out, and Mugwort helped solidify our beliefs. They killed your father by mistake, and you know that. There is much more to the d'rakken mahre than people understand. They must be kept apart from people so that they can complete their quest."

"But," interrupted Taire.

"No buts," Morgan abruptly cut off Taire. "This is important. Listen to what I have to say. That line of a poem that Mugwort recited, 'Many lives to learn the wisdom, to in the end redeem us all', it is part of an ancient poem concerning the k'aram mahre, the beautiful winged ones of the skies of Thulistan. The k'aram mahre left the skies to enter into the depths of the earth thousands of years ago, and somehow changed. I am sure now that they became the d'rakken mahre.

"It is said that the k'aram mahre were the blessed of Varsnya, seemingly an evolutionary creature whose destiny is the redemption of the world. Varsnya put much of her own life into their creation, and it is my belief that they travel on her path. They arise from the earth to continue this quest—to change again. The d'rakken mahre must be traveling towards their next step in the prophecy. Wherever this is, they must make it. The world is on the brink of war, greater than any ever known. The timing cannot be coincidence, the d'rakken mahre may be our only hope to survive beyond this war."

Taire sat, slumped in his chair, feeling the weight of the world on his shoulders. "It's so much to ask, though. I am afraid, and I really don't think I can do it."

Halnan smiled softly. "You will not be alone, Taire. As foretold, Morgan, Norin, his people, and I all are here to help, guide, and protect you. We must do it; therefore we can do it. Talk to Morgan, he is used to an inflated opinion of himself, he can help you deal with it."

Morgan simply raised his eyebrows in response. Taire smiled and felt some of the burden lighten. With his friends' help, and the help of the fearsome Clan Moncall, he could at least try.

"What do we do now?" Asked Taire.

"First, we eat," answered Halnan. "After that, we will rest tonight before heading back to north, to Thulistan."

Morgan nodded agreement. "We must find Norin and the rest of Clan Moncall. They will be in danger, both from the Tulisian armies, as well as the d'rakken mahre. From your description of the meeting between your Ruler, and the d'rakken mahre, they should be surfacing within a few days. I would like to reach them before they cross over into Barstol. With the Tulisian army in place, Norin will have to mount a full attack to make a path for the d'rakken mahre. Clan Moncall will be outnumbered ten to one. We must change these odds, or Moncall will not be able to create a free passage for the d'rakken mahre, and the prophecy will be lost.

"If the draks are attacked, I fear that they will respond by defending themselves. This would mean tens of thousands of Tulisian deaths."

Halnan finished for Morgan. "The destruction of the Tulisian army itself causes me little concern, but the d'rakken mahre may learn that humans are all hostile to their quest. If this happens, they will cut a swath of destruction wherever they go, and tens of thousands of innocent civilians could be killed before all countries are forced to unite in an attempt to destroy them. With a concentrated effort, they will be utterly destroyed, and their purpose lost from the earth. So you see, we must keep the d'rakken mahre from encountering any enemy armies."

Morgan spoke. "We will ride fast and hard. We will ride through western Barstol, where the Tulisians have minimized their defenses. Hopefully no one will take interest in three men heading north, towards the front. We must make it within a week. Halnan, you will purchase spare mounts, and we will ride day and night, resting only a few hours a day."

Their food arrived shortly afterwards, and they passed the meal with plans for the ride, and conjecture regarding the likely destinations of the d'rakken mahre. At the end of the meal, Taire was shown to his room upstairs, and Morgan and Halnan stayed in the dining chamber to make further plans over another glass of ale.

Taire found his room to be large and comfortable. He sat on the thick feather mattress and pulled off his shoes and socks. Hot water had been ordered for him, and a brass tub sat steaming in the middle of the room, calling out to his weary and sore body. Standing, he finished stripping before walking over to the tub and climbing in.

An unknown time later, Taire was awoken by a knock on his door. Groggy from sleep, he called, "come in," before realizing he was still in the now cool tub.

As the door open, he sank low into the soapy waters of the tub. With the water all the way up to his chin, it took him a moment to make out who his visitor was. As the identity registered, he gave out a whoop, jumping up from the tub and grabbing at a towel.

"Karrel, it's you!"

Karrel walked into the room and closed the door. The sight of Taire scrambling out of the tub and quickly wrapping himself in a towel was a bit surprising. "Well—yeah, I guess it is. Halnan found me out in the stable and said I should come talk to you..."

Taire scrubbed down quickly with the towel and scrambled into his breaches and a shirt as his visitor spoke. "I thought you hated me! Why did you take off like that? Wait a minute, why did Halnan talk to you?" Although Taire liked Morgan and Halnan, he knew they were adults, and adults could do things for their own reasons sometimes.

Karrel walked across the room and sat in a chair. "He just explained a few things about why you had to keep secrets from me. He also explained about your quest, and how you are just as scared about it as I was about hearing of the d'rakken mahre. I promised him I could keep secrets, and he told me that I should come see you. I am sorry I ran off, it's just that..."

"Don't worry," Taire broke off Karrel's apology. He was relieved that Halnan had helped explain things to Karrel, and resolved to thank him for his interference. "I'm just glad you're here. We have to go in the morning, but maybe I can come back when this is all over. I don't have any family, and only a few friends."

Karrel, caught up in Taire's enthusiasm, interjected. "Maybe we could live together! I always need help in the stable, and there is plenty of room in the loft. I'll just bet that Rialthi would let you work for him if I asked!"

Taire smiled. He knew he would never share a loft with his friend, and doubted he would ever even see him again. "Yeah, that would be great!"

They spoke for several hours before dropping off to sleep on Taire's bed. Taire slept deeply, and had many peaceful dreams, and one confusing one. In the dream, he stood under a great canopy of stars. The stars grew in his vision, coming closer at an alarming rate. The stars impacted around him in brilliant flashes of reds and golds, blinding him for a time. As the starbursts receded from his vision, he saw the sky overhead had darkened. Surrounding him, on a vast field of grass stood thousands of dimly glowing creatures.

Their shapes were shifting, from visions of d'rakken mahre, to lovely winged creatures, to long sinuous shapes with fins and flowing strands of glittering hair.

In the morning, he forgot the dream as Morgan shook him awake. Karrel was gone already, helping Halnan prepare the mounts. Taire dragged his body from bed and prepared for a long journey into his unknown destiny.

# TWENTY-TWO

## SOLDIER'S OATH

In the rubble of the partially cleared cavern directly east of the entrance through which the d'rakken mahre were soon due to emerge from the deep under earth, Major Tisen reviewed the two hundred crack troops he had assembled. The men were well aware of the importance of their role, and were selected for their loyalty towards General Nits, the commander of the castle forces. Major Tisen filled the time left before action by reviewing the instructions given by General Nits during their secret meeting.

Shortly after the traitorous meeting deep in the southern guard complex, Major Tisen had secretly made his way to the upper castle to meet with General Nits. He knew that General Ardra's plans were suicide, that the d'rakken mahre would never leave the city in peace. In the best interests of saving the city, not to mention his own hide, he had decided to turn coat on General Ardra.

General Nits met with him in his private salon on the second level of the castle. The salon was decorated with plush rugs and colorful wall tapestries. General Nits was a man of sophistication and taste, greatly different from the austere General Ardra. Major Tisen approved of General Nits, approved of his use of position. An officer deserved certain perks.

General Nits drummed his well-manicured fingernails on a

mahogany table next to his chair. Nits was a tall, lanky Desilian, in his late forties. His hair had gone to grey, but his long mustache remained a peppered black. His features were hawk-like and his eyes penetrating. "Well, Major Tisen—what brings you to the upper levels?"

Tisen cleared his throat. "Sir . . ."

General Nits leaned forward and cut off Tisen's answer with a curt wave of the hand. "Whatever it is—it better be good. I do not approve of breaking the chain of command this way. If I deem this a breach of chain of command, I will turn you over to General Ardra for discipline."

Major Tisen leaned back in his chair, away from the General. "Yes Sir, I understand that. If you will just give me a moment, you will understand—it is in regards to an act of treason sir."

The last statement seemed to catch the general's attention, and Tisen was allowed to have his say. It took some time to complete the story, General Nits interrupting frequently for clarification or elaboration.

"Well then, that explains the unusually long absence of The Ruler from the castle." General Nits looked thoughtful, but not really concerned. "I have long thought that he was an unstable, and ineffective leader, but the castle does belong to him, after all. Well, I suppose that has all changed now."

Tisen could not believe that the General had not even addressed the planned takeover of the city and storming of the castle. "Sir, perhaps I underrepresented the threat posed by the troops from the under-city. General Ardra plans no less than the complete assumption of power, both in the under-city, as well as the castle!"

Slightly raised eyebrows were the only indication of General Nits' annoyance. "Major, do not presume to lecture me. I fully understand all that you have told me. The fact is, now that I know, there is very little threat posed by the troops of the under-city. As a last resort, I could collapse the gates to the surface and let the draks consume the entire under-city."

Major Tisen, who had a wife and young child in the lower city, blanched at the thought. "But Sir, surely you can't mean to hold the entire city responsible for the actions of the military leaders?"

"No, Major—of course not. But understand—as a last resort, I could do so. Indeed though, there are a great many innocent civilians to be protected. Since you have seen fit to bring this plot to my attention, you will be assigned the role of protecting the city. Listen closely now, for we shall not meet again until after we crush this coup."

The general outlined all of his plans for Major Tisen, and assigned him several sub-officers along with their troops to undertake the mission. Tisen left the general filled with a grand purpose. He alone would save the city.

General Nits felt nothing other than disdain as he watched the Major leave. He hated traitors, and this man was even worse than those in the city below. Every military man owed allegiance to his commanding officer. To turn against a higher-ranking officer to protect ones own skin was a crime deserving of death. Still, he mused, the man had given useful information. The troops he provided should succeed in their mission, but Tisen would, unfortunately meet with an untimely end, perhaps a stray arrow from friendly forces.

General Nits smiled at the thought. He would prevail, and rid the world of a traitorous dog.

Major Tisen's reverie was ended by the sound of running feet coming down the empty corridor leading to the cavern in which he and his men were formed up. A runner burst into the cavern and identified himself with a codeword before the archers shot him down.

"Sir," the man panted, "the d'rakken mahre are reported to be within a quarter mile of the outer portcullis!"

Major Tisen turned from the man toward the two captains provided by General Nits. "You heard the man. Form the men up in columns. I want fifty to hold the northern portcullis. The rest are to accompany me to drop the eastern portcullis and hold it."

Within five minutes, the men were formed up in four long columns, marching out of the cavern at double time. As they broke out into the outer cavern, one column broke free under the leadership of one of the captains and moved north to hold the northern gate, which would be lightly guarded and already in the lowered position. The second three columns broke at a run towards the more heavily guarded, and open, eastern gate, through which the d'rakken mahre were due to emerge in less than ten minutes.

The twenty guards at the eastern gate barely had time to call for help before the overwhelming force was upon them. Half of the men were down before the others were able to form up and quickly retreat into the guard complex itself. To their surprise, pursuit was not given. Instead, the gate was slammed down from the outside, trapping them in the complex. It did not take long for the importance of that fact to enter into the mind of the corporal who had helped organize the retreat.

With something close to panic, he fled towards the barracks portion of the complex, hoping to bring enough help to retake the portcullis, and figure out some way to open it from the inside. The complex was designed to keep invaders out of the city, and the gates all operated from the outside. They were trapped in the complex, and the d'rakken mahre were about to arrive to find the gates closed against them.

Far above, in the bailey, Major Howat and his hundred men worked at their pretense of drilling. The men drilled with a precision brought on by the adrenaline that preceded battle. The plans were laid and the men were ready, Howat had selected the best, most seasoned, and most personally loyal troops he had available.

Despite all of this, he felt uneasy. Everything was going as planned, but something was just not right. It was not so much a something, as a number of something's. Despite the fact that the d'rakken mahre were to arrive within the hour, activity within the castle and bailey was minimal. Howat had expected there to be many other soldiers in the bailey, ready in case help was needed with the d'rakken mahre. He realized that Generals Nits and Ardra had met and confirmed plans dealing with the d'rakken mahre.

Ardra had assured Nits that The Ruler was personally running things in the lower city and that the d'rakken mahre would be held in the outer tunnels.

Even so, the men of the castle should be on alert, thought Howat. Even stranger than the lack of activity within the bailey was the lack of a guard at the inner castle gates. The gates were always held by four guards, but were currently unmanned. The outer gates, however, appeared to be more heavily manned than usual, as were the entrance gates to the under-city. There were a number of soldiers trying to give the appearance of lounging around the two entrances to the under-city. Nearby to each entrance were several covered wheelbarrows, being guarded by several alert men in peasant's clothing.

Howat knew these men were also guards, but could not figure out what the purpose of the wheelbarrows may be. Looking about the bailey and scratching his stubbled chin, Howat considered things. It seemed like the castle was offering an open invitation for him and his men, and yet all possible exits from the under-city to the surface, and from the bailey to the outside of the city, were well guarded. Somehow, he thought, General Nits had discovered General Ardra's plan. The castle was wide open to him—a trap, and the gates to the city, and those to the outside were held tightly.

If General Nits knew of the plan, he would have already made counter-plans to assure the d'rakken mahre never reached the city. Or, thought Howat with a grimace, plans to ensure they did reach the city, just not the surface. He looked again at the wheelbarrows, trying to discern their contents. It was too late to do anything about the under-city, he knew. The best he could do was neutralize the guards holding the gates to the under-city against the oncoming d'rakken mahre, as well as his reinforcements. Those below would have to do their part and overcome whatever obstacles were thrown their way.

Having come to a decision, he called his officers to him and began to outline a desperate plan. As he finished going over the plan, his runner emerged from the main entrance to the under-city. As the breathless guard emerged, the guards at the city gates began to move with forced casualness towards the wheelbarrows.

Without waiting for the runner to arrive with his news, Howat barked several short orders and set his men in motion.

Far below, General Ardra himself rallied a force of nearly one hundred men to attempt to retake the eastern gate. Captain Garteth led another force of equal size towards the northern gate.

Ardra's men met with stiff resistance, as archers showered arrows through the portcullis. Ardra and a dozen men reached the gate behind a wall of shields, only to discover that the gate was locked from outside, and quite unmovable. As arrows showered around them, they began a slow retreat behind their shield-wall; moving back to bring forward men who were arriving with picks and shovels.

At the northern gate, Garteth found that the gate itself was locked, and the mechanism jammed with a broken off dagger. The warriors outside did not even bother to fire arrows, so sure were they of the strength of the portcullis. Garteth moved his men back from the entrance and began to gather the remaining men from the nearby barracks rooms to assist at the eastern gate.

As General Ardra began to move back towards the gate with several score of men providing a shield wall for a score of sappers with picks and shovels and saws, a shout from the southern end of the complex caught his attention. "The draks are here! Clear the way, the draks are here!"

General Ardra began to shout orders. "Step it up men, we have to have this gate open! The draks will be here in a moment, and if this gate is closed, we're dead men!"

Under a hail of arrows, with the d'rakken mahre streaming into the southern tunnels, General Ardra held his men steady to their purpose. His steady demeanor calmed the men and kept them from panic. Unfortunately, the wall was stronger than his will.

The foremost d'rakken mahre, a large group of warriors under the leadership of several organizers emerged into the large cavern in which Ardra and his men struggled. Finding the gate closed, with a knot of armed warriors before it, the organizer sent the warriors to clear the way.

Ardra called for warriors with shields and spears to hold the rear against the d'rakken mahre. "Hold the line, men. The draks will slaughter us if we don't get this gate open. Someone try to break through to the southern gate and drop it before more of them arrive!" Ardra knew that he would have to hold off the d'rakken mahre until the gate could be opened. There would be no chance to explain the closed gate to the d'rakken mahre.

Garteth dropped the two sets of gates protecting the guards housing complex from the main passage and proceeded towards the sounds of battle through the smaller passages of the guard complex itself. At the end of a long narrow passage, he emerged into the mayhem of the large central guardroom in which the pitched three-way battle was taking place.

He emerged into the desperate battle with nearly two hundred men behind him. The cavern had filled with over a hundred d'rakken mahre already, and more rapidly poured into the enclosed space. To his left, General Ardra tried valiantly to hold a shield-wall while sappers worked at the gate. Ardra's force was being battered at by several dozen d'rakken mahre, and peppered by arrows from outside.

General Ardra, seeing the arrival of Garteth and his men, paused to shout orders. "Garteth! Try to drop the southern gate, we are betrayed! Major Tisen holds the gates with several hundred, we are . . ." Ardra's orders were cut off as an arrow found an opening in his armor and planted deeply in his neck.

Captain Garteth saw the General go down and watched the men dissolve into panic. A larger force of d'rakken mahre warriors arrived from the south. The men in the passage were badly outnumbered. Failing to see any way to save the trapped men, Captain Garteth ordered a retreat into the narrow passages of the guards housing complex.

The d'rakken mahre made quick work of the unorganized men remaining between them and the portcullis and began to press against the bars of the portcullis, seeking to lift, or break the bars.

Outside of the gate, a captain ordered the men to advance on the gate with pikes lowered. The Captain had taken over when an arrow accidentally embedded itself in Major Tisen's back. The long, razor sharp pikes pushed through the bars into the milling mass of d'rakken mahre. Many of the pikes penetrated the black carapace of the d'rakken mahre, increasing the fury of their attack upon the gate.

For every d'rakken mahre twitching in its death throes upon the ground, a score pressed upon the gates. Their hardened claws ripped into the very stone of the walls and floors, and the bars themselves began to buckle in some places.

Captain Garteth led his nearly two hundred men in an orderly retreat away from the masses of d'rakken mahre. A number of the creatures were pressing them, leaving a trail of dead warriors. As they approached the portion of the complex wherein the prisoners were kept, Garteth ordered the cells opened and the prisoners released.

He ordered the retreat halted long enough for the cells to be opened. A shout of "All cells clear!" set the men into a slow retreat again. Garteth, at the outermost line of defenders was unable to react in time as a shape pounded into his back, screaming in incoherent rage. He regained his feet amongst stout defenders just in time to see the corpulent form of The Ruler, screaming insanely, torn to shreds by the claws of several pursuing d'rakken mahre.

Taking advantage of the pause in pursuit, Garteth ordered the men to continue their retreat towards the officers' quarters. "But Sir," shouted a soldier nearby, "that's a dead end!"

"Just follow orders!" Garteth grabbed the man and bodily shoved him to the rear, taking his position on the front line. After another forty feet, they reached an intersection, leading either towards the jammed northern gate, or towards the officers' quarters. The men turned towards the officers' quarters and entered into the small complex through a stout wooden door.

Captain Garteth was the last to pass through the door, with several d'rakken mahre fiercely pounding on his buckler. As he cleared the door, several men with spears forced the d'rakken mahre back several paces before stepping back and allowing the door to be slammed and barred. Those on the inside could clearly hear the sound of claws gouging deeply into the door.

Garteth began to move down the narrow corridor past weary men, moving past many doors to officers' private quarters. "Hold the door as long as possible!" The statement was, to say the least, unnecessary to the group of trapped men.

At the end of the corridor stood the door to Garteth's own chambers. Garteth entered into his room and enlisted the aid of several of the dozens of men that were resting there. With the help of two men, he moved a large bookcase filled with scrolls and books of military history. After sliding the bookcase out of the way, he moved his hands along the base of the wall. After a moment, with an "Aha" of success, he found the small raised stone he was looking for and pushed it in.

A three-foot section of wall slid aside on a well-oiled track. Beyond the opening was a dark, low passage. "At the far end, there is a handle to open the outer door. You will find yourselves in a small open space behind the trading sheds. Wait for me there!"

Garteth pushed his way back into the outer corridor, where he found that the door had been torn down, and men were pushing forward to replace those that were constantly falling, trying to hold the d'rakken mahre at bay. "Retreat to the chambers at the end of the corridor! I want a slow, orderly retreat!" He pushed his way to the front line, repeating his orders all the while.

Men were pouring from the side chambers as he moved forward, all pushing towards the open door at the end of the corridor. Garteth pulled a spear from a dead man and helped hold the d'rakken mahre at bay, giving the men time to exit through the secret passage in his chambers.

The soldier next to him went down as a d'rakken mahre lunged forward and grasped him by the throat. In a spray of blood, the man's throat was torn out, while Garteth jabbed his spear into the soft spot at the base of the d'rakken mahre's neck. The spear slipped out of his hand as the creature toppled backwards. The Captain drew his sword just in time to intercept a clawed swing at his head.

Another man stepped forward to protect his flank and after forcing the draks back a few feet; the two turned and fled the last several feet to the open door. The door slammed behind them with a bang and was quickly barred. About thirty men remained in the room, awaiting their chance to press into the small secret passage. "Barricade the door!" Garteth shouted, pushing men aside in an effort to get to the toppled bookcases.

The men shook themselves into action, and soon there were a dozen men stacking every piece of furniture in the room before the door. By the time this was finished, the passage was clear and the remainder of the men rushed through, Garteth exiting last. Once inside, he turned and pushed an unseen lever. The door silently slid closed, blocking the oncoming d'rakken mahre behind a foot of solid rock. Garteth pushed his dagger between the track and the wheel and snapped off the blade jamming the door shut.


Major Howat and his men marched quickly toward the inner castle entrance, where they were expected to go. As his men neared the inner castle gates, he shouted the order, "now," and all hell broke loose.

A dozen men at the rear of the column turned, lifted crossbows and fired. Of the dozen men at the entrance to the western gates to the under-city, half were dead or wounded from the initial volley of bolts. The twenty men at the rear of the column broke away and rushed the remaining guards who were scrambling for cover and pulling weapons.

Howat led his men the remaining distance to the gates of the inner castle. The bailey was strangely quiet. Across the bailey, the guards holding the outer gates had pulled back, inside the gatehouse. With a protective ring of shields, Howat led a dozen men inside the entrance to the inner castle. Across the bailey, the guards in the gatehouse waited for all the men to enter before coming out to complete their trap.

Major Howat, however, had other plans. Once inside, he pulled closed the inner doors and spiked them closed from the outside.

As the two men finished spiking the door, a loud clanking warned General Howat. The portcullis came slamming down, supposedly trapping him and his men inside. Howat, however, had been prepared. Unfortunately, the two men spiking the inner doors had not moved quickly enough, and were trapped. The men, seeing their situation, showed remarkable bravery. One man began to pry at the chain that operated the portcullis, hoping to disable it entirely from being able to open, and the other continued to pound spikes into the inner door.

Howat nodded to the two men, acknowledging their sacrifice, and exited the inner castle, slammed the outer doors, and began to spike them, finishing the closing off of the inner castle.

Seeing their intended prey escape, the archers in the castle began to fire. Major Howat and the men accompanying him began a slow retreat towards the gate to the under-city, shields held high against the incoming arrows. Despite their defense, a dozen men were down; left behind to die, by the time they reached the under-city gate.

His men had secured the gates and had already sent runners down into the middle city levels to warn Major's Allin and Urnat of the change in strategy. They were to proceed with all speed towards the lower levels and ensure that the d'rakken mahre were able to reach the surface. There would be castle troops below, and Allin and Urnat would have to clear them out.

Major Howat had other plans for his men. He would leave a token force to hold the ramp open, and take nearly one hundred and fifty men into the gatehouse. There would be a large number of men in the barracks above the gatehouse, ready to re-take the bailey and close the entrance to the under-city.

With shield held high to intercept arrows fired from the inner castle, Major Howat led his men towards the gatehouse, and the hundreds of men he knew awaited him. Grimly, he prepared to uphold his bargain. His goal had changed, but not his commitment; he would hold the gates. The men in the gatehouse would not come upon his allies from behind, and the d'rakken mahre would not find the gates held against them.

Captain Garteth formed up the two hundred men that had survived the slaughter within the complex. He knew that over six hundred men were housed in the southern guard complex, and was afraid that even should the d'rakken mahre safely exit the city, the troops of the upper castle would overwhelm them quickly. Nonetheless, there were battles to be fought in the present, he thought. No reason to worry over tomorrow's fights when today's are yet to be survived.

With a shout of "attack," his men broke wildly from their place of concealment. The castle troops were unprepared for the attack, and were quickly forced back, away from the creaking bars of the portcullis. Garteth was amazed to find the mechanism left in working order, and released the lock. He began to raise the portcullis.

As soon as the gate was raised five or six feet from the ground, the d'rakken mahre began to push through. At this point the castle troops fled.

As the d'rakken mahre came out, they lashed out at everything nearby. They had been driven to battle frenzy. D'rakken mahre began to scatter in every direction. Garteth immediately saw the danger to the city. "Form up around me! Ready shields and spears, steady retreat towards the Southtown Ramp!"

Thus began a terrible, controlled slaughter of the men under Captain Garteth's command. The d'rakken mahre, seeing no other outlet for their hostility, regrouped and gave chase. It seemed that thousands of the creatures were pouring into the cavern, all following the men under the Captain's command.

By the time Garteth and his men reached the top of the Southtown Ramp, he only had fifty men surrounding him, all wounded and fatigued. Captain Garteth himself bled from dozens of wounds, several serious.

At the top of the ramp, he was met by a shout from a familiar voice. "Hold the barricades!" Other voices repeated the order into the distance. "Harriers form up, prepare for orderly retreat!" Major Urnat's voice was easily recognizable in the turmoil.

As Captain Garteth reached the top of the ramp, Urnat's fresh troops pushed by, taking over the job of leading the d'rakken mahre onwards. The Captain was ushered to the rear, where the Major awaited him. His men were led through a heavily defended barricade where they were allowed to rest in safety.

Major Urnat spoke as soon as the Captain was within sight. "What happened? Where are the rest of the men, and where the hells is Tisen?"

Garteth attempted to salute, but was unable to raise his hand. "Sir, Major Tisen betrayed us! He held the portcullis closed against the d'rakken mahre and we were slaughtered. General Ardra is dead. The men with me were the last survivors from all of the troops that were in the guard complex. We escaped through a passage in my private chambers and cleared the portcullis. The bulk of them should be following us."

"You have done well, Captain. Major Howat forewarned us of treachery, although we don't know how he fares. He said he was going to take the outer gates. Major Allin has taken troops to herd the d'rakken mahre away from the northern end of the cavern. He should be able to protect the northern portion of the lower city and drive the d'rakken mahre towards the path we have cleared. It is not over yet, and we may still prevail! The castle troops are bottled up, and we have recruited heavily amongst the local adventurers and guard companies. We have several surprises left!"

Further speech was cut short as the men were forced to move back, away from the advancing d'rakken mahre.

Major Howat met with stiff resistance at the outer castle gates. The momentum of his men's charge quickly brought them inside the large tunnel leading to the outside. As men set to work destroying the levers that controlled the portcullis and gates, attempting to lock them in their open positions, arrows began to rain down through arrow slots above.

"Shields overhead," shouted Major Howat. He grabbed a nearby Captain and pulled him near. Pointing to a stout set of doors near the entrance to the bailey, he shouted. "Don't let them close the door to the upper chambers! These arrows will be our undoing, we must get men into the upper chambers and deal with these archers!"

The Captain called out some orders and fifty men turned away from the fighting in the corridor and followed the still shouting form of Major Howat towards the still open door. Several dozen castle troops held the door. Major Howat and his men met them with a clash of steel. The enemy soldiers were still in disarray, not having expected an attack of any kind on their forces, and the Major and his men were able to break through the door into the inner complex of corridors.

Men were shouting and running in every direction. Some were still buckling on armor and unsheathing weapons, running to join the battle in the hallway. They were surprised to meet with enemy troops within the halls of the tower, and were quickly dispatched by Howat's men. Major Howat held his troops just inside the tower complex and quickly assessed his situation. He knew that no matter how many men he brought into the complex, he would be greatly outnumbered. Instead of risking any more men, he came to a decision. "Captain, spike the door!"

The Captain pushed through several soldiers to reach Major Howat. "But Sir, we will be locking our own reinforcements outside! We will be trapped—outnumbered."

Major Howat simply grabbed the man by the collar, turned him, and thrust him towards the door. "Execute my orders, Captain!"

As several men began to hammer spikes deeply into the cracks on all sides of the door, Major Howat sent a score of men to clear the half a dozen small chambers in the lower level of the complex. There were few men present in the lower chambers, and most of those surrendered without a fight. Major Howat himself, along with a half dozen hand picked men held the wide stairway leading to the upper chambers. So far, the castle troops were content to hold the upper complex, from where they could continue firing deadly arrows down onto the troops in the tunnel below.

The Captain came to the stairway with most of the remaining

men. "Sir, the door is heavily spiked and the other chambers are cleared. Several prisoners have been tied and left in one chamber, with the door locked from the outside!"

Major Howat looked behind him. There were just under sixty men with him. He estimated that close to three hundred would be in the series of chambers above. Directly at the top of the stairs was the long chamber directly above the exit tunnel. If he could clear that chamber and hold it, he would succeed in fulfilling his mission. He only need hold it until the d'rakken mahre exit, which should be within a half hour or less by now if all was well.

The Major raised his voice so that all could hear. "Men, we must take and hold the chamber directly above us. We are outnumbered badly. Nonetheless, the city, our families, friends and all of those we are sworn to protect, rely on our success. We have all taken the Soldier's Oath, and now we must live up to it. We will be victorious because we must. To victory!"

Major Howat charged up the stairs ahead of all, sword and battered shield held ready. Behind him, his men charged, shouting wildly. They swarmed up the short flight of stairs and burst around a ninety-degree turn into the open chamber above. With the clash of steel on steel, they crashed into the hundred men holding the chamber.

Major Howat was a whirling dervish of steel and death. He and his men fought with the valiant desperation of cornered animals. Many of the castle troops were unable to effectively use the bows and crossbows they held due to the close fighting, and had to pause to unsheathe their swords. This pause, for the most part, proved fatal.

Within minutes, Major Howat, and about thirty bloodied men stood panting in the now silent chamber. The floor was littered with the battered bodies of the dead and dying, both those of his men and his enemies. Most of those still standing bled from multiple wounds; Major Howat included. Slow to come out of the fog of blood and fury that had taken over during the fighting, the Major began to evaluate his victory. He saw no officers among those standing.

"Men; that was well fought. We cannot go on, though. It is my hope we can hold this chamber. Move all of those," he indicated a pile of casks and chests, "towards the end of the chamber. Form a defensive perimeter around the entrance to the stairway. Here we stand! Move quickly, they will be on us soon!"

Major Howat watched as all of the men shook off their fatigue and went to work. There remained near to two hundred troops in the complex, he knew, and they would attack in force shortly, as soon as they had time to organize. He had lost half of his men killing the hundred that occupied this chamber, and had freed those below from the downpour of arrows. Now, he had two hundred more to battle, but he only had thirty; most of whom were wounded. With a committed grunt, he sheathed his weapon and began rolling casks with his men.

As the last of the kegs and chests were put in place, the sound of booted feet could be heard coming from several of the corridors leading into the chamber. Major Howat looked at his fortification. It was chest high in most places and would force the enemy into several smaller areas where the barrier was lower. This would keep his men from being overwhelmed. Fatigue would quickly be an issue though, he knew.


Major Urnat and his forces were successfully leading the d'rakken mahre through the city. Intent upon the soldiers ahead of them, the d'rakken mahre left the barricades alone. Now that the retreat was under control, there were very few casualties. The last of the d'rakken mahre were now making their way through the lower cavern, carefully herded by a shield wall created by over five hundred soldiers and mercenary troops. The d'rakken mahre made no attempt to attack these troops, however, so intent were they upon exiting the caverns.

The line of d'rakken mahre stretched for over three miles through cavern and city streets. They traveled in a long, sinuous, dense, line; like herd-beasts, completely filling the space that the city streets allowed. In all, over twenty thousand of the alien creatures jostled through the city in their dense formation. The soldiers and city inhabitants holding the barricades watched in fascinated horror, realizing the hopelessness of resistance against the creatures.

The soldiers knew the danger of d'rakken mahre, knew that a thousand of them could gut the city and rout the army. They nervously fingered weapons and prayed to Varsnya that the procession would remain orderly; death would come soon enough without any mishaps in the under-city. They still had the castle to take.

As the troops at the forefront reached the surface, they passed by the guards left in place by Major Howat and fanned out to create a corridor towards the outer gate of the castle. Arrows from the inner castle reigned down, occasionally finding their target. Despite this, the d'rakken mahre were more important. The men held discipline and stood in position, shields and spears towards the d'rakken mahre, not defending against the less dangerous arrows of the castle troops.

The sinuous black procession continued for close to an hour. Major Urnat, seeing that the d'rakken mahre showed no interest in anything but exiting the castle had pulled his men out of bow range of the castle, giving the d'rakken mahre unrestricted access to the gates.

As the last of the d'rakken mahre cleared the tunnel entrance to the lower city, the troops that had been holding the barricades began to poor forth.

As soon as the d'rakken mahre were clear, Major Urnat, after being informed of the whereabouts of Major Howat by one of the men that had survived the battle for the gate tunnel, led a force of several hundred men to discover the fate of the Major.

He discovered the door to be secure, and was unable to open it. One of Major Howat's men brought forth a small round globe. "We found these in a wheel barrow near the entrance to the under-city, Sir. They're blow globes, Sir." Blow globes were expensive magical explosives used in heavy excavation. "It looks like they intended to close off the under-city entirely."

The Major took the globe and motioned for his men to back away. He pounded on the door and shouted. "Ware the door, we are going to blow it in!" He stepped back ten paces and handed the globe off to one of his men, who expertly hurled it at the door. The globe struck and exploded; the door breaking into splinters, and some of the rock of the jam fractured and fell to the ground.

Before the smoke cleared, Major Urnat and several hundred men were running, weapons drawn to the aid of Major Howat, whom they hoped was still alive.

All was quiet within the corridors inside the gate complex. Major Urnat and a few dozen men were the first to reach the top of the staircase where Major Howat and his men had made their stand.

Silence and bloody corpses were all they found.

Within the defensive perimeter were the hacked and still forms of Major Howat's men. Outside of the wall of casks and chests were the piled bodies of the attackers. "Hell and blood," swore Major Urnat. "There must be a hundred and fifty dead enemy soldiers! Varsnya take you, Major Howat, it must have been a valiant fight!"

Major Urnat's men were pouring into the chamber, and fanning out to secure it. Major Urnat began to examine the bodies. "Men, find the Major's body! He, and all of these men will be buried with all honors!"

From his left croaked a horse voice. "Save it for later, Urnat. I'm not finished with this fight yet."

Major Urnat, and several men turned to see a bloody form rising from the floor. Major Howat, bleeding from more wounds than could easily be counted, slowly rose and stood. "Sorry I didn't say anything sooner, but I didn't have the energy. The fighting didn't stop until the explosion at the door. There were several dozen men in the chamber—they fled through the northern door. There should be a few score of the rats hiding about the place. Send a hundred men and clean it out."

Major Urnat, relayed the orders and the men hurried to carry them out, buoyed by the display of bravery and prowess of Major Howat and his men.

Major Howat, trembling slightly, looked around. "Now, don't bury anyone yet. There were five men standing with me when you broke in, and they are in this mess, unconscious or resting somewhere. Find them!"

After a quick search, Major Urnat's men found four men alive, if barely, amongst the bodies on the floor. Major Howat himself located the fifth man. The man had opened his eyes and began to rise, holding his weapon in bloody fingers. Major Howat grabbed the man's sword arm. "It's all right, soldier. They are all dead, we have won a great battle today." The man looked about, eyes only half open. Finding himself surrounded by friendly soldiers, he nodded to Major Howat. "I have met my Soldier's Oath—I am tired, Sir. Permission to rest?"

Major Howat nodded to the man. "Permission granted, soldier." With a sigh, he lowered the man to the floor. The soldier, whose name he never knew, was dead before he reached the floor, his sword still grasped in locked fingers.

"Major Urnat," Major Howat spoke with the intensity of death incarnate, "ready the men to take the castle."

Accepting the other man's leadership, Major Urnat began to plan the assault that would free the city from the leadership of The Rulers military lackeys.

# TWENTY-THREE

## DIVINITIES FALL

As Morgan, Halnan, and Taire rode north, they found the weather quickly turning towards winter. Each morning, thick frost, like spun crystal, covered the grass. Taire was mesmerized by the frost; by the way the sun hit it and fragmented into thousands of tiny rainbows.

Breath steaming, Taire turned back towards Halnan and Morgan, who were riding close and discussing plans. "Where exactly are we?"

Halnan turned away from Morgan. "We are approximately twenty miles south of Thulistan. Those hills to either side are called the Moghin hills. That," he pointed to the north where the clouds partially obscured the steep slopes of a mountain range, "is the Moghin Mountain range. Somewhere in there is your home city of Torance. Somewhere between here and Torance, the d'rakken mahre should be moving towards us, hopefully under the watchful eyes' of Norin and his people."

Taire shivered, more from the thought of the d'rakken mahre than the cold.

"Anyhow," said Morgan, "we should travel quietly and alertly. There are a hundred thousand or so enemy soldiers ahead, and we have to make our way through them. If we meet up with anyone, let Halnan and me do the talking. Go along with whatever we say and we should get through."

In silence, the three rode into the coming winter, a winter that promised strife and change.

Norin jogged along, some miles ahead of his main force, with a small band of several dozen men. He and his men had rounded the southern end of the Moghin Mountains earlier in the day and were expecting to sight enemy forces soon. In breathless silence they ran, breath steaming in the cold, legs pumping tirelessly.

They ran up a small rise, and after passing through a small grove of pine trees, halted dead in their tracks. Ahead of them, several miles to the southwest, was encamped a huge army. Norin turned back towards his men. "Nuorn, you will accompany me. Gurdon, take the rest of the men back to the main force. Prepare the men for a running battle. We must round these mountains and pass up into the valley. You will likely meet stiff resistance. Don't get bogged down in a pitched battle, fight and run. Your goal is to reach the d'rakken mahre. Until you do so, don't engage."

Gurdon nodded wordlessly. After looking briefly towards the enemy forces, he turned and again ran with his men close behind.

Norin smiled at Nuorn. "No reason to involve all of them in a small fight like this. Let's go find if we can turn this army aside; it won't do for them to go getting themselves killed. This has nothing to do with them, after all."

Nuorn shrugged his shoulders. "As the S'hapur orders." With a sigh, he began to trot after Norin's retreating form.

Before they had traveled a mile, they met with a large Tulisian patrol. The mounted patrol split out and surrounded the two men, who had stopped running after sighting the thirty mounted men. One of the Tulisians dismounted and walked towards the two men. He wore a burnished chest plate with a white crest on its center. Standing before the two, he removed his plumed helm.

"Do not attempt to flee, or you will be ridden down and killed. Who are you?"

Norin spoke. "I am Norin, and I must see whoever it is that commands this army."

"Well, Norin. You have the looks of a Thulistan, albeit an odd one. Why should I take you to the Marshal General, instead of slaying you and your companion out of hand?"

"I have information for your Marshal General; information regarding enemy troop movement. I have been traveling for days, and possess knowledge that could prove invaluable."

The officer in front of them turned and gave a curt hand signal to his men. Several men dismounted and came forward. "We will take you to the Marshal General. You will be bound, however." He came forward, up close to Norin's face. "If you are lying about your information, I will find other methods to get information from you—understand?"

Norin smiled and held out his hands to be bound.

Two men bound him and removed his weapons, and two others did the same for Nuorn. They tightly bound his wrists with long cords and tied the other end to saddle pommels. "You seem to like running, so keep up!" The soldier chuckled at his cleverness.

The ease at which the two men kept up with trotting horses, despite their hands being tied, was a bit disconcerting to the mounted soldiers. The soldiers slung insults and tugged at his rope, trying to upset his balance. Norin simply held onto his chilling smile. Nuorn's black looks quickly caused the soldiers to stop taunting him.

After an easy jog of several miles up and down the rolling Moghin Hills, the patrol brought Norin and Nuorn within the Tulisian army camp itself. The two tattooed men were much commented upon by the billeted troops as they passed through the camp. After another half mile, they began to climb a hill slightly taller than the others around. At the top of the hill stood a large colorful pavilion, heavily guarded.

The patrol was halted by a troop of soldiers, pikes lowered. A heavyset soldier stepped to the forefront. "Stop and dismount. State your business."

The officer leading the patrol dismounted, as did his men. "I am Knight Captain Tith. I have brought two captives claiming knowledge of enemy troop movement. They insisted upon sharing their information with the Marshal General."

"Well now. If they have any information, they will share it with me first," growled the guard. "I will then decide if the Marshal General needs to hear what you have to say." The large guard moved in close towards Norin. "Now, what is this important information that you have?"

Norin looked the larger man in the eyes. "I will not speak with the likes of you. My information is for your Marshal General, not his lackeys." His voice was even and unconcerned.

The guard backhanded Norin across the jaw, knocking him from his feet. Blood flowed freely from a cut across Norin's jaw, opened by the man's steel gauntlets. Nuorn jerked reflexively in his bonds, but quickly quieted as he saw Norin calmly regain his feet.

"If you lay hands on me again, not only will you not hear what I have to say, but you will die by my hands before you even realize your mistake. Now, I will speak with the Marshal General."

Knight Captain Tith, still holding the short rope by which Norin was tethered, looked anxiously at Norin, and the now furious guard. "I think this man should be heard by the Marshal General, soldier."

The guard wiped a small amount of blood off of his gauntlet. "Knight Captain, with all due respect, you have no authority over me. I have full authority over this area, given by the Marshal General himself. So, why don't you just leave these two men with me and go about your business."

Knight Captain Tith, knowing better than to argue with the stubborn idiot, dropped the rope tether and turned towards his men. "I will be a moment visiting with the Marshal General, men. He has ordered me to report to him on movements in the field. Wait here for me." He turned back to the guard before moving. "You may have your fun, but be prepared to answer to the Marshal General for overstepping your bounds. Now, unless you would stop me from giving my ordered reports, I will be seeing the Marshal General."

The guard grunted and let the Knight Captain pass. After the Knight Captain passed, he turned back to Norin. "You dare to threaten me? You, a freakish looking Thulistan—no one threatens me!"

The guard pulled out a short, broad dagger and moved towards the unmoving captive. He held the dagger before Norin's face, almost touching his nose. "Now, then—why would I want to lay hands on stinking vermin such as yourself. That is what steel is for." He gently pulled the razor sharp dagger across Norin's jaw, adding a long thin line just above the bleeding cut.

Norin smiled. "Do you want to dance, then?" His voice was colder than the frost on the ground.

"Dance eh? No, I think not Thulistan scum. You know nothing, and probably simply seek to attempt the life of the Marshal General. Time to die pig!"

The guard plunged the dagger towards Norin's chest.

Before the blade could sink home, faster than belief, Norin turned sideways and brought a loop of rope into his bound hands. As the guard, lunging forward, passed by, he looped the rope over the man's head. Continuing his sideways roll, he turned until he was behind the guard, holding the rope snugly about his throat. The guard was pulled short by the tight rope. For a brief moment, he stood still, mind just registering how quickly the bound man had moved.

Further thought was cut off as Norin pulled mightily on the rope and drove a knee into the guards back. The large man's spine cracked loudly as he bent backwards at an impossible angle.

By the time the guard slipped the ground, dying, Nuorn had removed a dagger from a guard and removed the rope binding his hands. He jumped to Norin's side, tossing the dagger to Norin while removing a sword from the dead guard's body.

By the time the rest of the guards reacted, they found themselves facing two armed opponents, capable of killing while bound and unarmed. Recognizing dangerous foes, they lowered pikes and formed a loose circle around the two. Before they could advance, a loud voice knifed through the crowd.

"Step away from those two men!" It was the Marshal General himself, accompanied by Knight Captain Tith.

The circle of armed men loosened and backed away, allowing the Marshal General to come within the circle. Despite the presence of two armed men, one corpse, and warnings by the assembled guards, Davan 'av Carpea seemed unconcerned.

He approached Norin, who had stepped forward to meet him. "I understand you have information that you deem I desire. What possibly could a Thulistan be willing to tell me about his own people that I would desire to hear? Are you then a turncoat?"

Norin stiffened at the comment. "I do indeed have information, and information about Thulistan troops. It is not what you expect, however. My name is Norin, I am S'hapur of Family Caully, of Clan Moncall."

A man behind the Marshal General stepped forward and whispered in his ear. Davan's eye's widened in surprise. "If what my scout tells me is true, there is something unusual to your claim. Clan Moncall is a fable, he says. Extinct."

"A fable indeed," answered Norin. "The fable has come to life, and this is of what I have come to warn you. My people move in answer to an ancient prophecy, and an ancient debt to Varsnya. I have come to tell you that although you stand in our path, you are not our enemy. Your enemy stands to the north and east, and though they are brothers of blood, my people and I answer to a higher authority.

"The d'rakken mahre arise, and my people are chosen to escort them; keep them and those around them from conflict until the Tarcha and the Shepherd come. We must pass your army, and do not desire to cross blades. However, our purpose brooks no delay. Should your army interfere, it will be destroyed."

Davan listened carefully. He had heard of the d'rakken mahre, although only through the texts he had read during his years of schooling. He did not understand what the man meant. "I do not understand—are you, here in my camp, threatening me and my men?"

"No—I only seek to warn you against folly."

"Well, I know little of the d'rakken mahre; only that they are legends to scare children. But again, so it was thought that the

Clan Moncall extinct. Nonetheless, my army will not allow your men to pass. You are Thulistans, and my post is to hold this border against any intrusions. You are a fool to come here."

Norin looked at the Marshal General, and then looked to Nuorn, flashing several quick hand signals. Nuorn dropped his weapon and stood back several paces.

Norin spoke. "No, you are a fool to stand in the way of that which you do not understand. Your forces are no match for that which comes, to interfere will bring about your pointless destruction. I am but one of tens of thousands, try me, if you doubt my words."

Davan nodded and several guards stepped forward. They were friends of the dead guard, and eager to avenge their friend. They drew swords and readied shields, coming in from front and back. Norin stood calmly, dagger held ready, the short piece of rope still dangling from one wrist.

As the first man came within reach, Norin turn to face him. At this moment, the second man took the opportunity to lunge his short sword towards Norin's exposed back. Norin dropped and rolled forward, towards the nearest guard, away from the sword strike. He rolled just to the left of the first guard and past him. As he passed, he struck out with the dagger and hamstrung the man.

The guard fell with a scream.

Norin came to his feet several feet past the fallen guard. He stood casually alert, bloody dagger held in a reverse grip, the back of the blade resting along his wrist. Two more guards drew their swords and came forward. In a fluid motion, Norin threw the dagger. It buried itself in the arm of one of the men, and he fell back shouting for help. Before anyone could advance, Norin collected the sword from the still bleeding guard on the ground.

"I have no desire to kill all of these men. My point has been proven, has it not? If not, I can easily wound three or four more; but, if any die, I will not be held responsible."

Davan acknowledged the point and ordered the men back. Several, after disarming, came forward to help the wounded men.

Davan spoke. "Your competence is not at issue. Your right to enter into my camp—an enemy trying to threaten me—that is what is at issue. You are good, but at my orders you will die. I think, however, I will personally kill you. I have orders to see Thulistan taken, and my enemy killed, or if possible, subdued. I think you will not be subdued."

As Davan moved forward, Norin flashed a hand signal to Nuorn. Nuorn, away from the center of attention, nodded his assent to the order. As the attention turned towards the Marshal General, removing his winter cape and unsheathing his saber, Nuorn grabbed the pike of the guard watching him and reversed the thrust, knocking the man to the ground. Before he could shout, Nuorn was sprinting down the hill, dodging through men who were unaware of who he was.

A shout went up from the guard on the ground. Davan yelled above the din as men turned to pursue. "Let him go, a patrol will pick him up or kill him. If not, he will die with the rest of his army when it comes. Now, come friend Norin—do not trifle with my men, this is a contest of leaders, to determine the better man."

Norin smiled. "A worthy challenge. Varsnya will take you into her arms, should you prove worthy."

Norin, with his belief in his divinely gifted superiority, calmly awaited the confrontation. Davan 'av Carpea, with equal confidence in his abilities, was just as sure of the outcome. Neither man wore armor, disdaining it as a weakness. Davan's saber looked pitifully inadequate next to the heavy short sword that Norin held.

Norin moved first. He came forward with a wide overhead swing. Before Davan could counter it, Norin tucked into a roll, sword swing dropped down to cut at Davan's midsection. Davan, not willing to risk his blade against a direct thrust from such a heavy weapon, parried down and away, deflecting the heavy blade off on a steep angle. Norin swept his legs around in a semicircle. Unused to such maneuvers, Davan found himself dumped on the ground.

Norin sprang to his feet and brought his sword down in an overhand chop at the supine form of Davan. Before the swing was halfway complete, Davan curled forward under the cut, saber thrust point first before him. The saber's edge ripped along the exposed flesh of Norin's knee, opening a deep gash. Taking advantage of Norin's temporary shock, Davan scrambled away and to his feet, several paces away.

Norin, wide eyed, looked down at his leg. He put his weight on it, and found that it was still sound. "You have some skill. I underestimated you, but will not again. Now, you die."

Davan simply wiped his bloodied saber on his pant leg and circled warily. Slowly, he tightened the circle, looking for a weakness. Norin, shifting and changing hands with the short sword, presented none. Tired of waiting, Davan came in, saber blurring in a sequence of high and low slashes. Norin alternated between deflecting blows with his sword, and lashing out with feet and free hand in lethal chops. After several blows from feet and hands connected, Davan gained respect for the tactic, and began to guard equally Norin's blade, and his hands and feet.

Seeing no quick end to the fight, Davan began to set a strategy. As time progressed, he began to slow his pace. At first, the change was barely perceptible, but as time went on, he appeared to be struggling to counter Norin's lightning quick attacks. Several times, he allowed Norin to lay light scratches across his arms.

Norin saw his enemies' weakness, his inability to keep pace. It was no surprise that a soft-fleshed city bred man could not maintain the pace. He was impressed by the attempt, however. Surely Varsnya would take this man. Time pressed, and Norin knew he must finish this display and return to his army, to lead it around or through these weak men.

In a swirl of steel, he increased the pace of the fight, pressing the tiring Tulisian Marshal General. After several dozen high slashes, Norin quickly rotated in a lightning fast full revolution, slashing towards the neck. He expected Davan to counter, and he did. With an instant change of momentum, he went from a strait locking of blades into a counter rotation, sword swinging low as he dropped to his knees. Davan would barely be recovering from the initial parry, as his blade cut deeply through the man's mid-section.

Somehow, things did not work out as Norin had planned.

Instead of pulling back from the parry to ready his next, Davan anticipated the move. As the swords unlocked just above Davan's head, Davan dropped forward into Norin, his sword following with the weight of his bodies fall. Norin, in the middle of his quick reverse, found himself outmaneuvered, and outclassed. Davan, with speed previously unseen by his opponent, completed his downwards cut and opened Norin from upper chest to waist.

Norin's sword flung wide from unfeeling fingers as he completed his maneuver. Wide eyed, he could not credit the speed by which Davan had countered. Despite his ghastly wound, he stood and faced Davan. "Wha—what have you done? The prophecy—the d'rakken mahre will destroy you all. Do not interfere. I only sought to . . ."

He fell forward, into Davan, who caught him and lowered him to the ground. "I do not understand you or your prophecy. You asked for this fight, not I. May you find peace."

Norin opened his mouth and closed it several times before finding the breath to speak. "Peace . . . no peace—only the debt, still unpaid."

These were the last words Norin spoke, and to Davan 'av Carpea, the most disconcerting and confusing. "I want the scouts to attend me. Find Marshal Yith and have him brought to my tent. I will be in conference this afternoon and am not to be interrupted. Somebody bury this body!"

Davan's steel had been tested against the anvil of Norin. The steel had held, and the anvil cracked. In a world free of absolutes, things often went against the wishes of even the Gods. Davan acknowledged no need but his own, and such men made history.

# TWENTY-FOUR

## DUTY AND HONOR

Far to the east, another unsuspecting wolf was about to be consumed by the sheep.

In Carstan, the Knights of Saint Hespah, ten thousand strong, had already begun to entrench as the remaining twenty thousand knights rode forth northward. The knights were thoroughly encased in steel, carried pinioned lances, and rode massive warhorses. The thunder of their hooves could be heard for miles in every direction.

By the end of their first days travel, the war party had rounded the southeast tip of Long Bay and made camp within eighty miles direct travel of Jocko's Corner, the home of Clan Larrs. Having already seen several scouts riding northward, it was clear that the Thulistans knew they were coming.

Gnurth, the Marshal of the Knights of Saint Horathy, and chosen leader of the combined Knightly forces, called a meeting of the three other knightly orders, as well as the ten landholding Lords that had pledged men to the cause. The creaks of straps and the clang of steel forced Gnurth to shout to be heard.

"Sometime tomorrow," Gnurth shouted in his deep, harsh Carstan accent. "The pathetic Clan Larrs will pay for every border raid they have ever committed. We will greatly outnumber them on the field, and should utterly destroy them on our first charge. I desire their utter ruination. We will charge in the traditional line, ten deep, and two thousand across. We will draw by lottery to determine who gets lances to lead the charge, drawn by Lord, not knightly order."

A general commotion broke out within the large pavilion.

"Now, now, not everyone can ride lance, we need swordsmen to destroy the wounded and missed targets, and a final line of lancers to ride any stragglers into the ground. Battle can not be all fun and games, sound strategy must come first!"

The voices quieted, seeing the wisdom in the leaders words.

"By drawing by Lord, we will allow each knightly order to take part in all phases of the attack, giving cohesion to the forces. Now, before we draw, let us pray.

"We beseech you father, in the name of the Four Saints that the hacked corpses we leave upon the field tomorrow will come unto you."

The small crowd intoned. "May their blood be as oil to our blades."

Gnurth continued. "Only then can they live again as warriors fit to die under our hooves and swords."

Again the crowd answered. "To provide nutrients for the earth, and testament to our prowess."

Piously, Gnurth finished. "Only then will their lives gain value and meaning."

Each warrior raised a sword. "And through the holy communion of steel, may we come closer to your divinity." As the prayer ended, the chorus was shouting.

Several minutes of chaotic shouting ensued before the men set to drawing straws over the honor of first kill rights with the lance, the greatest privilege in the proud tradition of the Carstan knighthood.

In a field, not many miles to the north from the brightly lit encampment of the Carstan forces, over thirty thousand Thulistan warriors quietly mounted their warhorses. Each warrior was armed with the traditional cavalry bow, the arrows specially tipped with a heavy wedge, designed to pierce armor.

The combined forces of Clans Larrs, Traagson, Mckallinson, and Trakarie prepared for a night assault, a tactic unheard of among the Carstans. With an intensity brought on by necessity, the warriors prepared themselves. There was no need for commands or encouragements, the men were born raiders, and were fighting for the lives of their families.

Even with surprise tactics and numerical advantages, all knew it would be a close thing. The power of a Carstan cavalry charge was known to be devastating, and if the Carstan forces were allowed to regroup after the initial attack, the battle could still be lost, leaving the Frost Steppes open to invasion. Despite the risks, there was no time to wait for further reinforcements. If the battle were not fought now, it would be lost.

A running retreat would allow for reinforcements to cut the enemy up piecemeal as it approached the interior, but Jocko's Corner would be lost, and families killed or enslaved to work as indebted servants in the fields of the Carstan Lords. Thulistan had developed permanent cities since the last invasion it repelled, and tactics could not follow the course of the past; attack and withdraw indefinitely until the enemy was destroyed through attrition. The Thulistans now had land to protect, and it forced them into a type of battle they were little accustomed to.

At the loud call of a night owl, the men began to form up into predetermined regiments of several hundred men each. The regiments formed up as they rode, an artful maneuver that would have been impressive, had there been light to see it by. The regiments fell into predetermined columns and rode this way, until, about two miles from the enemy camp, the front twenty regiments split apart to encircle the camp. The remaining ten regiments, all ten thousand men armed with long steel tipped spears, drove directly up the middle.

The sound of the tens of thousands of horses warned the Carstans five minutes before the trap was sprung. The knights, who slept in armor and kept weapons in hand at all times, were upon mounts within minutes and prepared to repel the attack.

In the heavy fog of the late night, a cry in the dark brought Davan into immediate wakefulness. Several glowing braziers near his bed were the only light source in his bedchamber. The room was a large partitioned chamber to the rear of the huge command pavilion. The commotion outside was growing nearer, and voices could be heard calling out his name. A guard stepped inside his chamber and seeing the Marshal General awake, saluted crisply.

"Sir, the war party we sent north into Talon Valley has returned. There has been a conflict—the party has been decimated. The Knight Captain that led the party should be here shortly, he has men with him, Thulistans bearing tidings of another enemy. Can I assist you in dressing, Sir?"

"No, thank you. Let them in immediately upon arrival. I will meet with them here where it is warm. That will be all."

Davan found the news disconcerting, not in terms of losses, but in terms of other recent news. First the warning regarding Norin's unknown forces on the field and the warnings regarding the unknown d'rakken mahre, and now Thulistans come to warn him of another enemy on the field? It was all very disconcerting indeed.

Davan had finished dressing and lit several torches by the time many voices outside his pavilion forewarned him of the arrival of his Knight Captain and the Thulistans accompanying him.

The Knight Captain, a middle-aged officer of mixed Tulisian/Maldinian ancestry was the first to enter. The man was huge, well over six and a half foot tall, and proportionately large in the shoulders and chest. He was imposing in his burnished steel chest plate. His face bore many scars, both old and new, and was heavily pockmarked. Close behind him entered six more men, men of mixed ancestry wearing the livery of common soldiers, similar to that of his own soldiers.

Davan had never seen Thulistans such as these, if Thulistans they were. He had never seen a Thulistan in common soldiers armor, or lacking the characteristic tartan sash. One of the men wore the badge of an officer, and the other men stood slightly behind him in deference. Davan chose to address this man.

"I am Davan 'av Carpea, Marshal General and field commander of these forces. Who are you, what are your loyalties, and what message do you bear?"

The man removed his dented, conical helmet. He had the typical short stockiness of a Thulistan, but his facial features had a swarthy similarity to those of Desilian descent. "I am Captain Garteth, of Castle Torance. My loyalties are to my commander and Lord of the Castle, General Howat, the new ruler of the castle and the city of Torrance. Although our city is in Thulistan, it has existed independently from the Thulistan Empire for several generations, and seeks to continue doing so. As you can see, we are not Thulistans, but people of many lands.

"As to my message, it is this: The d'rakken mahre have risen, and they are on the move down Talon Valley, not two days march from this very spot. They number in the tens of thousands, and are powerful enough to threaten forces many times that number should they be provoked. I have come to warn you of this, although it may prove unnecessary now. Your Knight Captain here has met an advanced force less than a day away, and you should hear from him what he has seen."

Davan had listened without interruption to the soldier, trying to grasp the ramifications of the information. He turned his attention towards his Knight Captain. "Report."

"Sir," responded the Knight Captain. "What he says may be true. We met him and his men several days ago while scouting across the border; we were traveling up Talon Valley, trying to determine the risk of attack from there. They did not appear as common Thulistan soldiers, and after hearing their tale, I determined to bring them into camp. Shortly after meeting them, we camped for the night, despite the Captain's urgings to continue on without rest.

"Shortly into the night, a group of sentries raised the alarm; the camp was under attack. There were brief sounds of struggle in the dark, and then silence. By the time I pulled the men together into a defensive position near the fires, facing outwards, we got our first sight of the enemy.

"Sir—as they entered fully into our view, we saw only a dozen of them: black, bug like things, walking on two legs. Seeing no real danger to the command, I ordered the men to attack these d'rakken mahre creatures. For this error, I lost my command.

"I had a score of men with me, all veteran warriors, and they were slaughtered. By the time I realized what was happening, there were only a half dozen of my men standing. Only through their efforts, and those of Captain Garteth and his men, was I able to make it back to the camp to bring you this information. Sir, we outnumbered them two to one, and they cut through my soldier as if they were unarmed children." The Knight Captain's voice was rising in pitch.

"Sir, we only killed one of them that I could see. Barn, one of the last men standing, hewed its head off with a great sweep of his battle-axe. Short swords were useless against them!"

Davan stepped forward and slapped the panicking man, his gauntleted hand splitting the Knight Captain's lip.

"Sir," continued the Knight Captain, having regained his composure. "I failed my command and submit myself for punishment. I was warned, but ignored the warning. I was overconfident, and caused the loss of half a squad." He removed his sword and handed it to the Marshal General, the traditional gesture of submission.

Davan took the sword from the trembling hands. "You are to be stripped of all rank, titles and pay for a period of one year—should you survive that long. During that year, you will serve as a member of the forward scouts. Should you serve with bravery and dignity, your rank will be restored. That will be all soldier. Report to Knight Captain Rokes, he will assign you to your new squad. That will be all."

The man rose, trembling, and left the pavilion. He looked like a man bereft of all dignity and desire to live.

Captain Garteth understood the necessity of the act, and watched the entire scene impassively, although some of his men flinched as they saw a man's life destroyed. He understood that the Marshal General was a very dangerous man, one who posed a great risk to the world should he make the wrong choice regarding the d'rakken mahre.

Davan turned his attention back to Captain Garteth. "Well now, it appears I should hear more of these d'rakken mahre. You apparently have a greater understanding of them than any I have previously met. I believe I will need to hear your entire story before deciding how to meet this threat. Time is short, so tell it quickly."

Davan listened until the early hours of dawn as Garteth recounted his knowledge regarding the d'rakken mahre. When they finished speaking, he sent Captain Garteth and his men under escort to stay as guests within the camp. He had many decisions to make, decisions that went beyond anything the Emperor had envisioned.

At the crest of a round hill, slightly higher than those surrounding it, Morgan reigned in his horse. He motioned for Halnan and Taire to do the same.

Morgan spoke quietly. "Ahead and to the east, what do you see in the distance?"

Taire and Halnan peer into the mostly overcast horizon, searching for some clue as to what Morgan had seen.

Taire spoke first. "I don't see anything at all, just cold, empty hills!"

Halnan continued to search. "Ah, there it is! If you wait for passing rays of sun to break through the clouds you can see the glint of armor in the distance. I believe we have found a portion of the Tulisian army!"

"Indeed," Morgan stroked the scruffy growth of beard that covered his chin. "I would guess, by their position and by the extent of the camp that we have sighted the command position. I think it is time that each of us move to fulfill our individual tasks in this great game."

Taire interrupted, voice high and concerned. "What do you mean? You're going to do something drastic, aren't you?"

"Drastic?" Responded Morgan. "No, not drastic—necessary. Taire, you have a destiny you must meet, a destiny that I cannot help you with. I also have a destiny, one which I must meet alone." He glared at Halnan to forestall any objections. "Alone, I say! Taire must get north, past many Tulisian patrols to meet with Norin and his men. He can not get there alone, you must take him safely through the Tulisian lines, and in to this purpose I release you."

Halnan, sensing an end of something he had known his entire life, or perhaps a beginning of something else, saluted fist over heart. "It shall be as you require, S'hapur—Varsnya guard you in my absence."

Taire had never heard Halnan speak so seriously with Morgan. "Wait just a minute! Morgan, you can't just ride into their camp and leave us alone! They will kill you outright as an enemy spy or something—they will . . ."

Halnan brought his horse in-between Taire and Morgan and forestalled Taire's protestations. "Taire, do not make this any more difficult. It is as it must be; Morgan and I have long planned for this day. He is right; he has a task to complete as surely as do you. My heart, like yours, yearns to be with him. Despite this, you have another task. I have been released from my duties as the Torsch of Morgan's Quest, and I now vow to bring you safely to the conclusion of your quest, whatever that may be."

As they spoke, Morgan removed his tartan sash from a saddlebag and placed it over his shoulder. He quickly removed the leather thong from his ponytail and tied his hair into a true warrior's braid. He would meet the Tulisian army and its leaders as a Thulistan warrior, and S'hapur. The time for concealment was past.

Without a word, Morgan slapped Bran into a trot. He rode off into an unknown future, proud and undaunted.

Taire watched Morgan until the curve of another hill blocked him from view. He turned towards Halnan, and to his surprise saw Halnan sitting with downcast eyes, tears streaming down his cheeks.

Halnan, seeing Taire's attention turned towards him, wiped his cheeks with the back of a gloved hand. "He is a great man, like a brother to me, yet it is my thought that he rides towards a fate that even I can not help protect him against. It pains me to realize that he has grown beyond the need of my protection. Anyhow, we have a job—let's be about it."

With uncharacteristic force, Halnan kicked his mount into a gallop, away from his pain. Taire, speechless, followed. After about a mile, Halnan allowed Taire to catch up.

"Taire, things may get hectic soon. We are going to have to ride fast and without break. If we encounter any Tulisian troops, we are going to try to outrun them. We have no chance if we are caught, and I think that they will not bother themselves much over two men fleeing across the border. No matter what, however, do not stop; even should I turn to slow pursuers, you must continue north!"

Taire, having seen Halnan sacrifice once already for a friend, could not deny the urgency of Halnan's orders. "All right, I understand, just don't let it come to that!"

With a grin, more in character with the Halnan Taire knew so well, Halnan nodded and lightly kicked his horse into a gallop again. Taire, having no alternative, followed.

For over an hour they rode directly northward without seeing any sign of Tulisian troops. They were within a few miles of the Thulistan border, almost directly south of the western edge of the Talon Valley.

Halnan turned back towards Taire. "It is time for an all out sprint. By now, a scout must have spotted us. We can expect company soon, I suspect. Hopefully they will not be ahead of us! Come on now!"

Halnan's mount leapt forward into a full run, Taire's mount close behind. The trees and scrub brush whipped by as the continued towards where they assumed the border to be. After several minutes, Taire caught his first sight of pursuit.

A patrol of riders over a dozen strong angled towards them from the southeast. The pursuers were riding hard, and slowly gaining ground.

Halnan called over his shoulder, "They will not overtake us before we are into Thulistan! This is an unpopulated area, and they may still follow; either way, keep riding hard!" His voice was almost lost in the wind.

For ten long minutes the horses ran, unable to match the pace of the more rested pursuers. Taire continually looked over his shoulders at the increasingly gaining forms of the approaching Tulisian patrol. The pace of their flight precluded any further questioning of Halnan, however, and he faced his apprehension in silence.

They crossed over the strip of open grasses that Halnan had pointed out as the border, only a quarter mile ahead of the pursuit. Halnan turned on his lathered horse to look back past Taire towards the pursuers. They seemingly had no intention of stopping at the border.

"Taire," shouted Halnan. "We must make for the trees—perhaps we may lose them!"

The two turned slightly westward towards the forested slopes of the valley. Their urgency lent a burst of speed to the tiring horses, putting the pursuit temporarily further behind.

They passed into the heavier forest at a dead run, ducking low on their horses to avoid low hanging branches. After a hectic mile, Halnan slowed his mount to a safer speed; Taire's horse followed suit. The horses were nearly spent, and could not continue at their previous pace for much longer without suffering permanent harm. The forest would limit the speed at which any rider could safely travel, minimizing the advantage of the fresh Tulisian mounts.

Halnan began to believe that they were going to outpace their pursuit when a heavy weight knocked him blindly from his saddle. He landed hard on his side and rolled heavily over a few times before skidding to a halt in a spray of pine needles. With a grunt of effort he rolled onto his back, reaching for one of his knives. He stopped mid-reach as a spear point firmly pressed against his chest.

Blinking several times to clear the spots from his vision, he made out several dark shapes standing over him. His mind slowly registered the heavily tattooed faces of men of Clan Moncall.

"Wait, I am Halnan, companion of Morgan—friend of Norin and the Tarcha! Where is the boy? Don't harm him, he is the Shepherd of your prophecy—I swear if he is hurt..."

A tall, hooded man spoke arose from an impossible place of concealment several paces away. "The boy is not hurt," he said in a familiar voice, "and yes I recognize you Halnan, the return of the Shepherd is timely."

The spear was removed with a wave of the man's hand. As he pulled back his hood, Halnan recognize the grim face of Nuorn. "And where is the Tarcha?"

Halnan, remembering the pursuit, rolled onto his knees. "Nuorn, we have to get hidden. A dozen men pursue us. Get Taire and hide him!"

"Be calm, friend Halnan. Taire has already been taken safely away. I sent several men to handle the pursuing riders. They should be back shortly."

As Halnan rose carefully to his feet, brushing off needles and dirt, a hooded man ran out of the forest and stopped just before Nuorn. Nuorn gave the man a silent hand signal to report. The hooded warrior responded silently in hand language. When he finished, he turned and ran back into the boles of the trees, quickly melding into the greens and browns of the forest.

"Your pursuers no longer pose a threat. Now tell me where the Tarcha is."

It took Halnan a moment to absorb his new situation. "Wait a minute Nuorn. Why don't we get Taire and go find Norin. He needs to hear this too."

"Norin is dead," responded Nuorn. "I have taken the role as the leader of Clan Moncall, until a new S'hapur is selected—should we survive that is."

"Dead—how could he . . . ?" Sputtered Halnan. "What happened?"

"He is dead because he could serve the prophecy no other way. When last I saw him, he did battle with the leader of the Tulisian Army, one Davan 'av Carpea. Victory or defeat, he is now dead, and the Tulisian army understands better the threat of the d'rakken mahre. His debt, at least, is repaid. Now answer my question, where is the Tarcha?"

Halnan groaned. "The Tarcha is within the enemy camp by

now, I assume to meet with this Davan 'av Carpea should he still live. It's suicide! Ah, had we known he could have chosen another course."

"No, Halnan, he could choose no other course. He is the Tarcha. He acts as his destiny demands. Now, we have our own destiny to meet. The d'rakken mahre are close now. Come, let us gather up the Shepherd and look upon them together. Perhaps he may gain insight into his task."

Nuorn blew a piercing whistle through his thumb and forefinger. From all around them men began to arise from the scrub and remove hoods. Within several minutes, nearly a hundred men collected, one of the last groups bringing Taire with them.

Upon seeing Halnan, Taire ran over to him. "Halnan, what is happening?"

Halnan smiled reassuringly. "Everything is going to be all right Taire. We are going to go see the d'rakken mahre. I will explain on the way."

Taire flinched at the thought of going near the d'rakken mahre, but did not respond.

A half an hour later, Taire, Halnan and a score or so Moncall warriors, including Nuorn, stood upon a high bluff overlooking the valley floor, several miles below. To the north, only a few miles away, could be seen a moving, sinuous black line stretching for a mile or more, filling the valley floor. A half mile or less in front of the churning black procession, could be seen the darting forms of men, hundreds of them, coming in and out of the forest. Several thousand moved at a run before the black host a mile or so further south also.

Nuorn motioned towards the men. "Clan Moncall fulfills its purpose. We move before and around them, buffering them from all interaction. By nightfall tonight, they will reach the valleys end. It is my belief that they will turn east, as there is no path to the west. The armies of Tulisia will become an issue by tomorrow morning at the latest. The d'rakken mahre don't move fast, but they don't rest either." He turned towards Taire. "What think you Shepherd?"

Taire sat silently for a minute, wondering how he should respond. Deep within himself he felt a door opening, but he could not see what it revealed. He thought that he would know what to do when he saw the d'rakken mahre. Hidden away in his mind the answer lie; the door had opened, but still the answers eluded him.

He answered absently. "They are—they—well, I haven't the slightest idea of what they will do, or what I should do. Is that what you wanted to know? Just leave me alone—I don't have your answers—get them yourself"

Halnan blinked in surprise at Taire's outburst, Nuorn stared impassively at the young man.

"Then let us catch up," responded Nuorn. Your mounts are somewhat rested and are awaiting us at the base of the bluff." He turned towards one of their heavily tattooed guards. "Provide adequate escort for the Shepherd and his companion. I will be at the front."

Nuorn took off at a dead run without further ado, several men following him. A dozen men stayed with Taire and Halnan, walking them to their horses. Once mounted, several more men jogged out of the forest, bringing the party to over a score.

Halnan, sitting atop his mount, turned to Taire. "Come on Taire; we have a job to do, whatever it may be. Stop feeling sorry for yourself."

Taire nodded at Halnan's statement. "I know, it just seemed overwhelming for a minute. There is something there, I just can't grasp it, it is just so frustrating, and terrible! I'm fine now—let's go."

Taire chucked the reigns and started his horse into a canter, Halnan following closely to his left. The warriors around them donned hoods and split off to surround the two. Within a minute, many of them disappeared into the trees surrounding them. They were unseen but present, a comforting presence to the frazzled Taire and Halnan.

They rode uneasily in silence. The next day would provide many answers; determine many fates. Filled with questions, but dreading the answers, they rode south, towards the confrontation of the d'rakken mahre and the Tulisian army.

# TWENTY-FIVE

## ONE DESTINY UNVEILED

Morgan rode for several miles before attracting the attention of a Tulisian patrol. The patrol, approximately a dozen riders, immediately changed course to intercept the lone rider. Morgan reigned in Bran to a slow walk to ensure the riders would quickly reach him without having to try to shoot him out of the saddle, or shoot Bran out from under him. Seeing him slow, the advancing patrol fanned out to surround him, several riders unlimbering powerful crossbows.

After the riders formed a loose ring around Morgan, one of the men removed his helm and spoke. "I am Nathir, senior scout and leader of this patrol. Although you have made no efforts to evade us, or acted aggressively, I have to request that you disarm yourself and allow my men to take you into custody."

Morgan looked slowly at the men surrounding him. They sat nervously in their saddles, fingering weapons, ready for violence. "I am Morgan, S'hapur of Family Partikson, Clan Piksanie. I will speak to your commander."

Nathir and his men tensed at Morgan's declaration. "Well, Morgan, you tread upon Tulisian soil. This is a death sentence for a Thulistan, much less a leader. I may indeed take you to an officer, as queer as your request is—but first you will disarm yourself!"

"No—I will not. I have come bearing tidings for your commander, tidings of great importance to both my, and your peoples—I will not crawl on my belly to deliver it, however. You outnumber me twelve to one, and have crossbows, what risk can I pose?"

Nathir nodded to Morgan, sensing that this issue went beyond his authority. "As you wish. We will escort you, and if you should draw your weapon or seek to flee, you will be shot. I will take you to the Knight Captain, and he will decide what to do with you."

Morgan nodded his assent and waited for his escort to begin moving before nudging Bran slowly into a canter. They rode for several miles, skirting a low hill. As they emerged around the northern end of the hill, Morgan had his first sight of the Tulisian army up close. A wide valley stretched out for several miles before them, filled with bright officers' pavilions and drab brown soldiers' tents. Soldiers, armor shining in the afternoon sunlight, bustled like busy ants as far as the eye could see.

Many men paused in their various activities to watch Morgan and his escort pass bye. He could see aggression in the eyes of the Tulisian soldiers; their gaze contained a frightening mix of anger, hatred, and fear. Nonetheless, he rode proudly, his head held high, his tartan sash flapping lightly in the breeze behind him. He was quickly brought to one of the brightly colored pavilions among the many, and his escort tightened around him before halting.

Within a minute, a short, broad shouldered Knight Captain walked briskly out of the tent, his officers plume bending in the cold afternoon breeze. He walked directly over to Morgan, and took Bran by the bridle.

Bran pulled his head up, trying to release the unwanted grip, and finding himself unable to escape the tight grip, began to paw the ground nervously.

Morgan, sensing that Bran was preparing to kick, patted the horses back reassuringly. Bran quieted immediately, but his eyes remained wild.

Morgan spoke. "Knight Captain, standing in front of a trained war horse is not prudent."

Without moving an inch, the Knight Captain responded. "You will dismount to address me."

Morgan climbed down slowly from the saddle. "Sir, I am Morgan, S'hapur of..."

The Knight Captain interrupted. "I have been told who you are. I am not of a mind to listen to your story twice, so I will take you to the Marshal General directly. Strange things are afoot, and you are not the first Thulistan to enter the camp recently. You will be allowed to retain your weapons—but I warn you, to draw steel is to die a heartbeat later. Come along."

As the impassive Morgan was led through the throng of armed Tulisians, the Knight Captain called to a man Morgan could not see through the ring of guards around him. "Hurn, find Marshal Owans and have him meet us at the Marshal Generals pavilion—right away!"

A quick reply of, "Yes, Sir," rang out from the crowd.

A soldier stepped forward to take Bran's reigns from the Knight Captain. The Knight Captain released the reigns.

"Soldier, this horse is to be brushed down and cared for." He turned his attention towards Morgan. "Should matters allow, your mount shall be returned. In the meantime, he shall be well cared for."

Morgan nodded to the Knight Captain and scratched Bran on the neck lightly. "Go easy Bran. I will be back for you soon."

Without further word, the Knight Captain turned and began walking at a brisk pace, Morgan and his procession of guards following. For ten minutes they walked through the camp, heading towards a large hill, higher than the others. A huge, brightly colored pavilion crowned the hill, a crested flag flapping from a high pole above the pavilions sloping top.

As they began a circuitous climb up the hill, a second group of soldiers, led by a stolid middle aged officer who Morgan suspected was Marshal Owans, joined their large group. The Marshal joined the Knight Captain and they huddled together, speaking quietly as they climbed.

After another half circuit around the hill, they reached the large, relatively flat crown of the hill. They were met by a large contingent of guards wielding pikes. The Marshal spoke briefly with one of the guards, and a path was opened.

Morgan could not help notice the raw aggression on the faces of many of the guards. Their hatred went beyond what Morgan had seen from the other soldiers he had encountered; it was more personal, more immediate. He heard grumbles of "murderous dogs," and "hope the Marshal General skins this one too." The last statement sent shivers of dread through Morgan's spine. Who had been killed? Had another emissary come and been killed? Answers would have to wait.

Once past the ring of guards, the grassy hill lay wide open, free from the bustle of the camp below. They walked a hundred yards before reaching the entrance to the pavilion. The pavilion itself sat quietly atop the very crest of the hill, the flag snapping in the breeze the only sound. At each corner of the square pavilion stood an attentive guard, and two manned the entrance.

Marshal Owans, along with the Knight Captain, approached the two door guards, leaving Morgan and his guards several paces behind. One guard stepped inside. After returning, he motioned for the two to enter, leaving the rest of the party, Morgan included, outside.

After about five minutes, a guard from inside the pavilion stepped out through the flap, and conversed briefly with the two outside. He stepped back into the pavilion and emerged holding a large, loaded crossbow. He then pushed through the ring of guards to Morgan, who stood impassively awaiting his summons.

The soldier motioned to Morgan with the loaded crossbow. "You will accompany me. Walk before me and keep your hands away from your blade. Make a mistake, and I will punch a hole through your back big enough to see through. Let's go."

As Morgan began to move, the soldiers with him began to follow.

The crossbow wielding guard spoke. "I have taken command of this prisoner." Morgan stiffened at the term. "The Knight Captain will meet you all back in camp—you are to return to your duties."

As Morgan and his guard moved towards the pavilion, the milling mass of guards that had escorted him slowly broke up and walked back towards the route down the hill.

Morgan passed into the pavilion before the guard. Expecting relative darkness, he was surprised to find the pavilion brightly lit from sunshine above. Sunlight shone through the light, colorful material of the pavilion lighting the pavilion in a riot of bright colors. To the rear of the pavilion and the sides, several private chambers were hung with a heavier material for privacy.

Directly in the middle of the pavilion set a large table with benches to each side. The table itself boasted a large map of Barstol and Thulistan. Colorful wooden pieces were strewn about the map, mostly bunched up along the long border of Thulistan and Tulisia. A dozen braziers lined the walls, only a few lit for warmth.

The table commanded Morgan's attention, however. On the map, the positions of all of Tulisia's troops were revealed. It did not bode well that they allowed him to see the map.

At the far end of the table, in a large wooden chair, sat Davan 'av Carpea, flanked to either side by the Marshal and the Knight Captain. He examined the large Thulistan before him for a long minute before speaking. "Have you got all of those troop positions memorized yet, or would you like a few more minutes?"

Morgan smiled. "You are, I assume, the commander of these far reaching forces?"

Interested by the calm demeanor of the man, Davan stood and walked nearer. The Thulistan before him was clearly a warrior, yet lacked Norin's fanatic demeanor. The man proudly wore a clan tartan, and carried himself like a king, despite the fact that he was in an enemy camp, likely to die soon.

To his surprise, Davan decided he respected the man. "Yes, I am the Marshal General and field commander of these forces. My name is Davan 'av Carpea." Davan turned towards the table. "Our two peoples will soon begin to die wholesale, you know. I don't suppose you would care to show me your troop placements to return the courtesy I have done you by allowing you to see mine?"

Morgan turned and stood side by side with the Marshal General, looking at the table. He could sense the closeness of the guard with the crossbow. "Marshal General, my name is Morgan. I am S'hapur, or leader, of Family Partikson, Clan Piksanie. I have been long away from my people, and know little of how our forces are arrayed. I have come with a different purpose than to discuss the imminent war between our peoples.

"There are two things I can tell you, however. First, the border will be stoutly held by forces greatly outnumbering those you have arrayed here, however many reinforcements you call."

Davan turned to face Morgan with a wry grin. "Do you think to inform me, or dare to threaten me?"

"Marshal General, I seek only to instill caution. The second thing I know, perhaps, will give some recompense for your having allowed me to see the might arrayed against my people." Morgan motioned to the table. "May I?"

Davan looked from Morgan to the two officers standing impassively at the end of the table. He shrugged. "Please—feel free."

Morgan moved down the table, towards the western half of the map. He found the portion of the map labeled Talon Valley. He slowly reached for a long pointer lying on the side of the table and lifted it, giving the guard time to see what he was doing. Deciding he was not about to be shot, he grasped the pointer and used it to point to a spot in the middle of the Talon Valley.

"Somewhere around here, or even further south by now, a large army moves towards the forces you have collected along the border. These forces are comprised of what is left of an entire clan of Thulistans, and another force, more unknown, and more deadly. They will slaughter your men should they meet with them."

"You speak of the d'rakken mahre and Clan Moncall."

Morgan's eyes went wide at the statement. "But if you know, why haven't . . ."

"Why haven't I moved forces to intercept? Because I have met with the leader of Clan Moncall; and he taught me the power of his people. Of the d'rakken mahre, I have learned much, both from Norin, and others. The d'rakken mahre, and their followers will be upon my troops by tomorrow morning. I have no wish to engage this enemy, but do not find any choice. Can you tell me of their purpose, so that I may better select my course of action?"

Morgan shrugged. "Of the d'rakken mahre and their purpose, I can tell you little, though I have myself striven for months to discover it. There is much I can tell you however, that may help you to best select your course of action. For this, have I come to you. There is much to be spoken of, if you will hear me."

"Indeed—you speak fairly. I will hear what you say, although I will not vouch for your safety until all is told. There is much that together we may uncover. It is my belief, that there is more at stake than the conflict between our peoples."

Morgan nodded. "Than you see more clearly than most. Let me explain my Quest, one undertaken months ago. From there, only your wisdom stands between life and death, mine, and that of your forces."

Davan stiffened at the implied threat of the statement, but said nothing. Morgan, believing that the Marshal General showed qualities of a true leader, decided to throw caution to the wind and tell all.

Tell all he did. For several hours they spoke, two leaders discussing world affairs, and discussing the purpose and background of the d'rakken mahre. Davan learned of the history and of the generalized theory of what the d'rakken mahre sought to do. Morgan learned of the fates of Torance, a city he had never heard of, and of Norin.

Morgan mourned for Norin, but understood the purpose of the sacrifice. Norin, through his death, opened Davan's eyes to the seriousness of the d'rakken mahre threat, and the dedication of the men of Clan Moncall to their preservation.

After completing the sharing of relevant information, they ate a brief meal in a somewhat companionable silence. The pavilion had long since been cleared of all but the guard with the crossbow trained on Morgan's back.

After eating, Davan came to a decision. "Guard, send for Marshal's Owans and Yith. I want them here within fifteen minutes."

"But sir," protested the guard, "the captive..."

Davan stood up. "Guard, I can handle myself. I am not accustomed to having my orders questioned—now move!"

The guard then moved very quickly, and ten minutes later, the two Marshals were in attendance.

"Marshalls Owans, Yith," began the Marshal General. "We have come to a crisis, that I believe, takes precedence over our immediate orders. This question of the d'rakken mahre must be answered before we can complete our campaign. I believe that the d'rakken mahre may pose a direct threat to the Tulisian Empire if not countered. Yith, do you still contend that the Thulistans will not advance should we hold our ground?"

"Aye, Sir. I believe they will stay put."

"And Morgan," questioned Davan, "do you concur?"

Morgan nodded. "We will fiercely defend ourselves, but not attack in force unprovoked."

"But Sir," interjected Marshal Owans, "we must move quickly if we are to make our schedules rendezvous with the . . ." Owans left the sentence unfinished, looking at Morgan.

"With the Carstans, Marshal Owans? Yes, Morgan knows of this now. If this threat is not in earnest, we will still make our schedule, and our guest the S'hapur will not be alive to betray our plans. Should the threat prove real, the Carstans will be on their own, and we will involved in a far greater undertaking."

"But Sir," Marshal Owans began again, "the Carstans will be slaughtered if we do not meet with them. The Thulistans will be able to concentrate their efforts on wiping out the invaders, and we will have betrayed our trust with them. It is nothing short of mutiny against the will of the Emperor!"

Davan stroked his long mustache lightly. "Aye, what you say is true. Should we not meet our duty with the Carstans, it will be mutiny. Perhaps Marshal General Kratch and his two hosts will meet up with them. I think not though, as they do not have enough men to reach central Thulistan. The fact is, regardless of this, we must follow a different course for now. The d'rakken mahre pose a potential threat to the entire Empire. I see no other choice than to forsake our plan until this threat is nullified.

"So, it comes to this. For the greater good of the Empire, I ask you to go against the orders of the Emperor. The question is, do I have your loyalty? Will you follow me?"

Marshal Yith spoke first. "Sir, I have only been under your command for a short time, but I believe in your wisdom. You command, and I believe you have the greater good of the Empire at heart. It may be a death warrant, but so be it. I will lead my men down the path you have selected."

Marshal Owans stood slowly. "Sir, long have I known you, and you me. You need not even ask where my loyalties lie. You live under the grace of the God's themselves, and I will not question your orders."

Davan 'av Carpea, greatly relieved, smiled. "Very well. Now, how many men can we collect to move westward before midnight? We must leave at least a token force here of course, but most of the men must come with us."

Marshal Yith answered. "Sir, I am sure that your entire Second and Fourth Hosts can be assembled. I believe that we can safely collect a total of two additional hosts from our camped forces and the forces stationed along the border to the west. We will have to name acting marshals for the two hosts we piece together, but I don't anticipate any problems in that."

"Sir," interjected Marshal Owans. "I know of a number of loyal candidates from amongst the junior officers that can receive field promotions for the length of the campaign. I am confident that Marshal Yith's estimate of four hosts can be met without stripping the border defenses."

The Marshal General spoke. "Give the orders then. We march at midnight. At forced march, we will reach the eastern edge of the Talon Valley by dawn. That is all."

The two Marshals stood, saluted crisply and left.

The pavilion was empty except for Morgan and Davan. Davan stood and stretched his limbs. He drew his saber and pressed the tip to Morgan's chest. "If you have played me false, then it shall be a great victory for the Thulistans. You however will die."

Morgan stood slowly, eyes focused on the blade pressed deeply into his flesh. Slowly, he reached down and grasped the hilt of his sword. With a slow rasping sound, he drew the long sword free. Davan held the pressure on the point of his saber steady.

"By my S'hapur's badge of office," Morgan intoned. "I have treated fairly and truthfully with you." He slowly raised the bright blade before him. It gleamed in the bright light of the dozen glowing braziers that had been lit as daylight had passed into night. Slowly, deliberately, he straitened the blade before him. He then pulled his opposite forearm across the gleaming blade, leaving a long thin line that quickly began to seep heavy droplets of blood.

"If you seek greater assurance, then I would mingle blood with you. As such, you would be of my family and clan, bonded in purpose."

Davan removed his blade several inches. "As such, would not you be my leader then, S'hapur? It would be a clever trick indeed, but an empty one. To your offer, I say this. You seem a man of quality, and as such I have taken your word as you give it. In this, though, I say prove your worth.

"If you wish to seal your word with me, you will have to draw my blood yourself, if you are man enough. This is your chance. If you seek to kill me, you may try. If you seek to bond me to your family and clan, then prove that you are worthy to be my better in such an arrangement, though I will always retain leadership of my men. Never before have I met one worthy to mingle my blood with, prove that you are the one—now!"

As Davan said the last, he plunged his saber forward the half a foot that now separated it from Morgan's chest. As fast as lightning, Morgan's S'hapur blade swiped the saber aside and came to rest in a defensive position.

Morgan smiled. "I will strive to prove my worth."

Morgan's blade flashed in an overhead slice, which Davan expertly deflected. Morgan allowed the momentum of the swing to carry his body around and his trailing foot rose in a roundhouse kick, which Davan did not counter. Morgan's foot contacted with Davan's chest and sent him sprawling onto his back.

Before Morgan could advance, Davan arched his back and sprung to his feet without using his hands. "Very fast, faster than your friend Norin even. Now, let's see about your blade work."

Davan wade in, saber blurring in a series of cuts, high and low.

With practiced ease, and economical motions, Morgan countered and returned cuts of his own. Davan, seeing that this would be the toughest opponent he had ever faced, increased the pace immediately and put all of his strength into the blows.

Morgan gave ground and continued to parry blows. Several times he attempted to add high or low kicks into his attacks, but Davan, having seen this technique once, adapted and was adept at defending against it. Rather than risk losing a limb to a defensive slice of Davan's saber, Morgan decided to rely strictly on his blade.

The two circled; steel blurring in the ruddy light provided by the braziers. Their blades whined through the air and the rasp of steel on steel filled the room as the blades frequently met. Back and forth they tested their best routines, each unable to penetrate the other's defense.

After ten minutes, they separated. Morgan wiped his brow with his arm, leaving a streak of blood from his self-inflicted wound. "You are, indeed the greatest challenge I have faced with a blade. Do you find me equally worthy?"

Davan lowered his blade fractionally. "Worthy—yes you are worthy of respect. But I am not bloodied."

Morgan nodded. "Aye, this is true. There is one routine I have left to show you then."

Morgan stepped in, blade flashing through routines quicker than the ability of the human eye to follow. Davan was quickly forced back, his blade barely meeting each blow. Morgan, seemingly unfatigued, forced Davan to the far wall of the pavilion itself where he locked blades with Davan, blades pressing tightly together near the hilts.

Davan was winded and his arm numb from the solid impact of Morgan's blows. He rested, waiting for a chance to drive Morgan back, when with a grunt of effort, Morgan dropped down to his knee, holding steady pressure on Davan's saber as his blade slid down its length. It took only a second before only the tip of his blade pressed tightly against Davan's saber hilt, near his hand.

Before Davan could pull away, or otherwise react, Morgan rose in a swift motion; blade twisting strongly towards Davan's now unprotected fingers. Davan released his blade and rolled to the side, away from his fallen blade. Morgan raised his sword until the point was inches from Davan's chest, turning the tables from where the combat began. In a fluid motion he rotated his entire body fully around, his weight drawing his blade in a deadly arc at neck level towards Davan. In a natural defensive move, Davan's hands rose before him, trying if vain to fend the inevitably deadly stroke coming.

Morgan, in the blink of an eye, adjusted his sword stroke, and the whistling swing completed without apparent damage to the shocked Davan. Morgan re-sheathed his sword. "Now, I would still seal my fate with yours, should you find me worthy to share your blood."

Davan nodded and spoke in wonder. "Aye, you are the first to prove themselves a greater warrior than I. I will draw blood for you." He reached for a small dagger at his waist.

"I believe you will find that unnecessary."

Davan did not understand the words until he felt the stinging in his wrist. He turned his wrist towards himself and saw a line, five inches long, barely starting to seep blood. "How could you possibly control such a swing so perfectly? Indeed, I accept your offer, as long as you understand my duty to my men and to the Emperor."

Morgan stepped forward and grasped hands with the slightly shaky Marshal General. "Accepted." He then pressed their arms together, blood smearing between them.

Several hours later, they rode out together, Morgan riding Bran, at the head of over thirty thousand Tulisian troops, with more joining as they traveled. Many wondered at the status of the Thulistan warrior riding at the head of the army with their Marshal General, but none questioned.

The sun climbed over the mountain peaks to the east, shining brightly on the black carapace of the shuffling host of d'rakken mahre. They passed out of the southern mouth of the Talon Valley, the men of Clan Moncall to the front and sides, prepared for war.

Taire, at the head of a column of several thousand warriors, had heard over an hour ago that a large force of Tulisian warriors was moving quickly towards them, and that they would meet within the hour. The meeting would prove ruinous, he knew, and yet still could not place his finger on the knowledge bumping at the edge of his consciousness. It was becoming maddening, like a mosquito buzzing by your ear. Regardless of the intentions of the oncoming Tulisians, the d'rakken mahre would continue their southward movements, and bloody conflict would arise as forced their way through the oncoming host. The men of Clan Moncall would be outnumbered, and hard pressed to keep a clear route for the d'rakken mahre.

Further thought was cut off as a scout ran in, breathing hard, a rare occurrence for one of the hardy Clan Moncall. "Battle Leader, the forces to the southeast number near to forty thousand at best estimate. A group of several score ride hard ahead of them, flying a white flag. At present, they will meet with us in a half an hour, and their forces are about an hour behind. There is no way around them."

Nuorn nodded to the man and made several quick hand gestures. The scout saluted and ran off again southward.

"Nuorn," began Halnan. "We must ride to meet these men coming under the white flag. We must have time to respond to their message, regardless of its contents. If we wait for them to meet us, the d'rakken mahre will be too close behind to avoid disaster. It may be an impossible situation, anyway, but we must try." Halnan turned to Nuorn. "Will you join us?"

Nuorn nodded and increased his pace to keep up with Taire and Halnan as they kicked their horses to a fast gallop.

# TWENTY-SIX

## UNIFICATION

They rode hard for fifteen minutes before spotting the Tulisian party. The Tulisians were also riding hard, and quickly approaching across the open valley floor. As the distant shapes materialized into individually distinguishable human beings, Taire made out a familiar face at the head of the column.

"Halnan, it's Morgan! Morgan is riding with the Tulisians!" Taire shouted breathlessly from his saddle.

Halnan, upon seeing the familiar tartan flapping behind Morgan shouted back. "Something is afoot here! Nuorn, your Tarcha has been working miracles! We may make it yet." The last was spoken softly and lost in the wind.

As the groups came within a hundred paces of each other, the Tulisians reigned in their horses, as did Taire and Halnan. From the front of the Tulisian party, three figures continued forward at a statelier pace. A standard bearer rode several paces ahead of the other two, which consisted of Morgan riding Bran, and another figure, striking in gilded armor, riding a huge white war-horse.

Morgan, relieved at finding Halnan and Taire where he had hoped to find them, smiled a small welcome as he drew reign less than a dozen paces away. The standard-bearer and herald rode directly up to Halnan and Nuorn, who were closest and boldly began introductions.

"Hail, honorable adversaries." His voice was as pure and loud as the blowing of a trumpet. "We have come under a flag of truce, seeking parlay. Will you honor the truce, for as long as the parlay shall last, and until we may make such egress as needed to return to our forces?"

To Halnan and Tair's surprise, Nuorn responded. "I am Nuorn, chosen leader of those forces pitted against you. I accept your parlay, and grant your request of truce for such time as we parlay, and grant you safety until such time as we meet as enemies upon the field of battle."

The herald nodded acknowledgment. "That is well. May I introduce the Marshal General Davan 'av Carpea, field commander of the Thulistan campaign." The herald motioned to the armored man behind him, and turned his horse and moved a short distance away from the five men.

The Marshal General waited for the herald and standard-bearer to move away and then lightly kicked his horse forward, closing the small distance between the two parties. Morgan followed on Bran.

Both Halnan and Taire were full of unasked questions, yet held their tongues. They were unsure of how tenuous the relationship between Morgan and the Marshal General may be, and of its nature. Instead of risking Morgan's position, they waited for either Morgan or the Marshal General to speak first.

"Your friend Morgan is a very persuasive man." It was the Marshal General who spoke first. He turned his attention from the two mounted men towards Nuorn, whom he remembered from the earlier encounter. "I honor the memory of your S'hapur, Norin. His death opened my eyes to the importance of the story of the d'rakken mahre. Without his sacrifice, I would never have allowed Morgan to tell his tale."

Nuorn simply nodded.

"Now, to the point," continued Davan. "My forces have come to assist in your mission. I believe that the issue of the d'rakken mahre supersedes our current conflict in importance. I have nearly forty thousand men to assist in the shepherding of these creatures.

The men are due southeast of here currently. What is the position of the d'rakken mahre? Would it be possible for me to see them?"

"How can we trust you?" Asked Nuorn. "You invest our border unprovoked, and now ask us to accept your word?"

Morgan interrupted before Davan could become entangled in an argument with the unyielding Nuorn. "If you traveled with Norin, then you know who I am?" Nuorn nodded in response; the answer too self evident to require response. "Well then, all of you need to know that Davan 'av Carpea and myself have taken the bond of blood brotherhood, according to the laws of the clans. In this matter, we are as one in purpose. His honor is my honor."

Taire looked confused. Halnan stared openmouthed. Nuorn seemed pleased.

"The d'rakken mahre travel rapidly towards us, merely several miles up the valley. If we detour back to view their progress, they will come upon your troops unawares." Nuorn answered.

Morgan looked over their shoulders, as if expecting to see them across the valley basin.

Davan asked. "Where are they going? I must know if I am to keep my men clear!"

All eyes turned to Taire.

"I don't know! I really don't, but I know that you have all made a huge mistake!" Taire blurt out the thought that had plagued him since discovering the oncoming Tulisian army. Morgan and Halnan looked confused, and the Marshal General angry. Before any could speak, he continued his thought. "You have brought an army here to escort them like they are a group of pilgrims you wish to protect from robbers. The problem is, they are heading south, and your army is right in the way! They won't stop because you have come to help, they will begin to plow through and your men will defend themselves, it will be a massacre of your army, and Clan Moncall!"

Morgan turned white, the Marshal General sputtered. "Ruin, it will be ruin!"

Halnan began to yell. "Marshal General, your men must be warned! Turn them aside . . ."

Nuorn stood impassively, unaffected by the situation.

Morgan was the first to regain his wits. "Wait!" He shouted at the top of his lungs. "Taire, how do you know they are going south? Just a minute ago, you said you had no idea where they are going, and now you said they are going south. Which is it?"

Taire looked at Morgan. It was there, deep in his mind, the answer bounced around seeking to free itself. He knew the d'rakken mahre were going south, it was true. He shook his head, trying to clear his thoughts.

Meanwhile, Morgan rode over to him, bringing Bran alongside Taire upon his mount. He put his hand upon Taire's shoulder and shook him lightly. "Which is it, Taire? You and I must save these men somehow, it is our destiny, Tarcha and Shepherd."

The vapors of a thought solidified and crystallized in Taire's mind. An electric current pulsed through his body. Taire knew with absolute certainty where the d'rakken mahre were going, and why.

"It's southwest, right into the oncoming army," he whispered. "They are going to go southwest until they have a strait shot to the south. They are going to pass due south until they reach Telusian Ocean! That is where they will go. It's the cycle: air, earth, and sea! Then there is something more, something fantastic—it, well I can't explain it. It can't be stopped, it must not, they will reach the sea, no matter what gets in the way, Varsnya commands it of them! Oh, Morgan, they are all doomed!"

Morgan turned to Davan, who was already turning his horse to ride back to his men. "Davan, you must . . ."

Feeling rushed, the Marshal General interrupted. "Yes, I will go to the army and seek to turn it aside. It is a vast host, though, and will be near impossible to clear from the path. Morgan, Nuorn, you understand my course of action, if it comes to it, do not allow your Clan Moncall to engage my men, allow them to be slaughtered instead, but don't take action. It would be a declaration of war between our countries that would have immediate ramifications beyond even this situation. A war now would be devastating to Tulisia, and all of its peoples who I must protect!"

Without waiting for a response, he savagely kicked his horse into a full gallop, back towards his endangered forces.

Taire, Halnan, and Morgan came together briefly as the Marshal General faded into the distance, heading towards his army several miles distant. Halnan reached across from his saddle and grasped arms with Morgan.

"Well met friend Morgan! It seems you have managed nicely to fulfill your part of the prophecy. How did you manage to bind him with the bond of blood brotherhood? Does he even know what it means?"

Morgan smiled. "Mostly he does, but some he will learn after passing this immediate crisis. We don't have time for this though. We must get back to Clan Moncall, time is short." He released Halnan's arm and moved Bran over to Taire and slapped him lightly on the shoulder. "Taire, you have done well. You too have begun to fulfill the role intended it seems. I imagine this has all been a relief to Nuorn, who may have begun to despair of our ability to fulfill his Clan's prophecy." As he spoke the last, he turned towards Nuorn, eyebrows raised questioningly.

Nuorn shrugged. "All is as it was intended by Varsnya, and the prophecy was never in doubt—you doubt yourselves, but the prophecy will not allow this to interfere. Do not fear; you will not fail. Taire indeed begins to fulfill the prophecy, but your role has yet to be played out, Tarcha. Leading the Tulisians around by the nose is not your intended role. Come back to the clan with me now, and assume your role."

Morgan, slightly put off by Nuorn's confidence, simply nodded.

Taire spoke. "Yes, I have a feeling we should be getting back. Morgan, maybe you can find a way to turn the d'rakken mahre aside?"

Halnan turned his horse and looked back over his shoulder towards the other men. "Yes, Morgan, a little sweet talk and I am sure they will follow you anywhere. S'hapur, Tarcha, and Bug Savior; how can one help but envy your rapid elevation?" He winked at Taire and kicked his mount forward.

Taire chuckled and followed quickly. Morgan followed closely, his brow creased in consternation. Finally, Nuorn began to follow, striding effortlessly behind the horses. For some reason, he was upset by Halnan's behavior, and Taire's tacit approval of it. It was no way for companions of the Tarcha to behave. Nuorn determined to speak his concerns with Halnan when time permitted.

It was a ride of less than two miles to the Clan Moncall vanguard. The tattooed warriors had increased their numbers along the front of the d'rakken mahre procession, and close to ten thousand men were arrayed, jogging easily with spears and bows ready, before the exodus of d'rakken mahre. Nuorn, without saying a word, melded into the moving mass of warriors and began to speak with various other battle leaders regarding current events.

Morgan stopped Bran and sat high in the saddle, the warriors of Clan Moncall spreading out around the bulk of his horse. Both Taire and Halnan found their mounts unable to stand against the press of moving men, and were slowly separated from their companion.

Morgan, secure atop Bran's bulk, waited for a clear view of the d'rakken mahre. As the press of Moncall warriors began to thin, he heard an odd hissing noise growing from the north. At first, all he could see was a dark sea of moving forms. As the mass neared, details became clear. Hundreds upon thousands of the creatures walked packed tightly together at a steady, unrushed pace with the determination and surety of the advancing tide. A growing hiss could be heard.

The sound, Morgan realized, was the rasping of thousands upon thousands of chitinous bodies rubbing and jostling against each other.

Morgan sat, mouth agape, mesmerized by the oncoming d'rakken mahre. They were nothing like he had ever imagined. They were utterly alien and frightening; yet fantastic, and awesome. Their very motion spoke of an unnatural unity of purpose.

The d'rakken mahre were within several hundred paces of the Morgan before Halnan, who had ridden around the Moncall warriors to reach Morgan, slapped him on the shoulder to get his attention. His eyes were wild from the nearness of the terrible creatures.

"Morgan, come on! Move—they will be on us in a moment!"

Morgan, however, did not move. Halnan unsheathed one of his long blades and used it to slap Bran on the flank. The shock of the blow caused Bran to rear up onto his hind legs, almost unseating Morgan. Morgan, shocked into attentiveness, blinked his eyes and shook his head savagely.

He brought Bran under control and turned him towards Halnan. "All right, lets go."

With the d'rakken mahre within fifty feet, they turned and rode rapidly towards the retreating backs of the Moncall warriors. Morgan, having recovered from the shock of seeing the d'rakken mahre, was just beginning to register what he had seen.

"Halnan, we have to find Taire. There is nothing I can do about this. They have a terrible—well—purpose; I guess is the best word. Taire is the Shepherd, maybe he can do something, but armies, whether Thulistan or Tulisian have no hope."

Halnan was afraid. He had never seen Morgan admit to being hopeless. "Well, let's find him and ask."

They rode back through the thick knot of warriors, back towards the front, where they assumed Taire would be riding. As they rode, Morgan realized one thing he could do, must do.

Taire, upon horseback was easy to find. He was riding, looking very out of place and uncomfortable among the grim faced Thulistan warriors.

Morgan began to split away from Halnan after he saw Taire. "Halnan, you speak to him, see what he can do—if anything. I have something to take care of!" He had to shout to be heard over the rumble of thousands of running feet. Upon seeing Halnan's nod of acknowledgment, he maneuvered the last distance out of the advancing army and spurred Bran forward, to the south, towards where the Tulisian army was.

He rode for about a mile before seeing the first signs of the Tulisian forces. The ground was heavily trampled from the booted feet of the Tulisian soldiers. He followed the swath of trampled earth for another two miles before finding the bulk of the Tulisian army. They were in full retreat now, but moving too slowly! The size of the army hampered its movements, and its size prevented it from moving out of the way of the oncoming d'rakken mahre force. The army spread across the entire space between the Talon River to the west and the Moghin Hills to the east. They could not reach the open passage to the southern end of the Moghin Hills in time, and did not possess boats to cross the river. It was hopeless, and he knew that without some intervention, these men would all die!

Morgan sat for several minutes, unsure of what to do. There was no right choice. No matter what he did, men would die and the d'rakken mahre would be whipped into a killing frenzy that may last throughout their southward trek, bringing death to everyone in the way.

Finally he turned, resolved to find Taire, praying that Taire would have an answer. As he turned Bran back to the north, his blood ran cold. The Thulistan vanguard troops were within a half-mile of his current position. So soon, he thought! They were traveling twice as fast as the heavily burdened Tulisian army, and they were already in sight, only a half hour from the Tulisians.

Suddenly, Morgan understood something. The d'rakken mahre were not his problem! Nuorn had explained it all, and he had not listened. The prophecy would take care of itself, Taire to his part, and he to his own.

As the first men of Clan Moncall approached, he brandished his sword and called to them. "Turn aside! You must turn aside, into the hills, out of reach!" He knew that the mobile Thulistans could easily climb up out of the reach of the advancing d'rakken mahre. By doing so, he could eliminate one problem, allowing Taire to do his job—hopefully.

The Thulistans to the front slowed and spoke amongst themselves, unsure of what to do. Their role had been defined, and yet the Tarcha demand they break with their assigned role. For a moment, they stopped dead in their tracks, unable to decide their role.

Morgan suddenly felt a righteous fury beyond any he had ever experienced. "Men of Clan Moncall, here my words. I am the Tarcha, as ordained by Varsnya. You will turn aside, and you will ensure those behind you hear the word. You will soon be called back to your duties, but now you must turn aside and let the prophecy move forward on its own!"

The several hundred men within hearing distance decided simultaneously. Most turned to the east, where the steep foothills provided the nearest protection. Others turned back northward to spread the word. Morgan simply stood his ground, like a sentinel forbidding passage to any. Men split east and west, melting into the forested hills, disappearing like phantoms into the greenery.

About twenty minutes later, Halnan and Taire rode up, accompanied only by Nuorn.

Morgan spoke to Nuorn first. "Why haven't you gone with your people? I need someone to keep them together and bring them back southward behind the d'rakken mahre, ready to take position again when I command it."

Nuorn shrugged. "They will be ready when you need them. I belong here. One must bear witness to the fulfillment of the prophecy. It has truly begun. The Tarcha assumes his position. Now the shepherd must prevail."

His voice shaky, Taire spoke. "What do you mean prevail—how?"

"I do not know, that is your question to answer, not mine."

Halnan, looking back northward interrupted. "Whomever's job it is, it is time! Here they come!"

They all turned in unison, to find the d'rakken mahre moving purposefully towards them less than a half mile away.

Taire shouted. "I don't know what to do, I can't stop them!"

In a panic, he spurred his horse forward, away from the danger posed by the d'rakken mahre. The others followed him, all concerned, all but Nuorn, who seemed merely curious. They followed Taire for a mile or so before the bulk to the Tulisian army loomed before them. Now, the Tulisians filled the southern horizon, and the d'rakken mahre the northern. Hemmed hopelessly between,

Taire sat astride his horse, wild eyes darting from one army to the other.

"Morgan, Halnan—help me—please don't make me do this, I just can't. I am so scared, and confused! What do I do, how can I keep them all alive."

Morgan dismounted and moved over to Taire, pulling the trembling young man from his saddle. Holding him firmly by the shoulders, he looked him in the eyes.

"Taire, it may not be easy, but you must do something. Only you have this answer. You are the Shepherd! You must find a way to stop them or those soldiers will die!"

Taire, held firmly in Morgan's grasp, looked at the moving Tulisian army. Tens of thousands of men were marching, desperate to save their own lives. He thought of his father, killed by the d'rakken mahre for no other reason that being in the wrong place at the wrong time. This was no different—he could not allow this to happen. With a strength he did not know he had, he broke Morgan's grasp and pushed him away. Before Morgan could react, he turned and ran towards the oncoming d'rakken mahre.

Halnan jumped off of his mount and tried to stop Taire, but hit the ground too late; Taire had already passed by.

"Taire," shouted Halnan. "Wait! What are you going to do?"

Taire didn't listen, or answer, and there was nothing anyone could do, the d'rakken mahre were too close to retrieve Taire and make it safely away.

Taire ran without thinking. He was beyond fear, beyond thought. He still had no idea what it was he was to do, but determined to try. After a hundred yards, he stopped. The d'rakken mahre were only a minute from reaching him. They approached without seeming to see him, or acknowledge him. How could he stop something that did not even acknowledge his existence?

Then Taire began to laugh. Even the three men watching from a distance could hear his near hysterical cackling. Before they could even question each other as to what was happening to Taire, the laughter stopped. In the space of a heartbeat, Taire disappeared.

In the space where Taire had been standing, now stood a

motionless d'rakken mahre. For a moment, the creature that was Taire turned back towards the three men. There was no emotion or discernible humanity to the gaze it turned their way.

As it turned back, the front wave of d'rakken mahre split open and passed by him, engulfing him. Morgan and Halnan both audibly gasped. Nuorn smiled broadly.

To the south, the Tulisian army, having seen the hopelessness of flight, began to turn to prepare for impact with the black nemesis. Morgan, Halnan, and Nuorn, too involved in what they were seeing to move, were about to be trampled by the deadly press of d'rakken mahre.

Then, as one, the mass of oncoming d'rakken mahre stopped, the forerunners were just paces away from Morgan, Halnan and Nuorn. Their black carapace glistened with moisture, their limbs twitched with desire to move. Nonetheless, they remained frozen in place, held by a will greater than their combined desire to continue.

Morgan moved forward, compelled towards the mass of d'rakken mahre before him. Unafraid, he reached the nearest d'rakken mahre and touched its shiny carapace. It did not react in any way to his presence. Its shell was very warm to the touch, and moist with condensation forming in the crisp air. He looked into the creature's black eyes: black on black, deeper than the darkest obsidian, deeper than time. He became lost in those eyes.

A hard, sharp object poked Morgan's arm and startled him. Besides him stood a solitary d'rakken mahre, its long clawed hand reaching out towards him, touching him only lightly. Morgan turned towards what he knew was Taire, feeling a sense of awe at what his friend had become, and fear at what it meant.

"Taire, I know you are there. Can you hear me, can you understand me?"

Taire did not indicate any understanding at first, but after a silent moment, reached out and touched Morgan's forehead. "I see you, Tarcha. They can not see you, will not see you—understand?" The voice was sibilant, almost a hiss. "Now they see me—follow—wait. I cannot hold them long. You must go to them and move them—now." He paused for a minute. "It is different than the other forms. I can't come back. Everything is changing too quickly. I understand now, and must ensure the cycle is completed.

"You must do your part. Do not allow any to stand before us. They," he gestured behind himself, "cannot see them, only I can, and I can't be everywhere at once—keep them safe from us. I must move south—the ocean, it calls to me. We must change again. Go—now. Remember me. You have been like a father, and Halnan a brother."

Taire moved his forehead forward until it lightly touched Morgan's. He then stepped away and walked back into the throng of d'rakken mahre. Morgan, wide eyed, sorted through the visions that he had been granted: Men at war, cities burning, death, and rebirth. It flashed in rapid patterns through his mind—it was too much to process. He shook his head and wiped a tear from his cheek.

"Good-bye Taire, should I have a son, I hope he can be as kind and brave as you!" Morgan called into the still mass of black figures.

Although Morgan had no way of knowing it, Taire heard his call, and paused. His mind, quickly changing to suit his form, had great difficulty assimilating the statement. It became more difficult every minute to remember what he had been; it was fading so fast. His last thought as a human was one of love for Morgan and Halnan, and a hope that his father was proud of him. From there, he remembered no more, his past life shed like an old skin; forgotten until it could be granted meaning again through rebirth.

Morgan slowly turned and walked back to the stunned Halnan and the awed Nuorn. "Come on," he spoke absently to the two men, "we have a lot of work to do. Nuorn, have your people ready to move, find your fellow battle leaders and bring them to the Tulisian camp. I will meet you there. Come with me Halnan, there is much I desire to speak with you about."

Talking quietly about the goings on of the past hours, the two mounted their horses and rode toward the nearby Tulisian army. The Tulisian forces, having seen their opportunity to escape, had begun marching southeastward again.

By the time Davan met them at the in the rear-guard of the Tulisian forces, both men wore bitter smiles, smiles of pride and of loss. They would miss Taire, and mourned his loss to the needs of the prophecy. Despite this, they understood and applauded his sacrifice.

Morgan greeted Davan, and filled him in briefly on the events that had transpired.

"The lad has undertaken a great mission. We owe everything to him, let us make his sacrifice worthwhile." Davan paused and rubbed his chin, feeling the two days growth of beard. "I have pulled my army into the maelstrom. Although I know I have done the necessary thing, I will now be considered a traitor to my country. Yet, despite this, we must protect them from the d'rakken mahre, else tens of thousands of innocents will die. Think you, Morgan, that you can pull these two diverse forces together to achieve this goal?"

"I must," answered Morgan. "Taire has the hard part, he has sacrificed the greatest. How can I allow myself to fail in this? Have you then, given yourself to the prophecy, Marshal General Davan 'av Carpea?"

"Nay, but I have been taken by it, I think. I am lost in these matters. There is no going back now. I, and forty thousand men with me, submit myself to your will. You have proven yourself to me, and I will follow you, blood brother. My men will go where I lead them, without question. When the Moncall battle leaders arrive, we must conference with my marshals. We will have just over sixty thousand warriors, and the entire world will seek to bar our way. I have no home, and my enemies have become my people. What can I do but follow, for I know not whether I am fit to lead."

Morgan smiled. "Do not doubt your fitness. You must still lead your people; I will have enough problems dealing with Clan Moncall. The world changes, and you will have a place within it, friend Davan. For now, we must be content to assume our assigned roles. We will hold to our purpose, through war and fire. There can be no going back, or second thoughts. Let us indeed make Taire's sacrifice worthwhile. Perhaps in time, our sacrifices will grow to give value to what he has done."

Davan smiled. "Always I have sought to be challenged, to have something worthwhile to do. I fear I have been granted my request." He paused in his speech, and drew his sword, pointing it skyward. "I will see the d'rakken mahre to their destination, and should all the forces of the world unite against us, then let them beware. Davan 'av Carpea and Morgan of Clan Piksanie have united under the call of Varsnya's prophecy!"

Morgan raised his sword skyward next to Davan's. "Then let the world quake under the force of our unification. Let us go forward as blood brothers, to live or die, achieve or fail. Whatever fate befalls, let us meet it together!"

Davan lowered his sword, but did not sheathe it. "Aye, let it be known! Let all men witness," he cried, catching the attention of many of the hundreds of men attending him in the rearguard. "In all things, Morgan of Thulistan is my brother. His word is as my own, and his people are my people. We are as one, and will meet the challenge of the worlds need together! Let the word pass, and let all be warned. We have no land or property save what we carry. Despite this; we have something greater than property, we have honor and duty! Until our duty is fulfilled, we shall dwell within the protective shield of our honor, and form our own community of those who share our duty. Let all allegiances to symbol or country be forgotten until this duty is done. Our allegiance shall be to protect our families, and those of our enemies. Our duty goes beyond the bounds of border and nationality! The warriors of Varsnay's prophecy shall have rewards eternal!"

Word spread forward through all of Davan's command like wildfire burning across the valley floor. Allegiance to Tulisian army and host were shed like outgrown skin; attesting to the power of the prophecy. A new allegiance was born. Before the end of the day, Tulisian and Thulistan warrior alike were united under a greater cause, under a new allegiance.

By the next morning, all men throughout the two forces shared a new understanding of who and what they were. Into the dawn of a cold early winter day, the hosts of the Prophecy advanced to create a path for the again mobile host of d'rakken mahre to follow: A path leading to a bitter winter of strife and death.

Early the next morning, Halnan, sitting forlornly on his bedroll, watched Morgan and Davan walk together in the pre-dawn fog. With a deep sense of uncertainty, he looked east, wondering when the sun would rise to bring light and warmth to the world. In the chilled depths of his heart, he doubted that the sun would ever give warmth again. Light seemed like a forgotten memory, forever doused as both Taire and then Morgan moved beyond the need of his help.

With a sigh, he stood and prepared to meet the new day.

# AFTERWARDS

## FORGED IN THE DEEPS

An arm reached through a narrow crack in a pile of rocks and began to push away stones, widening the gap. The arm was etched with scars; both long healed ragged white ones, and lumpy pink, poorly healed more recent ones. Sinews bulged and a large rock fell away, creating a fair sized opening. First one arm reached through, and then a shoulder.

After a moment of scrambling and squeezing, the escape from the earth was completed, and a dirty, panting figure lay on the ground covering his eyes. The figure was lean to the point of emaciation, but massive in build. The remains of heavy leather leggings and vest hung loosely on the filthy tattered body.

The body was even more heavily covered in half healed and poorly healed wounds than the arm. Each muscle lay clearly defined through skin that seemed almost transparent.

A quarter of an hour passed before the man began to uncover his eyes. He wiped his tearing eyes with the back of his hand and rose determinedly to his feet. He stood over six and a half feet tall, and seemed to be constructed from steel, instead of fresh and bone. He tried to remember when he had last seen the open sky, and could only imagine that it must have been close to a year.

During that year he had wandered for hundreds of miles in the depths of the earth. He had clambered through tunnels of all sizes, clambered down a great chasm, and lived a short time on the shores of an under earth sea. He had found caves of fire, and great caverns filled with beautifully glowing fungi and lichens of every hue. He discovered the deepest homes of those that dwelt under the earth; the degan sahre, d'rakken mahre, and other even more incredible creatures that never ventured near enough to the surface to have been seen by a human before. A few of these creatures had given him aid, in the form of wisdom, information, or a place to dwell for a time. Mostly though, he had fought, fought for survival every day that passed. He had discovered many secrets in the womb of the earth, secrets he would hold close as long as he lived, and secrets that he was deeply compelled to make known to all of mankind. He had become the tool of those secrets, those truths, compelled to bring them to the light of the world.

The hammer of battle and the anvil of the earth had forged something unique in this man. Strength, wisdom, need, and desire had been melded together into something more than a man: He was mortal, yet almost godlike in his ability to adapt and survive.

His sense of humanity was almost buried underneath the instincts that had kept him alive. Two things were clear to him, however. These two things rang in his mind like a litany against insanity. One was a truth that he had learned in the deepest most secret places of the earth, a place he would never speak of, from a being who's very existence would rock the foundations of Tulisian society should it be revealed. The other was all that was left of his previous existence. At times, he muttered them to himself, a reminder of his humanity. Almost without conscious thought, he began to verbalize his mantra.

"The d'rakken mahre cannot be allowed to achieve their false purpose." His hand reflexively gripped his sword at the mention of the d'rakken mahre.

He took his bearings, and, after a moment remembering the relative positioning of the sun, turned southward. As he stretched his legs into a rarely practiced long stride, me muttered his second truth.

"I will find Taire."